Saint John Chrysostom

The life and times of Chrysostom

Saint John Chrysostom

The life and times of Chrysostom

ISBN/EAN: 9783337149765

Printed in Europe, USA, Canada, Australia, Japan

Cover: Foto ©Raphael Reischuk / pixelio.de

More available books at **www.hansebooks.com**

The Life and Times

OF

CHRYSOSTOM.

BY THE

REV. R. WHELER BUSH, M.A., F.R.G.S.,

RECTOR OF ST. ALPHAGE, LONDON WALL; SOMETIME SELECT PREACHER AT OXFORD;

Author of

"St. Augustine: his Life and Times;" "An Introduction to the Pentateuch," etc.

THE RELIGIOUS TRACT SOCIETY

56, PATERNOSTER ROW; 65, ST. PAUL'S CHURCHYARD;
AND 164, PICCADILLY.
1885.

CONTENTS.

INTRODUCTION.

SECT. I.—State of Christianity before and during the age of
Chrysostom 3

SECT. II.—Sketch of the Roman Emperors during Chrysostom's
life 6

BOOK I.

FROM CHRYSOSTOM'S BIRTH TO THE END OF HIS ASCETIC LIFE.

CHAPTER I.

ANTIOCH, THE BIRTH-PLACE OF CHRYSOSTOM.

1. Its splendid geographical Site 19
2. Its Founders and Embellishers, with a Sketch of its Decline
and Fall 22
3. Its Christian Associations and Memories, and its probable
effect upon the mind and feelings of Chrysostom . 30

CHAPTER II.

THE BIRTH AND PARENTAGE OF CHRYSOSTOM.

On the surname of 'Chrysostom' 34
His Father Secundus dies early 35
His mother Anthusa carefully directs his Religious Training . 36
She refuses to marry again 37
The Religious Influence at that time of Christian women . 38
Anthusa desires to give her son a solid education . . 40

CHAPTER III.

CHRYSOSTOM'S EDUCATIONAL CAREER.

PAGE

Anthusa seeks for a Tutor for her Son . . . 42
She selects Libanius, the eloquent Rhetorician, who was conversant with many men and cities 43
Libanius a Heathen, but Chrysostom was fortified against his influence by study of Holy Scripture and his Mother's teaching 45
Libanius praises his Oratorical Abilities . . . 46
Would have liked Chrysostom as his Successor . . . 46
Account of his Education meagre as compared with that of Augustine 46

CHAPTER IV.

THE CHOICE OF A PROFESSION FOR CHRYSOSTOM.

The Bar selected 48
The practices of the Bar repugnant to Chrysostom . . 49
He resolves to renounce the Law, and devote himself to a Religious Life 50
His determination confirmed by his friend Basil . . 51
Bishop Meletius also, to some extent, seconded Basil's views . 52
The Bishop's partiality for Chrysostom 56
After due preparation he is baptised by the Bishop . . 57
Postponement of Baptism common in that day . . 57
Chrysostom ordained 'Reader' by Meletius . . . 58

CHAPTER V.

THE ASCETIC LIFE OF CHRYSOSTOM.

Chrysostom's changed life after Baptism . . . 59
His desire for Monasticism opposed by his Mother and Meletius 60
The attractions of Monasticism to the young . . . 60
His Mother's appeal to him to remain at home successful . 62
From Diodorus he learns the grammatical interpretation of Scripture 63
His Influence on Theodore and Maximus . . . 63
Theodore lapses from the ascetic life 64
He is brought back by the earnest appeals of Chrysostom . 65
He afterwards became a learned Bishop and Preacher . . 66
The Influence and Work of Diodorus 66

CHAPTER VI.

CHRYSOSTOM GUILTY OF A 'PIOUS FRAUD.'

PAGE

Vacancies in several Syrian Sees 67
Chrysostom, by a 'Pious Fraud,' forces Basil into the Episco-
pate, he himself avoiding it 68
He glories in what he did 69
The nature of an 'Economy,' or 'Pious Fraud' . . 69
Advocated by many of the early Fathers . . . 70
It gave rise to Chrysostom's work on the Priesthood . . 71
Written in the form of a Platonic Dialogue . . . 72
Question as to the Date of its Composition . . . 72
A Summary of the Six Books 73

CHAPTER VII.

CHRYSOSTOM'S RIGID MONASTICISM.

A peril, in connection with magic, leads Chrysostom to a life
of stricter asceticism 76
Monasteries on the mountains near Antioch . . . 78
The probable cause of Monachism 79
Sketch of the life of the Monks outside Antioch . . 80
The Rule of Pachomius observed in the Syrian Monasteries . 80
Persecution tended to produce Monachism . . . 81
Chrysostom's inclination towards the life . . . 82
Opposition to Monks from different quarters . . . 83
Chrysostom's Treatise in reply to objections . . . 84
Different Treatises by him on the subject . . . 85
He retires into complete seclusion 88
His health fails, and he returns to Antioch . . . 88
Chrysostom writes in sympathy to Stagirius . . . 89
Two aspects of Monachism 90

BOOK II.

FROM CHRYSOSTOM'S DIACONATE TO HIS DEPARTURE FROM ANTIOCH.

CHAPTER I.

CHRYSOSTOM'S DIACONATE.

PAGE

Chrysostom ordained Deacon by Meletius at Antioch . . 95
Death of Meletius at the second Council at Constantinople . 95
He is ordained Priest by Flavian, the successor of Meletius . 96
His promise of eminence in the future 97
The five years of his Diaconate well spent . . . 97
His literary work during that time 97
His Letter of Consolation to a Youthful Widow . . 97
His Treatise on Celibacy 99
His Work on the Martyr Babylas 101
Account of sensuous Daphne 101
Martyr-Chapel of Babylas built there to raise the tone of
    religious feeling 101
Outline of his Treatise 103

CHAPTER II.

CHRYSOSTOM AS PRESBYTER AND PREACHER.

Chrysostom is ordained Presbyter 105
His fame as a Preacher predicted 105
Difficulties of a Preacher in a City where Heathenism coexisted
    with Christianity 106
Flavian generously affords him scope for Preaching . . 106
His Sermons, sometimes written, sometimes 'Extempore' . 108
His first sermon after his ordination as Presbyter . . 109
Too ornate, self-depreciatory, and eulogistic for our tastes,
    though full of promise 110

CHAPTER III.

CHRYSOSTOM IN THE PULPIT.

Only a portion of his Sermons can have come down to us . 112
He seemed to leave no subject untouched . . . 112

PAGE

Only a general review open to us 113
His Homilies naturally vary in excellence . . . 114
Wonderful knowledge of Scripture displayed in them . . 114
His reference to Scripture as a final appeal . . . 115
His indignant satire against vice, frivolity and pleasure . 116
His success arose from the depth of his Christian love . . 119
Dupin's opinion of him 120

CHAPTER IV.

CHRYSOSTOM AS A HOMILIST.

Homilies delivered in the year 386 A.D. . . . 121
Amongst these, Homilies on Genesis, on Meletius, against
    Anomœans 122
Arianism a product of Antioch 126
Homily on Anathematising 126
Panegyric on Philogonius 127
Homily on the Nativity 127
The Feast of Christmas only recently introduced into Antioch 127
The need of such a Preacher as Chrysostom . . . 128

CHAPTER V.

THE SEDITION AT ANTIOCH.

Threatened Taxation the cause of the Sedition at Antioch . 130
Destruction of the Statues of the Emperor and his Family . 131
Riot crushed by the Prefect 131
The Citizens dread the Emperor's wrath . . . 132
Chrysostom's influence over the people 132
He addresses them in twenty-one Homilies . . . 132
Flavian goes to Constantinople to propitiate the Emperor . 135
Commissioners from Theodosius arrive . . . 139
Judicial proceedings commence 140
City to be disfranchised, and Theatres and Baths closed . 140
The Monks come down from the mountains and appeal to the
    Commissioners 140
Flavian's mission successful 142
He returns before Easter Day with tidings of the Emperor's
    clemency 143
Sorrow converted into joy 143
Addition from ranks of Heathenism to Church . . . 145
Chrysostom's Homilies delivered in rapid succession . . 14

CHAPTER VI.

THE CLOSE OF CHRYSOSTOM'S PRESBYTERATE.

	PAGE
The Sedition the great event of Chrysostom's life at Antioch .	147
His Writings during this Period	147
(1) Homilies on St. Matthew, with Criticism on them, and Extracts from them	148
(2) Chrysostom's Illness from the anxieties of the Sedition .	153
Unable to share in Services at Martyr-Chapels with Flavian	153
(3) Homilies on St. John ; Criticism ; and Extracts . .	154
(4) Homilies on Epistle to the Romans ; his Fondness for St. Paul ; Extracts	164
(5) Homilies on Epistles to the Corinthians ; why Preached at Antioch ; Extracts	166
(6) Homilies on Epistle to the Galatians ; Remarks on them ; Extract	168
(7) Homilies on Epistle to the Ephesians ; why Preached at Antioch ; Extract	170
Chrysostom's Homilies adapted to all times and all places	171

BOOK III.

FROM CHRYSOSTOM'S ARCHBISHOPRIC TO HIS EXILE AND DEATH.

CHAPTER I.

CHRYSOSTOM'S CALL TO CONSTANTINOPLE.

	PAGE
Chrysostom's exalted position at Antioch . . .	175
His personal appearance familiar to all	175
Nectarius, Archbishop of Constantinople, dies . . .	177
Many eager aspirants for the vacant dignity . . .	177
Arcadius, under the influence of others, vacillates . .	178
Eutropius, his favourite, strongly recommends Chrysostom .	178
Chrysostom, by fraud and force, is carried off to Constantinople	179
Theophilus, of Alexandria, is compelled to consecrate Chrysostom	180

CHAPTER II.

CONSTANTINOPLE.

	PAGE
Remarkable that Chrysostom should have ministered in two such cities as Antioch and Constantinople.	182
Constantinople the creation of Constantine	182
Its site adapted alike for war and commerce	182
Its Buildings, Institutions, Architecture, and Art	183
The artistic wealth of other cities appropriated for it	184
Its people luxurious and pleasure-loving	185
Its ancient monuments have now departed	185
Its establishment an era in the history of Christianity	186

CHAPTER III.

CHRYSOSTOM'S ENTRANCE ON HIS EPISCOPATE.

	PAGE
Difficulties of Chrysostom's position as Archbishop	188
Nectarius, his predecessor, lax and luxurious	188
Chrysostom's rigid abstinence displeasing to all alike	189
The indolent Clergy irritated by his demands upon them	190
His reform of the Clergy wanting, perhaps, in conciliation	191
The unfortunate influence of his archdeacon, Serapion, over him	193
The lower orders and the Court still side with him	194
Eudoxia and Archbishop in close amity	194
Their Nocturnal Procession to a Martyr-Chapel	195
His Sermon extravagantly laudatory of Eudoxia	196
A second Sermon in which he equally lauds the Emperor	196

CHAPTER IV.

THE FALL OF EUTROPIUS.

	PAGE
Unaccustomed honours granted to Eutropius	198
His rapacity satirised by Claudian	199
He obtained a Law of Treason to protect himself	201
Danger threatens the favourite from Tribigild	201

PAGE

He flees to the Sanctuary of the Church . . . 202
Chrysostom screens him from violence 203
He delivers a striking Homily on him 203
Eutropius ultimately condemned to death . . . 204

CHAPTER V.

CHRYSOSTOM'S WORK AT CONSTANTINOPLE.

Chrysostom's religious zeal displayed in different directions . 206
Attends to spiritual wants of the Goths at Constantinople . 206
His missionary work among Goths on the Danube, and among
    nomad Scythians 207
Sermon on Festival of Theodosius 208
Sermon on Easter Day after violent rainfall . . . 209
Gainas demands the surrender of three noblemen from
    Arcadius 212
Chrysostom goes to camp of Gainas to plead for them . . 213
Refuses Gainas the use of a Church for Arian Services . . 213
Citizens of Constantinople attack Gothic troops who were
    swarming there 213
Gainas alarmed at the slaughter of his forces, and of Fra-
    vitta's appointment in his place 213
Gainas at length retires towards Scythia . . . 214
Is slain by Uldin, King of the Huns 214
Chrysostom labours to improve the religious condition of
    villages in his Diocese 214

CHAPTER VI.

CHRYSOSTOM'S EXPOSITIONS AT CONSTANTINOPLE.

His Expositions at Constantinople less finished than those at
    Antioch 217
This arose from want of time and pressure of business . . 217
His regard for Holy Scripture equally great as before . 218
  (1) Criticism on his Expositions on the Acts of the Apostles. 218
  (2) Homilies on the Epistles to Philippians, Colossians, and
      Thessalonians ; where Delivered ; Extracts from them . 220
  (3) Homilies on Epistles to Timothy, Titus, and Philemon . 223
      Doubts with regard to the Place and Time of their
      Delivery ; Extracts from them 223

CHAPTER VII.

OPPOSITION TO CHRYSOSTOM.

	PAGE
Chrysostom's reputation at zenith	227
Signs of opposition begin to appear	227
His rank as Archbishop defined, but not his jurisdiction	229
His visitation at Ephesus	230
Deposes Bishops and Clergy	231
Severian conspires against him	232
Chrysostom's rash language on his return	233
Reconciled with difficulty to Severian	234
Theophilus leads oppositon against him	234
Question of the 'Tall Brethren'	234
Theophilus summoned to appear before Council	236
Epiphanius deceived by Theophilus	237
Synod of 'The Oak' convened by Theophilus	240
Counter-Synod of Bishops favourable to Chrysostom	243
Frivolous charges brought against Chrysostom	243
Condemned at length as contumacious, and deposed	243

CHAPTER VIII.

CHRYSOSTOM'S FIRST EXILE AND RETURN.

	PAGE
Indignation of the people at the sentence pronounced upon Chrysostom	246
Secretly giving himself up to the officers, he is conveyed to Bithynia	247
A popular Insurrection imminent	248
An Earthquake shakes the City and the Palace	248
In alarm he is recalled	248
He is welcomed back by the acclamations of the people	249
Theophilus in fear withdraws from the City	250
A Synod pronounces Chrysostom the lawful Bishop of Constantinople	250
Reconciliation effected between Eudoxia and Chrysostom	251
A Statue of Eudoxia raised in front of the Church with Pagan revelry	251
Chrysostom denounces the Empress and all concerned	251
Her implacable indignation	252

CHAPTER IX.

CHRYSOSTOM'S SECOND CONDEMNATION AND EXILE.

	PAGE
Old foes rise up against Chrysostom	253
He is sentenced to deposition by a Council	255
He refuses, except by force, to quit his post	256
The soldiers brutally expel the Catechumens from the Church	257
Chrysostom is guarded in his palace by friends	258
On the command of Arcadius he secretly gives himself up	258
He is conveyed as exile to the coast of Asia	260
The Cathedral burnt down	260
The fire charged on the Joannites, who are cruelly treated	260
Arsacius, and then Atticus, appointed to the Archbishopric	261
Olympias and others persecuted	261
Appeal made to Innocent of Rome	263
Innocent persuaded of Chrysostom's unfair deposition	263

CHAPTER X.

CHRYSOSTOM'S EXILE AT CUCUSUS, AND DEATH.

	PAGE
Chrysostom banished to Cucusus	265
His painful sufferings on his journey	268
His ill-treatment by Pharetrius at Cæsarea	269
Isaurian marauders threaten his safety	271
Hospitable reception at Cucusus	272
His exile cheered by correspondence with his friends	273
His powerful influence there	274
His charity, liberality, and missionary spirit	276
His sufferings there physical rather than mental	278
Through fear of Isaurians he retires to Arabissus	279
Cucusus seemed to him a paradise on his return	280
Annoyance of his enemies at his survival	282
Ordered to go in cruel haste to Pityus	282
Reaches Comana and Martyr-Chapel of Basilicus	283
His death and burial there	284
Parallel between his and Henry Martyn's death	285
His remains afterwards brought back to Constantinople	286
Rationale of his persecution	286

BOOK IV.

THE CHARACTERISTICS, INFLUENCE, THEOLOGY, AND ASPECT OF THE TIMES OF CHRYSOSTOM.

CHAPTER I.

THE CHARACTERISTICS OF CHRYSOSTOM.

	PAGE
He was deeply imbued with the literature of Greece	291
His intellectual pre-eminence	292
His moral and theological character	292
Milner's estimate of him	293
The qualifications of a bishop and preacher contrasted	295
The affectionateness and sympathy of his nature	295

CHAPTER II.

THE INFLUENCE OF CHRYSOSTOM.

	PAGE
His marked influence at Antioch and Constantinople	297
The greater ecclesiastical authority of Bishop of Rome	298
Chrysostom's vast power as a preacher	299
Yet he sometimes complains of desertion of the Church for theatre and games	299
The effects of his scriptural preaching	300
A noble specimen of regenerated human nature	300
The true secret of his influence	302
His uncompromising character created opposition	303
A spirit of moderation needed	303
A martyr to the cause of Church discipline	304

CHAPTER III.

THE THEOLOGY OF CHRYSOSTOM.

	PAGE
His consideration for the relics of martyrs and saints	305
His unrestrained language liable to misconstruction	306
His views on Invocation of Saints	307
Invocation of Saints not held by early Church	308
Prayers for the dead common in first ages of Christianity	308
His views on Confession	309
Sacramental Confession not held by early Church	310
Confusion in his statements respecting free-will, grace, and original sin	310
Views of Apostolical Fathers wanting in clearness on subject of free-will and birth-sin	311
Neander's theory of Chrysostom's views on this question	312

PAGE

Dr. Shedd's philosophically expressed statement of Chrysostom's opinions 314
Chrysostom's views on the Sacraments 316
His very strong language in regard to the Holy Communion . 316
It exceeds that held by advocates of Transubstantiation . 317
Explained by Collier as rhetorical hyperbole . . . 318
The language of Chrysostom unchecked by creeds and formularies 319
His opinions on Monasticism and Celibacy modified by time . 320
Views of the Fathers on Celibacy 321
His exalted standard of the office of Bishop . . . 322
Many truly apostolic bishops in early days . . . 323
His view of the supremacy and value of Holy Scripture . 324
He held sound views on inspiration 326
The ' Liturgy of St. Chrysostom ' 326
The ' Prayer of St. Chrysostom ' in Liturgy . . . 327
The variety and excellence of his sermons . . . 328
His wonderful power over his hearers 329
Testimonies to his excellence as a preacher . . . 330
No advocate of persecution 331
His opposition to theatres and astrology . . . 332
His advocacy of almsgiving and prayer 332
He complains of noise and laughter in church . . . 333
His missionary spirit 334
Hampered by physical theories of Grecian philosophers . 334
The sign of the cross employed in Christian Church . . 334
Many doctrines and practices of the age of Chrysostom now rejected 335
Though not controversial, he was not latitudinarian . . 336

CHAPTER IV.

ASPECT OF CHRYSOSTOM'S TIMES.

Moral degeneracy had taken place 337
Low moral condition at Antioch and Constantinople . . 338
General demoralisation prevailed 339
Private luxury of dwellings of the wealthy . . . 340
Their personal luxury and extravagance . . . 341
The Emperor's follies reproduced 342
Chrysostom's caustic ridicule against such conduct . . 342
He attacks feminine follies 343
The rich ladies become his implacable foes . . . 343
He sacrifices everything to his sense of duty . . . 344

INTRODUCTION.

1. *STATE OF CHRISTIANITY BEFORE AND DURING THE AGE OF CHRYSOSTOM.*

2. *SKETCH OF THE ROMAN EMPERORS DURING CHRYSOSTOM'S LIFE.*

THE LIFE AND TIMES OF CHRYSOSTOM.

INTRODUCTION.

> ' So lay the World. So lie the frozen fields
> Before the dawning of the Arctic day,
> Sick for the sunshine, loathing wearily
> The cold, illusive gleam of fitful lights,
> That toy with darkness : then up-leaps the sun,
> And routs those mocking lights, and changes all.'

1. ITS own peculiar interest attaches to each different age of the Church of Christ.   In reviewing its history in the past, the mind reverts with feelings of devout reverence and chastened delight to the early dawn of Christ's kingdom upon earth.   We seem, as it were, to tread on holy ground, as we trace the upgrowth of Christianity in those primitive days, when inspired apostles and evangelists had only just quitted the scene of their earthly labours, leaving behind them many who had witnessed their miracles and listened to their words ; when even the echoes of that Divine voice that had brought life and immortality to light had not utterly died away, but still seemed to linger fondly, like some sweet song, in the ears of men. There is an indescribable pleasure in endeavouring to

recall those days, when a few illiterate fishermen and their successors won their triumphant way against the power of Rome, the intolerance of Judaism, and the deep-seated and long-cherished religious systems of the heathen world; when martyrs shed their blood in attestation of the faith to which they clung, and confessors were no less ready to offer up their lives in its defence; when persecution sifted the wheat from the chaff, and purified, as in the refiner's fire, the early professors of Christianity; when the power of working miracles and the gift of prophecy still remained in the Church; when Christians were ready to give up all that they possessed to the general fund, eager only to win Christ, and to be found of Him; when apologists fearlessly poured out their ardent words in vindication of the truth and Divine origin of Christianity, though summoned before kings, and rulers, and the princes of this world; when the disciples were wont to meet in upper rooms, and dens and caves of the earth, carrying their lives in their hands, to worship that God who seeth in secret; when, perhaps, the Church presented the holiest and the purest phase which she has ever exhibited on earth, and when to profess Christianity, and to be a Christian indeed, involved dangers, and trials, and a risk of life which no mere enthusiast would have been willing to encounter, and no false-hearted pretender would have been disposed to undergo.

Such was the aspect that the Church of Christ presented at the early dawn of the Christian era; and, bright as it was in itself, it stood out all the more brightly from the dark shadows which fell upon it from the surrounding gloom of heathenism.

But with the fourth century a new state of things

presented itself. A vast change had been ushered in. Christianity had now won its victorious way throughout the whole Roman empire, and made its influence felt not only in the great centres of civilisation, but in some of the wildest and remotest regions, extending even to Armenia and Iberia, to the land of the Magi, to the distant countries of Arabia, Ethiopia, Abyssinia, and India ; and, in the West, to the Goths and other barbarous tribes and nations. It had gained converts from the ranks of the nobles, in the schools of the philosophers, among the officers of the imperial army, and even from the select circle of the higher magistrates and governors of provinces.

But this was not all. Christianity had stormed the capital of heathenism itself, had laid its conquering hand upon the imperial palace, and had claimed as its own the occupant of the throne of the Cæsars. Kings had in very truth become the 'nursing fathers'[1] of the Church. Christianity now found itself the religion of the state. It was no longer the creed of an obscure section of the community, fighting its onward way against principalities and powers, and the rulers of this world ; but it was the religion of the sovereign, and rested under the shadow of imperial protection. No longer now did Christians stealthily meet in the secrecy of night in secluded chambers, or by some lone river's side, or in dismal catacombs ; but the word of the Gospel boldly sounded forth in richly-adorned basilicas, and from the pulpits of metropolitan churches. It now no longer acted on the defensive merely, or had to contend for existence with the organised power, civil and political, of the Roman world ; but it took its

---

[1] Isaiah xlix. 23, circ. 712 B.C.

own stand on vantage-ground, backed by the influence and authority of Cæsar himself. Now it could fearlessly gather its spiritual and ecclesiastical rulers from every quarter, convene its general councils, lay down its own laws, rightly divide the word of truth, and define with accuracy its faith in its own creeds and symbols of belief.

It had, indeed, much still to contend with. There was even yet a great leaven of heathenism at work in the world; superstition still prevailed, though its nature and its objects might be changed; heresy and false doctrine had sprung up within the pale of Christ's Church; ascetic notions were rife on the one hand, and lax views on the other; even then there was ground for fear lest the simplicity of the Gospel should be overlaid with the wood, hay, and stubble of man's devising; lest form should be substituted for reality, the shadow for the substance, the sign for the thing signified. Christianity, therefore, was still militant, though in a different sense and in a different degree from what it was in the earlier period of its existence on earth. Its foes were then chiefly external to itself; now they were, with some exceptions, of its own household. Still, however, it had its own peculiar conflict to wage; nor will this ever cease to be the case so long as the kingdom of Christ is a kingdom of this world, and until the time shall come when it is transplanted into its heavenly home, and the militant shall be converted into the triumphant Church.

2. The fourth century had already reached the middle of its course when Chrysostom was born. It had arrived at its close before he had attained the acme of his fame and his usefulness. But before

proceeding to trace his life and character, it would be well to glance for an instant at those who successively occupied the imperial throne during this period of the history of Christianity.

(1) Constantine the Great had been converted to Christianity, had taken the Church of Christ under his protecting care, had published a general edict of toleration, · had founded Constantinople, and had passed away from the stage of this life before the birth of Chrysostom, on May 22nd, 337 A.D. The reign of Constantine may very justly be considered as one of the great and prominent epochs in the world's history. It was the period of the disintegration of the Roman empire. A new dynasty now arose in the East, followed by the official institution of a new religion. The mighty influence of Rome was now on the wane. No longer did she continue the heart and core of the empire. She was no longer the centre of the great social and political system which had radiated from her throughout the vast extent of her wide dominion. The unity of the empire had ceased to exist. Instead of the one absolute independent sovereign at Rome, the paramount lord of the whole empire, two co-ordinate Cæsars—two who claimed the supreme title of Augustus—could be seen exercising a joint sway, by which the grand oneness and solidarity of the imperial authority had been gradually weakened and undermined. Thus, with a new capital in the East, the old traditions that had grown around Rome insensibly died out, and a new religion, patronised by the state, usurped the position of the ancient creed of paganism. It has been justly remarked [1] that the

---

[1] Milman, *History of Christianity*, ii. 245.

Roman religion sank with the Roman supremacy. The new empire welcomed the new religion as its ally and associate in the government of the human mind. The empire lent its countenance, its sanction, at length its power, to Christianity.

Whatever may have been the real motives and principles that produced Constantine's conversion to Christianity—whether his motives were perfectly pure and disinterested, as some have thought; or whether they were the outcome of hypocrisy, superstitious feeling, self-aggrandisement, or state policy, as others have not hesitated to assert; or whether they were of a mixed character, different motives swaying his mind at different periods of his life, as the influence of war, or statesmanship, or a religious feeling preponderated at the time—whatever the real motives of his conversion may have been, it cannot be doubted, that such an external recognition of Christianity on the part of the sovereign ruler of a mighty empire must have had a remarkable and powerful effect on the reception and propagation of the religion of Christ.

(2) During the reign of his son, Constantius II.—in whom the sovereignty finally merged on the death of his brothers, Constantine and Constans—John Chrysostom was born. Constantius, by nature cold-blooded, crafty, cruel, weak, and dissimulating, though professedly a Christian, did not walk in his father's steps; but after a chequered and stormy reign of nearly a quarter of a century, signalised by many massacres and great duplicity, and chiefly devoted to wars, either domestic or foreign, died suddenly at Mopsocrene in Cilicia, November 3rd, 361 A.D. During his reign, Arianism, to which he

himself leaned, was, with some checks, in the ascendant. He re-enacted some of his father's laws against paganism, his command being, ' Let superstition cease ; let the folly of sacrifices be abolished.' Moreover, several temples of the heathen deities were destroyed during his tenure of power, and pagans were persecuted, not so much from a religious as from a political stand-point.

(3) His successor was Julian, spared by Constantius at the sanguinary commencement of his reign, and brought up in the principles of the Christian faith, but kept in strict confinement during his early days, though he received a learned education in Greek literature at Athens. Summoned from thence to take the command of the army in Gaul, he was converted from a student into a soldier, and succeeded in gaining great popularity with the army, and, as a consequence, incurred the jealousy and suspicion of Constantius. He was compelled by his troops to accept the crown when summoned by the jealousy of the emperor to join him in Asia ; and only through the sudden death of Constantius, when marching against him, was the empire spared the desolation of a civil war.

Up to his twentieth year, Julian would seem to have been an outward professor of Christianity ; for the next ten years he concealed his apostasy ; and he did not, until he ascended the throne, make an open profession of the creed of paganism—the eclectic paganism of the Neo-Platonists. Still, he manifested a philosophical toleration towards Christians and heathens alike, though he displayed a more favourable disposition and spirit towards the latter, encouraging the worship of the gods of Greece and

Rome, instituting sacrifices, and rebuilding temples, and removing the monogram of Christ from the Labarum.

He visited Antioch, in which city Grecian licentiousness was blended with Syrian effeminacy. His reception, however, was far from warm or cordial on the part of the luxurious and pleasure-loving inhabitants of the place, whose feelings and inclinations were altogether opposed to the stern and severe manners of one who had long dwelt among the primitive and unrefined races that peopled Gaul. Nor did the suasive powers of Libanius himself exercise any influence over the mind of the hardy soldier, by whom the attachment of the citizens to pleasure and the games was viewed with philosophic contempt. Julian fell on the field of battle[1] in Persia, during a campaign which, though fraught with disaster, displayed the great military talents of the emperor; and so ended his brief but remarkable reign on June 26th, 363 A.D. It has been pointedly said, that 'the unchristian Christianity of Constantius must bear some part of the guilt of Julian's apostasy.'

(4) Jovian, the captain of Julian's life-guards, the son of one of the most famous Roman generals, was elected emperor immediately after the death of Julian. He avowed himself a Christian, and placed Christianity on a legal basis; he proclaimed anew a universal toleration; and he restored Athanasius to the Bishopric of Alexandria. He died most unexpectedly the year after his accession to the imperial

---

[1] The expression recorded by Theodoret (*Hist. Eccles.* iii. 25) as used by Julian when he received his death-wound, 'Thou hast conquered, O Galilean,'—Νενικηκας, Γαλιλαιε,—does not probably rest on trustworthy authority.

throne, at Dadastana, a small town of Galatia, February 17th, 364 A.D.,—the cause of his death being involved in uncertainty.

(5) Valentinian assumed the purple on the plain of Nicæa. He was a Christian, and when ordered by Julian at Antioch to sacrifice in a heathen temple, refused, and brought, it is said, exile upon himself by the refusal. He renewed, and perhaps extended, the edict of Constantine in regard to Christianity. He forbad certain magical rites of paganism to be practised ; he restored the cross, removed by Julian, and the name of Christ, on the chief standard of the army, named the Labarum ; he respected the Sunday ; but refrained from persecuting the Arians, and did not intermeddle in religious controversy.

His natural disposition was passionate, stern, even at times implacable. He occupied the throne nearly twelve years, dying in a fit at Bregetio, on the Lake of Constance, November 17th, 375 A.D. He possessed many great and distinguished merits, and well deserves a place amongst the ranks of illustrious Romans.

(6) Valens, who had been made Emperor of the East during his brother's, Valentinian's, reign (364 A.D.), adopted Arianism, and cruelly persecuted the orthodox, causing the death of eighty of their ecclesiastics in 370 A.D. He received baptism at the hands of Eudoxus, the Arian prelate of Constantinople, who is said to have exacted an oath from him to persecute the orthodox. According to Gibbon, he was 'rude without vigour, and feeble without mildness.' He perished at the sanguinary and disastrous battle of Adrianople, in which the Goths were victorious, August 9th, 378 A.D.

(7) Gratian, the son of Valentinian, on the death

of Valens, became master of the whole empire. He was gentle, amiable, chaste, and literary; but he was wanting in force and vigour of character, which caused him to sanction at times the persecution of those who were opposed to Christianity. He was the friend of the distinguished Ambrose of Milan, whose influence over the emperor's mind was great. In the year 379 A.D., he made Theodosius his colleague in the empire, and invested him with the government of the East. Gratian affirmed the principle of religious equality and toleration at the commencement of his reign, but afterwards (perhaps under the influence of Ambrose), was more severe in his attacks upon paganism than any of the emperors who preceded him had ever shown themselves. On August 25th, 383 A.D. Gratian was slain by Andragathius, at the instigation of Maximus, probably in the neighbourhood of Lugdunum. In his last extremity he is said to have uttered the name of Ambrose.

(8) Theodosius the Great, the son of a Christian father—a general who had restored Britain to the empire—was of Spanish descent, and his family had acknowledged the Creed of Nicæa. He was a warm friend of the orthodox, and previous to his expedition against the Goths, in 380 A.D., was baptised in the name of the Trinity, by the Archbishop Ascolius, at Thessalonica. His zeal for the unity of the faith, and uniformity of worship, was fanned by Ambrose, who exerted a powerful influence over him. He expelled the Arian Archbishop of Constantinople, and appointed Gregory of Nazianzum in his place. He convened a synod at Constantinople in 381 A.D. of 150 bishops, the second general or œcumenical council, to confirm the creed established

at the Council of Nicæa in 325 A.D., which Constantine the Great had convoked. Within fourteen years (from 380 to 394 A.D.) Theodosius published no less than fifteen decrees against heretics, especially against those who rejected the doctrine of the Trinity. A warrior himself, trained under his warlike father, successful against the Goths, and with a natural tendency to violence of passion, he showed more clemency than could have been expected towards the city of Antioch, upon being appealed to by the suppliant entreaties of the bishop and others in authority, when it rose in sedition in 387 A.D., and threw down the statues of the emperor, of his wife, and of his father ; but exhibited a cruel and treacherous severity towards the inhabitants of the city of Thessalonica, who had murdered the garrison that occupied the place in 390 A.D., for which sanguinary retaliation the emperor deigned to pay his celebrated penance to Ambrose, Archbishop of Milan.

After having established Valentinian II. in possession of the West, Theodosius returned to Constantinople in the year 391 A.D., but subsequently moved to the West, defeated Eugenius, and died at Milan on January 17th, 395 A.D., recommending his sons, Arcadius and Honorius, with his last breath to regard true religion as the great bulwark and protection of the imperial power.

It has been remarked by Gibbon, that ' the ruin of paganism in the age of Theodosius is, perhaps, the only example of the total extirpation of any ancient and popular superstition, and may therefore deserve to be considered as a singular event in the history of the human mind.' If Theodosius did not actually extirpate heathenism, he certainly entertained the design of doing so. He forbad heathen sacrifices, and the consultation . of the entrails of animals. In his reign many heathen temples were destroyed, and the lands of those temples given to Christian churches. His reign was undoubtedly one of the most important epochs in the history of the Latin empire, and he may fairly be regarded as the last emperor who honourably maintained the dignity of the Roman name.

(9) Arcadius, the elder of his two sons, was born in the year 383 A.D. His education was conducted partly by a heathen philosopher and partly by a Christian saint. In his twelfth year (395 A.D.) he received from his father the title of Augustus, and in the same year, on the death of his father, he became Emperor of the East, while the empire of the West was given to his younger brother, Honorius. Arcadius was the first of the line of emperors who reigned at Constantinople from the year 395 A.D. to the year 1453, when the city was taken by the Turks. Arcadius was not, as his father Theodosius had been, distinguished either for his personal appearance, his ability, or his manliness. He had no will of his own, and was successively under the influence of chamberlains, favourites, and women. He had made his favourite Eutropius—contrary to all precedent—both consul and general of his forces. On his favourite's fall he became subject to the will of his wife, Eudoxia, the daughter of a Frankish general in the imperial army, famous for her beauty, her arrogance, and the determination of her character. It was through her influence, to a great extent, that Chrysostom was banished from Constantinople.

Arcadius himself was sincerely attached to the Christian faith, and confirmed the various laws which his father had introduced for its protection. On May 1st, 408 A.D., Arcadius died, leaving the empire to his son, Theodosius II., who was then a minor.

Such is a brief sketch of the lives of the different emperors who occupied the throne about or during the age in which Chrysostom lived and died. Such a sketch is absolutely necessary for the right understanding of the history of the Church during that period.

The life of the great Christian orator of the fourth century, John Chrysostom, seems naturally to divide itself into three distinguishing periods.

The first embraces that portion of his life which extended from his birth to the time when he was admitted into holy orders. This may be regarded as the seed-time of that abundant harvest of piety, fame, and usefulness which afterwards displayed itself.

The second period comprises those years that elapsed from his admission to deacon's orders to the time of his departure from Antioch,—years spent in active ministerial work, when he acquired that marvellous reputation as a Christian orator which led to his elevation to one of the highest posts of dignity in the Church.

The third period includes the shorter space of time in which he filled the archiepiscopal throne at Constantinople, together with the sad, yet brilliant, close of his eventful life, when his sun went down in glory, though amid the dark clouds of exile and suffering.

BOOK I.

FROM CHRYSOSTOM'S BIRTH TO THE END OF HIS ASCETIC LIFE.

CHAPTER I.

ANTIOCH, THE BIRTH-PLACE OF CHRYSOSTOM.

Civitas gloriosa et nobilis, tertium vel potius secundum (nam de hoc maxima quæstio est) post urbem Romam dignitatis gradum sortita; omnium provinciarum quas tractus Orientalis continet, princeps et moderatrix.—WILLIAM OF TYRE.

CLIMATE and outward circumstances exert no slight influence upon the lives and dispositions of individual men, and even insensibly mould or modify the character of nations. Hence it would be a grave omission not to refer at the outset to the probable effect upon the tone of feeling and cast of thought, which the great city of his birth exercised over the susceptible nature of Chrysostom. Antioch was 'no mean city' either in situation, history, or associations. It deserves, therefore, more than a passing notice at our hands.

It stood highest amongst the cities of the East, until the rising fame of Constantinople cast its glories somewhat into the shade. It was, in the words of Chrysostom,[1] the 'head and mother of the Eastern cities.' Antioch was in fact an Oriental Rome, possessing alike the advantages and the disadvantages of the world's capital. In the vast throng of people that

[1] πολέων τῶν ὑπὸ τὴν ἕω κειμένων κεφαλὴ καὶ μήτηρ (*Hom. de Statuis,* iii. § 1. It has been styled πόλις βασίλισσα (Gothofred), and by Josephus, the third city in the Roman world.

flocked there from every quarter ; in its exaggerated refinement and civilisation that almost bordered on softness and effeminacy ; in the luxury, extravagance and sensuality, which followed in the train of its wealth, refinement, and ease ; in the striking contrast between abject poverty and boundless riches that its different inhabitants presented ;[1] in its abandonment to the pleasures of sense, and to everything that appealed to the eye or to the ear ; in its wild devotion to the struggles, contests, and factions of the hippodrome ; in all these respects it imitated with singular fidelity the characteristic features of the great Empress of the West, exerting even a certain degree of influence upon its powerful rival, so that Juvenal could say in his *Satires*—' In Tiberim defluxit Orontes.' (iii. 62).

1. The position of Antioch demands our first notice. Its geographical site tended greatly to its development and its eminence. It was situated at the sharp angle which is formed by the meeting of the two important countries of Phœnicia and Asia Minor, as the former runs upward from south to north, and as the latter trends from west to east. At the point of meeting or incidence of these two districts, some twenty miles from the Mediterranean Sea, under the shadow on the north-east of the great masses of the Taurus chain of Mount Amanus and Libanus—the one celebrated alike in Greek and Latin story, the other in the sacred poetry of the Jews—with Mount Casius rising up in a symmetrical cone to the height of almost 5,000 feet on the south-west, in a valley some five miles broad and ten

---

[1] Chrysostom says (*Hom. in Matt.* lxvi. § 3), ' The rich form one-tenth part of the citizens, and the poor, who have nothing, another tenth. The remainder are of the middle class.'

miles long, the city of Antioch was built. The Orontes—of old called 'Typhon,' from its mythic origin—which had hitherto flowed from its source in Cœle-Syria from south to north, here makes a rapid bend to the west, and sweeps either through or by the city, pursuing a meandering course till it empties itself into the Bay of Antioch.

A break in the mountain-chain of Amanus near the site of Antioch afforded an entrance into the lands of Asia Minor by the Beilan Pass, named the 'Amanides Pylæ,'[1] while great high-roads brought it into connection with Constantinople through Asia Minor, and with Alexandria by the famous coast-route, which ran southward along the borders of the Mediterranean Sea through Cæsarea to the Egyptian capital. It had also a communication opened out to all the rich countries of the East, as far as Zeugma on the Euphrates, along which route the loaded caravans were continually passing ; while its harbour at Seleucia, into which the Orontes flowed, brought in all the produce of the far-famed lands that bordered on the Mediterranean Sea. Thus it has been said to have 'united the inland advantages of Aleppo with the maritime opportunities of Smyrna.'[2]

The Orontes, with its deep bed and rapid stream, after receiving a tributary from a lake situated about a mile from the old city, encircled the island on which the new city was partially built, and greatly tended to its beauty and fertility. Like Damascus, Antioch was a city of waters. Not only were its

---

[1] Cf. Cicero *ad Fam.* xv. 4. As governor of Cilicia, Cicero knew the country well.

[2] Conybeare and Howson's *Life of St. Paul*, i. 132.

baths copiously supplied, but every house and garden of any importance had its fountains and trickling streams to temper the heat of the Eastern sun. The Orontes itself (over whose bed great physical changes have passed since the times of which we are speaking) made its noisy and murmuring way, like our own 'babbling Wye,' through precipitous cliffs and ravines, where grew in luxuriant richness the fig-tree, the vine, the arbutus, the dwarf oak and sycamore, the ilex, bay, and myrtle, all mingled together in extreme beauty, during its passage to the sea, towards which it ran in a navigable stream, widely distinguished from the ordinary scenery on the banks of Eastern rivers, 'vocal in its wooded walls.'

It was not to be wondered at that a city thus placed, 'beautiful for situation,' called emphatically 'Antioch the beautiful,' should have attracted residents from every quarter, and that not only the Graeco-Syrian kings, but also the Roman emperors and wealthy nobles, should have settled there. Lying beneath the vast and tumbled masses of the great mountains of the Taurus range, and within sight of the less severe and rugged outline of the heights of Libanus, the westerly breeze cooling its temperature, and the rapid Orontes refreshing and fertilising the soil through which it hurried in its course to the sea,—the very 'Gate of the East,' adapted for commerce, literature, refinement, and luxury,—with noble buildings and palaces, and pleasures of every sort to offer to its residents, it is no wonder that Antioch stood high in the estimate of the princes of the East and West, and the rich and powerful of the Roman world.

2. Such a situation naturally attracted the atten-

tion of Seleucus Nicator, *founder* of Antioch, so famous as a builder of cities, when looking out for a site for the capital of his Græco-Syrian kingdom. To distinguish it from other cities that bore the same name, it was sometimes called Antioch by Daphne, from the name of the notorious grove bordering on the city, where Apollo was worshipped, and sometimes Antioch on the Orontes, from its storied river. Of the sixteen cities in Asia of the same name of which Seleucus Nicator was the builder, Antioch (which was named either after his father or his son) occupied the highest and most distinguished place. The city became, in process of time, a tetrapolis, bearing testimony to the three additions which were made to the original city founded by Seleucus. He himself built his city, about 300 B.C., between the Orontes and the steep and craggy heights of Mount Silpius, which rose from the level of the river in two summits, separated from each other by a narrow gorge, through which in winter a mountain-torrent poured down. This was the site of the original city, around which the other parts grew up under the forming hands of different founders and builders, till at length it became a four-fold city.

Antioch could not, indeed, lay claim to the immemorial antiquity of Damascus—for to attempt, with Jerome, to identify it with Riblah of the Old Testament, has been shown to be a mere figment of the imagination—but it was one of the noble productions of the Macedonian era and of the Seleucidæ. As of old, at the foundation of Rome, auguries were taken by Romulus from the Palatine Hill, so also, at the building of Antioch, similar auguries were taken by Seleucus on Mount Casius from the flight of birds;

and the course of an eagle to the hill of Silpius settled the exact spot where the city should be founded,—a legend which is embodied in the coinage of the city, in which an eagle bearing the thigh of its victim is not unfrequently delineated.

In the depression or valley lying between the river and the hill, Seleucus, through the agency of the architect Xenæus, founded the original city. As we have already said, three other portions, severally encircled by their own walls, were subsequently added.

Antigonus, the rival of Seleucus, had originally intended that Antigoneia should be the capital of the Syrian empire; but when he fell in the battle of Ipsus, his successful opponent determined to find another metropolis for the kingdom, and built Antioch somewhat lower down on the Orontes, removing (it has been supposed) the inhabitants from the old and abandoned city to the new one which he founded. Not only does it seem probable that the natives of the surrounding district were subsequently admitted into citizenship in the new city, but that Jews were also permitted to partake of similar political advantages and rights. Hence arose a *second* portion of the city, due to the same founder. We learn not only from Tacitus, but also from Josephus, that an assembly of the people was held in the theatre in the days of Vespasian and Titus; and we gather from Julian's statement, that afterwards there was a senate consisting of 200 members. We find, also, that the inhabitants of the city were classified under eighteen local tribes. It is impossible to doubt that Seleucus Nicator built his city with magnificence and splendour, and that his son Antiochus contributed to the architectural beauties of the place ; but we have no specific or detailed information on which to rely.

The *third* part of the city, which was called the new city by Libanius and Evagrius, was built by Seleucus Callinicus on the island formed by the Orontes, according to the assertion of Strabo ; but according to Libanius the rhetorician, by Antiochus the Great, who is said to have colonised it from Greece, when engaged in war with the power of Rome, about the year 190 B.C. This portion of Antioch is described with considerable minuteness by Libanius. We owe also a good deal of what is known about it to the Church historian Evagrius (ii. 12), in his description of the destructive earthquake which took place in the days of Leo the Great. This part of the city was built, as we have seen, on the island. Hence it resembled that portion of Paris which was erected on the island formed by the Seine, though with this difference, that in the case of Paris it was the old city which was built on the island, while at Antioch it was the new city that sprang up there. This new city was attached to the old by five bridges which spanned the river. And thus the statement of Polybius (v. 69) is verified, that the Orontes flowed *through* the city of Antioch. The streets, as we may gather from Muller's excellent plan of the city, were constructed according to a definite and uniform design, with a four-fold arch or ' tetrapylum ' (as Dean Howson describes it), at the intersection of the streets, while the splendid palace hard by the river on the northern side commanded fine views of the outlying district and of the distant country.

The *fourth* part of the city was added by Antiochus Epiphanes, who inherited the architectural tastes of his predecessors of the Seleucid dynasty. The portion of the city constructed by him lay between the old wall and Mount Silpius, while the new wall which he raised stretched upward, and encompassed some of the steep crags which towered above the city. Epiphanes added much to the grandeur of Antioch. He erected a noble temple, consecrated to the worship of Jupiter Capitolinus, which Livy the historian (xli. 20) describes as rich with golden ornaments. He also built a house in which the senate could hold their meetings. But his grand and crowning architectural work was the glorious street with a colonnade on each side, which ran in an even and level line through the entire length of the city from east to west in an unbroken extent for the space of four miles. This formed a grand promenade in which the inhabitants could walk, sheltered either from the heat of the sun or from rain. It was intersected by other streets, symmetrically arranged at right angles to it, by which the river was reached on the one side, and on the other the groves and gardens that lay on the slope of the hill. Where the chief street cut through the Street of the Colonnades was the Omphalus, adorned by a statue of Apollo. Such was the fourth portion of the tetrapolis, — the magnificent work of Epiphanes.

A museum was afterwards erected near Mount Silpius, by Antiochus Philopator, and it is with this period that the fame for literature and the fine arts at Antioch is connected, which is described in such strong language by Cicero in his well-known speech in favour of Archias.

Antioch at this period must have almost equalled

Paris in size, and to the beauty of its architecture the different monarchs of the Seleucid dynasty, whom Milton calls 'the luxurious kings of Antioch,' had lavishly contributed with a generous rivalry.

Nor, again, did a long line of Roman emperors less zealously strive to render Antioch beautiful among cities. Freedom and independence were conferred upon it by Pompey, and it retained this self-government till it was converted into a 'colony' by Antoninus Pius. It was there that Cæsar built not only a theatre, amphitheatre, and baths, but also a basilica which claimed the title of Cæsareum ; there Agrippa added a suburb, and Herod the Great a colonnade ; there Caligula and other emperors erected additional baths, and Commodus formed a public promenade called Xystus, and Diocletian built a palace; and it was there that the noble Germanicus died, to the grief of all true-hearted Romans.

It suffered, indeed, from many earthquakes, especially the memorable one when Trajan fled for refuge to the Circus ; and in the year 260 A.D. Sapor and the Persians captured the city, taking the inhabitants by surprise when their attention was completely absorbed by the fascinations of the theatre.

After the foundation of Constantinople its political supremacy declined ; but it became more distinguished as a Christian city, and, like Constantinople and Alexandria, attained to the dignity of a patriarchal city. Within its walls no less than ten councils were held between 250 and 380 A.D., and it became distinguished for a new development of church architecture. One church there was which possesses a peculiar interest, commenced by Constantine and completed by his son, which was closed by Julian, but restored to the purposes of Christian worship by Jovian,—the great and famous church in which Chrysostom preached his heart-stirring sermons to a thronging and admiring crowd of listeners. It was (so he tells us) adorned with mosaic work, precious stones, and statues. Its dome, gilded within, rose to a lofty and imposing height. In its structure it was an octagon. Nor is it improbable that Antioch set the example in the East of churches of this peculiar form. The city was indebted to Constantine for other buildings also, among them for a prætorium, a basilica, and a hospice for strangers, erected close to the chief church. Constantine passed so much time at Antioch, that the city acquired the name of Constantia. His works at the harbour of Seleucia were many and various, and traces of them still remain. It is well known that Julian made great efforts to please the citizens, but, to his annoyance, signally failed, as we gather from his *Misopogon.* Valens added much to the architectural embellishment of Antioch, and erected a noble forum, adorned with marble columns and a marble floor. Theodosius took away from the city its metropolitical status, on account of the destruction of the statues in the famous sedition of 387 A.D., referred to in the Introduction.

We have now come down to the age of Chrysostom himself, in whose *Homilies* we can discover many allusions to different circumstances and incidents connected with Antioch. He states, for example, that the population of the city amounted to about 200,000, of which number half were Christians. Libanius also, so intimately associated with Chrysostom, furnishes us with full accounts of the different buildings in the city. The city was visited by a desolating earthquake in Justinian's day, just as it was rising out of a state of decadence into new glory and reputation, and this visitation was followed by its total ruin by Chosroes and the Persians. But notwithstanding all these misfortunes, a new city, called Theupolis, sprung into existence under the influence of Justinian, smaller, indeed, than the former one, and with a more contracted circuit of walls.

To make our sketch complete, it may be added, that during the Middle Ages its history is a record of a general but gradual decadence. It was taken from the Romans by the Saracens about the year 635 A.D., and recaptured in the tenth century by Nicephorus Phocas by means of a surprise similar to that by which we have already seen it was seized in former days by the Persians. No doubt many traces of the influence of four long centuries of Mahometan rule must have been discernible. Until the year 1084 A.D., it remained under the control of the Emperor of Constantinople, when it was captured by the Seljuks. Within fifteen years from this time it was besieged and taken by the Latins in the first crusade, the famous Godfrey and Tancred being prominent in the events that took place. Boemund I. then became its prince, and for well-nigh two hundred years it continued a Christian city. At length, in the days of Boemund VI., it fell once again under the sway of the Sultan of Egypt and his forces, 1268 A.D.

From this date its fall was rapid and complete. The modern town of Antakieh in the pachalik of Aleppo—the poor and miserable representative of the ancient splendour of Antioch—is a wretched place situated by the Orontes in the north-western portion of the old city, consisting, according to the census of 1835, of about 5,600 inhabitants, and with no church for its Christian population. The ancient walls and towers are still traceable in their ruins for a circuit of about four miles, stretching in parts over the rugged heights of Silpius.

3. The next question of importance is the position in the Christian Church that Antioch held, and the associations that are entwined around it.

Gradually in the narrative of the Acts of the Apostles, Antioch usurps the place of Jerusalem. The Christians were dispersed abroad in the persecution 'that arose about Stephen,' and this dispersion extended even as far as Antioch. There some of the Hellenistic Jews, who were natives of Cyprus and Cyrene, addressed the Greeks at Antioch, 'preaching the Lord Jesus,' in consequence of which preaching 'a great number believed and turned unto the Lord.' Barnabas — whose original name was Joses, a Levite of Cyprus, but named by the apostles the 'Son of Consolation,'—was accordingly sent from Jerusalem, the Mother Church, to the newly-enrolled Christians at Antioch, to exhort them to cleave unto the Lord, which mission he, being a 'good man, and full of the Holy Ghost and faith,' successfully accomplished. Seeing the importance of the work to be done there, he went to Tarsus to fetch his energetic and zealous friend Saul, feeling (as Chrysostom has expressed it in his twenty-fifth homily) that Antioch was more important than Tarsus, that the multitude there was great, and that the rich soil promised a fair and productive spiritual harvest.

Saul recognised the call of God in this appeal of Barnabas, and went with him to the metropolis of Syria, and there they tarried 'a whole year,' teaching 'much people,' so that the Christian Church there became well known and prominent. Gradually the Jewish character of the early converts disappeared, and the sect of the Jews was merged in the wider and more comprehensive title of 'Christian,'—a name given to them, no doubt, by the Gentiles, for Jews would not have been likely to employ in derision a term which was the Greek equivalent of 'Messiah,' and we know that the first followers of Christ called themselves 'saints,' or 'brethren,' or 'believers,' or 'disciples.' The term, too, has a Roman form about it (like Herodians, Pompeians, Vitellians, etc.), to express the partisans or followers of a certain person. It was thus that a name of derision became afterwards a title of glory.

It was, indeed, a characteristic fault of the citizens of Antioch, that they indulged in ridicule and scurrility, and were notorious for devising nicknames. Julian suffered from this evil habit of theirs, and in his vexation declared that 'Antioch contained more buffoons than citizens.' Apollonius of Tyana was also driven out of their city by the same bantering and jesting spirit on their part ; and when Chosroes invaded the city, the inhabitants brought destruction on their own heads by their suicidal folly in indulging in bitter raillery and jests at the expense of the Persians.

In the journeys of St. Paul, it was not Jerusalem but Antioch that was the place from whence he started and to which he returned.

Chrysostom invariably speaks of Antioch with

deep and singular respect.[1]   He tells the inhabitants that though they vaunted the pre-eminence of their city in having first enjoyed the Christian name, they were willing to be surpassed in Christian virtue by more homely cities.[2]   He speaks of Antioch as 'the patriarchal city of the Christian name.'

It is remarkable that Chaldæan astrologers found their most credulous dupes within the walls of Antioch, and Chrysostom complains that even Christians themselves were hurried away by their passion for horoscopes. It has also been observed, that Jewish impostors, common enough throughout the East, found their most favourable opportunities at Antioch. At the Grove of Daphne, which Gibbon[3] has graphically described, we can trace all the 'complicated heathenism' that then prevailed, 'where, under the climate of Syria and the wealthy patronage of Rome, all that was beautiful in nature and in art had created a sanctuary for a perpetual festival of vice.'

Antioch was represented, in a well-known statue, as a fair female figure, seated on a rock, with a crown on her head, and Orontes under her feet.

Such, then, was Antioch, the queen of the cities of the East, in her glorious prime. In form four-square (like most of the cities built by the successors of Alexander), and embellished by magnificent colonnades which extended from one end of the city to the other from the Gate of the Cherubim to the Gate of St. Paul. Surrounded by lofty and precipitous moun-

---

[1] See *Hom. on St. Matt.* vii.
[2] Cf. Conybeare and Howson's *St. Paul*, i. 132, note.
[3] In chap. xxiii. of his *Decline and Fall.*

tains, under whose broad shadow it rested, fertilised by the rapid waters of the restless Orontes, there floated around it imperishable memories of the early upgrowth of Christianity. Within those walls the title of Christian—that name above all other names in interest—first originated.   There Nicolas, one of the seven deacons, had lived : there the first Gentile Church was founded : thence St. Paul set out on his three great missionary journeys, which ended with his imprisonment at Jerusalem and Cæsarea : there Ignatius, the apostolical bishop, in the early days of Christianity discharged the duties of his office and episcopate.

How great, then, must have been the influence of such a city, both direct and indirect, on a character so ardent, and so susceptible to outward impressions, as that of Chrysostom !

High thoughts and feelings could not fail to have stirred within him as, day by day, he lived, and moved, and had his being,

> ‘ Where huge Taurus, with his brow
> High heaved above the clouds, eternally
> Keeps watch upon the sun, uplifting thought
> Beyond the sensual and the sublunary,
> The darkness, and the storm, and stir of earth
> To the unchanging peacefulness of heaven !’

CHAPTER II.

THE BIRTH AND PARENTAGE OF CHRYSOSTOM.

> ' 'Twere logic misapplied,
> To prove a consequence by none denied,
> That we are bound to cast the minds of youth
> Betimes into the mould of heavenly truth,
> That, taught of God, they may indeed be wise,
> Nor, ignorantly wand'ring, miss the skies.'

JOHN, surnamed from his remarkable and singular eloquence 'Chrysostom,'[1] or the 'golden-mouthed,' first saw the light in the famous capital of the Græco-Syrian kings. We are unable to fix with certainty the time when the characteristic epithet of 'golden-mouthed' was first bestowed upon him. It could scarcely have been given him during his life, since no allusion is made to it during that period of time by any writer, and we may fairly infer that so honourable a title would never have been passed over in silence by any one in their description of the great archbishop. He is simply known as 'John' at that period, and indeed for some considerable time afterwards. But when we come to the close of the fifth century, we find that writers almost invariably assigned to him the title of

---

[1] His Greek title was Ἰωάννης Χρυσόστομος.

Chrysostom,[1] and that his original name of 'John' is no longer employed to designate him, except in combination with the newer title of honour by which he was destined to be subsequently known through the long centuries down to the present day. It was a singular as well as an honourable cognomen. An Archbishop of Ravenna, who died about 450 A.D., famous also for his eloquence, and the author of many remarkable homilies or sermons, had, indeed, a somewhat similar surname bestowed upon him, having been designated 'Chrysologus.'

It is usually supposed that the year 347 A.D. was rendered famous by being the year of Chrysostom's birth, as it was probably also that of Jerome's. To this date the general consensus of opinion points. Some writers, indeed, have assigned his birth to the year 344 A.D., while others have regarded 354 A.D. as the more exact period. But it cannot be doubted that in favour of the year 347 A.D. we have the greatest weight of authority, and the most uniform verdict of tradition.

The family from which Chrysostom sprang was both noble and opulent. His father, Secundus, stood high as a general in the imperial army. He filled a distinguished post of command, being a *magister militum*, and by virtue of that honourable office he was designated *Illustris*. He would, in fact, appear to have been one of the limited number of eight generals, on whom devolved the important command of the imperial forces. He died so soon

---

[1] Subsequently to 437 A.D., he was called by one of his successors, namely Proclus, χρυσοῦς τῆν γλῶτταν. The surname of 'Chrysostom' is said by Gieseler to have been first employed by Joannes Moschus. Such is Dr. Wordsworth's opinion, *Church History*, iv. 123, note.

after his son's birth, that he could have done no more than leave him the legacy of an honourable name, the example of duty well discharged in the emperor's service, and an entrance into that high rank of society in which he himself had moved. So, too, many of the most distinguished fathers of the Church were descended from noble parentage and from wealthy families. We may refer to Jerome, Ambrose, Gregory of Nazianzum, and Basil the Great, who all sprang from noble or rich parents, or possessed relatives of distinction.

But the youthful Chrysostom found in his gifted and devoted mother, Anthusa, a compensation for the loss of his father in the tender years of his infancy. She, too, like Secundus, was descended from a family of distinction. A widow at a very early age—for she could not have been more than twenty years old when her husband died—she had to regulate the affairs of her household, and to attend to the management of her son's property, in the midst of the calumnies and temptations which assailed so young a widow in the profligate city of Antioch. But nobly did she discharge the duties that devolved on her. She devoted all her time, her energies, and her talents, to the training and education of her promising boy. No doubt, with the fortune which she possessed, with youth in her favour, and with a distinguished social position, she could not fail to have received many offers of marriage. But she remained true to her resolve of giving herself up entirely to the education of her young son, and to the superintendence of his fortune and estates. Proof against the different fascinations which wealth offered, and resisting all the invitations made to her to change her widowed state, she never married again.   All her efforts were directed to the absorbing desire which she felt to keep her son free from the enticements to evil which abounded on every side—to exert over him a moral and religious influence—and to super-intend and regulate the course of his education and the management of his estates. She was undoubtedly a woman of the highest Christian principle ; and, like Monica, was deeply anxious that her son should follow in her steps, and devote himself to the service of God.

With this great object in view, she spared no pains to inculcate in his young and docile mind the truths of religion, and strove with all the energy of a selfless and self-sacrificing love to shield him from the corruptions and contaminations of the luxurious and sensual city of his birth. In that self-pleasing and voluptuous capital her conduct was so singular, and differed so widely from that of the majority of young and wealthy widows, that it could not escape obser-vation, however much she, in her modesty, might shrink from anything that approximated to publicity. When Chrysostom was introduced to Libanius, who was not himself a Christian, for the purpose of attending his lectures, and when he mentioned to that famous professor of rhetoric that his mother, now in her fortieth year, had been a widow for half that period of time, having been only twenty years old when, in the bloom of her youth and beauty, her husband had died, he could not refrain from ex-claiming in astonishment, — ' What women these Christians have ! ' [1]

It does not, indeed, admit of dispute, that many

[1] Cf. Chrysost. *Ad viduam Juniorem,* i. 2.

of the Christian women of that age exercised a vast influence for good upon the community, and formed a 'sanctuary for Christianity.' Their bright example, · their admirable management of their children, their excellent regulation of their households, the high standard of their morality, their noble self-sacrifice, —all these distinguished qualities so added to the growth of true religion among those over whom their influence extended, and so strengthened the cause of Christianity, that, in their despair, the advocates of heathenism ridiculed the husbands for being subject to the sway of those whom it was their place to govern. The contrast, in too many an instance, between the pleasure-seeking, money-getting, licentious lives of the men, and the self-devoted efforts of the women in the retirement of family life to direct in the path of religious belief the hearts and minds of their sons and daughters, was too, marked to escape the attention of all the more thoughtful and virtuous of the heathen community. They could not help fearing for the prospects of the old faith, when they perceived in such women as these the power which the new faith could exert over its professors. They felt that all the influence which could be brought to bear upon the fathers and husbands by the advocates of heathenism would inevitably be neutralised by the wives and daughters, when converted to Christianity, and that nothing could resist their zeal and their persuasive teaching. It was to this cause —the influence, namely, exerted by Christian women over their male relatives—that Julian ascribed the failure of his scheme to bring Antioch back to the acknowledgment of heathenism.

Nor can it be doubted that the minds of some of

the most distinguished theologians were moulded, fashioned, and guided by the influence of Christian mothers, and that it was, under God, owing to the effects of such teaching that they became what they were in their after lives. Who can hesitate to ascribe to the prayers, the instruction, and the example of the pious and devoted Monica, the formation of the grand character of the great Augustine? Who can doubt the vast influence which the devout and zealous Nonna exercised over the mind of Gregory Nazianzen in his very earliest days,—the son whom she had devoted, even before he was born, to the service of God? Who can deny the powerful influence on the mind of Theodoret (who, like Chrysostom, was a native of Antioch) which his pious mother exerted, training him, as a special ' gift of God,' granted to her prayers, and consecrating him from his earliest infancy to a religious life with a care and an earnestness, to which he often bears the most grateful testimony?

Nor was Chrysostom's debt to his widowed mother, Anthusa, at all less than that which the other great fathers of the early Church, to whom reference has been made, owed to the loving care and affectionate teaching of their pious mothers. Anthusa felt that in the religious education and training of her son she was doing that which her affection for her departed husband demanded at her hands. She seemed to trace in the child the likeness of his father, and to renew her old love and regard in her affection for her son. She had, indeed, another child, a daughter older than John Chrysostom, who no doubt participated in her tender care; but this daughter was apparently taken from her in early childhood, and thus Chrysostom concentrated in himself all the loving devotion of his widowed mother.

It was from her that he received his first religious impressions, which he imbibed at so early a period of his life, that his Christian principles were formed gradually and almost imperceptibly, nor have we any account of his having passed through any such violent struggle of soul and body as that which rent and agitated St. Augustine.

This gradual and almost imperceptible growth and progress in Divine things, this almost insensible advance, day by day, in the religious life, was no doubt, in the providence of God, owing to the gentle, loving, Christian influence, and the persuasive teaching of his devoted and affectionate mother from his earliest childhood.

Anthusa did not, like the mother of Gregory Nazianzen, dedicate her son from infancy, either to monasticism or to the special service of the Church. Such a consecration to holy things no doubt produced in sensitive and susceptible natures a deep impression, and thus we are told that before the mind of Gregory there constantly floated in his infancy the form of Samuel. Nor did she imitate the example of the great majority of parents amongst the higher classes, and merely propose to educate her son superficially in that kind of knowledge which at that time was the chief passport to political distinction and valuable appointments. She placed a higher standard of intellectual excellence than this before her. As she had striven with heart and soul to build up his young mind with a deep and solid groundwork of religious teaching, and to fix all the tenets of Christianity firmly and steadfastly in his inmost nature, so

she could not rest contented with the shallow
intellectual training with which the wealthy at
Antioch were satisfied for their sons. Her aspirations and desires took a higher range than this ; and,
as we shall see in the sequel, her wishes were realised
in the case of her favourite son, and her highest
aspirations more than gratified in the future results
of that more solid system of education which she had
carried out in his case.

CHAPTER III.

CHRYSOSTOM'S EDUCATIONAL CAREER.

INFLUENCED, as we have seen, by a high and exalted estimate of what an intellectual education ought to be, Anthusa was not satisfied with placing her son under the care of mere superficial teachers or dilettanti professors of science. She desired to see her fondly-loved and talented boy deeply acquainted with the whole range of Grecian literature and philosophy, that thus he might be enabled, in process of time, to form his own judgment on the different problems that agitated the world in that age. Acting upon this view, we cannot doubt that she carefully examined into the claims of the different teachers who then occupied the foremost place in Antioch. Her choice was unlimited in such a city, which would be likely to attract eminent professors from every quarter. As it was said that any one who sat in the market-place at Antioch might learn · the manners of many cities, so no doubt every class of instructors could be found to teach the children of so many wealthy and illustrious inhabitants the different branches of a refined and elegant education.

The anxious mother, therefore, must have been subjected to much care and labour in her choice of a tutor for her boy, in whom the germs of talent and the promise of much future distinction could not fail to have been apparent. After rejecting many professors on various grounds, and hesitating in her decision respecting the rival claims of others, she at last fixed upon the famous sophist and rhetorician Libanius, whose reputation was world-wide. He was himself a native of Antioch, which circumstance we can readily imagine enhanced his claims in her estimation ; and, moreover, he was a member of a noble family in that city. He had studied profoundly at Athens, and was deeply imbued with the literature of Greece, to which he had devoted particular time and attention. His reputation at Athens was so great, that it was thought highly probable that had he remained in that classic city,—

> ' The eye of Greece, mother of arts
> And eloquence, native to famous wits,
> Or hospitable,'—

he would have been appointed to fill the chair of rhetoric. From Athens he went to Constantinople, in which city he set up a private school ; but such was the estimation in which he was held, that in a short time he had emptied the classes of the various professors in that city, and brought upon himself such an amount of envy and ill-will from those with whose interests he so materially interfered, that he was charged by them with being a magician, and through their active influence was expelled from the city. Thence he went to Nicomedia, where he realised an equal amount of success, and, after a delightful residence in that place of about five years, he was invited to return to Constantinople. He neither liked his reception there, nor did he accept the professorship of rhetoric which was offered him at Athens, and after a period of ill-health at Constantinople, he obtained permission from the emperor to take up his abode in his native city of Antioch. He was regarded with much favour and esteem by the Emperor Julian, with whom he corresponded, and with the Emperors Valens and Theodosius he maintained equally friendly relations. He was tolerant of Christianity, though himself a pagan, and was probably the instructor of Basil the Great.

The experience of Libanius was very extensive, stretching over Athens, Constantinople, Nicomedia, and Antioch. He had seen many cities and many men. It is probably a true estimate of his capacities that Dr. Schmitz has formed : ' Libanius,' he says, ' is by far the most talented and most successful among the rhetoricians of the fourth century ; he took the best orators of the classic age as his models, and we can often see in him the disciple and happy imitator of Demosthenes, and his animated descriptions are often full of power and elegance ; but he is not always able to rise above the spirit of his age, and we rarely find in him that natural simplicity which constitutes the great charm of the best Attic orators.' Such was the teacher under whom Anthusa placed her talented son.

The brilliant powers of Libanius as an orator, his firm belief in the mythology and religion of heathenism, and the wide range of his acquaintance with the classic literature of Greece, might perhaps have proved detrimental to the faith of his devoted and ardent disciple, had he not been fortified against such influences by the persuasive teaching of his mother, and by his own constant and deep study of Holy Scripture, which, like Timothy, he had been taught from his earliest days. To the value of such study of Holy Scripture Chrysostom often bears the strongest testimony. It has been supposed, from what he has himself told us,[1] that he possessed some knowledge of Hebrew, with which language scarcely any of the fathers of the Church were acquainted.

To the Sacred Scriptures may be directly traced his ardent love for all that was pure and holy ; his intense dislike to everything which savoured of untruthfulness, or fraud, or deception ; his love of justice, honesty, and righteous dealing ; his determined opposition to all sin, whether disguised in a fairseeming dress, or revealing itself in its native ugliness and deformity. To that sacred volume throughout his whole career, from his very earliest days, Chrysostom invariably appealed, as the source from which he drew the portraiture of the Christian life and the victory of faith, and from which he derived the support and consolation which alone could have cheered and sustained him in his varied trials, dangers, sufferings, and persecutions.

We can trace the influence of the teaching of Libanius in the ornate and rhetorical style of Chrysostom's preaching, and in his constant allusions to the literature

---

[1] *Hom. in Psal.* xlvii. § 2.

of heathenism, whether poetry or prose, as well Homer as Plato. We cannot also fail to remark how all this was, in his case, toned down and modified by the simplicity of his Christian character, the depth and earnestness of his personal piety, as well as by the real breadth of his knowledge and his high intellectual powers. Such progress did he make under Libanius, such striking abilities did he display, and such latent powers as an orator did he manifest, that Libanius was reported to have said on his death-bed, that he should have desired Chrysostom to be his successor in his school of rhetoric, ' if the Christians had not stolen him.'

' He was thus,' it has been remarked, ' prepared in a school of heathen eloquence to become a preacher of the Gospel.' Heathenism, according to the well-known simile, was like the eagle wounded by an arrow feathered from its own plumage. Libanius was unreserved in his praises of Chrysostom's early efforts at oratory, and was especially unqualified in his commendation of one particular panegyric that he is said to have delivered on Constantine and his sons, in imitation of the style of the Sophists, as an oratorical exercise. Such was the training which the youthful Chrysostom received from the famous rhetorician of Antioch, and such was the result of that training.

The name, indeed, of another tutor is mentioned by Socrates and by Sozomen—namely, Andragathius —who would seem to have been a Platonist, as instructing him in philosophy ; but of him and of his influence over Chrysostom nothing is known.

This account of Chrysostom's early training is undoubtedly meagre, but it is perhaps as full as we might expect to have been handed down to us. In the case of Augustine, the account given us of his training is more extensive and varied. We possess, in his autobiography, a record of the schools at which he was taught, and of his education continued through a college or university career.

We have every reason to suppose that Libanius not only endeavoured in every way to develop the intellectual faculties of his brilliant pupil, but also indulged in the fond belief that, after his removal, Chrysostom would be not only qualified, but also disposed to continue the conduct of his school, and to undertake 'the office of maintaining the dignity of paganism' in their native city. He was doomed, however, to lament, as we have seen, 'the sacrilegious seduction of the young orator by the Christians,' and the consequent disappointment of the hopes which he had formed of Chrysostom as a worthy successor in his professorial chair. He could scarcely have escaped a pang of regret, could he have looked forward with prescient eye into the future, and have seen how his favourite pupil would become the 'greatest preacher of Christ to ancient Christendom,' as well as the most distinguished champion of the faith of the Gospel in opposition to the cause of heathenism, which was doomed to a swift destruction.

George, Patriarch of Alexandria, in his life of Chrysostom, which is far from trustworthy, speaks of him as having gone to Athens, outstripped all his contemporaries there, and returned in triumph, having converted even some of his most bitter opponents, who were envious of him, to the Christian faith.

CHAPTER IV.

THE CHOICE OF A PROFESSION FOR CHRYSOSTOM.

Honos, an dulce lucellum,
An secretum iter, et fallentis semita vitæ?

HOR. *Ep.* i. 18, 103.

CHRYSOSTOM having now completed his early training, the question as to his future course of life and the choice of a profession had to be decided. It was an anxious and important crisis in his life. It was a choice that might naturally exert an overwhelming influence upon his career.

One of the learned professions would obviously have been thought of. We cannot suppose that, after such a display of brilliant powers and abilities as he had already exhibited, any profession or calling would for a moment have occurred either to his mother, his tutor, or himself, which was not of an intellectual character. A secular calling was designed for him. He had not been brought up with the idea of being devoted, like Gregory, to the strict service of the Church, and consecrated to it from his early days, like the infant Samuel. It was deemed best that he should move among men, amid the public affairs of the world, in some profession in which laymen were engaged.

He was accordingly introduced into the Forum

and the courts of law as an advocate, and began to practise there with every prospect of attaining the highest eminence which that popular and lucrative profession could hold out to a distinguished practitioner.

Evidently—from what may be gathered from Libanius—his oratorical powers, his brilliant abilities, and his persuasive eloquence, soon acquired for him a high reputation. His speeches attracted the greatest attention, and were listened to with admiration and delight. A distinguished future was opening out before him, though he was now only eighteen years of age. The prospect of honour, fame, wealth, and position, lay spread out before him with tempting distinctness. What men were most eager to attain seemed placed within his grasp. The goal of mature ambition appeared already close at hand. But such worldly prospects of distinction were never destined to be realised. He was not to reap the fruits of fame and eminence in such a field of labour and exertion. A different vocation in life was in store for him.

Very soon after his entrance into the profession of an advocate, he became first pained, then disquieted, and afterwards disgusted at the practices among the members of the bar in that age. The low tone of morality which prevailed in the law courts, and the corrupt practices which he there saw justified, so grieved and offended him, that he felt (as in our day Dr. Arnold[1] felt) that the life of an advocate was likely to prove injurious to his Christian character. The sordid aims which were there set before him, so different from the exalted standard of Gospel excellence, as well as the base and degrading conduct

---

[1] *Life of Dr. Arnold,* ii. 74, by Dean Stanley.

which he saw commonly prevailing amongst advocates in that day and in that city, were thoroughly repugnant to the noble simplicity of his character, and to the religious training which he had received from his earliest days.

His mind, therefore, was soon made up. He determined at once to abandon that which had seemed to be 'gain to him,' and to renounce the pleasures and the attractions which the bar held out, however congenial in some respects to his training and his temperament, since they could not be secured with safety to the higher life of his soul, and to devote himself to some more quiet and secluded life, in which he might—untrammelled by the world and unaffected by its seductions—give himself up more entirely to the exercise of piety and holiness. Socrates, the Church historian, tells us that he determined to follow this more quiet course of life in imitation of Evagrius, who was, perhaps, Chrysostom's schoolfellow, though it is difficult to assert positively who this Evagrius was. The same writer adds that Evagrius, having been educated under the same masters, had long before betaken himself to a more sedate and quiet course of life.

The eloquence of Chrysostom (as Dean Milman has observed[1]) was not destined to waste itself in the barren litigations of the courts of justice in Antioch, or in the vain attempt to infuse new life into the dead philosophy and religion of Greece. He felt himself summoned to a nobler field.

There can be no doubt that this growing aversion to the duties he had begun to undertake in the exercise of his profession as an advocate, was

[1] *History of Christianity*, iii. 119.

greatly fostered by the advice and example of his intimate and dearly-loved friend Basil. The two had been most closely united together in their pursuits, their aims, their work, and their recreation. The bond of friendship and affection attached them to each other by the strongest chains. They were one in heart, in thought, in feelings, and in aspirations.

But Basil, at the time when Chrysostom had re-solved to devote himself to the pursuit of the law, had determined to give himself up to the monastic life, and to abandon all thoughts of worldly and secular advantage. This divergence in the pursuits of the two friends, who up to that time had shared in common thoughts, hopes, and wishes, produced a temporary suspension of that delightful intimacy and affection which had subsisted between them. No wonder, therefore, that Basil, when he saw that his friend Chrysostom was wavering, and that a disgust for his present calling was gaining ground in his mind, endeavoured all the more earnestly to lead him towards that ' true philosophy,' to which at first Chrysostom could not devote himself, being shackled by the love for the things of sense, passionately given up to the emulative struggles of the law courts and the fascinations of the theatre, as well as attracted generally by the pomps and pleasures of this world. Nor can we doubt that, when this change of feeling and sentiment was passing over the mind of Chry-sostom, he once again sought for the society and advice of his trusted friend, and that he was stimu-lated by him to relinquish the world, and devote him-self to a religious life, and to the practice of ascetic or monastic austerities. And thus he, who was destined to be the great Christian orator, was 'almost self-doomed to silence, or to exhaust his power of language in prayers and ejaculations heard by no human ear.'

Accordingly, under the powerful influence of his friend, he was gradually led, not only to renounce the life of an advocate, but also to desire to devote himself to a life of religion, and to consecrate his whole body, soul, and spirit to the immediate service of God. He forthwith (remarks Socrates) changed his dress and his gait, and applied his mind to the reading of the Sacred Scriptures, and frequently went in great haste to the church, probably for the sake of prayer.

Such was the change that was now passing over him,—a change that may fairly be regarded as a conversion from the secular to the religious life, from the pleasures and gratifications of a popular profession, to the devotion of his whole heart to the pursuit of piety and the formation of holiness of character in the seclusion of some monastic retreat.

The advice of Basil[1] received, to some extent, confirmation at the hands of Meletius, who then occupied the episcopal throne at Antioch. Meletius, whose very name, said Gregory, expressed the ' sweetness of his character,' was born at Melitene, in Armenia Minor, which lay near the right bank of the Euphrates. He inherited an estate at Melitene from his parents, who were persons of rank and position there. He won

---

[1] His friend Basil must be distinguished from Basil, the Bishop of Cæsarea in Cappadocia, who was his senior in age, and from Basil, the Bishop of Seleucia, who was his junior. Valesius, in his note to Socrates (*Hist. Eccles.* vi. 3), agrees with Baronius in regarding this Basil as afterwards Bishop of Raphanea, or else as Basilius, Bishop of Byblus, who were both contemporaries of Chrysostom. How deep and sincere was Chrysostom's affection and regard for Basil may be seen in the opening pages of his work *De Sacerdotis.*

golden opinions from all sorts of men in consequence of his mild and gentle character, his integrity of conduct, his strict piety, and his suasive eloquence. From the possession of these estimable qualities he was appointed Bishop of Sebaste, in Armenia, but owing to the factious disposition of the people of the place—many of whom espoused the cause of Eustathius, who had been deposed in consequence of his ascetic notions and practices—he relinquished the bishopric and retired to the Syrian Beræa, the modern Aleppo, of which city, according to the opinion of some, he was never made bishop. Meletius would seem to have veered in his doctrinal views—in consequence, perhaps, of the non-combative gentleness of his nature—from a modified Semi-Arianism to the Homoousian or orthodox doctrine ; but was still regarded with favour and esteem by both parties, each of whom, on account of the moderation of his views, and the practical character of his teaching, claimed him as an adherent. Still, his general bias towards the Homoousian doctrine was well known to many. He was, nevertheless, invited to occupy the episcopal chair at Antioch in the year 360 A.D., through the influence of Acacius and the Arian party, and was cordially accepted by the clergy and laity of the place. They, aware of his great eminence and the esteem in which he was previously held, went out in crowds to welcome him to their city.

For a time, in consequence of the practical character of his addresses, his views were not clearly known ; but, at last, at his installation, Constantius, the emperor, who was present, wished to ascertain his exact sentiments on the vexed question of Arianism that then agitated the Church.

Constantius, accordingly, selected some of the most distinguished preachers of the day to state publicly their views on Prov. viii. 22, 'The Lord possessed ($\check{\epsilon}\kappa\tau\iota\sigma\epsilon$) me in the beginning of His way, before His works of old,' which was regarded as a crucial test. When George of Laodicea, and Acacius of Cæsarea, had spoken from the pulpit in favour of the Arian or Semi-Arian interpretation of the passage, Meletius, who had to deliver his inaugural address last of all on the same thesis, advocated that view on the subject which was regarded as orthodox, indifferent to the violent opposition of many, and to the unpopularity of the opinions he maintained. On account of his outspoken advocacy of the views of the orthodox party, in opposition to Arian or Semi-Arian opinions, he was deposed by the emperor, and banished from his see, and Euzoius appointed in his place.

As a result, schisms and divisions arose in the Church at Antioch, and it was not till the reign of Julian, in 362 A.D., that Meletius was invited to return to Antioch. No reconciliation, however, could be effected between the opposing parties, though vigorous efforts were made to bring about such a result, and at length, during the reign of Valens, Meletius was again banished, at least on one occasion, and as some think, more than once, from his episcopal chair. On his return he again endeavoured, though ineffectually, to heal the schisms and divisions that prevailed.

The Church of Antioch, about the time when Chrysostom was young, was torn and rent by theological controversy. The Arians had secured the bishopric in more than one instance; they had gained the ascendency in synods, and they had prevailed to

so great an extent that Jerome forcibly remarked,
' The world groaned and found itself Arian.'   At one
time there were actually four bishops presiding at the
same moment in the ill-fated diocese.   Euzoius, the
Arian bishop, had his followers ; Paulinus, one of the
party of Eustathius, had been appointed through the
agency of a Sardinian bishop named Lucifer ; the
Apollinarians had set up a third ; and Meletius still
reigned in the affections of the people and the feelings of the Eastern Church.   Thus supported, he
was able to hold his position and prevail over the
rival claimants.   We can readily see, therefore, what
an atmosphere of storm and tempest prevailed at that
day in the Church of Antioch.   Creed succeeded to
creed, and banishment and exile fell upon the weaker
side.   It may be that such a distracted, agitated, and
unsettled condition of thought, feeling, and creed
caused the postponement of· Chrysostom's baptism for
so long a time.

In 381 A.D., when attending the second general
council at Constantinople, Meletius died. His body was
subsequently conveyed with much pomp to Antioch,
where he was buried near the tomb of the martyr
Babylas, and a funeral oration, still extant, was pro- ·
nounced over him by Gregory Nyssen, in which he
asked, ' Where now is that sweet, calm look, that
radiant smile, that kind hand which was wont to
second the kind voice ?'

Whether Meletius carried his gentleness of disposition to the extreme limits of toleration, or whether he
is justly liable, in his earlier career, to the charge of
modified dissimulation, there can be no doubt that,
during the time of his bishopric at Antioch, he firmly
adhered to the truth, and that from his mildness of

character and kindness of heart, from the practical tone of his preaching and his powers of persuasion, he was held in great honour and respect by vast numbers at Antioch. One saying of his that is handed down indirectly marks his character and the views which he held in regard to asceticism. Addressing one day a monk, whose body was clothed in an iron tunic, he is reported to have said, ' There is no need of iron : determination of mind is sufficient to invest the body with chains of reason.' Meletius was at this time the orthodox bishop of the city, and had once again been restored to the see from which he had been driven by the adversaries of the faith.

Gentle in his disposition, holy and blameless in his life, sympathetic in his nature, the bishop was admirably fitted to attract the interest and to draw forth the feelings of the youthful Chrysostom. Nor was the bishop, on his part, unattracted by the brilliant powers, the ardent aspirations, the vigorous energy, and the pure life of the young advocate. He saw in him the germs of much future benefit to the Church, and instinctively felt that such talents were destined to bear much fruit in the after time. He was not only willing to receive Chrysostom and advise him as to the course which it was best for him to take, but he himself anxiously invited his confidence, and devised means by which he might acquire a greater intimacy with him. He was well adapted in many respects to form the mind and guide the religious opinions of Chrysostom at this important crisis of his life. He would seem to have taken him under his especial charge ; and from the wide charity that filled his heart, the experimental character of his piety, and the sympathetic tone of his nature and disposition, he was likely to prove of the greatest service to Chrysostom, as his spiritual guide and counsellor. We can, in fact, trace a strong degree of resemblance between the character of the mind and disposition of Meletius and that of his disciple Chrysostom. The aged bishop's love of truth was remarkable, his moderation in regard to the controversies of the day great, and his freedom from mere speculative views of Christian doctrine was most unusual in that disputatious age and country. In consequence of his holy, pure, genial, and amiable character, he was deeply beloved at Antioch ; and we find that his likeness was engraven on many a signet-ring, painted in many a picture, and that not a few children were called after his honoured name.

For three years, it is said, Chrysostom was guided by Meletius in the study of the doctrines of Christianity, and he was then, according to Palladius, after much careful preparation, baptised by him. This took place about the year 369 or 370 A.D.

It may, perhaps, appear remarkable at first sight that Chrysostom, whose parents were Christians, and who was brought up by his pious mother in the principles and practices of Christianity, should not have been baptised before. But it was not uncommon to postpone baptism to a late period of life, and sometimes even to the very closing scene. The practice arose from the then prevalent notion that every past sin was washed away by baptism, and that all sin willingly committed after baptism was regarded as sin against the Holy Ghost, and therefore unpardonable.

We know that in after times Chrysostom himself, as well as many of the most famous divines in that age, set their faces most strongly against this putting off of baptism to the close of life.

After the period of preparation, to which we have already referred, under the superintending care of Meletius, Chrysostom deemed it right to make a public profession of his faith, and to show by such an act that he had resolved to give himself up to a religious life. This reception of baptism at the hands of Meletius undoubtedly formed a marked and critical epoch in the life of Chrysostom.

After his baptism, Meletius, according to Palladius, ordained him to the function of 'reader' in the Church at Antioch, a position which was then regarded as 'an honourable office' in the Church. Chrysostom was now twenty-three years of age.

CHAPTER V.

THE ASCETIC LIFE OF CHRYSOSTOM.

> ' We need not bid, for cloistered cell,
> Our neighbour and our work farewell,
> Nor strive to wind ourselves too high
> For sinful man beneath the sky :
> The trivial round, the common task,
> Would furnish all we ought to ask ;
> Room to deny ourselves ; a road
> To bring us daily nearer God.'

FROM his baptism Chrysostom became, in the fullest sense of the words, 'a new man.' He devoted himself at once to the prosecution of a higher and holier life. We learn from his biographer, Palladius, that from the moment in which he dedicated himself to God's service in baptism, he never swore, never defamed any one, never uttered a falsehood, never even tolerated questionable witticisms. He desired intensely to join his dear friend Basil, and retire with him from the sins, the follies, the amusements, and the temptations of the world. And, doubtless, he would have carried out this resolution, had he not been checked by the weeping entreaties of his mother not to leave the home of his childhood and abandon her, who had sacrificed so much for him, to the loneliness of a second widowhood.

To this desire for a monastic life he may have been impelled — apart from his own inherent convictions at the time of its greater excellence and advantage—by the prevalent custom of the young men at Antioch when affected by religious impressions, who at once became eager to betake themselves to the cells of the hermits on the hills outside the city, and there give themselves up to meditation, prayer, the study of Holy Scripture, and a severe and self-denying life.

Meletius, however, wished to win him over to the active services of the Church, and to draw him off from the recluse and contemplative life to which he longed to resign himself to the more active and stirring duties of practical existence.

There was, no doubt, something peculiarly striking and captivating in the sight of young men dedicated to prayer, and study, and self-denial, as contrasted with the luxurious, unrestrained, undisciplined, and licentious lives which so many of the same age were spending close at hand, within the walls of the gay and dissolute city. Such a contrast could not fail to appeal to the better instincts of many men of an impressionable temperament, who visited these young monks in their retirement, where they lived secluded lives separated from the cares, the vexations, and the various enticements to a lower life, with which the sensuous city of Antioch abounded.

Meletius, by appointing him to the office of 'reader' of the Scriptures, gave Chrysostom a definite bond of attachment to the outward service of religion among men, and endeavoured to impress him with the importance of such a vocation in the midst of his fellows. His mother also strove to retain him in her own home, and, in order to do so, took all personal trouble off his hands. Her appeal to his feelings, as given in his work on the priesthood (*De Sacerd.* I. 5), is most touching, and very dramatically told by Chrysostom. ' If,' she says, ' I have done my very all to provide for thee a passage through this life in unbroken · leisure, though no other chain can bind thee to me, yet let this. Yea, even if thou didst say that ten thousand loved thee, there is not one that will afford thee the enjoyment of such a liberty ; for indeed there is not one among them all whose care for thy reputation is like unto my care.' [1]

Hear, again, how his weeping mother pleaded, as recorded by her eloquent son :—' When she perceived that this was my intention, she took me by the right hand, and led me into her own private chamber. She made me sit down beside her . . . . and unlocked the fountain of tears, adding thereto words more piteous far than tears ; and such was the mournful burden of woe that she poured forth to me :—It was for no long time, my son, that I was permitted to enjoy thy father's excellent nobility of soul. God willed it so. For his death followed hard upon thy birth ; and brought down untimely orphanhood on thee, untimely widowhood on me.' [2]

Once more she appeals. ' I beg of thee one sign of gratitude, that thou wouldest not involve me in a second widowhood, nor stir up again the grief that begins already to be lulled in sleep ; only wait for the time of my departure. . . . . Therefore, when thou hast given · my body to the earth, and mingled my

---

[1] Moule's translation, in his *Essay on Christian Oratory, etc.* p. 137.

[2] *Ibid.* p. 135.

bones with the bones of thy father, then set forth on long travels, and sail whatsoever sea thou wilt, no man forbidding thee. But until I have breathed my last breath, suffer the abiding with me ; and rush not blindly on an offence against God, by involving in such miseries thy mother who hath never done thee wrong.'[1]

In the seclusion of his mother's home, and within the walls of Antioch, he lived in devout study of the Holy Scriptures. Efforts—increasing efforts—were made by his friend Basil, who had taken, as we have seen, to an ascetic life outside the walls, and who appeared to Chrysostom to have attained to a far higher standard of piety than that which he himself had reached, to induce him to join the monks; but, notwithstanding his deep and true sympathy with his friend, his mother's prayers prevailed, and he still continued to be the companion and solace of her widowed life, recalling to her saddened memory the likeness of the husband whom she had lost.

The affectionate nature, it has been well said,[2] of Chrysostom was not one that could resist a mother's tears. In spite of Basil's urgency, he yielded so far as to consent to remain at home. But in all other respects his resolution was unchanged. If, out of filial regard, he abstained from deserting his home for a monastery, he would make a monastery of his home. He practised the most rigid asceticism. He ate little and seldom, and of the plainest food. He slept on the ground, and rose frequently for prayer. He rarely left the house, and, lest he should fall back

---

[1] Moule's translation, in his *Essay on Christian Oratory, etc.* pp. 136, 137.

[2] By the Rev. E. Venables, in the *Dictionary of Christian Biography*

into his habit of slander, he kept almost unbroken silence. It is not surprising that his former associates should have called him morose and unsociable.

But, at this period in his career, his friend Meletius was banished by the Emperor Valens, about 370 A.D., and two presbyters, Evagrius and Diodorus, were appointed to supply his place and discharge his duties.

Diodorus exerted a very considerable influence over the mind of Chrysostom. It was from him that Chrysostom learned that practical and grammatical method of explaining Scripture which eminently characterised him. The eloquence of Diodorus is compared by Theodoret to a limpid river, and the style of his language is described by Photius as clear and perspicuous. He wrote a treatise on the distinction between ' Allegoria ' and ' Theoria.'

At this particular time Chrysostom was thrown into the society of several young men at Antioch, zealous like himself, and devoted to the ascetic life, over whom he exercised a singular ascendency. Foremost in this select circle were Theodore and Maximus, between whom and himself a strong bond of friendship existed. They were natives of the same city; had been fellow-pupils of the same tutor, Libanius; and had embraced the same kind of religious life. Socrates also informs us that Chrysostom persuaded them to leave their pursuit of gain, and to follow after a more simple course of life, as though the change were due to his inducement alone. They must, however, have had an evident leaning to such a life, even though his influence may have been great in their selection of it.

Theodore, who was younger than Chrysostom, had devoted himself with all the enthusiasm of his ardent nature to the study of ancient literature and philosophy; but he was so affected by the devout consecration, on the part of his friend Chrysostom, of all the powers of his mind to heavenly things, that he forsook the career of worldly distinction that opened out before him, and joined a body of young men, who, under the superintendence of Diodorus and Carterius, had given themselves up to a life of strict and rigid asceticism.

This zeal, however, on the part of Theodore, proved only transitory; and, to the grief of his friend Chrysostom (who wrote to him most strongly on the subject in a letter[1] which is deeply interesting, as being the first of his treatises which have come down to us), he went back to his former pursuits and to a secular life. There are two letters in Chrysostom's works, generally supposed to have been addressed to Theodore, one of which is not so much a letter as a treatise, the style of the one being much more severe than that of the other. They are written with all the fervour a young enthusiast would feel. Scattered through them we find many passages of real eloquence. They exhibit, moreover, a striking knowledge of Holy Scripture.

In his correspondence Chrysostom pressed upon him the superiority of the ascetic over the secular

---

[1] As to the question whether Chrysostom wrote one or two letters directly to Theodore, see Stapleton's translation of Neander's *Life of Chrysostom*, p. 20, note. Cave, in his *Life of Chrysostom*, says—'He pursued him with two set discourses.'

life : he asks him whether to have his mind distracted by such a multiplicity of objects, while unable to live for himself, can really be called, in the strictest sense of the term, *life.* He reminds him of the calm joys he had experienced during the time that he consorted with the brethren ; and he tells him that he alone is a freeman who lives for Christ.

Theodore, however, had a strong tie which bound him to the world, the force of which Chrysostom could not fully appreciate. He was devotedly attached to one Hermione, and his love for her held him back for a time from the ascetic life, and induced him to resist the appeals of his friend. Chrysostom could not sympathise with him in such a line of conduct. He pressed him, as he valued his salvation, to cast aside such a stumbling-block, to renounce such a temptation, and to flee from the world. He lavished all the wealth of his eloquence and his persuasion on his friend. He did not cease from pouring out all the impassioned language of his fervid nature in his attempts to bring back his friend from his lapsed condition, and to restore him once more to the holy brotherhood from which he had seceded. His earnestness, his fervour, his holy ardour, his burning words, and his terrible denunciations, at length prevailed, and Theodore was induced to sacrifice the girl to whom he was engaged, and return once more to the ascetic life.

With the grief of Hermione at her desertion little sympathy would have been felt by those who were interested in the escape of Theodore from the shackles of the world and the flesh. The single life stood, in their judgment, so immeasurably above the married state, that such a desertion

of the object of his affection would, in their estimation, have deserved praise rather than blame.
The higher and the nobler life must not, in their
views, be sacrificed for any consideration of private
feelings, or personal affection, or individual sorrow
and regret.

In the after time, Theodore developed into a
learned and scientific man, distinguished for his
ability and judgment, and is said to have fashioned
into a system the doctrines which his master,
Diodorus, had propounded.

He was afterwards consecrated Bishop of Mopsuestia in Cilicia, an office which he held for thirty-
six years. He maintained the same clear, simple,
and natural views with regard to the interpretation
of Scripture which Diodorus, his master, had adopted,
and which Chrysostom also held.

There can be no doubt that Diodorus exercised
no inconsiderable influence over those with whom
he was associated, especially over Chrysostom and
Theodore.   Like Chrysostom, he was of noble family,
and was made Bishop of Tarsus by Meletius, whose
duties he had undertaken to discharge at Antioch
during the time of his exile.

Though often in danger from the ill-will of the
Arians, Diodorus never hesitated to go to the old
town of Antioch, where Meletius was accustomed
to hold meetings and address his people. He was
fearless in his visits to the flock left under his especial
charge. We may add that he was so well known
as a Christian controversialist and writer, that the
Emperor Julian directed against him personally his
sarcastic and acrimonious wit.

CHAPTER VI.

CHRYSOSTOM GUILTY OF A 'PIOUS FRAUD.'

' I have an especial dislike to the expression, " pious frauds." Piety, indeed, shrinks from the very phrase, as an attempt to mix poison with the cup of blessing. One of the most seductive arguments of infidelity grounds itself on the numerous passages in the works of the Christian fathers, asserting the lawfulness of deceit for a good purpose.'—*The Friend*, by S. T. Coleridge.

OUR moral sense is shocked by an episode in the life of Chrysostom that took place at this time.

Several vacancies in different Syrian sees had just then to be filled up. Meletius had been expelled about 370 A.D. by Valens, who sided with the Arian party, and who was himself expected very shortly to visit Antioch. Consequently the people, as well as the bishops and clergy, were anxiously looking out for fit persons to be nominated for these episcopal vacancies.

At this time the reputation of Chrysostom and Basil stood so high for learning, piety, and eloquence, that it was regarded as highly probable that they would be selected for the vacant offices, although Chrysostom, at any rate, had not then been ordained deacon, and they were neither of them, probably, more than twenty-five or twenty-six years old, while the age of thirty had been fixed by councils as the lowest limit of age at which a bishop might be elected.

History, indeed, informs us that afterwards Rhemigius of Rheims had, in 471 A.D., been consecrated bishop when he was not more than twenty-two years old ; and that others—as, for example, Cyprian, Ambrose, and Nestorius—had been made bishops when laymen.

When the friends heard of this intention they were filled with alarm and consternation, and agreed to act in concert in regard to the dignity which was likely to be thrust upon them; for this violent seizure of candidates for the ministry was far from being uncommon at this time. We know that Augustine was thus forced to accept a clerical office in spite of his reluctance. The friends agreed to act in concert, and either accept or decline the honour which would be probably forced upon them. Chrysostom, however, had secretly, in his own mind, determined that, while he himself avoided the proffered distinction, for which he felt in his own judgment that he was utterly unfit, his friend Basil, whom he deemed eminently suited in all respects for such a high office, should be forced to accept it. He consequently sought a place of concealment. But when the agents employed to seize Basil discovered him, he anxiously inquired of them what was the course that Chrysostom had adopted. He was deceived into the belief that his friend had accepted the office, and so, in this belief, reluctantly allowed himself to be appointed to the episcopate. Shortly afterwards, however, he learned that Chrysostom had deceived him, and had concealed himself, while the agents were made acquainted with the hiding-place of Basil.

He was naturally most deeply grieved and pained to find that he had been thus entrapped, and severely blamed his friend, and censured him for his deception and perfidy. But, to our indignant surprise, his complaints were only met by laughter on the part of Chrysostom, who expressed his satisfaction at the deceit which he had practised—gloried in the fraud—and argued in its defence that he had only deceived with a good motive, and with a sure prospect of benefit to the Church and the world from the fraud which he had designed and executed. He regarded what he had done as a 'pious fraud'—if such a contradiction in terms can exist—and justified it by the custom of the age, the example of the fathers of the Church, and even of the apostles themselves. He advocated the principle that a deception, and even a falsehood, is justifiable, if the object sought by such a deception is a good one. He argued that every action must be regarded as moral or immoral, according to the intention ($\pi\rho\text{oa}\acute{\iota}\rho\epsilon\sigma\iota\varsigma$) with which it is done; and, in accordance with this principle, he would even justify suicide, if committed with the pious object of endeavouring to alienate the body from the service of sin. The exceptions to this justification of the 'pious fraud' were, in the Eastern Church, few and far between.

Our moral sense is shocked by such an artifice, and still more, perhaps, by the line of argument by which its justification is attempted. It is repugnant alike to our ideas of right and wrong, and of the sacred character of truth. But still, in judging of the moral character of an action in that age, we ought to assume a different stand-point to that from which we should naturally judge of it in the present day. At that time, even among the most distinguished of the early Christian fathers, it was regarded as justifiable to deceive, if the object sought after by the deception was a good one.   It was then only deemed an 'economy' —a 'pious fraud'—a justifiable artifice.   This was especially considered to be the case, if the intention was supposed to be legitimate and honourable.

But (remarks Coleridge) 'an honest man possesses a clearer light than that of history.   He knows that by sacrificing the law of his reason to the maxims of pretended prudence, he purchases the sword with the loss of the arm to wield it.'

Still, however, it must be pleaded, that we should be acting harshly, if we did not pass a more lenient judgment in the case of Chrysostom—influenced as he was by Eastern notions, and the principles and practices of the age in which he lived—than we should on the conduct of men of our own day and nation.   We know that such 'pious frauds' were then sanctioned by the conduct of persons eminent for their piety and learning.   History tells us that Ambrose, when desirous of escaping from being appointed bishop, did not scruple to employ such deceit ; that Jerome, in his correspondence with Augustine, advocated it by an appeal to the teaching of the apostles, to which he referred as being in his favour. When such was the tone of feeling, and such the practical conduct of men eminent for their virtue and piety in that generation, we should learn to be more lenient in our judgment of individuals when they fell in with the motives, principles, and practices which were at the time popular.   The moral atmosphere in which men lived in that age had, in this respect, a deteriorating effect upon their moral character. They learned to forget the truth that 'no real greatness can long co-exist with deceit,' and that 'the whole faculties of man must be exerted in order to noble energies ; and that he who is not earnestly sincere, lives but in half his being, self-mutilated, self-paralysed.'

It may be added that Chrysostom (in his exposition of the Epistle to the Galatians, chap. ii.) thinks that St. Paul and St. Peter were laudably engaged in fraud, because their views were charitable and pious. It is, however, the judgment of the learned author of *The Friend* that ' the imputation of such principles of action to the first inspired propagators of Christianity, is founded on a gross misconstruction of those passages in the writings of St. Paul, in which the necessity of employing different arguments to men of different capacities and prejudices, is supposed and acceded to. In other words, St. Paul strove to speak intelligibly, willingly sacrificed indifferent things to matters of importance, and acted courteously as a man, in order to win affection as an apostle. A traveller prefers for daily use the coins of the nation through which he is passing, to bullion or the mintage of his own country ; and is this to justify a succeeding traveller in the use of counterfeit coin ?"[1]

But this episode, painful as it is in many respects, derives a deep interest from its having been the originating cause of Chrysostom's remarkable treatise on the priesthood, a work which Bishop Burnet has characterised as one of the ' best pieces of antiquity.' In its deep fervour of spirit, its singular eloquence,

---

[1] We may refer for information on the question of ' economy ' to what has been said by the learned author of the *Arians*, i. § 3, pp. 72-87. It is there stated ' that the obvious rule to guide our practice is, to be careful to maintain substantial truth in our use of the economical method.' Cf. also his (Newman's) *University Sermons*, xiv. p. 343, note. But, chiefly and principally, as a corrective, see Coleridge's *Friend*, vol. i. essay v. p. 38, *et seq.*

and in the instructive matter which it contains, it stands pre-eminent among the works of that age, or even perhaps of any age. Suidas assigns to it the palm amongst all his treatises for learning, sublimeness, and elegancy.

It was written after the manner of a Platonic dialogue, in which Chrysostom and his friend Basil are the speakers. We cannot hesitate to believe that the work contains a true statement of the conversation which took place between them on this important subject. Additional matter was no doubt introduced by Chrysostom when it was committed to writing, although the original spirit of the conversation was preserved.

We find Augustine, in his retreat at Cassiacum, writing dialogues of a similar character. We have, in fact, every reason to believe that the Platonic dialogues exercised a great influence over the minds of the thoughtful and the intellectual for many centuries. Their style and form have been reproduced by writers of our own day and generation.

It is difficult to decide positively when this treatise on the priesthood was put into actual shape and reduced to writing. Socrates, the Church historian, speaks of it as having been composed after Chrysostom had been appointed by Meletius to the office of deacon, in 381 A.D. ; but it would seem, perhaps, more probable that Chrysostom actually reduced it to writing in its present form during the time of his rigid monastic life preceding his diaconate, to which mode of life allusion is constantly made in the work. A similar ascetic retirement was also the fruitful time of literary production in the case of Augustine.

In the *Dialogue on the Priesthood*—which might

be fairly named, 'On the episcopate'—Chrysostom dwells with impassioned earnestness on his own complete unfitness for so high and exalted a position as that of bishop. When he thought of the vast responsibilities which it involved ; the intense love for God which should actuate the holder of such an office ; the sound judgment, purity, discretion, and piety which were required, he shrank from assuming such a function, as much as a man would shrink from undertaking the management of a vessel who had no skill in, or even any acquaintance with, the art of navigation. A power, he thought, was placed in the hands of the priest greater than any power that was intrusted even to the angels. It was, indeed, from no sense of pride—a feeling which had been attributed to him—that he declined to undertake the duties which it was intended to force upon him when all unworthy to bear them, but from a deep and overpowering sense of his own sinfulness, and his incompetency to discharge such duties aright. He shuddered, too, at the idea of the violence, the turmoil, the ambition, the rivalries, and the actual bloodshed that often occurred at the election of bishops. Who was competent to the due discharge of such obligations ? He felt convinced that he was personally unequal to such responsibilities, and that he did not possess those mental, moral, social, and religious powers which would enable him to steer his bark successfully among the rocks and quicksands and breakers of so stormy a sea as that amidst which a bishop had to guide his perilous course.

On the other hand, he felt that his friend Basil was eminently fitted to undertake such duties, and to discharge with ability an office, than which no other position, either in itself or in its bearings upon others, could be more exalted.

As, in the first book, he dwelt generally on the whole subject by way of introduction, so in the following books he enters into greater and more particular detail.

In the second book—grounding his observations to some extent on our Lord's words to Peter, ' Simon, lovest thou Me ? '—he shows from the distinctive features of the character of shepherd, and also of physician, what difficulties and dangers a bishop had to encounter ; what caution, care, and prudence he needed ; and what attention was requisite in the selection of fit men for the office.

In the third book he dwells in eloquent language on the privileges, honour, and almost angelic dignity of the priestly office, an office from which even St. Paul drew back in dread.   He instances the different virtues, and high qualities of mind and heart, which the due discharge of the episcopal office demanded ; speaks of the great things which were expected from bishops; of all that they had to do, or refrain from doing, in their social relations, in the midst of that ' fierce light ' which beat upon them, and of the calumny to which their conduct was perpetually exposed.

In the fourth book he shows that if, in the different arts and professions, both skill and toilsome effort were needed, they were *à fortiori* required in that calling which was more important than all others,—a calling in which all the distinguishing qualities of a Paul were imperatively needed, not only in refuting heresy, but also in maintaining sound doctrine.

In the fifth book he treats of what was expected in a bishop as a preacher.   He was neither to court the flattery of his audience, nor to disregard their judgment and opinion, but to keep to a middle course, in which his reputation would not be sacrificed. He must not seek applause for eloquence ; but his great aim must be, by careful study and preparation, to build up his hearers in the true faith.

In the sixth book he works out the idea that to live a life of the severest monasticism and self-mortification in the desert is far easier than to direct and guide aright the Church of Christ as a bishop, and to conduct himself blamelessly in so dangerous a position.

Such is a brief and necessarily imperfect sketch of that marvellous work—all the more marvellous when we think of the age and country in which it was composed—in which Chrysostom strives to kindle in the minds of the young and the inexperienced a due sense of the awful danger of rashly, presumptuously, and thoughtlessly undertaking the ministry of the Word, and to prove not only the dignity, but also the responsibility, of the episcopal office.

CHAPTER VII.

CHRYSOSTOM'S RIGID MONASTICISM.

Bonum est nos hic esse, quia homo vivit purius, cadit rarius, surgit velocius, incedit cautius, quiescit securius, moritur felicius, purgatur citius, præmiatur copiosius.—BERNARD.
(This sentence is usually inscribed on Cistercian monasteries.)

A STARTLING and singular peril was encountered, about the year 373 or 374 A.D., by Chrysostom, who always viewed his deliverance from it as due to the mercy of God, to whom, in consequence, he ever felt that he owed a deep debt of gratitude and thankfulness. It may be fairly supposed that this escape, through the providence of God, from an extreme danger, had no slight influence in leading him to devote himself to a still stricter mode of ascetic life, and in inducing him to join the monks outside the city of Antioch. It therefore probably initiated a new epoch in his career.

A most severe decree against all who directly or indirectly practised any arts of magic, or who were in possession of any books of a magical character, had been passed by Valentinian and Valens. This decree was being enforced at this time with great rigour and cruelty at Antioch. Those charged—oftentimes on the most frivolous grounds—with any complicity with such practices were liable to exile, torture, and even death. Soldiers were employed in carefully searching for suspected persons, and dragging them before the legal tribunals. Informers, too, abounded on every side. And not only soldiers and informers, but judges also were eager to court imperial favour by carrying out the decree with rigour and severity. No age or sex escaped. The prisons, not only in the capital, but also at Antioch, were filled with persons of all ranks and professions charged with offences connected with magical rites, or with having in their possession books either actually bearing on magic or supposed to bear upon it. Men, in their terror, destroyed their whole libraries in order to avoid all suspicion.

When such was the state of feeling at Antioch in connection with magic, it happened that one day Chrysostom and a friend were walking on the outskirts of the city, in the gardens by the banks of the Orontes, towards the chapel of the martyr Babylas. As they were proceeding along the margin of the river, they saw some leaves of a book floating down the stream. In emulous sport they tried to catch the leaves as they passed along upon the surface of the water. They succeeded in securing some of them, when, to their consternation, they discovered that they were filled with magical signs and symbols. At this critical moment a soldier was observed approaching them. What could they do with those fatal leaves? Should they hide them about their persons, or cast them back again into the river? If they hid them, the soldier might prosecute a search, and discovery might lead to the most fatal consequences; if they threw them into the river again, the soldier might see the act, recover the leaves, and fasten a charge upon them for having had such a book in their possession. They hesitate in alarm as to their course of conduct, rapidly weighing and balancing in their mind the probable effect of either line of action. At last they determine to commit those perilous leaves once more to the river. Fortunately for them their conduct was unobserved by the soldier, who passed on in ignorance both of their terror and of what they had done. They thus escaped ; but the fears of Chrysostom were greatly excited by the event, and he could not refrain from attributing his escape to the merciful providence of God.

A very short time must have elapsed between this startling incident in Chrysostom's career and his devoting himself to the severity of a monastic life on one of the mountains outside the city of Antioch, living after the pattern of an aged and devout Syrian monk, with whom he had been thrown into contact.

At that time the mountains to the south of Antioch— the steep slopes of Mount Silpius and Casius—were occupied by many Cœnobia, or monastic fraternities, who were living in seclusion amid the solitudes of that wild region. The monks found many votaries from among the young men of the city, who had before been living in luxurious ease, consulting merely the dictates of their senses and their pleasures. This tendency towards the ascetic life showed itself in the East from the earliest times. We read of the Therapeutæ in Egypt, and of the Essenes in Judæa, and the Solitaries in India, even before the existence of Christianity. The inhabitants of the East—with their fervid temperament, their warm and genial climate, their natural inclination to fanaticism and superstition, and their proneness to run into extremes —would be even more likely than the more sober peoples of the West to devote themselves to the fascinations of a monastic life, in which they thought they would be enabled to bring the desires of the flesh, and their lower nature, into subjection to the higher law of the spirit.   The precision, therefore, of the *régime*, and the more methodical rules of the monastic system, might naturally be expected amongst the more formal nations of the West; but the fire and the enthusiasm which would prompt men to sacrifice present pleasures to a life of ascetic rigour, and to resign their wills, thoughts, and feelings to an iron despotism that exacted from them an unhesitating and implicit obedience, might fairly be more looked for in the East than in the West.   And so in very early times Egypt was densely peopled with ascetics and monks, living either as Anchorites in solitude, or as Cœnobites in communities, devoted to a religious life, to prayer, fasting, reading the Scriptures, as well as to manual labour for the supply of their daily wants, scanty though their wants might be.

The growth of monachism may probably be traced to the belief entertained, in the religions of the East and in the Platonism of the West, in the 'inherent evil of matter.'   A natural affinity existed between this principle and the use of the expression 'world.' Both were called alike the 'irreclaimable domain of the adversary of good.'   It has been remarked, that ' the importance of the soul, now through Christianity become profoundly conscious of its immortality, tended to the same end.   The deep and serious solicitude for the fate of that everlasting part of our being, the concentration of all its energies on its own individual welfare, withdrew it entirely within itself. A kind of sublime selfishness excluded all subordinate considerations (as, for example, the softening and humanising effect of the natural affections, the beauty of parental tenderness and filial love). The only security against the corruption which environed it on all sides seemed entire alienation from the contagion of matter and estrangement from the world.'

We learn from Chrysostom's own writings, especially from his homilies and sermons, the mode of life which was then practised by the monks outside the city. He tells us how, before sun-rise, they left their straw pallets, and sang hymns and offered prayers and praises to God for all His bounties ;[1] how they afterwards read with care and diligence the Holy Scriptures, and how, after performing their task of daily labour, they partook of their frugal meal of bread and water, and sometimes of herbs and vegetables,[2] which was followed by prayer and thanksgivings for all the bounties of God's providence bestowed upon them.[3]

In the Syrian monasteries the rule of Pachomius prevailed. He was an Egyptian, born about the year 292 A.D., and was divinely warned (so tradition affirmed) to extend to others that system of ascetic discipline which he had found so beneficial to himself. He had only recently passed away from the stage of life, having, however, lived to see eight monasteries founded during his life-time, with 3,000 devotees, the first monastery having been established

---

[1] Cf. *Hom. in Matt.* lxviii.   [2] *Hom. in* 1 *Ep. ad Tim.* xiv.
[3] *Hom. in Matt.* lv.

at Tabennæ, an island on the Nile, and that number very shortly afterwards increased to 50,000.   Hilarius is said to have introduced the system of Pachomius into Syria.

Monasticism in Egypt had been actually due, in the first instance, to persecution.   Paul had retired to the solitudes of the Thebaid during the persecution of Decius in 251 A.D. ; and Anthony, in a similar manner, had withdrawn there during that of Maximin in 312 A.D.   Around these primitive Anchorites the earliest monastic fraternities grouped themselves, and from thence the monastic system gradually developed. Held in honour by their contemporaries—regarded as 'more elect than the very elect'—they quickly (like Anthony) found many followers.

It is to Oriental monasticism that we shall chiefly confine our remarks.

In the monastic institutions founded after the Pachomian rule, the neophytes, who, after three years of strict discipline, were deemed fit to be elected, were, after making a declaration of conformity and obedience, admitted to the full privilege of membership.   We have no reason to believe that they took any irrevocable vow of devotion to the order, otherwise it would seem unaccountable that Chrysostom could leave them and return once more to the city after a long residence among the brotherhood.

Each part of their dress (so we are informed by Sozomen) had a peculiar symbolical significance. The meal which they took about three in the afternoon, after having fasted up to that time, was eaten in silence.   Only travellers were admitted to share it. The brethren were separated in different divisions, according to their progress, and employed themselves

G

in different trades and callings, all being engaged in some definite pursuit, in order that idleness might not lead them into sin.

We meet in the writings of Chrysostom with many accounts of the life, occupations, and exercises of these monks on the mountains near Antioch. He delighted in drawing vivid pictures of their mode of life, and in contrasting it with the luxurious habits of the wealthy inhabitants of the city. They had, he says, no fear of robbers, for they had nothing to lose — *cantabit vacuus coram latrone viator.* They had no reason to contend about that unfailing source of contention, namely, their private property, for they possessed none. They did not weep and sorrow over him who died, for they thought that by death he was 'perfected,' and could only pray that their own course might speedily be brought to a similar end.

It was in such a society, actuated by such principles, and guided by such rules, that Chrysostom lived at this time. His natural tendencies led him to follow such a life. He always looked back to it with peculiar interest. It was congenial to his tastes and feelings, and it afforded him time and opportunity for that close and diligent study of Holy Scripture, the advantage of which he realised throughout his whole after life. It was during this period of seclusion from the outer world that he acquired that deep insight into human nature and the workings of the human heart, and learned that most difficult lesson of self-knowledge, which was so valuable to him as a preacher—a knowledge which some of the greatest and best men have acquired in the solitudes and seclusion of the desert, and amidst a life of loneliness and isolation from the outer world.

The monks, however, in process of time relinquished the peaceful prosecution of their calling, and mixed themselves up with the religious disputes and controversies that raged in the city. They took their side in these theological contests with all the enthusiasm of fanatics, and used the greatest violence in vindication of what they regarded at the time as the cause of truth, not hesitating to employ brute force in maintaining the principles which they advocated. It is the remark of a learned writer,[1] that 'it is impossible to survey monachism in its general influence, from the earliest period of its interworking into Christianity, without being astonished and perplexed with its diametrically opposite effects. Here it is the undoubted parent of the blindest ignorance and the most ferocious bigotry, sometimes of the most debasing licentiousness ; there, the guardian of learning, the author of civilisation, the propagator of humble and peaceful religion. To the dominant spirit of monachism may be ascribed some part at least of the gross superstition and moral inefficiency of the Church in the Byzantine empire ; to the same spirit much of the salutary authority of Western Christianity, its constant aggressions on barbarism, and its connection with the Latin literature.'

We find that in 365 A.D. Valens introduced a law against those who adopted the monastic life with a view to idleness and inactivity, and with the object of shirking the duties which fell upon them as citizens, compelling them to come forth from their retreats, and take their part in the work of life, and in the discharge of those obligations which a citizen owed to the state.

Amongst the worldly and the wealthy there was

---

[1] Dean Milman, *History of Christianity*, iii. 223.

often a strong prejudice against the monastic life, since they were indignant at their sons, not unfrequently through the influence of Christian mothers, devoting themselves to the religious life, instead of following some honourable and lucrative calling which they had designed for them. In reply to the objections raised by such parents, Chrysostom wrote a long treatise in three books. He censures such parents for merely holding up before their sons the idea of worldly honours, distinctions, and wealth. 'Of heavenly concerns,' he says,[1] 'no mention is made, and he who ventures to allude to them is banished as the disturber of society. If, therefore, from childhood, ye hold up such example to your sons, ye lay the foundation of all that is evil; for ye instil into their minds the tyrant passions of avarice and ambition. Either of these passions is sufficient to overset the virtuous principles of the youth ; but when united they fall upon his tender mind, they annihilate each germ of good. And the worst is, that ye not only teach things opposed to the doctrine of Christ, but ye disguise vices under specious names ;—ever to be loitering in the circus or theatre, ye call the tone of good society ; striving after wealth, the seeking an independence ; ambition, a high feeling ; recklessness, courage : and, as if this deception were not sufficient, ye designate virtues by opprobrious appellations ; temperance, ye call rusticity ; modesty, cowardice ; unassuming manners, servility ; patience, weakness. Ye spare no expense to adorn your houses with fine statues, and to cover your roofs with gold ; but that the most precious of all statues, the soul, should be of gold, never engages your thoughts.'

[1] See Neander's *Life of Chrysostom*, by Stapleton, p. 33.

Chrysostom expresses' indeed, his desire that it were not necessary for the devout Christian to live a monastic life, but declares that such was the wickedness of the world, that it was almost impossible for a man of genuine piety to live in cities. He shows that the monk is free from the desire of those things which worldly men crave after; that he has resources which even the rich do not possess; that real honour and distinction do not consist in the splendid apparel with which the body is clothed, but in the beauty and perfection of the soul; that the monk can exert a power greater than that of the rich and noble, and even of the sovereign himself.

He moreover strongly advocates the education of children in monasteries by monks, where they would be trained apart from the contaminations of the outer world, be brought up in Christian habits and modes of thought, become at an early age conversant with Holy Scripture, and have a solid foundation laid of Christian knowledge and principle.

It was at this period, when Chrysostom was so ardently in favour of monastic institutions, that he wrote a treatise, in which he endeavoured to show that there was more dignity and happiness in the life of a monk than in that of an emperor. ' The monk,' he said, ' combateth against evil spirits for the sake of piety and the worship of God, seeking to free cities and villages from idolatry; the emperor contendeth with barbarians for lands, boundaries, and spoil,— avarice and an unjust desire of empire urging him to the conflict. The monk seeketh nought from the wealthy for himself; he asketh alms only for the poor, by which he benefits those who give and those who receive. He is the common physician both of the rich and poor, liberating by his good advice the former from their sins, and relieving the poverty of the latter. The monk by his prayers delivereth those possessed of evil spirits, and emperors themselves in seasons of calamity take refuge in his cell.'

Amongst the other works composed by Chrysostom during his monastic life, was a letter addressed to Demetrius, which we can gather from internal evidence was clearly written very shortly after his entrance on the monastic life, for he speaks of the difficulty which he felt in mastering the desires of the flesh, and the longing for personal comfort and ease which possessed him, which he had not yet been able to overcome. He endeavours also to arouse and stimulate in the heart of those whom he addressed greater and intenser longings after the higher Christian life, which could only be attained by prayer, zeal, and earnestness, together with the assistance of the Holy Spirit. He shows how the precepts, and spirit, and tone of Christianity and of the Sermon on the Mount were violated in the world; he urges them to strive to attain to the high standard of Christian life which he had set before them, and brings forward the example of the apostles themselves, alleging that their conduct might be followed and imitated by us.

Another treatise, addressed to Stelechius, is written in a still more rhetorical style, and dwells in a more fervid and impassioned manner, and with a holy rapture, upon the blessedness of the life of the monk, and on his exemption from those anxieties and vexations to which the man of the world was exposed.

These different treatises evidently show that it was the marked distinction between the religion of Christ and that Christianity which passed current in the world, which led men of thoughtfulness and piety in that age to monasticism. It seemed to them to be the only means by which they could flee from sin, and attain to that standard of holiness which Christ set forth.

There can be no doubt that Chrysostom, in his after life, modified and toned down the almost extravagant praises of the monastic life in which at this time he indulged. He did not stand alone in being thus, in his younger days, enamoured of monasticism. Though he did not formally relinquish the principles which he at this period advocated, nor ever cease to admire this fancied perfection of the Christian life, yet he afterwards became more liberal and practical in his views. And it has been truly said that then his ambition was not so much to elevate a few enthusiastic spirits to a high-toned and mystic piety, as to impregnate the whole population of a great capital with Christian virtue and self-denial.

But, be this as it may, it is impossible not to be struck with the exalted tone of the morality and piety which he taught in these writings to which we have referred ; with the deep love for God and Christ which they breathe ; with their unflinching denunciations against worldliness and a low standard of piety; with their unfailing recognition of the providential dealings of God with man ; and with the earnest desire expressed in them to train the soul in a higher philosophy than could be found in the outer world. Chrysostom felt that if monasticism could, and, as he thought, did effect all this, it ought to be followed by him with all the devotion of heart, and soul, and spirit.

· To this kind of monastic life he devoted himself for

four years ; but finding that even thus he could not entirely root out the different faults and blemishes of his nature, he adopted a still more rigid and severe mode of life. He became an Anchorite ; dwelt in a cave high up on the side of the mountain ; practised still more rigorous self-denial and self-mortification ; lived on a still more sparing diet ; and gave himself even less sleep and rest than he had done before. There, in his rocky cell, with no human voice to break the intense silence, with no companionship to cheer his loneliness, supported only by the wretched food which the mountain could supply, he passed, in rigid mental and bodily discipline, and in secret prayer and lonely meditation, this period of his eventful life. But now nature asserted herself. His health failed him after he had carried on this severe struggle with the appetites and desires of his lower being for two years ; and he was obliged to submit and return to the city with shattered frame and broken strength. There can be no doubt that during this time he seriously injured his bodily constitution, weakened his vital powers, and created that irritability of temper to which he was not unfrequently subject, and to which, as to a cause, many of the principal miseries of his subsequent life may be fairly attributed.

When thus suffering from illness, and obliged to return to Antioch, tidings came to Chrysostom of the sad condition of a young friend of his, with whom he had lived in the same monastery. He was reported to be suffering from a species of demoniacal possession—the result, no doubt, of his severe and rigid austerities. Stagirius—that was the young man's name—had, at the instigation of his mother, but in opposition to his father's wishes, devoted himself very

zealously to monastic life. Accustomed hitherto to
the luxury and refinement that were usual in the
residence of a noble family, he had forthwith given
himself up to a rigid asceticism.   The strain, however,
was too great for him, and he had fallen into a morbid
state of mental paralysis, and was completely unable
to regulate and control the impulses and desires of
his mind.   Some of the symptoms enumerated by
Chrysostom were 'wringing of the hands, rolling of
the eyes, foaming of the mouth, and a condition of
complete prostration.'   He was sent to famous monks
in order to be cured, and to have the demon exorcised;
he was taken to the most celebrated churches and
chapels; but all in vain. Chrysostom wrote to console him, and bade him regard his present affliction
as a chastisement from God. He assured him that
the will can be restrained by no external power;
that the ascribing to evil spirits the condition in which
he then was, indicated a faulty method of arguing;
that the temptation to suicide of which Stagirius
complained, was the result of his own despondent
feelings; that many of God's saints had undergone
greater sufferings than he had; that the one only
thing of which he need be ashamed was sin; and that
those were real demoniacs who were hurried away by
their impulses and desires, which they could neither
restrain nor curb.

In this correspondence we trace a remarkable
feature in the character of Chrysostom,—the singular
power which he possessed of sympathising with the
sufferings of others, even when he himself was involved in affliction and misfortune of no ordinary
kind.

There is much—to employ the language of Canon

Robertson[1]—that is beautiful and attractive in the idea of monasticism :—A life dedicated to prayer and contemplation, varied by labours for the good of mankind ; a bond of brotherhood, linking together as equals all who should enter into the society,—from the man who had resigned rank and wealth, the commander of armies, or the counsellor of emperors, to the emancipated slave ; renunciation of individual possessions for a community of all things, in imitation (as was supposed) of the first Christians after the day of Pentecost.   But while we acknowledge this, we cannot close our eyes, even thus early, to the evils which were mixed with it.   Foremost among these may be placed the danger of the distinction between an ordinary and a more exalted Christian life.   This idea Chrysostom strongly and forcibly opposes.   But the distinction was too commonly adopted, to the relaxation of religion and morals among the multitude. Moreover, the institution was not of Christian origin. It was common to Eastern religions ; the scriptural patterns of it were all drawn from the days of the Old Testament ; a New Testament warrant for it was only to be found by distorting the meaning of some passages, or magnifying them beyond their due proportion.   The monk was to renounce the charities and the discipline of the world, and to become a stranger to his natural affections.   Virginity should be embraced, in spite of the will of parents ; celibacy was over-valued.   The means taken to avoid temptation often served to excite it.   Many were driven into positive insanity by excessive fasting, working on enthusiastic temperaments ; many to despair, with thoughts of suicide, which were sometimes carried

[1] *Church History*, i. 308.

into act. With many the outward imitation of the founders of monachism was all in all, while unhappily the spirit which preserved such men as Anthony from the evils of their system was wanting. Austerities frightful to think of were too often combined with a want of true Christian faith and purity of heart. Chrysostom mentions that he had known some who made continual progress as monks, but who deteriorated when brought into active life as ecclesiastics. The monastic training failed to prepare them for functions which required a knowledge of men and a sympathy with human feelings.

Such is the close of the first period in the life of Chrysostom. His career as a layman has now terminated.

BOOK II.

*FROM CHRYSOSTOM'S DIACONATE TO HIS
DEPARTURE FROM ANTIOCH.*

CHAPTER I.

CHRYSOSTOM'S DIACONATE.

'Only, since God doth often vessels make
Of lowly matter for high uses meet,
I throw me at His feet.'

WITH Chrysostom's return from his hermit-life to the crowded city of Antioch commences the second great period of his remarkable career.

He had returned as a layman; for the position which he had before held in Antioch as ' reader ' was not regarded as a clerical office in the full sense of the term. But he was neither likely of himself to remain idle, when he saw that there was much work to be done all around him, nor was it probable that he would be suffered by others to continue long without a definite sphere of labour.

Almost immediately, therefore, after his arrival in his native city, in the year 381 A.D., he was ordained deacon by Meletius. Very shortly after Chrysostom's ordination as deacon, Meletius was summoned to Constantinople to preside over the œcumenical or general council that was held there in that year. During the time in which this council was still holding its sittings, Meletius died. As we have already seen, Meletius was greatly esteemed during his life for his gentle and winning disposition, his persuasive eloquence, and his high tone of Christian principle. Nor was he less honoured after his death. His remains were brought to Antioch with great pomp, amidst the display of much popular affection and regret.

Meletius was succeeded by Flavian in the episcopate. As yet—during the five years of his diaconate—Chrysostom had no scope for the exhibition of his powers as a preacher. He gained, indeed, the respect of those around him by his remarkable abilities. The eloquence of his after days might even then have been predicted. His high moral tone, the exalted character of his piety, his singular influence over those associated with him, his marvellous skill in teaching and instructing others,—all these characteristics could not fail to make him known, valued, and esteemed, even though he had enjoyed as yet no field for the exercise of his powers as an orator or as a preacher. But Flavian no doubt detected the mighty energies that were slumbering within him, and perceived that hitherto during those five years no position had been assigned to him commensurate to his great abilities. He, therefore, in the year 386 A.D., not only ordained him to the office of presbyter, but appointed him a sphere of work in his own church, in which he shared with Flavian many of the different duties of the ministerial office.

At some of the great cities in that age, as, for example, at Rome and Alexandria and some other large capitals, there appear to have been different parish churches, each under its respective presbyters ; but this division did not, so far as we can learn, exist at Antioch, where the services were performed by the staff of clergy connected with the chief church. Chrysostom was now under the eye of his bishop, sharing the duties of the church with him, and consequently in a prominent position. His reputation had been gradually and silently growing during the five years of his diaconate. His powers as a speaker and preacher, so far as opportunity had been hitherto afforded him, were becoming felt and appreciated. The high religious tone of his daily conversation was manifest to all. The influence which he possessed over the minds of men in his intercourse with them, was increasingly felt. Hence, when he was appointed to act as presbyter in the chief church of Antioch, in conjunction with his bishop, his abilities and talents could no longer be kept in the background, and he entered upon the duties of his sacred office with the sympathy of many in his favour, and with high expectations formed of his future career in his more enlarged and prominent sphere of action.

But before we speak of the way in which this expectation of high things on the part of the citizens of Antioch was responded to by Chrysostom, we may say that those five years of his diaconate, though years of no great notoriety for him, were far from mis-employed or wasted. Not only was he then laying the foundation for his after-work among men, and establishing that reputation which no doubt aided him in his ministry, when called to a more important field of labour ; but he also employed that period of comparative quietness and retirement in studying the secrets of the human heart, and in literary work.

(1) Though some have placed his *Letter to a Young Widow* 'a little earlier, yet the year 381 A.D., when he was just made deacon, would seem to be the

more probable time at which the epistle was written. It was a letter of consolation. We have already seen, in the account of his correspondence with Stagirius, how singularly fitted Chrysostom was to minister comfort to the mind diseased. We could not but observe the delicacy of his treatment of the case of his disconsolate friend ; how true and heartfelt was his sympathy; how wise and discriminating he showed himself in his efforts to check the grief of Stagirius, and to restrain him from the thought of self-destruction in which he indulged.

And now, in the present case, he directs his sympathy in another channel. In the epistle with which we have now to do, he endeavours to console the young widow of Therasius in the bitter loss which she had sustained by her husband's premature death, after a married life of only five short years. He, too, was young and distinguished, and on the eve, as it seemed, of being appointed to the honour-able rank of prætorian prefect. His widow, still in early womanhood, was disconsolate under the blow from which she was suffering. Chrysostom's method of consolation was essentially Christian. Having dwelt on the high character, the piety, and the excellence of him who had been snatched away in his early manhood, so full of future promise, he bids her think of him, not as having ceased to exist, and as having sunk into annihilation, in which case she might indeed have mourned and grieved, but as having gone before to his Almighty King, to a sphere of happiness and joy, to the society of angels and the spirits of the just made perfect, having ex-changed earthly care for heavenly peace, the anxious rivalries of this world for the security of the celestial paradise, and as having entered into an inheritance which no change could affect, and of which nothing could deprive him, which was eternal as its Author. How different *his* peaceful security to the condition of many emperors whom she had known or read of, either stripped of the purple, or slain in battle, or falling by the sword of the murderer, or burnt to death by barbarians, while their widows had to mourn their fate with broken hearts, uncheered by the hope· which animated her of one day, in a better home, with more glorious surroundings, meeting him again from whom for a short season she was severed.

His mind seemed impressed when writing the letter with a sense of the insecurity of all earthly things, and filled with 'sad stories of the death of kings,' arising from the terrible inroads of the Goths at that time, their slaughter and destruction of the imperial forces, and the ruin and loss which their devastation had occasioned.

This epistle was followed by another, addressed to the same person, *Against a Second Marriage.*

(2) He wrote also, at this period of his career, a treatise rather than an epistle, on the subject of *Celibacy.*

In the estimation of Chrysostom, when he wrote this work, celibacy was the higher state, though, at the same time, he never (as the Manichæans and Marcionites did) regarded the marriage state as sinful. He is not, therefore, to be classed among those who were justly condemned by the apostle (1 Tim. iv. 1-3) as 'forbidding to marry.' No doubt, from the ascetic notions which then prevailed in his mind, he viewed celibacy as ranking above the state of marriage,—as a sort of heaven on earth.

But as he advanced in life, and in intercourse of a more practical character with the world, his views experienced no little change and modification. It is possible that the early opinions of Chrysostom may have been in some degree influenced by the very condition of the women in the East,—a condition, speaking generally, of inferiority, ignorance, and even servitude. They were, too frequently, objects of jealousy to their husbands, watched and guarded by servants in the pay of their lords and masters, who reported to them all their actions, words, and imagined thoughts and feelings. They indulged, no doubt, in dress and in extravagance; but they had little else to occupy their minds. They adorned themselves with jewels, which, as Chrysostom insisted, were useless, if they themselves were really beautiful; but which, if they were themselves plain, only tended by contrast to enhance that plainness, and cause it to be brought forth more conspicuously into the broad light of criticism. What a contrast, he says, to this fashionable beauty did the virgin who devoted herself to God present. She was clad in the robe of modesty, humility, gentleness, and virtue. Her inward graces shone forth in her outward demeanour. All could take knowledge of her excellences and admirable qualities. Much, in Chrysostom's opinion, was expected under the Christian dispensation. A higher standard must be sought for than that which existed in the times of the Old Testament saints. Undoubtedly the patriarchs and other holy men married under that dispensation. What was deemed perfection under that more elementary system could scarcely, in his estimation, be regarded in the same light under the kingdom of the Gospel. The thoughts and feelings must be raised above the low level of human nature. Nature, in fact, must be eliminated rather than exalted.

(3) About this period, 382 A.D., he composed his work *On the Martyr Babylas.* Its object was to make evident to the heathen world, by the example of such a saint as Babylas, how great was the inherent power of the Christian faith. Babylas had been once Bishop of Antioch, and in the Decian persecution had been a martyr to his belief in Christ. When Gallus Cæsar held the reins of government in that quarter of the world, he had been persuaded by the Christians to convey the bones of Babylas to the neighbourhood of the grove of Daphne and the temple of Apollo, and to raise a chapel over the spot where they were interred, in order that the idolatrous and sensual rites that prevailed there might be neutralised—at least to some extent—by the associations which gathered round the tomb of the martyred saint.

The grove of Daphne was essentially connected with Antioch, which was often described as Antioch near Daphne. It was, in fact, a suburb of the capital, of about ten miles in circumference, lying to the south-west, at a distance of not more than five miles from the city, and situated on a higher level than Antioch itself. The existence of this 'Versailles' of Antioch was due to Seleucus Nicator, who endeavoured to increase his own fame and that of the family by the religious and mythical associations of the grove. It was he who built the famous temple of Apollo in its midst, where towered the colossal statue of the god, made partly of marble and partly of wood, formed by the skilful hands of the great Athenian artist,

Bryaxis. The god of light was represented (so Libanius tells us) with a harp in his hand, as though in the act of singing. Subsequently, Antiochus Epiphanes raised an additional statue in honour of Jupiter, in the same sanctuary, of equally grand proportions as that of Apollo, composed of ivory and gold. To Commodus was due the establishment of the Olympian games at Daphne, when the morals of the Roman soldiers suffered from the corruptions of the place. The village of Daphne grew into a town in consequence of the 'perpetual resort of pilgrims and spectators' to the place.

The grove of Daphne, through which cool streams and rivulets ran within their own grassy banks, and in which the boughs of the cypress and the laurel screened the sun's rays from the worshippers of Apollo; where sense reigned supreme, and sensuality followed in its track; where art rather excited than elevated the feelings and passions, and where the inhabitants of luxurious Antioch sought a voluptuous enjoyment,—the grove of Daphne, with all its Grecian and mythical accessories, exerted a demoralising influence over those who were brought within its reach, 'where pleasure, assuming the character of religion, imperceptibly dissolved the firmness of manly virtue.'

Hence the idea of endeavouring to counteract such influences by raising a Christian chapel almost in its midst, where a purer faith and a holier worship might be exhibited than that which prevailed all around.

The tombs of the martyrs had, from the very first, been regarded and invested with a peculiar sanctity of their own. A holy emulation (says Chrysostom)

had always been called forth by such hallowed spots.'
The tone of feeling had thus been raised, and the
spirit quickened to higher flights of love and worship.
Hence those who had been fascinated by the insidious
witcheries of the voluptuous grove would, it might
reasonably be expected, be brought back to a purer
tone of mind, and to more chaste and refined
thoughts when they stood by the tomb of that holy
martyr, and when their hearts were affected by all
the sanctifying influences which prevailed around
such a shrine.

When Julian, in his eager zeal for paganism, wished
to resuscitate the worship of Apollo at Daphne, which
was then dying out, he asked what was the reason of
the silence of the oracle? Being told that it arose
from the presence of the dead, he disinterred the
bones of the martyr Babylas, which the Christians,
amidst the sound of chants and hymns, conveyed for
burial to another place.

This act of spoliation on the part of Julian was
quickly followed by the destruction by fire of
Apollo's temple, which was viewed by the Christians
as a nemesis following his sacrilegious act.

In his treatise on the martyr Babylas, Chrysostom
shows that cruelty and violence cannot extinguish the
religion of Christ ; that all the attacks on Christianity
by the enemies of the faith have proved useless ; and
he lays down the general principle that the attempt
to suppress by outward force and violence any religious system, even though false, is not permitted
to Christians, and that persuasion and conviction, in
a spirit of love, are the only legitimate instruments
by which such a work of reformation may be lawfully
carried out. He also points out that Christianity

diffuses itself abroad when most assailed through the Divine power within it ; while heathenism, when attacked, unaided by any support from without, falls into decay and ruin.

Chrysostom, moreover, dwells on the moderation exhibited by the martyr in moments of peril and in the excitement of contest. He points to the Christian love which he displayed, so different from the cold cynicism of heathenism—his humility as contrasted with the contemptuous conceit of the cynical philosophy—and brings forward the conduct of Babylas as a pattern for all Christians to follow.

CHAPTER II.

CHRYSOSTOM AS PRESBYTER AND PREACHER.

'They that have used (or "ministered," marg.) the office of a deacon well purchase to themselves a good degree, and great boldness in the faith which is in Christ Jesus.'—1 Tim. iii. 13.

CHRYSOSTOM'S diaconate was now over. He had served for what appears to us a long time in that subordinate office,—from 381 to 386 A.D. Little, if any, scope had as yet been afforded him for exhibiting his powers as a preacher. He had, no doubt, discharged the duties which he had to perform in the most satisfactory manner. His time had been spent, so far as his office as a deacon was concerned, in reading the services of the Church, in the visitation of the sick and of those who needed spiritual comfort and assistance, and in the administration of the Sacraments.

But his fame at the Bar, after he had left the school of Libanius, had not yet passed away. Instances of his eloquence and forensic ability would even still, after the lapse of twenty years, be remembered by many. Moreover, during the five years of his diaconate he had shown himself to be a learned, vigorous, and powerful writer, and had given indications of those peculiar gifts and talents which were likely to fit him in due time to become an able, eloquent, and instructive preacher. Consequently great expectations were naturally formed of him,— expectations which were destined not only to be fulfilled, but even to be surpassed.

The duties of a preacher were no light ones in such an age and in such a city. Paganism had not yet received its death-blow. Such men as Libanius and Julian had endeavoured, with earnestness and zeal, to rekindle the dying embers of the ancient faith, and to give it a new vitality and power. There were many learned heathen in such a city as Antioch—the resort of the inquisitive Greek, of the thoughtful yet practical Roman, and of the subtle and disputatious Asiatic—many of whom were weighing the two creeds in the balances, and had not yet come to a formal and definite decision as to their rival claims. Hence it followed that much responsibility rested upon a prominent preacher in those days, perhaps even a greater responsibility than that which would rest upon a popular preacher now, when the principles of Christianity are generally admitted by his hearers. We cannot doubt that such a solemn responsibility would be deeply felt by one whose heart and mind were moulded and trained as Chrysostom's were. He would realise the importance and the value of human learning ; not viewing it, indeed, as a substitute for Christianity, but regarding it as a handmaid and assistant in teaching and enforcing the higher wisdom, and as a means by which to 'convince the gainsayers,' but never as a means of displaying his own rhetorical powers and eloquence.

Flavian was not blind to the eminent qualifications of Chrysostom as a preacher. Without envy, or any narrow-minded feeling of jealousy or exclusiveness, the bishop appointed him to address, from the chief pulpit of the city, at least once or twice a week— probably, it has been supposed, on Sunday and on Saturday (the Sabbath)—the crowded congregations which then assembled in the church.

So large-minded was Flavian, that he even, on one occasion, permitted Chrysostom to answer and refute, at their desire, the objections of unbelievers and heretics, after he himself had preached the sermon in which the controversial subjects had been treated. Nor did he refrain from requesting Chrysostom, even though fatigued by previous efforts in preaching, to address the expectant crowd of hearers, and to remain himself as a listener.

Chrysostom's reputation and popularity as a preacher were almost at once firmly established. His eloquence attracted all classes, and men of every phase of thought and religious sentiment. They crowded round the bema or pulpit from which he preached, in order that they might not lose any of his utterances. So closely were they packed together, and so absorbed in listening to his golden words, that pickpockets found it a favourable field for plying their craft, and Chrysostom had to warn his hearers to leave their purses at home.

The congregation signified their appreciation and approval of his burning words by outward signs of their commendation, which grew louder and louder as he proceeded; and not unfrequently they indicated by their plaudits that, so far from being wearied by the length of his sermon, they were ready and willing to listen to him for a still longer time. Such preaching as this, coming from the heart, and confirmed by the holy life, produced very marked effects upon his hearers.

It was not by lowering what has fairly been called the 'dignity of the pulpit'—however much some in the present day may sneer at the expression—that he gained his great success and his mighty dominion over the minds of men. He was, not unfrequently, ironical, sarcastic, and satirical; but he never descended to vulgar witticisms, or low buffoonery, or questionable jests, or unsuitable familiarity, in order to gain that mastery which he possessed. He endeavoured, on the contrary, to raise to somewhat of his own exalted level the tastes, and tone, and feelings of his hearers. He did not court popularity by placing himself on the low standpoint of the masses he was addressing; nor did he aim at arresting attention, and attracting notice, by singularity, or eccentricity, or by humouring current tastes of a questionable character. There was nothing in his sermons which, though it might please the ears of the ignorant, would offend the tastes of the educated. His unrivalled charm (it has been said), as that of every really eloquent man, lay in his singleness of purpose, the firm grasp of his aim, and his noble earnestness.

Chrysostom sometimes wrote his sermons; at other times he either preached 'extempore' after previous thought and preparation, or 'extempore' in the strict sense of the word, grounding his discourse upon incidents which presented themselves to him at the moment and arrested his attention. Thus, on one occasion, he appeals to their charitable feelings by a picture of some miserable beggars whom he had observed, sunk in wretchedness, as he came to the church; and, on another occasion, when preaching an evening sermon, he points the attention of his hearers, whose interest was distracted by the lighting of the

lamps in the church, to a greater and purer light than that on which they were gazing. His words were :—
'I am expounding the Scriptures, and ye all turn your eyes from me to the lamps, and him that is lighting the lamps. What negligence is this, so to forsake me, and set your minds on him! For I am lighting a fire from the Holy Scripture; and in my tongue is a burning lamp of doctrine. This is a greater and a better light than that, for we do not set up a light like that moistened with oil, but we inflame souls, that are watered with piety, with a desire of hearing.'

On the appearance of a sudden storm he once remarked :—'The concourse of clouds has made it somewhat overcast for us to-day. But the presence of our teacher—the bishop, Flavian, who had just returned from his mission to Theodosius—has rendered it brighter. For the sun, when he darts his beams from the midst of the central summit of heaven, casts no such light upon our bodies as the presence of paternal affection pours a brilliance into our souls, darting its beams from the midst of the [episcopal] throne.'

But we must not pass over in silence the first sermon which he preached after his ordination, in the presence of his bishop and of a vast throng of persons drawn together by the reputation which he enjoyed as a distinguished orator and rhetorician. This sermon, like the first sermons of many men of genius and eloquence, is very ornate in its style, and more rhetorical than those which he afterwards delivered. It carries to an extreme length his depreciation of himself and of his own powers, and is, in an equal degree, extravagant in its praises of Bishops Flavian and Meletius. In these respects the sermon is scarcely in keeping with the tastes and feelings of the present age. Nevertheless, it exhibits clear indications of that masterly eloquence, and of that copiousness of thought and matter, for which he became afterwards so deservedly celebrated. In this sermon, in his self-depreciation (which almost amounts to the 'irony' of the Greek writers), he refers to himself as a mere youth, although he was at the time nearly forty years old, and entreats their indulgence for any failure of power on his part, since he felt unmanned by the sight of so many eager and anxious listeners. He asks their prayers that strength may be given him to praise God aright, and that, though a sinner, he may be enabled to attempt the work of preaching, in which he was as yet inexperienced. He then expatiates on the virtues and excellences of Flavian, who, though rich and of noble family, had devoted himself to the service of God, and sacrificed everything that men hold dear for the cause of Christ. He speaks of him as a second Meletius, possessed of all the virtues which had adorned his predecessor. And he concludes by once more begging their prayers, that he might be enabled to render to God at the last a good account of his stewardship.

If Chrysostom is, in this sermon, too fervid, too elaborate, and too rhetorical for our tastes, we must nevertheless remember that he was addressing those whose standard of judging differed from our own, whose tone of mind was more impassioned, whose tastes were formed on a different and an Oriental model, and to whom such a laboured and ornate style would not be offensive, because in harmony with their early training in the schools of orators and sophists.

His was, no doubt, an eloquence that has rarely, if ever, been equalled. Florid, ornate, impetuous, and declamatory, it combined, at the same time, depth of thought, vivid conception, fertility of illustration, striking imagery, logically reasoned argument, and profound learning. It was a style that carried away before it the feelings of the middle classes of Antioch and Constantinople, while at the same time it gratified the fastidious tastes of the more intellectual citizens, and satisfied also the deeper spiritual wants of the more religiously disposed of those two metropolitan cities. There was the spiritual earnestness and fervour, as well as the richness of Scriptural illustration, of a Whitefield; the argumentative and thoughtful cast of preaching of a Wesley; the vehement and even turgid oratory of a Savonarola; the profuse illustration, and the reference to the stores of ancient learning, which characterised a Jeremy Taylor. In him, the golden-mouthed, all appeared united. He could expose the latent excuses of the heart; lay bare the hypocrisy that lurked there; reveal to men secret sins and corrupt motives, of whose presence they were before almost unconscious, with the most marvellous power of mental dissection. Each one seemed to take the preacher's words as addressed especially to himself.

CHAPTER III.

CHRYSOSTOM IN THE PULPIT.

Ce père est un des plus éloquens orateurs Chrétiens, et son éloquence est d'autant plus estimable, qu'elle est sans affectation et sans contrainte. Il a une fertilité et une abondance de paroles et de pensées qui lui est tout à fait naturelle.—DUPIN.

AT this period, and for more than ten years, the mind of Chrysostom must have been continually on the stretch. The great mass of the theological literature which has come down to our day as the product of the unflagging mental and spiritual energy of Chrysostom, must have been composed during this portion of his life, when engaged as presbyter in preaching at Antioch. Nor can we doubt, when we remember how often Chrysostom was called upon to occupy the pulpit,—commonly twice a week, frequently on two or three occasions besides, as well as during Lent and on the great festivals,—that the homilies which have come down to us can only represent a very small portion of all the sermons which he must have delivered during those ten years and more of active ministerial life.

During that time he could have left but few theological subjects untouched, or few portions of the Bible unexplained. He had to contend with the enemies of the faith who lay outside the pale of the

Christian Church. He was called upon to refute the erroneous tenets of those within the pale, who had adopted many and diversified false views. He had to denounce the corruptions into which the Church had fallen, and the follies and the vices which disgraced her. Not only had he to oppose the Jews, but to contend for the true faith with Arians, Manichees, Sabellians, and Marcionites. He was called upon to address men of every sort. He had a word for each. He warned the careless and negligent professors of Christianity that their corrupt conduct and unholy lives tended to support the cause of heathenism. He pointed to the life of the soldier—many of which class were among his hearers—and drew the moral from it, that both soldiers and civilians alike should strive with earnestness to fight the good fight of faith. His task, therefore, was no light one ; but he did not shrink from the labour which it entailed. He had placed before him a noble and an exalted end and aim, and from that object he never allowed himself to be turned aside.

Homily followed homily in quick succession during those ten years. It is difficult to arrange them all under the different years in which they were delivered ; nor is it necessary to spend time in such an attempt. We can attain to a general idea of the period when the great mass of his discourses was composed, sufficient to give us a comprehensive notion of what he was doing at different stages of those ten or twelve years, and to enable us to form a rough and general classification of his writings. And this is quite enough to furnish us with the means of marking the progress which he was making, during that time, in his grasp and perception of religious truth, and of tracing out the changes and the modifications which took place in his views on different points of theory and practice. To attempt to analyse with care and accuracy all the sermons which have come down to us, would be incompatible with the scope of the present volume. We would desire to leave no important or salient point untouched ; to omit nothing which tends to exhibit the peculiar complexion of the mind and sentiments of Chrysostom ; to pass over in silence no characterising feature in his writings or in his career; but laboriously to attempt to dwell upon every single treatise or homily which he composed at this time, would be not only alien, as we have said, to the object of this work, but would, in all probability, only tend to confuse our notions respecting him, and to weaken, rather than strengthen, the general impression which we would desire to leave both of him and his works.

All his homilies do not, of course, stand on an equal level of excellence. This it would be impossible to expect from any man, especially from one as unceasingly engaged as Chrysostom was, in the arduous duties of an active ministerial life. Some must necessarily surpass others in argumentative or suasive power; in the fulness or the condensation of their subject-matter ; in their scriptural clearness of statement; in the tone of their religious feeling ; or in the wisdom and sound practical sense which they display.

But in all his homilies we cannot fail both to notice and to be astonished at the remarkable knowledge of the Scriptures which is manifested throughout them,— a knowledge which not only extends to their general bearing and scope, but which equally reaches to the minutest points, and what may appear at first sight merely trivial details,—a knowledge not confined to the New Testament, but extending with no less accuracy to the different writings of the Old Testament. He never seems at a loss for quotations, but from the treasure-house of his scriptural information is able to draw forth the argument or illustration which is best suited to the question under consideration, and to apply it with consummate dexterity on each occasion. Nor does he ever omit to make Holy Scripture the basis as well as the touch-stone of his arguments. ' To the law and to the prophets ', is with him the invariable appeal. In such cases he discards tradition ; he casts aside all *à priori* arguments ; he never refers either to human intelligence or to any verifying faculty in man. He falls back at once upon the unchanging rock of scriptural truth, and he makes the Word of God his court of final appeal.

And these Sacred Scriptures which he so carefully and diligently studied, himself, he earnestly pressed upon the attention and consideration of his hearers. He prays them to read the Scriptures at their homes constantly and seriously ; never to plead in excuse want of time or opportunity ; not to be deterred by the apparent difficulty of passages in God's Word, but to read them again and again, till the difficulty which they felt vanished away, and they became clear and plain ; not to confine themselves to certain portions of the Bible, lest their views of Divine truth should become distorted and incomplete. Such was the estimate of the Divine Word which he consistently presented to his hearers.

Nor can we fail to be struck with the intensely practical tone of his sermons. He never seems satisfied until he has made some earnest appeal to the hearts of his hearers. He is not content with

their simple appreciation or recognition of the arguments he may lay before them, or with their earnestness in following the oratorical appeals which he may
make. His intense desire was that, by means of his
preaching, they should become better men and
women, better citizens, better fathers and mothers,
better husbands and wives, better sons and daughters.
His great aim was to impress the truths of religion
deeply in their hearts and consciences, so that the
fruits of their faith might be seen in their daily
Christian walk and conversation. To this end he
never ceased to warn, exhort, encourage his hearers.
Nor did he ever flinch from rebuking them even
sharply and sternly when such censure was necessary.
He held up their vices before them, as in a mirror,
with unsparing severity. If the 'terrors of the law'
did not suffice to keep them back from indulgence
in what was wrong, he employed at times the
most withering sarcasm, the most biting irony, the
most caustic ridicule, unmasking their secret sins,
revealing to them, in all their naked ugliness, the
vices to which they were addicted, and lashing them
with scorpion-whip for their offences against the law,
against their higher nature, and against their God.
No language is at times too strong for him to employ
—no allusions either too trenchant or too homely—
no descriptions either too vivid or too outspoken.
Their vanities, their love of amusements, their frivolities, are all put before them with unsparing open-
ness and severity, and denounced with all the power
of a practised satirist. No Horace, or Juvenal, or
Aristophanes, no Massillon or Latimer, could surpass
him in his pungent satire on the empty vanities of
the people of Antioch. He raised his indignant

voice against their besotted devotion to the public games, and to the frenzied infatuation with which they took their different sides in the factions and rivalries of the hippodrome. He utters indignant complaints against them for giving up their attendance at church for the excitement of the race-course, and bitterly grieves over his labours, as though all in vain. He also censures them for the trifling and futile excuses which they were in the habit of making for not attending the services of the Church, when they would never think for an instant of offering such frivolous reasons for absenting themselves from the races in the circus.

Chrysostom was indeed the 'pattern of preachers and missionaries in great towns.' Augustine's sphere lay among humbler congregations in provincial towns. He, great as he was as a preacher, had no Antioch or Constantinople in which to deliver his sermons.

Chrysostom never permitted the force of his sermons to be frittered away in bare generalities, but always pointed his preaching by a personal application. It has been said of him,[1] that he threw aside the subtleties of speculative theology, and repudiated, in general, the fine-drawn allegory in which the interpreters of Scripture had displayed their ingenuity, and amazed and fruitlessly wearied their unimproved audience. His scope was plain, severe, practical. Rigidly orthodox in his doctrine, he seemed to dwell more on the fruits of a pure theology (though at times he could not keep aloof from controversy) than on theology itself.

Nothing escaped his observation ; nothing was either too high or too low for his notice. No fears or

---

[1] *History of Christianity*, by Milman, iii. 123.

scruples ever deterred him from unmasking every form of vice that fell under his eagle eye, however exalted the persons might be in whom the vices appeared. A great mission had been assigned to him at his ordination—the conversion and edification of those among whom he was called upon to minister—and from this great work he never for an instant shrank.

It has been truly said that ' events of public interest, the cares and occupations, the recreations and amusements, of social and domestic life, have a place in the cosmical panorama which is surveyed by Chrysostom from the pulpit. The court, its splendours, its follies, and its vices ; the magnificent costume of the emperor in his golden car of state ; its purple curtains, and precious stones ; the royal cortège and equipage, and armed cavalcade ; the brilliant costume of the courtiers,—all these are displayed to the audience, and moral lessons are drawn from them. The wealth of the princely palaces, their furniture, statues, and pictures ; the retinues of fair slaves in brilliant attire ; the luxury of their banquets ; the musical concerts with which they were enchanted ; the aromatic perfumes with which they were refreshed,—these are not forgotten. In a word, the brilliant magnificence and sumptuous voluptuousness of the scenes he describes are such as might be supposed to be drawn from an Eastern seraglio, or from a Persian paradise. These were pictures of the nobler and wealthier classes ; but the humbler and poorer were not forgotten by him. The vast multitude of his hearers were entertained by other delights. The immense hippodrome, the frenzied excitement of the rival partisans at the race-course, which lay open to thousands of spectators from the roofs of the neighbouring houses ; the

athletic and gymnastic games in the arena; the
sensual allurements of the theatre, and the dissolute
scenes there enacted, by which the virtue of many
was corrupted, and the happiness of many fond parents
was destroyed, were not beyond the range of the
preacher's view, but were pressed into his service;
even the rope-dancers, jugglers, conjurers, fortune-
tellers, buffoons in the streets, mountebanks, mingled
with grave philosophers, with long beards, staff, and
cloak, were grouped together in his homiletical
sketches: all these gave occasions for enlarging on
the wonderful pains which men take to acquire mean
arts for amusing others, and for their applause, and
for gaining a little money in this world; and the skill
they display in those arts is contrasted with the care-
lessness of most men, and their indifference and lack
of zeal to please God, and to win His approval, and
for their own everlasting salvation. We can thus
trace the marvellous versatility of Chrysostom's style,
the liveliness of his imagination, and the richness of
his fancy. But, after all, his grand success as a
preacher arose from the intense depth of the Christian
love which pervaded all his discourses. In this he
resembled his namesake, St. John the Evangelist.
He understood the hearts of his people, and delighted
them even when he censured them. He brought
tears from their eyes at will; he reproved and corrected their vices, and confirmed their faith; he
refuted Jews and heretics, and was frequently interrupted by the rapturous applause of his hearers, and
gained for himself the title of "the preacher with the
mouth of gold." But not unfrequently he rebuked
his hearers for testifying their pleasure by such
rapturous applauses, and told them that 'he rejoiced

not in their applauses, but in the effects which his discourses had on their minds, in making them become new men.'

' Chrysostom's eloquence,' says Dupin, ' is popular, and very proper for preaching ; his style is natural, easy, and grave ; he equally avoids negligence and affectation ; he is neither too plain nor too florid ; he is smooth, yet not effeminate ; he employs all the figures that are usual to good orators very properly, without employing false strokes of wit. His composition is noble, his expressions elegant, his method just, and his thoughts sublime. He speaks like a good father and a good pastor. He teaches the principal truths of Christianity with a wonderful clearness. His discourses, how long soever, are not tedious : there are still some new things that keep the reader awake, and yet he has no false beauties nor useless figures. His only aim is to convert his auditors, or to instruct them in necessary truths ; he neglects all reflections that have more of subtilty than profit ; he affects not to appear learned, and never boasts of his erudition ; and yet, whatsoever the subject be, he speaks with terms so strong, so proper, and so well chosen, that one may easily perceive he had a profound knowledge of all sorts of matters, and particularly of true divinity.'

The remark is a sound one,—that Chrysostom's example may be commended to those who are commissioned to do the work of evangelists in an age and country like our own, when rural populations are gravitating to great towns, and when towns are assuming a paramount importance in relation to politics and religion, and when the stimulants to vice are becoming more energetic.

CHAPTER IV.

CHRYSOSTOM AS A HOMILIST.

' With eloquence innate his tongue was armed ;
Though harsh the precept, yet the preacher charmed :
For letting down the golden chain from high,
He drew his audience upward to the sky.'

THE earlier years of the presbytership of Chrysostom are those in which the larger number of his extant homilies were composed. To the year 386 A.D.—the year in which he was ordained presbyter—a very considerable number have been referred ; while to the year 387 A.D. a still larger collection is attributable. In the following year, 388 A.D., there is a falling off in regard to numbers, and from 389 to 398 A.D., there is a very sensible and decided diminution in the list of his homilies and expositions. This may, indeed, arise from the loss of the treatises composed or the homilies delivered in those latter years. They may have been—and perhaps we may say they probably were—as fruitful in intellectual productiveness as the earlier years of his presbytership.

Moreover, a considerable number of homilies have come down to us which are of uncertain date. The precise time when they were delivered cannot be accurately fixed, either from internal evidence or

121

external authority.   We only know that they were delivered at Antioch some time between the years 386 and 398 A.D.

The following homilies are referred, on the best authority, to the year 386 A.D. :—

1. The homily, of which we have already spoken in the second chapter, delivered by Chrysostom at his ordination to the priesthood in the beginning of the year 386 A.D., stands foremost on the list of his homiletical works.   It is to be regarded, accordingly, as his first public effort in preaching.

2. The four homilies (*Homiliæ de Oziâ*) mentioned next on the list, which are said to have been delivered in January or February of this same year, would seem to be justly relegated to the year 388 A.D. by the author of the *Life of Chrysostom*, written in Latin in Migne's *Patrologia* (vol. xlvii. p. 100).

3. The sermons on Genesis, which are said to have been delivered in the beginning of Lent, 386 A.D.— though clearly, from internal evidence, some of the very earliest that Chrysostom delivered—evince not only a fulness of matter, a polish, an eloquence, and a happy originality, but also a remarkable power of extemporaneous utterance and ready facility of expression.   Thus, in one of the sermons (No. 3), we observe how, on the spur of the moment, he riveted the attention of his audience, distracted by the lighting of the lamps, to a higher and a better light, as we have already seen.

4. In the *Chronological Compendium* of the writings of Chrysostom, recently referred to, we see mentioned, as delivered during Lent in the month of March, two homilies on the *Obscurity of the*

Prophets, a third against the Manichæans, a fourth against idleness, and a fifth concerning the devil as tempter.

The homilies, however, named in this section are not alluded to as the work of this year in the *Life of Chrysostom* in the *Patrologia.*

5. The homily on Meletius was delivered in this year about the end of May. Chrysostom himself fixes the time of its delivery when he says: 'The fifth year has now passed away since Meletius departed to Jesus;' and we know that Meletius died at Constantinople in the year 381 A.D.

This homily was delivered in view of the casket in which the remains of Meletius were placed, perhaps on the anniversary of the day when those reliques were conveyed to Antioch, rather than on the anniversary of his death. History informs us that the inhabitants of Antioch entertained so great a feeling of respect and affection for Meletius, that very many of them called their sons 'Meletius' in his honour; and, as we have remarked before, pictures of him were to be seen everywhere on their walls, and his likeness was perpetually engraven on their signet rings.

In this homily he dwells with force and severity on the dissolute morals of the inhabitants of the city, and on their unbridled licentiousness; on the false doctrines of the Anomœans; and he also speaks against the Jews. Seeing, however, that the Anomœans were attracted by his preaching, he restrained himself, in order that he might perchance catch them in his net.

It is impossible to read the Church history of the days of Chrysostom without observing the intense respect, and even devotion, that was paid to the 'commemorations' of saints and martyrs. It is scarcely to be wondered at that such semi-adoration passed soon afterwards far beyond all the limits of a legitimate respect for their memory, and ended in a 'cultus' for which no scriptural authority can be adduced.

6. In August of the same year his first homily against the Anomœans was delivered; but his course of sermons was interrupted by the insertion of his first two addresses against the Jews at the end of the same month. In his first homily against the Anomœans, after showing that he had refrained from attacking them, in order that he might perchance win them over to the true faith, inasmuch as they attended his preaching, he explained that he had entered again into the controversy on their request, and with friendly feelings.

7. At the end of August or the beginning of September he probably delivered his first two sermons against the Jews. The series of sermons on this subject was now commenced, but we find that it was afterwards continued in several additional homilies which were not preached in this year.

8. In November and December he resumed his controversy with the Anomœans, and delivered his second, third, fourth, and fifth homilies against them. In these homilies he treats of the subject of the *Incomprehensible Nature of God.*

In his second homily he informs us of the nature of the interruptions from different causes — the presence of neighbouring bishops, and the celebration of the memory of martyrs—to which he had been subjected, which broke the thread of his discourse.

In his third homily, at its close, he sharply rebukes his audience for leaving the church after the sermon and not remaining to communicate.

In the fourth homily he congratulated them because they had attended to the advice which he had given them in the former homily, and had stayed after service for the Holy Communion.　He expressed his regret at its close that pickpockets had disturbed their devotions.

In the fifth homily, after a recapitulation of what he had said before, he brings forward fresh arguments against the Anomœans.

In these homilies not only does the eloquence of Chrysostom shine forth, but also his argumentative powers and his caustic wit in replying to the objections brought forward by heretics and unbelievers. It may be fairly considered that these homilies against the Anomœans rank among the very foremost of the works of Chrysostom.

He points out in this set of homilies that not only the essence of God, but also His wisdom, were alike incomprehensible to prophets and to angels.　He shows how we must employ faith, not reason, in Divine subjects ; how the Anomœans rashly ventured to say that they knew God, and how they dared too curiously to investigate His essence ; how the praises of God are profitable to man, not to God ; how men cannot understand the nature of angels, or even that of their own souls ; and how such complete knowledge of God is confined to the Son and the Holy Spirit.　He concludes by referring to the prudence of St. Paul in his teaching ; by specifically answering the objections of the Anomœans; and by showing the efficacy of prayer and the blessing of humility.

Arianism—inasmuch as it may, in germ and spirit, be traced backward up to Paul of Samosata, who was once Bishop of Antioch—may be viewed as the heretical product of that city. It was there that Lucian, the friend of Paul of Samosata, when a presbyter of Antioch, taught not only Eusebius, Bishop of Nicomedia, and Leontius of Antioch, but very possibly Arius himself, who, in a letter addressed to Eusebius, called him a 'fellow-Lucianist.' It was at Antioch that Aëtius and Eunomius, his pupil, at first lived,—men who advocated the most advanced views on this subject. The party who followed Eunomius were sometimes named Eunomians; but they were also designated Anomœans, because they denied the 'similarity' (namely, ὁμοιότης) as well as the equality of the Persons of the Father and the Son.

9. The homily respecting *Anathematisms* would, from the language employed at its commencement, seem to follow immediately after the homilies on the *Incomprehensible Nature of God.* Tillemont, however, places it at a later period in Chrysostom's ministry, namely, 388 A.D.

This homily denounces the custom, which was not uncommon at that time, of anathematising those who were in error. Chrysostom, however, quotes the example of St. Paul, who only in one single instance pronounced an anathema against others. It is the duty of Christians, he adds, to instruct, to warn, to exhort those who are in error, since peradventure they may be thus led to repentance and an acknowledgment

of the truth. Christians ought neither to anathematise
the living nor the dead. Such conduct is wrong in
either case. Heresy itself, in the abstract, you may
denounce and anathematise; but the holders and
advocates of such heretical tenets should be treated
alike with forbearance and love.

10. On December 20th, the Feast of St. Philogonius,
Bishop of Antioch, he pronounced a panegyric upon
him, which he did not finish, but left it to Flavian to
conclude. He closes the homily with an exhortation
to his hearers to prepare for the due celebration of
Christmas.

Philogonius had been first a lawyer, like Chrysostom,
and then had been made Bishop of Antioch about the
year 320 A.D. He is referred to by Athanasius with
commendation, as a sound and orthodox believer.

In this sermon Chrysostom shows the superiority
of the future over the present life; and narrates how
Philogonius, though a married lawyer, became Bishop
of the Church of Antioch.

11. On December 25th he delivered a homily,
which is generally classified under his panegyrical
orations, on the nativity of Christ. A peculiar interest
attaches to this sermon from the fact of our discovering
from it that the Feast of the Nativity was only a recent
introduction into the Eastern Church from the Western;
that, in fact, the festival had not been celebrated for
more than ten years at Antioch. Its observance had
been gradually gaining ground in the city, and now,
when Chrysostom preached, the church was full. He
declares his love for the holy day, which he warmly
welcomes; and he solemnly warns his hearers against
all irreverence, and crowding, and noise, in their
approach to the table of the Lord.

Such is a brief outline of the chief homilies and sermons delivered by Chrysostom in the first year of his presbytership, 386 A.D., which have been handed down to us. They evince the richness of his intellect, his fertility of resource, his untiring energy, his wisdom, prudence, and caution, as well as his distinguishing eloquence.

The title given him in the homilies of the Church of England—'the great clerk and godly preacher, St. John Chrysostom'—is seen from these specimens alone to be most fairly deserved.

'The history of the Church,' says one of her historians, 'was, if we may so say, like a beautiful tesselated work, in which the lives of her saints were set, as fair and precious stones and jewels with different colours, each in its proper place, to form a symmetrical and harmonious whole. But in this spiritual πολυποικιλία,[1] or variegated mosaic of Christian gifts and graces, one thing was still wanting, namely, a clear manifestation, in large cities, of Christ, the great Prophet or Teacher, Priest and King, who should come into the world. Something, indeed, had been done in this respect by great Christian orators, such as Basil at Cæsarea, Ambrose at Milan, Gregory Nazianzen at Constantinople. But they were theologians rather than homilists; their preaching, for the most part, was dogmatic rather than practical; it dwelt more on Christian verities in the abstract, than on their application to the ordinary duties of daily life. Augustine was a wise teacher of Christian duty, but his sphere as a preacher was limited to congregations in provincial towns; and he did not aspire to

[1] Cf. Eph. iii. 10 (in Greek).

lofty flights of eloquence. We hear of no great preacher at Rome before Leo the First, in the middle of the fifth century, and he was an imitator of Augustine. A person was raised up, in the providence of God, to supply the desideratum. This was John Chrysostom.'

CHAPTER V.

THE SEDITION AT ANTIOCH.

Ac, veluti magno in populo quum sæpe coorta est
Seditio, sævitque animis ignobile vulgus ;
Jamque faces et saxa volant ; furor arma ministrat
Tum, pietate gravem ac meritis si forte virum quem
Conspexere, silent ; arrectisque auribus adstant .
Iste regit dictis animos, et pectora mulcet.

VIRG. Æn. i. 148, et seq.

THE most noteworthy and memorable event that
took place during Chrysostom's ministry at Antioch
occurred in the second year of his presbyterate. This
was the famous sedition, occasioned by the oppressive
taxation laid upon the city by an imperial decree of
Theodosius, on February 26th, 387 A.D., in order that
he might by this means defray the heavy expenses
incurred by the celebration of the fifth year, upon
which his elder son, Arcadius, had now entered, from
the time when the title of Augustus had been given
him, and of his own tenth year of government ; and
also that he might meet the cost of the war against
the usurper, Maximus, in the West, and other necessities of state.

Theodosius had anticipated the tenth year of his
reign, which fell in 388 A.D., in order to associate the
two events together, and so lessen the expenses
attendant upon their celebration. The army alone,

on these occasions, expected a gift of five gold pieces a head for each soldier. All this was a severe burden upon the royal purse, and so it was resolved to levy a tax upon the cities of the East to meet this expenditure.

A general panic was created at Antioch by the announcement of this subsidy. Citizens of all ranks, from the highest to the lowest, flocked to the churches imploring Divine aid. The lower classes of the city, together with a foreign and degraded element of the population connected with the theatre, were excited to fury. This discontented and irritated crowd first sought (as was the custom then) the bishop, in order to obtain the redress of their grievances, which bishops of those days were often able to procure from the emperors. Not being able to find the bishop, they returned to the prætorium, and after having committed various injuries at the public baths, and attacked the prefect's palace, they threw stones at the painted tablets of the emperor, besmeared them with dirt, heaped curses on the Augusti, and then, in their rage and fury, tore down the statues of the emperor, and even of his dearly-loved wife, Flaccilla, whom he had lost, and dragged them ignominiously through the streets.

The following legend is found in Cave's *Life of Chrysostom* :—' The night before the sedition broke out, a *spectrum* (they say) in the shape of a woman, of an immense bigness, and a terrible aspect, was seen flying up and down with a swift motion through the streets of the city, lashing the air with a whip that made a dreadful noise.'

The sedition was crushed, after the excited mob had set fire to one public building, by the prefect of the city, who despatched a band of archers to quell it. Those taken in the act of outrage were condemned and executed by the governor of the city, who dreaded the emperor's indignation. Theodosius was informed by means of messengers both of the riot and of the indignity to which he had been personally subjected.

But no sooner had the populace indulged in this violent outrage, than they were terror-stricken at the prospect of the emperor's vengeance. Their panic-dread even exceeded their senseless fury. A gloomy silence prevailed throughout the city.

It was during the interval that elapsed between the deed of shame which they had wrought, and the manifesto of the emperor—an interval of the greatest alarm, in which suspense heightened and exaggerated their fears—that Chrysostom delivered his famous *Sermons on the Statues.* They were twenty-one in number, and are justly celebrated as some of the most interesting, instructive, and effective of the many sermons which he delivered. The first, and some at least of the others, were preached in the old church of Antioch, which was so named because it was situated in the more ancient part of the city, near the Orontes. It was sometimes called the apostolical church, as being that founded by the apostles.

It was a singular circumstance that on the Sunday preceding the riot, in the first of these sermons, when dwelling on the subject of blasphemy, he had strongly appealed to them to let no one who was their equal blaspheme God in their hearing without at once rebuking and checking him for the insult done to their Heavenly King, assuring them that if those who heard him watched over, and were anxious for, the salvation of their fellow-citizens, even though they were in a minority, the whole city would speedily be amended. 'One man,' he added, 'inspired with a holy zeal, sufficeth to amend an entire people.'

In these discourses Chrysostom turns to a practical use all the circumstances which then surrounded the Antiochians. The people were almost paralysed with alarm, not knowing what steps Theodosius might take in his just anger and fury. Their fears summoned up the most terrible presentiments in their minds. The unknown terrified them more than the actual reality. The forum was deserted, the schools abandoned, the theatres empty ; men looked with suspicious fear one upon another ; the higher classes left the city, the philosophers decamped, the young students fled. Chrysostom's account of 'the agony of those days is in the highest style of dramatic oratory.'

Soon tidings were brought from Constantinople that the emperor had resolved to take away the franchise from the city, to constitute Laodicea the metropolis of Syria, and to raze to the ground their beloved Antioch.

Upon this, alarmed at what was about to happen, and conjuring up even the vaguest sources of terror, those who had never entered the doors of a church before, now in their abject dread crowded the old church and offered prayers and supplications which were new and strange to them. It was then that the genius and the oratorical power, as well as the piety, of Chrysostom shone forth so conspicuously. For a week he had kept silence ; but at the end of that time he addressed the people with words of exhortation and comfort.

He endeavoured, in his second homily, to utilise the

present crisis and to employ their present state of mind and feeling—their fears, their anxiety, their dread of the anger of Theodosius—as 'stepping-stones to higher things,' and to lead them to look away from the just wrath of an earthly monarch to the still more just and righteous indignation of a high and holy God who was offended at their many and grievous transgressions, and thus to induce them to fix their minds upon the more awful punishment—irreversible and eternal—which they would suffer from an indignant God, unless they humbled themselves before Him for their sins, and repented of their evil doings. He vividly put before them their besetting sins—luxury, self-indulgence, blasphemy, swearing, amongst others —and urged them to repentance, pointing out God's mercy to those who, with contrite hearts, humbled themselves before Him. But all their tears and all their mortifications would be of no avail unless they produced the true fruits of penitence, namely, a holy and consistent walk and conversation. The true Christian, he assured them, stood upon a rock superior to all the assaults of earthly sorrow and misfortune, unalarmed and unterrified. Had they carried out the advice which he, with almost prophetic prescience, had given them in his first homily before the insurrection took place, they would have been able to repress these daring blasphemers, and perhaps have rescued the city from its present miserable condition.

When his hearers applauded what he said, he indignantly exclaimed that the church was no theatre, to which they went merely to be pleased and amused, but that the true object of their attendance there was their spiritual edification and improvement in their lives and actions. 'What need have I,' he asks, 'of these plaudits, these cheers, and tumultuous signs of approval? The praise I seek is that ye show forth all I have said in your works. Then am I an enviable and happy man, not when ye approve, but when ye perform with all readiness whatsoever ye hear from me.'

Earthly riches, he told them, were held on an uncertain and precarious tenure. Abraham's tent beneath the spreading oak surpassed the gilded dwellings of the wealthy, for angels made his rude abode bright and splendid. They should adorn, not their houses, but their souls. Of wealth we have but the use, not the ownership. The rich lose the pleasure of their wealth, because they lack the relish. Water is sweet to the thirsty, and sleep to the weary. Elijah's leathern mantle was more splendid than the purple, and the cave of the just man more so than the halls of kings. 'Let us not then,' he adds in conclusion, 'be cast down. Let us not lament, nor fear the difficulty of the times, for He who did not refuse to pour out His blood for all, what will He refuse to do for our safety!'

Meanwhile Flavian, their bishop, had quitted the city in order that he might appeal to the emperor in their behalf. He was now advanced in life, suffering from infirmity and ill-health, and his only sister—the object of his fond affection—was stretched apparently on her death-bed. It was winter too; and therefore all the more trying for their bishop, old and feeble as he was, to take a long journey of more than 800 miles at so inclement a season of the year. 'On this account,' Chrysostom says in his third homily, 'I trust there may be a good hope; for God will not disdain to look upon such earnestness and such efforts.

I know that when he has barely seen our pious emperor, and been seen by him, he will be able at once, by his very countenance, to allay his wrath. For not only the words of the saints, but their very aspect, are full of grace. He will also call in to his aid the season, and bring forward the sacred festival of the Passover; and will remind him of the season when Christ remitted the sins of the whole world. He will exhort him to imitate his Lord. He will also remind him of the parable of the ten thousand talents and the hundred pence. He will, moreover, inform him that the offence of the city was not a general offence, but that of certain strangers and adventurers; and that it would not be just for the disorderly conduct of a few to extirpate such a city, and to punish those who had done no wrong. These things, and more than these, the bishop will say with still greater boldness; and the emperor will listen to them; and one is humane, and the other is faithful; so that on both sides we entertain favourable hopes. But much more do we rely upon the mercy of God, than upon the fidelity of our teacher and the humanity of the emperor. For our city is excessively dear to Christ, both because of our ancestors, and of your own virtue.'

We have seen that not a few of those who had been guilty of rioting were brought before the imperial magistrates of the city, and after being scourged, were put to the torture. Hence still greater panic had taken place. The citizens in their alarm had fled in numbers to the mountains that surrounded the city, and so great and abject was the terror, that it seemed possible, if not likely, that the entire population might leave the devoted city. Sad rumours, too, had come from Constantinople of what was meditated by the emperor, and these rumours were converted into realities in their present alarmed and agitated state of mind. The fast of forty days preceding Easter had now commenced, which ordinarily produced considerable effect for good upon the citizens. But, at this time of alarm, the effects of the solemn season were heightened. Fasting was now more rigidly observed. They felt, in their hopelessness of all human aid in their miserable condition, the greater need of humiliation and repentance.

In the absence of the bishop, the authority of Chrysostom was more paramount.

He took occasion, in the same third homily, to dwell upon the personal as well as the paternal character of their holy-minded bishop, who had gone on his mission of love to the distant seat of government. Such conduct on his part was to them an ornament, to himself a crown. With such a bishop and such an emperor, they might justly entertain high hopes of success attending this mission. ‘Upon God, therefore,’ he adds, ‘should we call, that He may help and defend us in our hour of danger and peril.’

It was to him, he tells them, a source of joy that both the theatres and the circus were abandoned, and that ‘the whole city had become a church,’ the day being passed in public prayer, and in calling upon God.

‘Let not such deep religious impressions be momentary and transient. Ponder these things well in your hearts, when you meet your friends, in the family circle. Take these thoughts home with you, as you might bring back with you a garland of flowers for those who remained behind in the house. Such advice and such counsels are of more value than any perishable nosegay of flowers.'

'Practise then (he adds) the real fasting—not merely an abstinence from meats, but from sins too—for fasting is of little avail, unless it be accompanied by a fit state of mind. Fasting is unprofitable, except all other duties follow with it. It is a medicine ; but a medicine, though it be never so profitable, becomes frequently useless by the unskilfulness of him who employs it.'

He urged them, in the fourth homily, as well as in very many others, to abstain especially from all rash swearing and thoughtless invocation of the name of God. He assured them that he lived only for them ; that his great care was for their salvation ; and that he always carried them and their interests in his heart. Nothing, in his opinion, which is merely outward can either benefit or hurt any one ; that can alone result from their own free will. He quotes the example of the three youths in the fiery furnace for their comfort. Death may indeed be regarded as the greatest evil by men, but the true evil is to offend God, and that which displeases Him (*Hom.* v.). Nor did he hesitate to upbraid them for being quieted and tranquillised by the imperial magistrates, who endeavoured to remove in the church the abject fears of the people, when they ought, as Christians, to have listened to him, their spiritual pastor, rather than to a civil magistrate who was a heathen (*Hom.* xvi.).

It was at this time that the power of Chrysostom over the people was most strikingly exhibited. He did not quit his post. He was to be seen Sunday after Sunday, nay, day after day, in the church, endeavouring to calm their fears, and induce them not to quit the city. He preached to them on the subject of Paul's imprisonment, and how he was ready to endure suffering and even death in his Master's cause (*Hom.* v.). 'But give me,' saith one, 'to be like Paul, and I shall never be afraid of death. Why, what is it that forbids thee, O man, to become like Paul? Was he not a poor man? Was he not a tent-maker? Was he not a man of mean rank (ἰδιώτης)? For if he had been rich and well-born, the poor, when called upon to imitate his zeal, would have had their poverty to plead ; but now thou canst say nothing of this sort. For this man was one who exercised a manual art, and supported himself, too, by his daily labours. And thou, indeed, from the first hast inherited true religion from thy fathers ; and from thy earliest age hast been nourished in the study of the sacred writings; but he was "a blasphemer, and a persecutor, and injurious," and ravaged the Church! Nevertheless, he so changed, all at once, as to surpass all in the vehemence of his zeal, and he cries out, saying, "Be ye followers of me, even as I also am of Christ." He imitated the Lord ; and wilt not thou who hast been educated in piety from the first, imitate a fellow-servant, one who by a great change was brought to the faith at a later period of life ?' (*Hom.* v.).

Flavian did not succeed in forestalling the messengers sent by the angry emperor. Before the bishop's arrival at Constantinople, the commissioners appointed by Theodosius reached Antioch. They met, indeed, on their respective journeys. They were two in number, Cæsarius and Hellebicus by name, both men of high character, of clemency and moderation, and also Christians.

Zozimus, in his history (lib. iv.), reports that Libanius, the rhetorician, and Hilary (afterwards made governor of Palestine), were sent by the senate of Antioch, as delegates, to the emperor at Constantinople, to use all the means that eloquence, and learning, and distinction could afford, in order to appease his righteous anger. They were sent, in the opinion of Cave, by the Gentile portion of the population. The oration cf Libanius, in which he strove to mitigate the anger of Theodosius, and to lead him to a merciful estimate of an act which he represents as the 'effect of frenzy and madness, and the instigation of some malignant demon,' proves that he at least went to Constantinople.

The two commissioners speedily entered upon the work for which they were sent. It was now the middle of Lent. They announced to the weeping crowd of citizens that their city was deprived of its franchise—that its baths, in which they delighted, its theatres, in which they revelled, and its places of public entertainment, which were their boast, were to be all alike closed. The guilty were sought out and imprisoned ; men of the highest rank were dragged in chains through the public streets to the judgment-seat ; and the lists of the proscribed were long.

It was about this time that the monks came down from the mountains and their solitudes, that they might intercede for the city 'when just about to be overwhelmed,—to sink under the waves, and to be utterly and instantly destroyed' (*Hom.* xvii.). It must have seemed a strange apparition, when those wild-looking devotees, in uncouth rough garments, who had been shut up so many years in their cells, at no one's entreaty, by no one's counsel (as Chrysostom tells us), left their caves and their huts, when they beheld such a cloud overhanging the city. One of these monks, named Macedonius, an unlearned man, but enlightened by the Holy Spirit, seized the cloak of one of the commissioners when riding to the tribunal, and bade them dismount. They hesitated at first, but having heard who he was, they obeyed and embraced his knees. 'Tell the emperor, my beloved, that he is not only an emperor, but also a man; that being a man, he ruleth over those who partake of the same nature with himself; and that man is created after the image of God. Let him not then command that the image of God be so unmercifully and cruelly destroyed. Let him reflect that in the place of one brazen image we can easily fabricate many; but that it is utterly beyond his power to restore a single hair of the murdered victims.'

The commissioners were much struck with the way in which Macedonius uttered this, although they did not understand what he said (as he spoke in the Syrian language); and when his words were explained to them in Greek, they agreed that one of them should go to the emperor, to tell him how things were at Antioch, and to beg for further instructions.

The appeal, therefore, of the monks was not made in vain. The final and irreversible sentence on the city was postponed. Cæsarius himself departed to Constantinople as the bearer of the letter of intercession to Theodosius, which was signed by the monks.

Chrysostom was greatly struck with admiration at the courage of the monks, whose conduct he contrasts with the pusillanimity of the cynic philosophers at Antioch, who, when danger threatened, forsook the city, and all hasted away and hid themselves in caves.

'Such a thing is philosophy of soul, rising superior to all things, and to all prosperous or adverse events.' The accused had no legal advocates to plead for them. All had fled, with the exception of Libanius, who appeared in court with distressed and anxious countenance.

Again we find Chrysostom ministering consolation and encouragement in the midst of the sufferings of the people. The true glory of Antioch, he assured them, did not consist in its baths, or theatres, or public buildings, or in its being 'the capital of Syria,' but rather in the fact that in it the disciples were first called Christians, and that their deed of charity to the famine-stricken saints at Jerusalem had thence emanated. The piety of its inhabitants is the truest glory of a city. Such distinctions as those which have been recorded render it a metropolis not in earth but in heaven (*Hom.* xvii.).

But soon a change takes place in their condition. The clouds pass away. The prospect brightens. The darkness of night rolls off, and joy comes, as it were, in the morning.

Flavian's visit to the emperor had not been made in vain. He had appealed with the greatest earnestness to Theodosius on behalf of his beloved city and people. He had put before him the beauty of forgiveness ; had said that no punishment could be so severe as undeserved mercy ; had declared that he could never return to his people, unless the favour which he requested was granted ; had confessed the shameful ingratitude of his citizens, who had received such favours at the hand of the emperor, and that they now had no one from whom they could look for help, and were an object of contempt to the whole world; had assured him that no precedent for rebellion could be drawn from his clemency, but that both Jews and Gentiles would regard it with satisfaction; and had reminded the sovereign that he, too, had a Master in heaven, who was both merciful and just. His prayers were heard: the anger of the emperor passed away: the city was saved from destruction and ruin.

The emperor, as we learn from the twenty-first homily, was affected even to tears, and 'gave utterance to one only sentiment, which did him much more honour than the diadem. And what was that? How, said he, can it be anything wonderful or great, that we should remit our anger against those who have treated us with indignity—we, who ourselves are but men—when the Lord of the universe, coming, as He did, on earth, and being made a servant for us, and crucified by those who had experienced His kindness, besought the Father on behalf of His crucifiers, saying, " Forgive them, for they know not what they do? " What marvel, then, if we also should forgive our fellow-servants? '

Winter was now over. Flavian had despatched by post the gracious letter of the emperor, so that the citizens might receive the joyful news as quickly as possible, as Theodosius, in fact, himself desired. At the commencement of spring Flavian returned from Constantinople, and was able to share in the blessings of Easter with his rescued flock and people. He found, too, that his beloved sister, whom he never expected to have seen again in this world, had recovered from her illness. His people, most naturally, were deeply grateful for what he had done for them; but he declined to accept all personal thanks from them, saying, ' It was not my doing, but God who melted the heart of the emperor.'

In a sermon which Chrysostom preached on Easter-day (namely, the twenty-first and last of the *Homilies on the Statues*), in allusion to the conduct of the Antiochians after receiving the welcome messenger sent forward by Flavian to announce the emperor's clemency, he thus concludes:—' What, therefore, ye then did, in crowning the forum with garlands ; in lighting lamps, in spreading couches of green leaves (στιβάδας) before the shops, and keeping high festival, as if the city had been just now born, this do ye, although in another manner, throughout all time ; being crowned, not with flowers, but with virtue ; lighting up throughout your whole souls the lustre that is from good works ; rejoicing with a spiritual gladness. And let us never fail to give God thanks continually for all these things, not only that He hath freed us from these calamities, but that He also permitted them to happen ; and let us acknowledge His abundant goodness !'

Such a termination reflects the greatest credit on the justly-offended emperor, and on the powers of persuasion evinced by the aged Flavian. Nor does the character of Chrysostom shine forth with less brightness during the whole transaction. He neither quitted the post of danger himself, nor did he cease to strive to keep his flock at their posts, and endeavour to console, comfort, and strengthen them in the midst of the cruel sufferings, as well actual as anticipated, which they had to endure.

Theodosius was justly styled the Great. He was a Christian, orthodox in his views, of high and noble character, brave and patriotic, and a distinguished soldier and general. His military instincts led him to desire to see a uniformity of religious faith throughout his empire. We have remarked in the sketch of his character, in the introductory chapter, that he endeavoured to extirpate paganism and establish Christianity in its place. In all that was good, philanthropic, and Christian, Theodosius was much aided by his wife, the Empress Flaccilla, who was a sincere Christian, and of a noble simplicity of character. Her example and advice had great influence over the conduct of her husband, and tended to keep within due bounds the impulsive violence of the temper of Theodosius. She died in 385 A.D., and in her death the emperor sustained a grievous personal loss.

As the result of the sedition, no small accession from the ranks of paganism to the Church of Christ took place. They had been led—when the places of amusement were closed, and when their own hearts were sad—to frequent the church, and to hear the sermons of the great preacher. They had listened to his outspoken denunciations of vice, to his calls to repentance and amendment of life, to his contrast between the earthly and the heavenly treasure, to the proofs which he marshalled before them, from the nature of the universe,[1] and the formation of the human body, of the existence of a beneficent Creator ; and thus many were led to abandon heathenism, and were admitted into the ranks of the Christian Church. That no small number of converts must have joined

---

[1] Cf. *Hom.* ix. x. xi. xii. ' Not only,' he says, ' does the greatness and beauty of the creation show forth the Creator, but the very manner likewise in which it is compacted together, and the mode of creation being beyond the power of any natural consequence ' (*Hom.* x.). Parts of the eleventh homily are an admirable treatise on natural theology.

the Church would seem evident from the fact that Chrysostom speaks of the arduous nature of the task which was imposed upon him, after the return of Flavian, of building up in the true faith those who had, during the time of their great calamity, come over from the ranks of heathenism.

The homilies which Chrysostom delivered to the people during these fluctuations, on their part, of hope and fear, were obviously almost entirely the production of the moment, and therefore unpremeditated. Such sermons clearly did not admit of any definite preparation. They were, in the strict sense of the term, 'extempore.' At one time he had to console his hearers in their distress and alarm and despair ; at another time to urge them to cast away the sins which had brought down God's vengeance upon them. They were delivered in rapid succession, with only an interval of a few days between them. They are often masterpieces of the truest and highest eloquence, if the definition of Professor Blunt be true :—' Eloquence must be the voice of one earnestly endeavouring to deliver his own soul. It must be the outpouring of ideas rushing for a vent. It must be the poet's experience—

> " Thoughts that rove about,
> And loudly knock to have their passage out." '

CHAPTER VI.

THE CLOSE OF CHRYSOSTOM'S PRESBYTERATE.

'The great clerk and godly preacher, St. John Chrysostom, saith, whatsoever is required to salvation of man, is fully contained in the Scripture of God. . . . If it shall require to teach any truth, or reprove false doctrine, to rebuke any vice, to commend any virtue, to give good counsel, to comfort or to exhort, or to do any other thing requisite for our salvation; all these things, saith St. Chrysostom, we may learn plentifully of the Scripture.'—*The Homilies.*

THE sedition at Antioch, with all its varied excitement, and with all its fluctuations from hope to despair, and from despair to hope, was no doubt the great and signal event of Chrysostom's life during his ministry at Antioch. In comparison with it, the other incidents in his career at this time seem tame and almost colourless. It could, however, scarcely be expected that he would again have had such a field for his Christian oratory during the remainder of his presbyterate as that event furnished. But, nevertheless, we must not suppose that the rest of his course at Antioch did not afford many and great opportunities for the exercise of his unrivalled powers as a preacher.

We know that during this period of his life he composed a large part of those numerous works which have come down to us.

1. His ninety homilies on St. Matthew[1] were some of the fruits of his preaching at this time. They may be fairly reckoned as among his best productions. Commenced, in all probability, either at the close of the year 389 A.D., or the beginning of 390 A.D., they were probably completed either during the last named year, or at the commencement of the following one.

In these homilies he adopts the plan of first carefully and diligently inquiring into the exact meaning of the passage under review, and then concludes with a pointed and forcible application of it, exhorting his hearers to the practice of some particular virtue or grace that seemed to flow from the place under his consideration. His explanations of the sacred text are critical, sound, and reliable. They are in strict harmony with its spirit; but there is no 'servile literalism' (such as that in which the rationalising school has indulged) traceable in them, which makes the human element preponderate over the Divine. Nor, on the other hand, did the eloquence of Chrysostom ever roam into those 'wild extravagances of fantastic allegories, which blemished the homilies of Origen, and undermined the historical foundation of Holy Scripture itself. On this solid exegetical basis Chrysostom built a structure of sound moral teaching, which did not expend itself in vague generalities, but with wonderful vivacity and vigour dealt with popular errors and the vices of the day.'

In these homilies not only does he press upon the

---

[1] These homilies, which occupy vol. vii. of the Benedictine edition of Chrysostom's works, have been admirably edited by Field, in three volumes, in which edition great pains have been bestowed upon the revision of the Greek text.

attention of his hearers the duty of almsgiving, but he dwells upon the example of self-denial and devotion which the monks displayed. Not only does he attack, with all his vigour, the vices of the theatre, but he also comes into collision with the extreme phase of the Arian heresy,—namely, the Anomœan,—and sometimes, though far more rarely, he refutes the Manichæans.

We give, in his own words, some specimens of the mode in which he inculcates different virtues and duties, and in which he brings before his hearers different vices to be avoided. When dwelling, for example, on Matt. xix. 16, in which the rich young man is brought under our notice, and speaking of the injurious consequences of avarice on the soul of man, he says :—' Seeing, perhaps, the brightness of the silver, and the multitude of the servants, and the beauty of the buildings, the court paid in the market-place, art thou bewitched thereby? What remedy, then, may there be for this evil wound? If thou consider how these things affect thy soul, how dark, and desolate, and foul they render it, and how ugly; if thou reckon with how many evils these things were acquired, with how many labours they are kept, with how many dangers: or rather they are not kept unto the end, but when thou hast escaped the attempts of all, death coming on thee is often wont to remove these things into the hands of thine enemies, and goeth and taketh thee with him destitute, drawing after thee none of these things, save the wounds and the sores only which the soul received from these before its departing. When thou seest any one resplendent outwardly with raiment and large attendance, lay open his conscience, and thou shalt see many a cobweb within, and much dust. Consider Paul, Peter. Consider John, Elias, or rather the Son of God Himself, who had not where to lay His head. Be an imitator of Him, and of His servants, and imagine to thyself the unspeakable riches of these' (*Hom.* lxiii.).

Again, when speaking of the holy conversation of the monks, he says :—' And their conversation is full of the same calm. For they talk not of these things whereof we discourse, that are nothing to us : such a one is made governor, such a one has ceased to be governor ; such a one is dead, and another has succeeded to the inheritance, and all such like; but always about the things to come do they speak, and seek wisdom ; and as though dwelling in another world, as though they had migrated unto heaven itself, as living there, even so all their conversation is about the things there, about Abraham's bosom, about the crowns of the saints, about the quiring with Christ ; and of things present they have neither any memory nor thought, but like as we should not deign to speak at all of what the ants do in their holes and cliffs, so neither do they of what we do; but about the King that is above, about the war in which they are engaged, about the devil's crafts, about the good deeds which the saints have achieved ' (*Hom.* lxix.).

Or listen to him, when speaking of the different dangers that beset the several ages of our life :—Our present life, he observes, is an outstretched ocean. And as in the sea here, there are different bays exposed to different tempests, and the Ægean is difficult because of the winds, the Tyrrhenian Strait because of the confined space, the Charybdis that is by Africa because of the shallows, the Propontis, which is without the Euxine Sea, on account of its violence and currents, the parts without Cadiz because of the desolation, and tracklessness, and unexplored places therein, and other portions for other causes, so also is it in our life. And the first sea to view is that of our childish days, having much tempestuousness because of its folly, its facility, because it is not stedfast. Therefore also we set over it guides and teachers, by our diligence adding what is wanting to nature, even as there by the pilot's skill.

After this age succeeds the sea of youth, where the winds are violent, as in the Ægean, lust increasing upon us. And this age especially is destitute of correction; not only because he is beset more fiercely, but also because his faults are not reproved, for both teacher and guide after that withdraw. When, therefore, the winds blow more fiercely, and the pilot is more feeble, and there is no helper, consider the greatness of the tempest.

After this there is again another period of life, that of men, in which the cares of the household press upon us, when there is a wife, and marriage, and begetting of children, and ruling of a house, and thick-falling showers of cares. Then especially both covetousness flourishes and envy.

When, then, we pass each part of our life with shipwrecks, how shall we suffice for the present life? How shall we escape future punishment? For when first in the earliest age we learn nothing healthful, and then in youth we do not practise sobriety, and when grown to manhood we do not get the better of covetousness, coming to old age as to a hold full of bilge-water, and as having made the barque of the soul weak by all these shocks, the planks being separated, we shall arrive at that harbour, bearing much filth instead of spiritual merchandise, and to the devil we shall furnish laughter, but lamentation to ourselves, and bring upon ourselves the intolerable punishments.

That these things may not be, let us brace ourselves up on every side, and, withstanding all our passions, let us cast out the lust of wealth, that we may also attain unto the good things to come, by the grace and love towards man of our Lord Jesus Christ, to whom be glory for ever and ever (*Hom.* lxxxi.).

One more quotation will serve to illustrate the character of these remarkable homilies. Chrysostom is showing that poverty is nobler than riches.

' Hear these things,' he says, ' as many as are poor, or rather also, as many as desire to be rich. It is not poverty that is the thing to be feared, but the not being willing to be poor. Account poverty to be nothing to fear, and it will not be to thee a matter for fear. For neither is this fear in the nature of the thing, but in the judgment of feeble-minded men ; or rather, I am even ashamed that I have occasion to say so much concerning poverty, and to show that it is nothing to be feared. For if thou practise self-command, it is even a fountain to thee of countless blessings. And if any one were to offer thee sovereignty, and political power, and wealth, and luxury, and then having set against them poverty, were to give thee thy choice to take which thou wouldest, thou wouldest straightway seize upon poverty, if, indeed, thou knewest the beauty thereof' (*Hom.* xc.).

No quotations will, of course, give any complete

and adequate idea of these homilies. This difficulty results in great measure from the singular grace and elegance, as well as the rich copiousness of the Greek language, which admitted of a delicacy in the shades of meaning, as well as a peculiar play upon words and expressions, which cannot generally be expressed in a modern tongue.

It is said that Thomas Aquinas declared that he would sooner have composed them than have been master of Paris. And the Benedictine editor has affirmed that there is no book extant which contains so many precepts of Christian morality as these homilies on St. Matthew. In none of his writings has Chrysostom shown more, if as much, power of rooting out vice, of inculcating a high moral tone, and of regulating the Christian life.

2. The labours and the excitement which Chrysostom underwent during the eventful days of the sedition, would seem to have told upon his health and strength. That he was suffering from illness about this time we learn from the homily which he delivered on the Sunday preceding Ascension Day. He was, consequently, unable to take any share in the services which Bishop Flavian held, between Easter and Whitsuntide, at the different chapels erected over saints and martyrs, either in commemoration of their death, or to indicate the spot in which their death had taken place.

It can scarcely be doubted that the observance of the days of the deaths of martyrs, and of the martyrs themselves, had already degenerated from the early simplicity by which such observances had been characterised. Nor can it be denied that Chrysostom held the notion that the prayers of the martyrs possessed an intercessory power,—that they were able to procure benefits and blessings from God for those who appealed to them ; he did not, indeed, hold that they were the *immediate* dispensers of blessings, but that they had power mediately to procure them for the faithful. It was reserved for an after age and generation to look up to the saints and martyrs as the primary and direct bestowers of spiritual benefits to men. This excessive veneration for saints and martyrs, which was at that time felt, and in which we cannot doubt that Chrysostom shared, would seem to have paved the way for the simple and unmistakable worship and 'cultus' of the mediæval times. The feasts which were held at the graves of the saints and martyrs, and which were called 'love feasts,' degenerated very speedily into scenes of riot and excess, and had to be prohibited from taking place. It is well known that Augustine, by his earnest entreaties and persuasive eloquence, caused them to be abolished in his diocese; and Ambrose was compelled to introduce a similar prohibition at Milan.

3. During this period, about 388 or 389 A.D., Chrysostom delivered his eighty-eight homilies on St. John. They differ somewhat in their structure from his other homilies. They are less practical, and more controversial. This has been reasonably assigned to the early morning hour, at which they would appear, from the close of the thirty-first homily, to have been delivered; at which time his audience would have been more select, and therefore would not need, to the same extent, to be instructed in the more common and elementary truths of Christianity, and in the more ordinary duties of life.

They have no definite note of time attaching to

them ; but they seem to be alluded to in his seventh homily on 1 Cor. ii. 8, as having been published while Chrysostom was still at Antioch. Some writers have referred them to the year 390 A.D., regarding them as composed after the homilies on St. Matthew, and prior to those on the Epistles of St. Paul.

The subject-matter of St. John's Gospel furnished Chrysostom with many opportunities of refuting the Anomœans, who, as we have already seen, held that the Son was not of *like* substance with the Father. But, as it has been well remarked,[1] Chrysostom, in these homilies, is continually meeting with texts which the Anomœans perverted to the support of their heretical views, and turning them into weapons for their confutation. And this he usually does with great success, since the Catholic doctrine of true and perfect Godhead, united in one Person with true and perfect manhood, affords a key that easily opens texts which most stubbornly resist any confused notion of an inferior Divinity, or an unreal humanity. The texts urged by the heretic, put to this test, are found not really to belong to him. They are not even arguments so far for his view of the case, but perfectly consistent with the truth always held by the Church of Christ. If Chrysostom anywhere fails, it is from some over-refinement in rhetorical analysis, and not from any want of apprehension of the main truths concerned. Chrysostom commences the homilies on St. John with the following striking preface:—
' They that are spectators of the ฺheathen games, when they have learned that a distinguished athlete

---

¹ Cf. preface to translation of *Homilies on St. John*, part i., in the *Library of the Fathers*, from which translation generally many quotations have been made.

and winner of crowns is come from any quarter, run all together to view his wrestling, and all his skill and strength ; and you may see the whole theatre of many ten thousands, all there straining their eyes, both of body and mind, that nothing of what is done may escape them. So, again, these same persons, if any admirable musician come amongst them, leave all that they had in hand, which often is necessary and pressing business, and mount the steps, and sit listening very attentively to the words and the accompaniments, and criticising the agreement of the two. This is what the many do.

' Again, those who are skilled in rhetoric do just the same with respect to the Sophists, for they too have their theatres, and their audience, and clapping of hands, and noises, and closest criticism of what is said.

' And if in the case of rhetoricians, musicians, and athletes, people sit in the one case to look on, in the other to see at once and to listen with such earnest attention, what zeal, what earnestness ought ye in reason to display, when it is no musician or debater who now comes forward to a trial of skill, but when a man is speaking from heaven, and utters a voice plainer than thunder? For he has pervaded the whole earth with the sound ; and occupied and filled it, not by the loudness of the cry, but by moving his tongue with the grace of God. And what is wonderful, this sound, great as it is, is neither a harsh nor an unpleasant one, but sweeter and more delightful than all harmony of music, and with more skill to soothe ; and besides all this, most holy, and most awful, and full of mysteries so great, and bringing with it goods so great, that if men were exactly and with ready mind to receive and keep them, they would be no longer mere men, nor remain upon the earth, but would take their stand above all the things of this life, and, having adapted themselves to the condition of angels, would dwell on earth just as if it were heaven' (*Hom.* i.).

Again, when inquiring why the doctrines of St. John were more lasting than those of the philosophers, he says:—' For this reason, too, he did not hide his teaching in mist and darkness, as they did who threw obscurity of speech, like a kind of veil, around the mischiefs laid up within. But this man's doctrines are clearer than the sunbeams, wherefore they have been unfolded to all throughout the world. For he did not teach as Pythagoras did, commanding those who came to him to be silent for five years, or to sit like senseless stones ; neither did he invent fables defining the universe to consist of numbers ; but casting away all this devilish trash and mischief, he diffused such simplicity through his words, that all he said was plain, not only to wise men, but also to women and youths. For he was persuaded that the words were true and profitable to all that should hearken to them. And all time after him is his witness, since he has drawn to him all the world, and has freed our life, when we have listened to these words, from all monstrous display of wisdom ; wherefore, we who hear them would prefer rather to give up our lives than the doctrines by him delivered to us ' (*Hom.* ii.).

Chrysostom also forcibly dwells upon the need which children have of spiritual instruction :—' And yet when you take your children into the theatres, you allege neither their mathematical lessons, nor anything of the kind ; but if it be required to gain

or collect anything spiritual, you call the matter a
waste of time. And how shall you not anger God,
if you find leisure and assign a reason for everything
else, and yet think it a troublesome and unseasonable
thing for your children to take in hand what relates
to Him? Do not so, brethren, do not so. It is this
very age that most of all needs the hearing these
things ; for from its tenderness it readily stores up
what is said, and what children hear is impressed
as a seal on the wax of their minds. Besides, it is
then that their life begins to incline to vice or virtue ;
and if from the very gates and portals one lead
them away from iniquity, and guide them by the
hand to the best road, he will fix them for the time
to come in a sort of habit and nature, and they will
not, even if they be willing, easily change for the
worse, since this force of custom draws them to the
performance of good actions. So that we shall see
them become more worthy of respect than those who
have grown old, and they will be more useful in
civil matters, displaying in youth the qualities of the
aged ' (*Hom.* iii.).

Again, in answer to the inquiry why St. John
speaks immediately of the eternal subsistence of the
Word, he replies :—' I will now tell you what the
reason of this is. Because the other evangelists had
dwelt most on the accounts of His coming in the
flesh, there was fear lest some, being of grovelling
minds, might for this reason rest in these doctrines
alone, as indeed was the case with Paul of Samosata.
In order, therefore, to lead away from this fondness
for earth those who were like to fall into it, and to
draw them up towards heaven, with good reason he
commences his narrative from above, and from the

eternal subsistence.   For while Matthew enters upon his relation from Herod the King, Luke from Tiberius Cæsar, Mark from the baptism of John, this apostle, leaving alone all these things, ascends beyond all time or age ($\grave{\alpha}\iota\hat{\omega}\nu o\varsigma$).   Thither darting forward the imagination of his hearers to the " was in the beginning," not allowing it to stay at any point, nor setting any limit, as they did in Herod, and Tiberius, and John ' (*Hom.* iv.).

We can perceive Chrysostom's practical method of preaching in the following passage, where he shows that men cannot serve two masters:—' Return, then, at length to your sober senses, and rouse yourselves, and calling to mind whose servants we are, let us love His kingdom only ; let us weep, let us wail for the times past in which we were servants of Mammon ; let us cast off once for all his yoke, so intolerable, so heavy, and continue to bear the light and easy yoke of Christ.   For He lays no such commands upon us as Mammon does.   Mammon bids us be enemies to all men, but Christ, on the contrary, to embrace and to love all.   The one having nailed us to the clay and the brick-making (for gold is this), allows us not even at night to take breath a little ; the other releases us from this excessive and insensate care, and bids us gather treasures in heaven, not by injustice towards others, but by our own righteousness. . . . How, then, is it not extremest folly to slight a rule so mild, so full of all good things, and to serve a thankless, ungrateful tyrant, and one who neither in this world, nor in the world to come, is able to help those who obey and give heed to him?   Instead of riches upon earth, let us collect treasures impregnable, treasures which can accompany us on our journey to heaven, which can assist us in our peril, and make the Judge propitious at that hour, whom may we all have gracious unto us, both now and at that day' (*Hom.* viii.).

The following passage is of a more critical character, in which he is showing the unchangeable nature of God. 'Nay,' he says, 'to show that he uses the expression "was made" only that you should not suppose a mere appearance, hear from what follows how he clears the argument, and overthrows that wicked suggestion. For what does he add? "And dwelt among us." All but saying, Imagine nothing improper from the words "was made;" I spoke not of any change of that unchangeable nature, but of its dwelling and inhabiting. But that which dwells (or tabernacles) cannot be the same with that in which it dwells, but different; one thing dwells in a different thing, otherwise it would not be dwelling; for nothing can inhabit itself. I mean, different as to essence; for by an union ($\dot{\epsilon}\nu\dot{\omega}\sigma\epsilon\iota$) and conjoining ($\sigma\upsilon\nu\alpha\phi\dot{\epsilon}\iota\alpha$) God the Word and the Flesh are one, not by any confusion or obliteration of substances, but by a certain union ineffable and past understanding. Ask not how, for it "was made," so as He knoweth' (*Hom.* xi.).

Again, when pointing out to us how riches are to be used, he says:—'I blame not those who have houses, and lands, and wealth, and servants, but wish them to possess such things in a safe and becoming way. And what is "a becoming way?" As masters, not as slaves; so that they rule them, be not ruled by them; that they use, not abuse them. This is why they are called "things to be used" ($\chi\rho\dot{\eta}\mu\alpha\tau\alpha$), that we may employ them on necessary services, not hoard them up; this is a domestic's office, that a master's; it is for the slave to keep them, but for the lord, and one who has great authority, to expend. Thou didst not receive thy wealth to bury, but to distribute. Had God desired riches to be hoarded, He would not have given them to men, but would have let them remain as they were in the earth; but because He wishes them to be spent, therefore He has permitted us to have them, that we may impart them to each other' (*Hom.* xix.).

His observations on the variety of Holy Scripture are striking and apposite. 'The Word,' he says, 'is spoken indeed to all, and is offered as a general remedy to those who need it; but it is the business of every individual hearer to take what is suited to his complaint. I know not who are sick, I know not who are well, and therefore I use every sort of argument, and introduce remedies suited to all maladies, at one time condemning covetousness, after that touching on luxury, and again on impurity; then composing something in praise of, and exhortation to, charity, and each of the other virtues in their turn. For I fear lest when my arguments are employed on any one subject, I may, without knowing it, be treating you for one disease while you are ill of others. So that if this congregation were but one person I should not have judged it so absolutely necessary to make my discourse varied; but since in such a multitude there are probably also many maladies, I not unreasonably diversify my teaching, since my discourse will be sure to attain its object when it is made to embrace you all. For this cause also Scripture is something multiform (πολυειδής), and speaks on ten thousand matters, because it addresses itself to the nature of mankind in common, and in such a multitude all the passions of the soul must needs be, though all be not in each' (*Hom.* xxiii.).

When proving that life is a time of preparation for an everlasting state, he says:—'If now a woman of Samaria is so earnest to learn something profitable, if she abides by Christ though not as yet knowing Him, what pardon shàll he obtain, who both knowing Him, and being not by a well, nor in a desert place, nor at noon-day, nor beneath the scorching sunbeams, but at morning-tide, and beneath a roof like this, enjoying shade and comfort, yet cannot endure to hear anything that is said, but is wearied by it. Not such was that woman ; so occupied was she by Jesus' words, that she even called others to hear them. Let us then imitate this woman of Samaria ; let us commune with Christ. For even now He standeth in the midst of us, speaking to us by the prophets and disciples ; let us hear and obey. How long shall we live uselessly and in vain ? Because not to do what is well-pleasing to God is to live uselessly, or rather not merely uselessly, but to our own hurt ' (*Hom.* xxxi.).

Speaking of the sanctifying effects of the Scriptures, Chrysostom remarks :—' The Scriptures were not given us for this only, that we might have them in books, but that we might engrave them on our hearts. For this kind of possession, the keeping the commandments merely in letter, belongs to Jewish ambition; but to us the Law was not so given at all, but in the fleshy tables of our hearts. And this I say, not to prevent you from procuring Bibles ; on the contrary, I exhort and earnestly pray that you do this ; but I desire that from those books you convey the letters and sense into your understanding, that so it may be purified when it receiveth the meaning of the writing' (*Hom.* xxxii.).

In speaking of affliction as a trial of faith, Chrysostom observes :—' I see many persons even now become more pious, when, during the sufferings of a child or the sickness of a wife, they enjoy any comfort; yet they ought, even if they obtain it not, to persist just the same in giving thanks, in glorifying God. Because it is the part of right-minded servants, and of those who feel such affection and love as they ought for their Master, not only when pardoned, but also when scourged, to run to Him. For these also are effects of the tender care of God : " Whom the Lord loveth He chasteneth, and scourgeth, it says, every son whom He receiveth "' (*Hom.* xxxv.).

Once more, on the fear of God being true wisdom, Chrysostom remarks :—' If then to fear God is to have wisdom, and the wicked man hath not that fear, he is deprived of that which is wisdom indeed—and deprived of that which is wisdom indeed, he is more foolish than any. And yet many admire the wicked as being able to do injustice and harm, not knowing that they ought to deem them wretched above all men, who, thinking to injure others, thrust the sword against themselves,—an act of extremest folly, that a man should strike himself and not even know that he does so, but shall think that he is injuring another, while he is killing himself' (*Hom.* xli.).

But besides the two important series of homilies to which attention has been already directed, Chrysostom also delivered, about the same time, and while resident in the same place, his expositions on the Epistles of St. Paul to the Romans, Corinthians, Galatians, and

Ephesians. Those on Timothy, Titus, etc., were, in the opinion of Tillemont, delivered at Constantinople; but it should be mentioned that the author of the *Life of Chrysostom* in Latin in the Benedictine edition thinks that the homilies on the Epistles to Timothy and Titus were composed at Antioch.

Of these expository addresses we must content ourselves with a briefer notice than we have bestowed upon the homilies on St. Matthew and St. John, which latter seem not only to claim precedence in point of time, but also, to a certain extent, in the special interest of their subject-matter.

4. His thirty-two expository addresses on the Epistle to the Romans were the product of this period of his ministerial career. They are, like the subject-matter of the Epistle itself, most carefully reasoned out. Chrysostom's early training as a rhetorician enabled him to appreciate and to grasp the force of St. Paul's argumentative and dialectical style of composition better than most men. Moreover, St. Paul had a peculiar attraction for him. The composition of these homilies is, accordingly, very careful and elaborate,—too careful and elaborate (it has been supposed) to have admitted of their being composed when he was involved in the cares and labours of his life as archbishop. From other internal evidence they would undoubtedly seem to have been delivered at Antioch, when he was pastor there, and where his hearers could have had access to the spot where St. Paul taught and was bound, which would be compatible, to some extent, with his residence at Antioch, but certainly not with his residence at Constantinople.

He commenced his homilies on the Epistle to the

Romans with the following preface :—'As I keep hearing the Epistles of the blessed Paul read, and that twice every week, and often three or four times, whenever we are celebrating the memorials of the holy martyrs, gladly do I enjoy the spiritual trumpet, and get roused and warmed with desire at recognising the voice so dear to me, and seem to fancy him all but present to my sight, and to behold him conversing with me. But I grieve and am pained that all people do not know this man as much as they ought to know him ; but some are so far ignorant of him as not even to know for certainty the number of his Epistles. And this comes, not of incapacity, but of their not having the will to be continually conversing with this blessed man. For it is not through any natural readiness and sharpness of wit that even I am acquainted with as much as I do know (if I do know anything), but owing to a continual cleaving to the man, and an earnest affection towards him. For, what belongs to men beloved, they who love them know above all others, inasmuch as they have them in their thoughts.'

Again, when speaking of the obedience of the people as being the preacher's crown, he says :—'Let us then lay all these things to heart, and not be contented with passing mere praises upon them, but let us even accomplish what I have been speaking of. For what is the good of these applauses and clamours ? I demand one thing only of you, and that is the display of them in real action,—the obedience of deeds. This is my praise, this your gain ; this gives me more than a diadem. When you have left the church then, this is the crown that you will make for me and for you, through the hand of the poor ; that both in the present life we may be nourished with a goodly hope, and after we have departed to the life to come we may attain to those good things without number, to which may all of us attain (*Hom.* xv., *ad fin.*).

5. Chrysostom's homilies on St. Paul's Epistles to the Corinthians have been regarded by many men of learning and piety as occupying a very high place amongst his works. In elegance of style and in weight of matter they will fairly rank with the best of his homiletical treatises. And this praise is peculiarly applicable to those which are based upon the First Epistle. They may, perhaps, appear too redundant and too copious to our modern taste ; but they charmed and captivated the hearers to whom they were addressed, and thus succeeded in riveting their attention, and laying hold, with a firm grasp, of their hearts and consciences.

Though the exact date at which these homilies were delivered is uncertain, yet there can be no doubt, both from other reasons, and especially from what is stated in *Hom.* xxi., sect. 9, that they were preached at Antioch. 'And all this,' he says, 'in Antioch, where men were first called Christians, wherein are bred the most civilised of mankind, where in old time the fruit of charity flourished so abundantly.'

It is very probable that the different allusions which Chrysostom makes to the evils arising from schism and party-spirit, may have reference to the differences which are well known to have existed at Antioch about this time, in regard to the claims put forward by the respective followers of Meletius and Paulinus to the succession to the episcopate in that city.

Let us hear Chrysostom speaking on the subject of

God's punishments, when preaching on 1 Cor. iii. 13-15 :—'Consider, for example, how long a time, but for one single sin, our race abides in death. Five thousand years[1] and more have passed, and death hath not yet been done away, on account of one single sin. And we cannot even say that Adam had heard prophets, that he had seen others punished for sins, and it was meet he should have been terrified thereby, and corrected, were it only by the example, for he was at that time first, and alone; but nevertheless he was punished. But thou canst not have anything of this sort to advance, who, after so many examples, art become worse; to whom so excellent a spirit hath been vouchsafed, and yet thou drawest upon thyself not one sin, nor two, nor three, but sins without number! For do not, because the sin is committed in a small moment, calculate that therefore the punishment also must be a matter of a moment. Seest thou not these men, who, for a single theft, or a single act of adultery, committed in a small moment of time, oftentimes have spent their whole life in prisons, and in mines, struggling with continual hunger and every kind of death? And there was no one to set them at liberty, or to say, " The offence took place in a small moment of time; the punishment, too, should have its time, equivalent to that of the sin " ' (*Hom.* ix.).

Again, let us hear his description of a rich and, at the same time, generous man :—'Therefore, as teachers, however many scholars they have, impart some of their love unto each, so let thy possession be, many to whom thou hast done good. And let all say,

---

[1] According to the calculation of the times of the generations in the LXX. in Gen. v.

"Such an one he freed from poverty; such an one from dangers. Such an one would have perished had he not, next to the grace of God, enjoyed thy patronage. This man's disease thou didst cure; another thou didst rid of false accusation; another, being a stranger, you took in; another, being naked, you clothed." Wealth inexhaustible and many treasures are not so good as such sayings. . . . And, what is greatest of all, favour from God waits on thee in every part of thy proceedings. What I mean is, let one man say, he helped to portion out my daughter; another, and he afforded my son the means of taking his station among men (εἰς ἄνδρας ἐμφανῆναι); another, he made my calamity to cease; another, he delivered me from dangers. Better than golden crowns are words such as these, that a man should have in his city innumerable persons to proclaim his beneficence. Voices such as these are pleasanter far, and sweeter than the voices of the heralds marching before the archons; to be called saviour, benefactor, defender (the very names of God); and not covetous, proud, insatiate, and mean. . . . For if these, spoken on earth, make one so splendid and illustrious, when they are written in heaven, and God proclaims them on the day that shall come, think what renown, what splendour thou shalt enjoy! Which may it be the lot of us all to obtain, through the grace and loving-kindness of our Lord Jesus Christ' (*Hom.* x.).

6. The *Commentary on the Epistle to the Galatians* was written at Antioch, not earlier, probably, than 395 A.D. The evidence for this depends in part upon the fact that he alludes to other writings, which were composed at Antioch at about the same time (see ch. i. v. 16). In this commentary he not unfrequently

refutes the tenets of the Anomœans, and also those of the Marcionists and Manichæans. There is one particular circumstance to be noticed in his commentary on this Epistle, which separates and distinguishes this work from all his other works of a similar kind, namely, that the exposition is continuous, and is therefore unlike his other homiletical addresses, in which practical exhortation invariably succeeds to the exegesis of the passage under consideration.

In his commentary on the first verse of the third chapter, ' O foolish Galatians, who hath bewitched you ? ' etc., he remarks :—'When you hear of jealousy in this place, and in the Gospel of an evil eye, which means the same, you must not suppose that the glance of the eye has any natural power to injure the beholders. For the eye,—that is, the organ itself,—cannot be evil ; but Christ in that place means jealousy by the term. To behold, simply, is the function of the eye, but to behold evilly belongs to a mind depraved within. As through this sense the knowledge of visible objects enters the soul, and as jealousy is for the most part generated by wealth, and wealth and sovereignty and pomp are perceived by the eye, therefore he calls the eye evil ; not as beholding merely, but as beholding enviously from some moral depravity. Therefore by the words, "Who hath cast an envious eye on you ?" ($\epsilon\beta\acute{a}\sigma\kappa\alpha\nu\epsilon\nu$), he implies that the persons in question acted, not from concern, not to supply defects, but to mutilate what existed. For envy, far from supplying what is wanting, subtracts from what is complete, and vitiates the whole ; and he speaks thus, not as if envy had any power of itself, but meaning, that the teachers of these doctrines did so from envious motives.'

7. That Chrysostom delivered his homilies on the Epistle to the Ephesians at Antioch seems clear from internal evidence, though some critics have thought that, from their somewhat imperfect condition in regard to style and finish, they were delivered at Constantinople, when he would have had less leisure for composition ; and, moreover, that there is a passage in the eleventh homily which might fairly be applied to Eudoxia, and to his position at Court. The reasons, however, in favour of these homilies not having been delivered at Constantinople, appear fairly to outweigh the arguments that have been adduced in support of the opposite view. The internal testimony to their having been delivered at Antioch is of the following kind :—He alludes in them to a schism, not of a doctrinal character, as in existence, which would find its parallel at Antioch ; he speaks of the superstitious feeling that prevailed among his hearers, which would also well apply to Antioch ; he familiarly speaks of St. Babylas (*Hom.* ix.) and St. Julian (*Hom.* xi.), both of whom were Antiochian saints ; and he refers, moreover, to monastic establishments as existing in the mountains near the city, which would exactly apply to the case of Antioch.

When commenting on Ephesians iv. 17, in his twelfth homily, he says, by way of exhortation :—
' Let it not be so with us. But scorning all these things, as men living in the light, and having our conversation in heaven, and having nothing in common with earth, let us regard but one thing as terrible, that is, sin, and offending against God ; and if there be not this, let us scorn all the rest, and him that brought them in, the Devil. And now for these things let us give thanks to God. Let us be diligent,

not only that we ourselves be never caught by this slavery, but if any of those who are dear to us have been caught, let us break his bonds asunder; let us release him from this most bitter and contemptible captivity; let us make him free and unshackled for his course toward heaven; let us raise up his flagging wings, and teach him to be wise for life and doctrine's sake. Let us give thanks to God for all things. Let us beseech Him that we be not found unworthy of the gifts bestowed upon us; and let us ourselves withal endeavour to contribute our own part, that we may teach not only by speaking, but by acting also. For thus shall we be able to attain His unnumbered blessings, which God grant we may all attain, by the grace and loving-kindness of our Lord Jesus Christ, with whom, to the Father and the Holy Ghost together, be glory, might, and honour, now, henceforth, and for ever and ever.'

The homilies of Chrysostom are peculiarly adapted to be types and patterns of preaching in all ages and in all countries. The reason of this is, not only the absolute excellence of these discourses, as well in their subject-matter as in their style, but also their practical, uncontroversial, and scriptural character. They were neither delivered to hearers who were suffering under persecution for their profession of Christianity, nor to those who were, to speak generally, disputatiously carrying on a controversy with others on doctrinal topics. His hearers, on the other hand, were unaffected, for the most part, by such influences as these, and were anxious rather to promote their own progress in spiritual things, and to urge on others to holiness of life and conduct.

It was a different matter with Athanasius or with

Augustine. The former had to confront, almost in single combat, all the forces of Arianism ; while the latter had to contend with Manichæism, Donatism, or Pelagianism. Hence *their* discourses naturally assumed a controversial character and complexion. But in the age of Chrysostom, and in the cities of Antioch and Constantinople, the state of religious feeling was different. Christianity of an orthodox character was acknowledged, and heresies were not so much in the foreground. There was now a greater scope for the exhibition of the Christian character and the Christian graces, and for developing the latent powers of Christianity on the hearts and lives of its professors.

Chrysostom's homilies, therefore, are of a more catholic character. They appeal more to men as men, with all the wants and desires of a common humanity. They are, no doubt, wonderful specimens of homiletic addresses, whether we regard his remarkable eloquence displayed in them, his marvellous command of language, his deep sympathy with his hearers, his richness of illustration, his poetic imagery his devout piety, his practical application of all the current events of the day to the peculiar case of those whom he addresses, and the dramatic character of his style, which must have had the greatest charm for hearers so accustomed to the beauties of Greek oratory, with its delicacy of thought, its refinement of expression, and its rapid changes of feeling and sentiment. All this has contributed to render the homilies of Chrysostom the most popular and valuable of any similar discourses that have ever been uttered. It is clear to all how much of their grace and beauty such addresses must lose when they are translated into a foreign language.

BOOK III.

FROM CHRYSOSTOM'S ARCHBISHOPRIC TO HIS EXILE AND DEATH.

CHAPTER I.

CHRYSOSTOM'S CALL TO CONSTANTINOPLE.

> 'From thee the glorious preacher came,
> With soul of zeal and lips of flame,
> A Court's stern martyr-guest.'

ABOUT twelve years had now elapsed since Chrysostom had been admitted as a presbyter of the Church of Antioch.   They were twelve years of active, zealous work in his Master's service.   He had not spared himself during that time.   He had laboured, in season and out of season, in diffusing the knowledge of Christianity among every class of the community at Antioch, and had no doubt been the instrumental means of bringing many from a course of careless ease and pleasure to a life of devotion and self-sacrifice in the cause of Christ, and of converting many from the creed of heathenism to a purer and a nobler faith. All this time he had been the conspicuous figure in the city of Antioch.   His fame as a Christian orator and preacher had eclipsed that of all his contemporaries there, whether their rank in the Church was more exalted or more humble than his own.   He was the cynosure of all eyes.   No governor, or commander, or bishop, or advocate, possessed the reputation which he enjoyed.   He was known of all men, from the lowest to the highest there.   He occupied the loftiest position which it was possible to reach at Antioch.   He was, as it were, an epistle known and read of all men. His eloquence was universally acknowledged and admired. His sincerity, his self-sacrifice, his nobleness of character, his straightforward simplicity, his untiring energy, his high personal piety, were all alike admitted, respected, and revered. He was the idol of the common people, and his influence extended over all ranks in the city.

Such was the exalted pedestal of reputation on which he stood in the year 397 A.D. He appeared to all to be an integral part of Antioch, and to have done more for its well-being and reputation than any other of its citizens.

The inhabitants little suspected that his residence among them was all but ended, and that the voice to which they had listened so long, and with such rapt attention, would soon, very soon, so far as they were concerned, be silent. When others had fled from their city under the influence of terror and alarm, they remembered how he had remained firm at his post, even when that post was one of extreme peril. He had continued staunch to the call of duty, and had never ceased, during their hour of extreme peril, to comfort, encourage, and animate the hearts and minds of his fellow-citizens. That slight and attenuated frame, those deep-set eyes, that wrinkled though ample forehead, those hollow cheeks, that short grey beard, and that eloquent voice, were familiar to every one in Antioch.[1] No one among those 200,000 citizens was

---

[1] Palladius (chap. x.) speaks of his head as bald; that he had τὸ Ἐλισσαϊκὸν κρανίον, *i.e.*, a *bald-pate*, like Elisha. ' It was the look of a man,' says Cave (ii. p. 525), ' truly mortified to the world ; one that by the admirable strictness of his life had subdued the flesh to the spirit, and had brought the appetites of sense in subjection to the laws of reason.'

better known than he was to man, woman, and child in that fair city, which he was destined so shortly to quit.

On September 17th, 397 A.D., in the consulate of Cæsarius and Atticus, Nectarius died; and thus the throne of the Archbishop of Constantinople became vacant. Nectarius had succeeded the celebrated Gregory Nazianzen in the year 381 A.D. He was a prelate of gentle and amiable disposition, and constitutionally inclined to indolence. Many abuses had consequently crept into the Church during the laxity of discipline that had of late prevailed.

The archiepiscopal chair of Constantinople was a position of great dignity and importance, and therefore there were many aspirants for the vacant office. No post in the Eastern Church was more coveted and sought after. The appointment of the successor to Nectarius accordingly occupied much public interest and attention. Expectation was aroused in regard to the person on whom the honour was likely to be conferred. It is said that the more devout members of the Church at Constantinople earnestly entreated Arcadius to nominate to the post a man who was personally deserving of so high and influential a position, irrespective of all private feelings and inclinations. Socrates (vi. 2) informs us that the clergy, as well as the people, selected Chrysostom, and that the Emperor Arcadius was disposed to fall in with the choice that they had made.

However this may be, there was one who had no slight influence in the matter. This was the eunuch Eutropius, the iniquitous as well as contemptible favourite of the emperor. He had not long been in power, having succeeded the crafty and cruel Rufinus, who had fallen by the sword of one of the soldiers of Gainas the Goth, on November 27th, 395 A.D.

The feebleness and vacillation of Arcadius were notorious. He inherited none of the great qualities of his father, Theodosius, and was wholly unfitted to wield the vast power which he had acquired by his illustrious father's death in 395 A.D. He was, therefore, likely to fall under the power of any vigorous and designing favourite. Eutropius is said by his management to have relieved Arcadius from a marriage with the daughter of Rufinus, by substituting in her place Eudoxia, the beautiful, high-spirited, intellectual but imperious daughter of Bauto, a general of the Franks, who very speedily gained a complete ascendency over the feeble mind of her husband, Arcadius.

Eutropius had many candidates for the archbishopric brought under his notice, who were pushing forward their claims with an eager, indecent, and importunate zeal. 'Presbyters,' says Palladius, 'in dignity, but not worthy of the priesthood, having recourse to bribery, and falling on their knees even before the people.' But Eutropius set them all aside, and selected, for recommendation to Arcadius, one whom it was *à priori* most unlikely that he would have chosen. It so happened, however, that when he had been recently sent to Antioch on business of state, he had heard Chrysostom preach. His eloquence and his popularity had left a deep impression on his mind, and he determined to recommend him strongly to the notice of Arcadius for the vacant office. It seems strange that such a man as Eutropius, the licentious favourite of a weak and feeble-minded emperor, should have been the means of appointing Chrysostom to the archbishopric of Constantinople; just as

Symmachus, the stout advocate of expiring heathenism, should have been instrumental in sending Augustine to Milan. The bishops, who were summoned to Constantinople in order to give dignity and importance to the consecration, were delighted with the choice of Eutropius, and most ready to sanction it. It received their almost unanimous approval.

A twofold difficulty was, however, foreseen, and had to be met. How would it be possible to withdraw a man so universally beloved as Chrysostom from the scene of his manifold labours and successes in spite of the popular will? They would never willingly allow their favourite preacher to be taken away from them. The attempt would assuredly produce a serious disturbance. Another difficulty also presented itself. What if Chrysostom himself, with the high ideal of the episcopal office which he entertained, and which he had put before the world in his treatise on the priesthood, should decline to accept the position thus offered to him? In order to obviate both these difficulties, Eutropius induced the Emperor Arcadius to send special instructions to the governor of Syria to convey Chrysostom by stealth to Constantinople. A popular outbreak would thus be avoided, nor would Chrysostom himself, if thus suddenly brought to the capital, have equal time or opportunity afforded him to decline the proffered honour.

Stratagem was employed to effect the contemplated object. Chrysostom was induced by the invitation of Asterius—the *Comes Orientis*, the count, or military commander at Antioch, who had received his instructions from headquarters—to go to the Martyr's Chapel, which was situated outside the walls of the city. He went there in consequence of the invitation which he had received, having no idea of the deception which was meditated. No sooner had he reached the rendezvous than he was apprehended by government officers, to whom the task had been assigned. They immediately conveyed him to Pagræ, which was the first stage on the road towards Constantinople. Naturally indignant at such treatment, he inquired what was the meaning of this forcible abduction. He put the question again and again, but could gain no information from his guards, who maintained a dogged and persistent silence as to their intentions. They placed him in a public conveyance, and hurried him on with all the haste they could possibly make towards Constantinople. Stage after stage was rapidly passed in that long and wearisome journey of 800 miles. He was kept a close prisoner all the time, and no opportunity for escape was afforded him. Thus escorted and guarded he reached the capital. When the meaning of all that had been done was explained to him, and when the high position was offered for his acceptance, he felt that resistance would be vain, and that it would be more seemly and becoming to accept the honour which was almost forced upon him. To acquiesce with grace seemed therefore to him the most dignified course to adopt.

Accordingly, on February 26th, 398 A.D., Chrysostom was both consecrated and enthroned as Archbishop of Constantinople. Upon Theophilus, the Patriarch of Alexandria, devolved the unwelcome task of consecration—unwelcome, because he had not only endeavoured to detract from the reputation of Chrysostom, but had also used every effort to secure the appointment for a presbyter of Alexandria, named

Isidore, who had been a secret agent of his in more than one discreditable affair. We are informed by Socrates of the nature of one of these transactions. When the Emperor Theodosius was engaged in a war against the tyrant Maximus, Theophilus sent presents by Isidore to the emperor, and delivered two letters to him, ordering him to present the gifts and letter to him who should be conqueror. Isidore, in obedience to these commands, arriving at Rome, stayed there; expecting the event of the war. But this business could not be long concealed, for a reader who accompanied him stole the letters, on which account Isidore, being in great fear, fled forthwith to Alexandria. This was the chief reason why Theophilus was so anxiously concerned in favour of Isidore for the vacant dignity. It is said also that Theophilus, from his knowledge of physiognomy, clearly saw that he could never expect to find a tool in Chrysostom.

Many letters were addressed to the bishops against Theophilus, which got into the possession of Eutropius, who threatened to bring him to trial if he hesitated to consecrate Chrysostom. It was only this threat of the disclosure of his conduct—of which the proofs were forthcoming—that induced him to carry out the distasteful task. He at length consented to consecrate Chrysostom, but he resolved in his dark and ill-regulated mind that he would have his revenge in the future. A vast crowd attended at the consecration, not only from the desire to see the spectacle, but also from their wish to hear the famous preacher, whose praise was in all the Churches, deliver his inaugural sermon. Unfortunately this address is not extant.

CHAPTER II.

CONSTANTINOPLE.

<blockquote>
' Beautiful Queen ! unlike thy high compeers,
Thou wast not cradled in the lap of years ;
But like celestial Pallas, hymn'd of old,
Thy sovran form, inviolate and bold,
Sprung to the perfect zenith of its prime,
And took no favour from the hands of Time.'
</blockquote>

IT is a conspicuous fact in the life of Chrysostom, that he was called upon to minister in two such famous and remarkable cities as Antioch and Constantinople.

Constantinople, to which Chrysostom was now introduced, was the creation of Constantine the Great, who founded it on the site of the ancient Byzantium, which had during so many ages maintained a highly distinguished place amongst the great cities of the world, and was rich in historical recollections, as Thucydides, Xenophon, Polybius, and other writers so frequently attest.

Built on a 'gently-sloping promontory, which serves as a connecting link between the Eastern and the Western worlds, and which nature intended for the centre of a great monarchy,' the new Rome arose, like the old one, based on its seven hills, with the sea at its gates, and with a noble harbour, named the Golden Horn, in a matchless position, alike for self-defence and for commercial enterprise, bearing the name of its illustrious founder. 'Such a prospect,' says Gibbon, 'of beauty, of safety, and of wealth, united in a single spot, was sufficient to justify the choice of Constantine. A particular description, composed about a century after its foundation, enumerates a capitol or school of learning, a circus, two theatres, eight porticoes, five granaries, eight aqueducts or reservoirs of water, four spacious halls for the meetings of the senate or courts of justice, fourteen churches, fourteen palaces, and 4,388 houses which, for their size or beauty, deserved to be distinguished from the multitude of plebeian habitations.'

The foundations of Constantinople were laid with great pomp, and with a singular mixture of heathenism and Christianity, Constantine himself, with a spear in his hand, leading the long procession; and thus Constantinople sprung up into existence, a Christian city. Its population, according to Chrysostom, numbered at least 100,000 Christians. The city itself was about ten or eleven miles in circumference. What Constantine left unfinished was completed—and what he had erected was, after suffering from earthquakes, restored—by Constantius, Arcadius, Theodosius II., and especially by Justinian, called *reparator orbis*, its second founder. The city was surrounded by massive and lofty walls of stone, flanked by strong towers, and was divided into fourteen regions. On his new city Constantine conferred various privileges, in order to draw inhabitants to the spot. He established a species of state hierarchy, derived more from Asiatic than from Roman sources. He instituted three ranks of honour; he selected consuls for it; he revived the title of patricians; appointed prætorian prefects, together with pro-consuls and vice-prefects; and gave the rank of 'illustrious' to the seven ministers of the palace.

In government it widely differed from ancient Rome. A despotic rule took the place of free republican institutions. It was Oriental rather than Roman, alike in its conception and its organisation. And this Oriental tone of thought and feeling affected not only its architecture, its arts, and its literature, but also its religious thought and sentiment. Its literature, it has been well remarked, was 'learned, artificial, florid, but deficient in elegance and grace, and without a spark of genius to illumine it ;' its art was 'deficient in all deep and sincere feeling, and showing, under the hardness of the shape, and the sameness of the expression, the dull and slavish constraint to which it was subject ;' its architecture was peculiarly its own, in which 'the cupola was the great characteristic, to which every other feature was subordinate.'

Constantinople stood upon the border-land of the East and West, and was, to a great extent, separated from European and Roman civilisation by marked differences in its tone of thought, its language, its customs, and its institutions.

Its foundation was the grand object of Constantine's ambition. He spared no expense and no pains to make it a city worthy of his name, and a rival of Rome itself. He desired to reproduce, in many ways, a likeness in its palaces, its public buildings, its baths, and its aqueducts, to the seven-hilled city on the Tiber. Its buildings sprang up as if by enchantment. The famous works of Phidias and Praxiteles adorned its streets and squares. The images of the tutelary deities of different cities were brought to Constantinople, and centralised there. The statue of Constantine himself, standing on its marble and porphyry pillar, to the height of 120 feet, with the palladium, it is said, buried beneath it, towered in its midst. It was by Constantine's command that the various cities of Asia and Greece were stripped of their different specific ornaments to add to the splendour of the new city.

'The trophies of memorable wars,' writes Gibbon, 'the objects of religious veneration, the most finished statues of the gods and heroes, of the sages and poets of ancient times, contributed to the splendid triumph of Constantinople, and gave occasion to the remark of the historian Cedrenus, who observes, with some enthusiasm, that nothing seemed wanting except the souls of the illustrious men whom these admirable monuments were intended to represent.'

Its upper classes were immersed in luxury, indulged in lavish expenditure, and were characterised by a spurious refinement of civilisation. The lower orders of the people were devoted to the wild excitement and the frenzied rivalries of the circus and the chariot races in the stately hippodrome, and to exhibitions of an acrobatic rather than athletic character. No gladiatorial shows, however, disgraced the new city, built under Christian auspices.

Considerable remains of its ancient buildings and architecture yet exist to tell their tale of what the city once was, although nature and man seem to have conspired together for its destruction. Earthquakes, fires, sieges, domestic insurrections, have all contributed to obliterate its ancient buildings. And last of all, the Latin crusaders utterly demolished the works

of art that had up to their time survived extinction.
A fine double wall which surrounded the city on the
land side may still be seen, and two of the reservoirs
for water constructed underground, and supported on
their marble pillars, exist to our day.   The marvellous
temple erected by Justinian, and dedicated to eternal
wisdom, still exists as the great mosque of St. Sophia
(Santa Sophia).   But the noble works of art fashioned
by the hands of the most celebrated of Grecian artists
—the golden gate, of exquisite beauty and workmanship, through which the emperors entered the city in
state—the colossal statue of himself which Justinian
erected, as well as his palace, richly adorned with
bronzes and precious marbles—all have perished.

The establishment of Constantinople was a great
and important epoch in the history of Christianity.
Its foundation proved, without doubt, advantageous
to the spread of the religion of Christ.   'It removed,'
as Dean Milman has remarked,[1] 'the seat of government from the presence of those awful temples, to
which ages of glory had attached an inalienable
sanctity, and with which the piety of all the greater
days of the republic had associated the supreme
dominion and the majesty of Rome.   It broke the
last link which combined the pontifical and the imperial character.   The Emperor of Constantinople, even
if he had remained a pagan, would have lost that
power which was obtained over men's minds by his
appearing in the chief place in all religious pomps
and processions, some of which were as old as Rome
itself.   The senate, and even the people, might be
transferred to the new city ; the deities of Rome
clung to their native home, and would have refused to

[1] *History of Christianity*, vol. ii. book iii. chap. 3.

abandon their ancient seats of honour and worship.
Constantinople arose, if not a Christian, certainly not
a pagan city. The new capital of the world had no
ancient deities, whose worship was inseparably connected with her more majestic buildings and solemn
customs.'

CHAPTER III.

CHRYSOSTOM'S ENTRANCE ON HIS EPISCOPATE.

'Preach the word; be instant in season, out of season; reprove, rebuke, exhort with all longsuffering and doctrine.'—2 Tim. iv. 2.

THE position to which Chrysostom had been elevated was no easy one to fill, especially to a man of his religious character, habits, and disposition. For sixteen years Nectarius had occupied the archbishop's chair, and during those years Church discipline had been increasingly relaxed, many evils had crept in, and a general lethargy prevailed. Nectarius had never entertained the idea of being made a bishop, until he was suddenly chosen, at the Council of Constantinople, as Gregory's successor. He was not even at that time baptised; so that he had at first to receive baptism, and then, within a week, to be consecrated bishop of the second church in the whole Christian world. He had been appointed, to a great extent, through the influence of the emperor, and had exhibited towards his patron so cringing and servile a spirit, that his sycophancy was noticed with contempt even by the emperor himself. He was a man of high rank, and had lived in great state and magnificence as archbishop. His table had been loaded with costly foods; his equipages and domestic arrangements were all on a luxurious and extravagant scale; his palace was furnished with corresponding expensiveness and prodigality.

Such a mode of life as this was in complete antagonism with that rigid simplicity to which Chrysostom had always, on principle, been accustomed. His own tendencies were towards asceticism, and consequently all the luxury which he saw prevailing in the episcopal palace was opposed to his own notions of fitness and propriety. From the very first, therefore, he set his face resolutely against such a luxurious mode of life. Plain and frugal fare now took the place of the luxuries indulged in before. He is said to have dismantled the bishop's palace, to have sold the rich furniture, carpets, and plate, and perhaps even some of the ornaments of the church, and to have given the proceeds to the poor and to the hospitals of Constantinople.

He usually dined in solitude, in his own private chamber, on the plainest food. He declined, for the most part, all invitations to the banquets of the rich and noble. It was but rarely that he could be seen at Court. He felt that he had no time to give to such entertainments. Nor did he usually ask the strange bishops who visited Constantinople to partake of his hospitality. His health was weak, and he felt sure that they could secure attention in other houses besides his own. Nevertheless, he did not on that account suffer less ill-will and odium at their hands.

It is not, therefore, to be wondered at, that his conduct proved displeasing to those who had been in the habit of receiving the archbishop at their tables, and of partaking of his hospitality. Chrysostom was regarded by them as ascetic, morose, parsimonious, and as falling short of the duties belonging to his high station. Such perfect simplicity in his mode of living was even misunderstood by the poorer classes, who had been accustomed to the state and splendour in which the archbishops of Constantinople had uniformly lived. He was consequently looked upon with disfavour, not only by the wealthier, but even by the lower classes, who both appeared equally incapable of attributing his conduct to a right motive.

To those, however, who were conversant with the former life of Chrysostom, such conduct on his part would only have appeared the natural outcome of his previous habits and character. They could have seen that there was no new assumption of asceticism, and nothing unreal or affected in his present mode of life. He did not, as archbishop, put on the garb of religious strictness or formalism, as something claimed by the duties of the high office on which he had entered. He was simply carrying out, in a higher and more influential sphere, the same habits and the same mode of life, which had become habitual to him during all his preceding lifetime.

But Chrysostom's mode of life proved also equally displeasing and offensive to his clergy. Their duties had of late been easy. Nectarius had ruled them with a light hand. They had done, for the most part, what seemed good in their own eyes. Their standard of duty had greatly deteriorated. They seemed unequal to the effort and the labour which the energy of Chrysostom imposed upon them. They had indulged in many questionable practices, especially in regard to the spiritual sisters,[1] who had been introduced

---

[1] Called συνείσακται, *subintroductæ*, 'subintroduced sisters.' Like some of the widows of the Church, they indulged in dress, and bestowed more

into the houses of many of the clergy. They had sunk into a pleasure-seeking, idle state. They consequently opposed, in the first instance, a *vis inertiæ* to the call which he made upon them for increased diligence and earnestness in their spiritual work.

At this time Arianism extensively prevailed in Constantinople. It had many zealous advocates, who drew away many of the more orthodox members of the Church by means of open-air services, or by the singing of hymns and chants within the public colonnades of the city, or by other means. In order to meet them on their own lines, Chrysostom instituted, or perhaps restored, the custom of holding assemblies by night in the different churches, at which the chanting of hymns and psalms largely predominated in the services. In his efforts to repress Arianism—efforts parallel to those which had been employed at Milan by Ambrose—Chrysostom received considerable help from Eudoxia, who joined in these services and in different midnight processions. Nor was he less active in his opposition to Novatian errors, being sometimes carried, in the strong language which he employed against their tenets, to the very borderland of Pelagianism. Still there can be no doubt that he was fully conscious of the need of Divine grace to aid our infirmities.

Such efforts as these tended to increase the labours of the officiating clergy, and imposed a burden upon them which was incompatible with that love of idleness in which the majority had lately indulged. But when this call to greater activity was repeated with

than needful care on their personal appearance. We afterwards hear of these rich widows forming a party against Chrysostom, though some of them, like the pure and holy Olympias, were devoted to his service.

increased energy, and when they could no longer shelter themselves under the cloak of passive indifference and apathy, they then roused themselves into an active and outspoken opposition to their energetic superior. They ascribed his conduct to pride, and charged him with churlishness and austerity. His life of active duty was a tacit censure on their inactivity and worldliness. His frugality was a reproach to their fondness for luxury, and to the court which they had paid to the rich and noble.

When, however, Chrysostom saw that neither his appeals, nor expostulations, nor threats could effect a reformation in their conduct, he deemed it right to adopt harsher and severer measures. He felt that it was his duty to cleanse and purge his diocese of such clerical inactivity, worldliness, and sin. Consequently, when his expostulations proved useless, he prevented some of his clergy from partaking of the Holy Communion, and deposed others from their sacred offices.

It is quite possible that these reforms were not carried out in a gentle, conciliatory, or even judicious spirit. With the great object before him of his own duty, the claims of God's Church, and the good of the people, Chrysostom was hurried along in an impetuous course, like some mountain torrent, and could not endure either opposition or indifference to his wishes. In the energetic execution of his measures he often forgot that suavity and long-suffering which would have proved of the greatest service in winning obedience to his instructions. Though he could not have been deficient in that general knowledge of and acquaintance with human nature without which he could not have been the preacher that he was, yet he

seemed at times quite incapable of appreciating the
character of individual men, or of understanding how
to treat them. He could not brook opposition to his
will. Firmly persuaded himself of the certainty of
the principles which guided his own conduct, and
resolute in carrying out such principles when persuaded of their truth, he could neither appreciate nor
tolerate any divergence of views on the part of those
with whom he had to deal, and endeavoured to over-
ride all opposition.

Possibly, too, his manner may not have been conciliatory or agreeable to his clergy. We have already
seen that the ascetic and rigorous discipline to which
he had formerly subjected himself had tended to
injure his bodily functions, and to create an irritability
of temper, which was the result of physical disorgan-
isation of system, rather than of any defect of moral
constitution and temperament. It is, indeed, a rare
thing to find a placid, equable, and conciliatory
temper coexisting with the nervous excitement which
naturally belongs to the organism of an orator so
eloquent, so swayed by the impulse of the moment,
so sympathetic, and so susceptible to outward impressions, as Chrysostom was.

But, though it may seem strange at first sight, men
of Chrysostom's temperament are not unfrequently
under the influence of some strong-willed, selfish, and
systematic dependant. Such was, unfortunately, the
case with the archbishop. He had an archdeacon
named Serapion, who exercised too great an influence
over him, and in whose hands he left too much to be
done in his dealings with his clergy. Serapion was a
man of violent temper, arrogant, and self-willed. He
would have desired to drive the inferior clergy into

O

obedience, and to have ruled them with a rod of iron. Socrates tells us (vi. 4) that at a time when all the clergy were present, Serapion spoke aloud to the bishop after this manner :—'You will never be able, O bishop, to get the mastery over these persons, unless you drive them all out with one rod.' Such an expression naturally excited an odium against the bishop. The faults and harshness of the subordinate were charged upon the principal. The archbishop was held responsible by his clergy for the faults of his archdeacon. Opposition was fostered in the ranks of the clergy, which almost amounted to mutiny or rebellion.

But though the clergy were thus disaffected towards their head, the people stood loyal to their great and favourite preacher. They went in crowds to hear him preach ; felt the sway which his unrivalled eloquence exerted over them ; and listened with no little delight and satisfaction to the portraiture in his sermons of the vices and the follies which characterised their superiors in rank and station, and their ordinary spiritual guides and teachers. Such preaching, however much it was needed, was perhaps scarcely judicious. It may have had a tendency to set class against class. It certainly undermined the influence of the higher ranks, and of their spiritual superiors, in the judgment of the people.

Chrysostom, however, had still the influence of the Court on his side. Not only was Arcadius favourably disposed towards him, but the Empress Eudoxia was a strong and determined partisan of his at the commencement of his career. No language seemed too strong on the part of Chrysostom when praising and commending the empress. Nor did she fail in reciprocating the praises bestowed on her by the archbishop. Her ambitious mind was at this time occupied with the attempt to free herself and her husband from the domination of Eutropius. She had profited herself by his recommendation and patronage, but she now wished to extricate herself from the thraldom to which such services on his part subjected her. She desired also to gain for herself the power which Eutropius now exerted over her husband.

At this time, at the close of the year 398 A.D., an opportunity was afforded for the public display of this mutual feeling of respect and admiration for each other on the part of the archbishop and the empress. A violent shock of an earthquake had been felt at Constantinople. The buildings in the city were rudely shaken, and so great was the alarm caused by it, that many hastily fled from the city in their terror, and not a few thought that the end of the world was close at hand. The Empress Eudoxia was much moved by this startling event, and would seem to have invited the archbishop to unite with her in a solemn processional service. The remains of some un-named martyrs were conveyed by night from the great church to the Martyr Chapel of St. Thomas, which was situated on the shore at Drypia, about nine miles from Constantinople—a chapel which Eudoxia had herself founded under the influence of religious feeling. A long procession accompanying the relics left the city at midnight. The empress herself, with her regal coronet and purple robe, attended by a noble and distinguished retinue of gentlemen and ladies of the Court, walked by the side of Chrysostom, while in front of them was borne a coffer in which the bones of the martyrs were deposited. The procession stretched to a great distance, composed of persons of all grades in life, of every profession, young and old, the feeble and the strong, and of either sex, while the lighted torches which were carried aloft added largely to the effect of the pomp.   Chrysostom compared the appearance of the procession to a stream of fire. The Martyr Chapel was not reached till early dawn.   It was then that Chrysostom preached a sermon containing most extravagant praise of the empress, and an excessive outburst of congratulation on the part she had taken.   The style of this extempore address differed considerably from that which he usually employed.   This address was afterwards made the ground of accusation against him at the Synod of the Oak.

'What shall I say?' he began, 'and what shall I speak?   I exult and am mad, but with a madness which is better than wisdom.   I am borne aloft; I am, in short, intoxicated with spiritual pleasure. What shall I say? and of what shall I speak?   Shall it be the virtue of the martyrs? or the alacrity of love? or the zeal of the empress? or the madness of Satan? or the destruction of evil spirits? the nobility of the Church? the virtue of the cross? the miracles of the Crucified One? the glory of the Father? the grace of the Spirit? the pleasure of all the people? the exultation of the state?'

On the following day Arcadius himself, attended by his nobles, paid a visit to the Martyr Chapel, and, divesting himself of his royal crown, his followers laying aside their weapons, reverentially reviewed the remains of the martyrs. On this occasion Chrysostom preached another sermon, full of excessive laudation of the emperor for the religious feeling and the humility which he had displayed, the emperor himself not

being present. After having praised the piety of
Arcadius, and spoken of the service which he had
paid to the martyrs, he compared the present life with
the future one—the one brief and toilsome, the other
infinite and delightful, in which we shall enjoy crowns
of immortality.   He pictured the dignity of man in a
state of innocence, and added that a future resurrection
was obscurely intimated in the old Law, but was
now clearly and manifestly revealed.   He begged his
hearers not to pray to the martyrs, but to emulate
their zeal, and faith, and courage, and their contempt
for earthly things.

CHAPTER IV.

THE FALL OF EUTROPIUS.

'To him the Church, the realm, their powers consign ;
Through him the rays of regal bounty shine ;
Turned by his nod, the stream of honour flows ;
His smile alone security bestows :
Still to new heights his restless wishes tower,
Claim leads to claim, and power advances power:
At length his sov'reign frowns : the train of state
Mark the keen glance, and watch the sign to hate.
Where'er he turns he meets a stranger's eye ;
His suppliants scorn him, and his followers fly.'

IN January, 399 A.D., very shortly after Chrysostom's appointment to the archbishopric, Eutropius, the favourite of Arcadius, who had been the instrument of Chrysostom's election to the see of Constantinople, was hurled from the proud position to which only a few short years before he had been raised. He had, as we have already seen, succeeded the proud, bold, and vigorous Rufinus, whose vices he too faithfully imitated.

Before the time of Eutropius, the power of the eunuchs of the Court had been concealed and secret. They had not ventured to obtrude themselves upon the public gaze. Their intrigues had been confined to the palace, and their services to the bed-chamber of the emperor. But Eutropius had ventured to break through this acknowledged and customary precedent. He had stepped boldly forward into the presence of the nobles and the people. He had dared to claim the office of a Roman general, to assume the rank of a patrician, and even to invade the consulship itself. He sometimes, remarks Gibbon, (chap. xxxii.), in the presence of the blushing senate, ascended the tribunal to pronounce judgment, or to repeat elaborate harangues, and sometimes he appeared on horseback at the head of his troops, in the dress and armour of a hero. Men were naturally disgusted and offended that one, utterly unacquainted with the laws and the exercises of the field, who had been born in abject servitude, and before his admission into the imperial palace had been the slave of a hundred masters,—old, deformed, and decrepit,— should be received within the sacred limits of the senate, have statues in brass and marble erected to his honour in every place, however dignified, and even be styled in inscriptions the third founder of Constantinople. Such honours appeared as strange and monstrous as showers of blood, or double suns, or speaking animals ; so that Claudian, in his satirical writings on Eutropius, declares, when speaking of prodigies,—*Omnia cesserunt eunucho consule monstra.*

Nor was the avarice of Eutropius less notorious than that of Rufinus. It was not so much noticed at first, when he spoiled those who had gained their wealth by the spoliation of the people. But when he proceeded to plunder those who had honestly acquired their fortunes by their own industry and efforts, then he brought down upon himself a storm of reproach and indignation.

Claudian has given us the following dramatic sketch of the public auction of the state :—' The impotence of the eunuch,' says the satirist, as quoted by Gibbon, ' has served only to stimulate his avarice: the same hand which, in his servile condition, was exercised in petty thefts to unlock the coffers of his master, now grasps the riches of the world ; and this infamous broker of the empire appreciates and divides the Roman provinces from Mount Hæmus to the Tigris. One man, at the expense of his villa, is made pro-consul of Asia ; a second purchases Syria with his wife's jewels ; and a third laments that he has exchanged his paternal estate for the government of Bithynia. In the ante-chamber of Eutropius a large tablet is exposed to public view, which marks the respective prices of the provinces. The different value of Pontus, of Galatia, and of Lydia, is accurately distinguished. Lycia may be obtained for so many thousand pieces of gold ; but the opulence of Phrygia will require a more considerable sum. The eunuch wishes to obliterate, by the general disgrace, his personal ignominy ; and as he has been sold himself, he is desirous of selling the rest of mankind. In the eager contention, the balance which contains the fate and fortunes of the province often trembles on the beam ; and till one of the scales is inclined by a superior weight the mind of the impartial judge remains in anxious suspense. Such are fruits of Roman valour, of the defeat of Antiochus, and of the triumph of Pompey.'

In order to effect such a confiscation of their pro-perty, the blood of many noble Romans had been shed, and the most distant extremities of the empire were crowded with distinguished and innocent exiles.

The wealthy Abundatius, who had introduced Eutropius into the palace, was despoiled of his riches, and banished to the inhospitable shores of the Euxine. The powerful Timasius, the master-general of the armies of Theodosius, next fell under the favourite's hand. Arraigned before Saturninus and Procopius,—the former of consular rank, the latter the father-in-law of the Emperor Valens,—he was condemned, his wealth confiscated for the benefit of Eutropius, and he himself doomed to perpetual exile at Oasis, in the midst of the sands of the Libyan desert.

Such acts as these necessarily excited a great amount of popular odium against the favourite, so that he must have entertained fears for his personal safety. To guard himself as much as possible against attempts on his life, he persuaded Arcadius to introduce a most cruel and unjust law of treason, by which those who should conspire against any of the members of the emperor's personal retinue, not only in act, but even in thought and intention, should be liable to death, together with the confiscation of their effects, and their sons should also be disqualified from inheriting or holding any personal property.

But danger threatened Eutropius in a quarter from which he could little have anticipated it. A colony under Tribigild the Ostrogoth had been planted by Theodosius in the rich province of Phrygia. Discontented with the slow returns of agriculture as compared with the rich and immediate rewards of war and rapine, the Goths made an insurrection, and desolated the country with fire and sword. After a successful campaign against the two generals whom Eutropius had appointed to resist their attack—namely, Gainas the Goth; and Leo, who from his size and dulness was named the Ajax of the East, both of whom really and practically played into the enemy's hands, and assisted rather than opposed their efforts—the determined and arrogant Tribigild dictated himself the terms of peace, and these terms included the demand for the head of Eutropius. Worked upon by the passionate entreaties of his wife, who complained of some insulting treatment on the part of Eutropius, the weak emperor was induced to sign the condemnation of his favourite, which was immediately followed by a loudly-uttered demand for his death.

In the hour of his fall and of his abject wretchedness, he fled to the sanctuary of the Church—the privileges of which he had previously endeavoured to curtail, which was now his only refuge, and grasping convulsively the altar, he strove to shield himself from the fury of the people, who were eagerly clamouring for his execution.[1] At this supreme moment of his destiny, the archbishop, whose position was chiefly due to the favour of Eutropius, mounted the steps of the ambo, in order that he might be seen and heard by the vast multitude that was assembled in the church, and delivered a splendid and unpremeditated homily on the instability of human affairs, and on the duty of forgiveness of injuries. He illustrated and accentuated his sermon on the vanity of all human greatness, by pointing to the late successful and prosperous

---

[1] Many whom Eutropius had wished to plunder or imprison, especially from the poorer classes, had fled to the Church as an asylum, and hence his desire to curtail the privilege. The right of asylum was an institution common to all religions, Jewish, Greek, and Christian, and had its origin in what has been called the 'universal religious sentiment of man.' But what had its commencement in the spirit of love and charity subsequently degenerated in character, and interfered with the righteous demands of justice.

favourite now crouching in servile fear at the foot of the altar, entreating help and assistance from the anger of the emperor, over whom he had formerly ruled, and importunately soliciting the archbishop to throw his protecting shield over him. 'Vanity of vanities!' exclaims the great preacher, 'all is vanity. Where now is the pride of state, the pomp of office, the luxury of him who was lately lord of all? Where the plaudits of the city, the acclamations of the games, the adulations of the spectators? All, all are gone. A sudden blast has swept off the leaves of the tree, which is bare and stricken to the roots. All that earthly grandeur has vanished like a dream. The shadow has flitted away; the bubble has burst. "Vanity of vanities! all is vanity." Let these words be inscribed on our houses, in our markets, on the walls and gates of our city.' Then reminding Eutropius of his former exhortations, which he had scornfully rejected, he adds:—'Thy friends who flattered thee have forsaken thee, but the Church, whom thou treatedst as an enemy, opens wide her arms to receive thee in her bosom.'

'Do not think that I would reproach him or exult over him,'[1] said the preacher, addressing the people. 'No; God forbid! I look on him with compassion and sorrow, and I invoke your sympathy for him, and would persuade you, by his example, to cast away your own love of earthly things, and to long and to labour for those which are eternal, and to learn a lesson of forgiveness of injuries from God and His Church, and to act in the spirit of Christ, who prayed

---

[1] This shows how little he was disposed, as some have affirmed (cf. Socrat. v. 5, and Sozom. viii. 7), to triumph over Eutropius in his calamity.

for His murderers, "Father, forgive them ; for they know not what they do." '

' The powers of humanity' (once more to quote Gibbon's language), ' of devotional feeling, and of consummate eloquence prevailed. The Empress Eudoxia was restrained, either by her own sentiments or by those of her subjects, from violating the sanctuary of the Church ; and Eutropius was tempted to capitulate either through the influence of persuasion or in consequence of an oath that his life should be spared. An edict was forthwith published, in which it was declared that the property of Eutropius, who had disgraced the names of patrician and consul, should be confiscated, and that he himself should be sent away into perpetual exile in the island of Cyprus.'

Though Chrysostom protected Eutropius from the indignation of his enemies when he sought the asylum of the Church, yet he had not proved the compliant bishop that Eutropius hoped to have found in him. He had fearlessly denounced his designs when opposed to what he judged to be right, nor did he ever gloss over any wickedness in Eutropius, nor refrain from reprobating his conduct even from the pulpit. Such honesty of purpose and outspoken truthfulness naturally provoked the indignation of the favourite ; but his insolent conduct towards the empress had called forth another and a more powerful enemy against him.

It may be added that the refusal on the part of Chrysostom to give up one who had claimed the right of sanctuary in the Church turned the indignation of the soldiers and people against himself, and he was, in consequence, conducted, under military escort, to the imperial palace, in order that his refusal to surrender Eutropius might be laid before the emperor. The persuasive powers of Chrysostom prevailed in the first instance with Arcadius, and the sentence of death upon Eutropius was then commuted into banishment. His fate, however, was merely postponed. He was subsequently ordered back from Cyprus, to which island he had been exiled, and eventually put to death at Pantichium, which lay between Chalcedon and Nicomedia, being brought to his trial before Aurelian,[1] the prætorian prefect, and other illustrious persons who were constituted judges for that purpose. His name was erased from the *Fasti Consulares*, and the law which he had procured respecting the asylum of the Church was removed from the records.

[1] According to Cave, ii. 468.

CHAPTER V.

CHRYSOSTOM'S WORK AT CONSTANTINOPLE.

'Feed the flock of God which is among you, taking the oversight thereof, not by constraint, but willingly; not for filthy lucre, but of a ready mind.'—1 Pet. v. 2.

CHRYSOSTOM'S energy and Christian zeal were displayed in various directions, and were not confined to the more regular lines in which episcopal efforts at that time commonly moved. Wherever he saw an opening for the spiritual good of any class committed to his charge, he never failed to take advantage of it. He had received a commission to 'feed the flock' of Christ intrusted to his care, and therefore he never neglected the duties of his pastoral office.

It was in consequence of this earnest Christian love towards the souls of all within his diocese, that he was led, at this time, to attend to the spiritual wants of the numerous Goths who were then resident at Constantinople. The views of some of them were orthodox; but the majority inclined towards the errors of Arianism. This fact, no doubt, contributed not a little to stimulate his efforts on their behalf. For the use of the Goths he procured translations of different portions of Holy Scripture in their own language, and engaged a Gothic presbyter to read the Word of God to his fellow-countrymen in their own tongue in the church of St. Paul, and to preach to them also in their native language. The archbishop himself was in the habit of occasionally addressing the Goths by means of an interpreter. We cannot doubt that such efforts as these must have been productive of very great good among the Gothic population at Constantinople. But Chrysostom's efforts did not rest here. Having heard that there were many Gothic tribes who remained in their original settlements on the banks of the Danube, he ordained native catechists and clergy, and sent them out to these tribes to bring them over, if possible, to the true faith. Nor was this all : for he consecrated one of their number, whose name was Unilas, as their bishop.

Tidings, moreover, reached him that some tribes of nomad Scythians, who also lived on the banks of the Danube, were anxious to receive spiritual instruction, and immediately he sent out missionaries from Constantinople to teach them the truths of Christianity, and wrote also to the Bishop of Ancyra, named Leontius, entreating his co-operation in this spiritual work.

We find, too, that his feelings were excited by the prevalence of heathen idolatry, and that he persuaded the emperor to issue an edict for the destruction of temples in the district of Phœnicia devoted to pagan idolatry ; which edict was carried out through the aid of some Christian women at Constantinople, who were always ready to supply funds for missionary undertakings and for religious work in general. To such missionary efforts Chrysostom was always most favourably disposed throughout his whole life, even in the midst of persecution and exile. Whenever an opening presented itself for the inculcation of truth, or for the refutation of error, it was always seized upon by him. It was his ardent desire not only to propagate Christianity in its best and purest form, but also to expel heresy of every kind, whether Arian, Marcionite, or Novatian.

There is perfect truthfulness in the remark, that Chrysostom's ambition was not so much to elevate a few enthusiastic spirits to a high-toned and mystic piety, as to impregnate the whole population of a great capital with Christian virtues and self-denial. It was never his wish to captivate the attention of the people by mere religious displays and by sensational spectacles. The principal object which he had at heart was to produce among them holiness of life and conversation. Though he was well-disposed towards the monastic life, yet we find him most severe in his censures of those monks who led an easy, self-gratifying life, passing their days in idleness, and indisposed for any good work.

In the beginning of the year 399 A.D., Chrysostom preached a sermon on the festival of Theodosius, four years after his death. In this sermon he boldly and unflinchingly proposed the character of Theodosius as a pattern for his son Arcadius, the reigning emperor. 'We are debtors,' he said, 'to the blessed Theodosius, not because he was an emperor, but because he was a good man; we are debtors to him, not because he wore the purple, but because he was clothed with Christ, and with the panoply of spiritual arms—the breastplate of righteousness, and was shod with the preparation of the Gospel of peace (Eph. vi. 15), and wore the helmet of salvation, and wielded the sword of the Spirit. With these weapons he routed two tyrants, Maximus and Eugenius—the one without toil or bloodshed, the other by his prowess and his prayers. When the two armies had engaged, and his own troops were flying before the enemy, he leapt from his horse, and laid his shield down on the ground, and knelt on his knees, and prayed to God for help. The plain became a church; his weapons were tears and prayers. Then a tempest arose; the winds blew furiously, and flung the weapons of the enemy back upon themselves; some of their troops, who had breathed out fire and slaughter against him, turned round and hailed him emperor, and delivered their leader bound into his hands. Thus Theodosius was glorified, not only by his victory, but by the manner of it. He conquered by faith. Do not therefore suppose that he is dead; no, he is not dead, but sleepeth. For Christ says, " He that believeth in Me, though he were dead, yet shall he live: and whosoever liveth and believeth in Me shall never die "' (John xi. 25, 26).

During the season of Lent in this same year, which was the second of his residence at Constantinople, a very violent rainfall occurred, which created an alarm of a general deluge. Penitential hymns and inter-cessions were poured forth in the Church of the Apostles, in consequence of this terrifying visitation. But on Good Friday there was a race in the circus, which attracted great interest; while on Easter Eve the theatres were crowded, but the churches only partially filled. On Easter Day Chrysostom ad-dressed the people who had been witnesses of the games and spectacles on the previous days in a very severe style. 'Is this to be borne patiently?' he indignantly asked. ' I appeal to you in the words of Almighty God to the Hebrew nation—"O My people, what have I done unto thee? and wherein have I wearied thee?" (Mic. vi. 3). "What iniquity have your fathers found in Me, that they are gone far from Me?" (Jer. ii. 5). Is this, I say, to be borne? After so much teaching in successive sermons, some of you have left us for the hippodrome, others have gone to revel in bacchanalian orgies, and here I sit down and mourn. Even on Good Friday, when thy Lord was being crucified, and Paradise was opened, and the curse abolished, and sin effaced, and the ancient war of ages was ended, and God was reconciled to man ; aye, on that very day when men ought to fast and confess their sins, and join in prayer and thanksgiving for the blessings poured out upon the world, then it was that thou didst leave the church and the spiritual sacrifice, and the assembly of thy brethren ; then it was that thou wert led captive by the devil to those worldly spectacles. Is this, I repeat, to be borne? How can we hope to appease the wrath of God? For three days we had a deluge of rain, sweeping everything before it, and snatching the food from the mouths of the farmers, and laying prostrate their ripe crops, and their litanies went up to heaven, and all the population streamed, like a winter's torrent, to the Church of the Apostles. And yet, after the short interval of a day, thou didst allow thy soul to be carried away captive by vicious passions ; and, not content with the frenzy of the circus, thou didst rush on the next day (being Easter Even) to the theatre, running from the smoke into the fire. Old men disgraced their hoar hairs ; young men cast their youth headlong down a precipice ; fathers led their own sons to those gulfs of iniquity. . . . . Think of the worth of a single soul. Each single soul is precious in the sight of God and of Christ. For its sake God made the world, and furnished it, and gave laws to it, and worked many miracles. For its sake He spared not His only-begotten Son. For every soul Christ shed His blood. Think what a price was paid for each, and haste and spare no pains to bring that one lost soul back to the fold. But if you are remiss, I at least must be zealous, and I will use the power which God has given us for edification, and not for destruction. If any one after this warning falls away to the theatrical pestilence, I will not administer to him the holy mysteries, or suffer him to approach that holy table. I will separate him as a diseased sheep from the flock. I have tried gentler means. A year has passed away since I first came to this city, and I have never ceased to exhort you on this matter. But remember, though we have power both to bind and to loose, I do not desire to cut off our brethren from the Church ; but I do desire to wipe off this reproach from it. Jews and Gentiles now scoff at us for winking at sins. But when we have corrected them, they will admire the Church, and revere her laws. . . . . As for myself, I must mourn till this is done, although I may be irksome to you, in order that I may be able to stand before the dreadful tribunal of the Judge. Would to God, therefore, that the diseased may return to us, and that they who are whole may be strengthened, and that ye may attain eternal salvation, and that we may rejoice together, and God be glorified, now and for evermore. Amen' (Wordsworth's translation).

But an event occurred at this time, 400 A.D., which clearly evinced the influence, the zeal, and the boldness of Chrysostom. The Gothic commanders were then objects of terror and alarm to the emperor and the Court of Constantinople. They ventured to dictate their own terms to Arcadius. From colonists, permitted to dwell within the limits of the empire, they had become the conquerors of imperial armies. The victories of Alaric are well known to all, together with his crowning success at Rome itself. At the present time the Emperor Arcadius had, under similar dictates of fear, created Gainas the Goth[1] the master-general of his armies, who introduced into the capital an overwhelming number of his followers, on whom he bestowed honours and rewards with a lavish hand. Stimulated by the success which had attended his efforts in the case of Eutropius, the Gothic general—relying on the influence which he possessed over his troops—ventured to demand from the emperor the surrender of three of his principal ministers of state, namely, Aurelian the consul ; Saturninus, of equal rank ; and Count John, the favourite of Eudoxia. The meeting between Arcadius and Gainas took place at the Church of the Holy Martyr Euphemia, which was situated on a high and commanding position near Chalcedon. The three nobles already named voluntarily surrendered themselves to Gainas, in order to extricate the emperor from the difficult position in which he was placed, and their lives were no doubt exposed

[1] Gainas was born near the Ister in Scythia, and from being a common soldier in the Roman army rose to the rank of general.

to extreme peril. Then it was that Chrysostom courageously went to the camp of the Gothic chieftain, urgently pleaded for the lives of the three noblemen, and strove to induce Gainas to modify the terms which he had proposed to the emperor. But though Chrysostom was thus ready to entreat the Gothic general to act leniently towards his prisoners, and to moderate his own arrogant proposals, yet he would not yield for an instant to the request of Gainas, that one of the churches in Constantinople should be given up to him for Arian services and worship. No entreaties could induce the archbishop—in the conference which took place between them in the presence of the too-compliant emperor—to consent to a demand which, in his opinion, cast a slur upon the religion of Jesus Christ. So resolute was his opposition, that Gainas was compelled to yield, and to abandon, for the time, his claim.

Meanwhile the alarm of the inhabitants of Constantinople for their property, on which the Gothic troops that swarmed in the city had fixed their covetous glances, induced them to take courage from despair, and, in the absence of Gainas, suddenly to fall upon the Goths, of whom they slew not less than seven thousand. Some of them, who had fled for refuge to the building in which the Arians had held their services, were attacked by their pursuers, who stripped off the roof, and threw down upon the fugitives crowded within the walls burning logs of wood, till they had entirely destroyed them. Gainas was struck with the greatest astonishment and alarm when he heard of the massacre of his best troops, and that he himself had been declared a public enemy.

and that his countryman, Fravitta, had assumed the command of the imperial forces by sea and land. After various efforts on the part of Gainas to retrieve his shattered fortunes, his attempt on rafts to force the passage of the Hellespont was frustrated by Fravitta and the Roman forces under his command, and his armament was totally destroyed, the Hellespont being strewn with the wrecks of his flotilla. Gainas, upon this, resolved once more to return to the independence of savage life. With a body of troops devoted to the fortunes of their general, he retired by forced marches to the banks of the Danube and the wilds of Scythia; but his onward progress was arrested, not by Fravitta, who gave himself up to the delight of a popular ovation and the honours of the consulship, but by Uldin, the King of the Huns, by whom he was opposed in his march, and slain on the field of battle. Within eleven days of the naval victory in the Hellespont, the head of Gainas was received at Constantinople amid the rejoicings of the people, Arcadius enjoying the honours of a triumph which Uldin had himself gained.

But Chrysostom's efforts were not confined to Christianising the Goths, the Scythians, and other tribes,—his missionary efforts (as he tells us) having reached even as far as the British Isles; but he aimed also at consolidating the Church at home within his own peculiar diocese. Having discovered that the outlying villages within his diocese were deficient not only in places of worship, but also in spiritual teachers, he set himself to repair this want. He made an

---

[1] Cf. Gibbon's *Roman Empire*, ch. xxxii. Slightly different accounts of these transactions are given by different historians.

earnest application to Christian landowners and pos-
sessors of property in these districts to furnish the
means for building churches and supplying preachers.
He entreated them not merely to devote their property and their attention to the construction of
splendid mansions, and baths, and markets on their
property, but to strive to improve the spiritual condition of their labourers, and endeavour to win them
over to Christianity. He pointed out to them that
God would bless their worldly property, if they
devoted some portion of their wealth to the further-
ance of His worship, and the benefit of the souls of
their dependants. The erection of a church to God's
glory and man's good was, he said, an ornament to
their estates; and not only an ornament, but also the
truest safeguard and protection which they could
devise. Thus would their estates become a very
Paradise. Quietness and peace would reign within
them, and discord, theft, and heresy would flee away.
The husbandry and tillage on their estates would be
sanctified by the act of prayer, and a harvest of souls
would be brought into the spiritual garner.

It was thus that the archbishop, with untiring labour
and unflagging zeal, endeavoured to bring within the
pale of the Church those who lived within the limits
of his diocese, as well as those who dwelt beyond its
boundaries. He left no stone unturned in his efforts
to win souls to the obedience of the Gospel of Christ
We may, perhaps, add, in the words of Canon Robertson,[1] that Chrysostom's 'influence was beneficially
exerted to heal the schism of Antioch. On the death
of Paulinus, who had been acknowledged as bishop by
Egypt and the West, his party consecrated Evagrius ;

---

[1] *Church History*, i. 349.

but this bishop did not long survive, and they were again left without a head. Through the intervention of Chrysostom, in the first year of his episcopate, both Innocent of Rome and Theophilus were persuaded to acknowledge Flavian, who thereupon inserted the names of both Paulinus and Evagrius in the diptychs of his church. Thus the later separation—that which Lucifer had occasioned by consecrating Paulinus—was brought to an end, although some remains of the old Eustathian party continued to exist without any bishop. The schism was eventually terminated by the conciliatory measures of Alexander, Bishop of Antioch, in 415 A.D.'

CHAPTER VI.

CHRYSOSTOM'S EXPOSITIONS AT CONSTANTINOPLE.

'To hold the multitude as one, breathing in measured cadence,
  A thousand men, with flashing eyes, waiting upon thy will;
  A thousand hearts kindled by thee with consecrated fire;
  Verily, O man, with truth for thy theme, eloquence shall throne
    thee with archangels.'

THERE can be no doubt that we must look to Antioch as the scene of the larger number and of the most perfect of the productions of Chrysostom as a homilist and expositor. He had there somewhat more leisure to devote to literary work, nor was he so constantly occupied by the labours and anxieties which his more exalted position at Constantinople brought upon him. The care of the Churches there pressed heavily upon him, as it had aforetime pressed upon St. Paul. His preaching, when he was archbishop, would not, however, seem to have declined. He possessed no less a degree of mastery over the minds and hearts of men than he had wielded in his most palmy days at Antioch. His powers as an extemporaneous preacher, as one capable of unpremeditated efforts, were probably as great as they ever were. But it would seem that there was less of finish in his oratory, less of that careful preparation and premeditation which is so clearly traceable in his earlier efforts. This, as has been remarked, was the natural result of the altered circumstances in which he was placed—circumstances that precluded him from taking the pains and bestowing the attention which he had done at first, during his presbyterate at Antioch, when the time at his disposal was greater.

His love for the Holy Scriptures never lessened. His earnest exhortations to his hearers to study the Word of God continuously never flagged. This was a special characteristic of Chrysostom. We perpetually find him urging those who listened to his preaching to give themselves frequently to the reading of God's Word. He was in the habit of insisting upon this study, more especially in the case of those who were immersed in trade and business, and who were inclined to excuse themselves from such reading on this very account. He assured them that they, with all their business cares and distractions, were the very persons of all others who needed the comfort and support in trial and temptation which the Scriptures furnished. They would find the Bible, which was written in some parts by publicans and illiterate fishermen, respond to the different wants and necessities of the poor, the unlearned, and the busy, while it also answered the deeper cravings of the learned and the philosophical.

1. It is difficult to state with any precision the exact time when the homilies on the Acts of the Apostles were delivered. Some writers believe that several at least of them were preached at Antioch towards the end of Chrysostom's presbyterate ; but a larger number of writers have concluded, from internal evidence, that these homilies were preached in the Easter week of the third year of his residence as Archbishop of Constantinople, 400 A.D.

The text of these homilies is, in many cases, very imperfect, and it is often difficult to establish with anything like certainty the true reading. The style, also, is less elegant and finished than that in which most of his homilies are written, and bears evidence of wanting his final correction. There can be detected in it an abruptness and ruggedness not like Chrysostom's ordinary writing, so that Erasmus throws out a hint of the work not being Chrysostom's.[1] The matter, indeed, is good, and quite equal to that of Chrysostom's ordinary expositions. It is possible, as has been suggested, that about the year 400 A.D., the Eastern capital was kept in constant alarm by the revolt of Gainas and the Goths. Ecclesiastical questions also continually occupied the attention of Chrysostom about that time—questions which even compelled his personal attendance at Ephesus. He was consequently unable to give to the transcriber's copy of his sermons any care or revision.

The Acts of the Apostles, moreover, was a book which, though read in the Church from Easter to Pentecost, was very rarely made the subject-matter of preaching, and would therefore be less known and familiar to those who took down his sermons at the time, or to those who endeavoured to revise them after they had been taken down.

It has been remarked that this work on the Acts of the Apostles stands alone among the writings of the first ten centuries. No other treatise on the subject is extant. Hence arose an imperfect and doubtful text, which it is difficult in places to translate; the older text being the better of the two, the more recent

---

[1] His words are—*Quod stylus concisum quiddam et abruptum habeat, id quod à phrasi Chrysostomi videtur alienum.*

one being apparently an attempt of some reviser to smooth down the ruggedness of the style, and render it more easy of comprehension.

2. Chrysostom's homilies on the shorter Epistles of St. Paul, namely, the Philippians, Colossians, and Thessalonians, were undoubtedly the production of this period of his career. They contain internal evidence of having been delivered at Constantinople. We find in them reference to the responsible office which he held as president of the Church, and to the duty which devolved upon him of maintaining discipline and order.

In the ninth homily on the Epistle to the Philippians, he says :—' I ought then to have exacted from you this penalty for your negligence in the Scriptures. But what shall I do? I am a father. Fathers freely give to their sons many things beyond what is fitting.'

Again, we hear him saying, in the third homily on the Epistle to the Colossians :—' So long as we sit upon this throne, so long as we have the first place, we have both the dignity and the power, even though we are unworthy. If the throne of Moses was of such reverence that for its sake they were to be heard, much more the throne of Christ. It we have received ; for it we speak ; since the time that Christ hath vested in us the ministry of reconciliation. Ambassadors, whatever be their sort, because of the dignity of an embassy, enjoy much honour. And we now have received a reward of embassy, and we are come from God, for this is the dignity of the episcopate.'

Again, in the eighth homily on the First Epistle to the Thessalonians, he says :—' I could wish also myself that there were no punishments,—yes, myself most of all men. And why so? Because while each of you fears for his own soul, I shall have to answer for this office in which I preside over you.'

We may notice, in these homilies, evidences of a greater severity in tone and style, as well, perhaps as a fuller ripeness in judgment and knowledge. He also dwells with increasing harshness of language on the luxury which existed at the time, and on the ostentatious display of wealth then prevalent, in consequence of which strong expressions he is said to have incurred the anger of the Empress Eudoxia.

We may give the following specimens from these homilies:—(*a*) In the introduction to the homilies on the Epistle to the Philippians, he says:—'Such is the power of Mercy. She brings in her nurslings with much boldness. For she is known to the porters in heaven, that keep the gates of the bride-chamber; and not known only, but reverenced; and those whom she knows to have honoured her she will bring in with great boldness, and none will gainsay, but all make room. For if she brought God down to earth, and prevailed with Him to become man, much more shall she be able to raise man to heaven; for great is her might. If, then, from mercy and loving-kindness God became man, and she persuaded Him to become a servant, much rather will she bring her servants into His own house. Her, then, let us love, on her let us set our affection, not one day, nor two, but all our life long, that she may acknowledge us. If she acknowledge us, the Lord will acknowledge us too. If she own us not, the Lord too will disown us, and will say, "I know you not." But may it be ours to hear no such voice, but that happy one instead, "Come, ye blessed of My Father, inherit the kingdom prepared for you from the foundation of the world." '

(*b*) In the twelfth homily on the Epistle to the Colossians he thus speaks of tears :—' Remember me these tears: thus let us bring up our daughters, thus our sons ; weeping when we see them in evil. As many women as wish to be loved, let them remember Paul's tears, and groan : as many of you as are counted blest, as many as are in pleasure, remember these ; as many as are in mourning, exchange tears for tears. He mourned not for the dead ; but for those that were perishing whilst alive. Shall I tell of other tears? Timothy also wept ; for he was this man's disciple ; wherefore also, when writing to him, he said, " Being mindful of thy tears, that I may be filled with joy." Many weep even from pleasure. So it is a thing that resulteth from pleasure, and pleasure of the utmost intensity. So far are the tears which proceed from such sorrow from being painful : yea, they are even better far than those which come of worldly pleasure. Hear the prophet saying, "The Lord hath heard the voice of my weeping." For where are tears not useful ? in prayers? in admonitions? But we get them an ill name by using them not to what they are given us for. When we entreat a sinning brother, we ought to weep, beating our breasts and groaning; when we exhort any one, and he giveth us no heed, but goeth on perishing, we ought to weep. These are the tears of heavenly wisdom. When, however, one is in poverty, or bodily disease, or dead, not so ; for these are not things worthy of tears.'

(*c*) Speaking of the ' strait and narrow way,' he says, in the ninth homily of the First Epistle to the

Thessalonians:—'Let not any one, therefore, expect that he shall see heaven with ease, for it cannot be. Let no man hope to travel the narrow road with luxury, for it is impossible. Let no one travelling in the broad way hope for life. When, therefore, thou seest any one luxuriating in baths, in a sumptuous table, with attendance of guards, think not thyself unhappy, as not partaking of these things, but lament for him, that he is travelling the way to destruction. For what is the advantage of this way, when it ends in tribulation? And what is the injury of that straitness, when it leads to rest? Tell me, if any one invited to a palace should walk through narrow ways, painful and precipitous, and another led to death should be dragged through the midst of the market-place, which shall we call happy? which shall we commiserate? Him, shall we not, who walks through the wide road? So also now, let us think happy, not those who are luxurious, but those who are not luxurious. These are hastening to heaven, those to hell.'

3. There is another group of homilies which Chrysostom delivered on the Epistles of St. Paul to Timothy, Titus, and Philemon.

As to the place and time at which they were delivered, critics are undecided.

Whether the homilies on the Epistles to Timothy were preached at Antioch or Constantinople is still a moot point. While Montfaucon thinks that they were delivered at Antioch, because Chrysostom speaks much of the monks in them, and because, in referring to Timothy's episcopal office, he never alludes to his own; and because (it may be added) he seems in *Homily* viii. to refer to the burning of the Temple of Apollo at Daphne: Tillemont, on the other hand, considers that their somewhat rude and unpolished style points out Constantinople as the place at which they were delivered.

The homilies on the Epistle to Titus are assigned also to different places, as regards their delivery, by different writers. The conclusion of *Homily* i. § 4 would seem to point to the preacher as a bishop. 'Great indeed,' he says, 'is the danger of such a station, and it requires the grace and peace of God. Which that we may have abundantly, do you pray for us, · and we for you,' etc. At the same time it must be acknowledged that, in *Homily* iii. § 2, he speaks of Daphne, and the cave of Matrona, and the plain in Cilicia that is called Saturn's, which point rather to Antioch as the place of their delivery.

The homilies on the Epistle to Philemon have nothing in them definitely to mark the time or place of their delivery. It is natural that they should follow those on the Epistles to Timothy and Titus.

The style in which they are composed is, in the judgment of Hemsterhusius, negligent and careless; and this leads him to suppose that they were purely extemporaneous, and that possibly they were, in addition, carelessly reported by others. Nevertheless, the subject-matter of the commentary is thoughtfully handled, and the exegesis is careful and accurate.

(*a*) In the commencement of *Homily* iv. on the Epistles to Timothy, Chrysostom says:—'The favours of God so far exceed human hope and expectation, that often they are not believed. For God has bestowed upon us such things as the mind of man never looked for, never thought of. It is for this reason that the apostles spend much discourse in securing a belief of the gifts that are granted us of God. For as men, upon receiving some great good, ask themselves if it is not a dream, as not believing it,—so it is with respect to the gifts of God. What, then, was it that was thought incredible? That those who were enemies, and sinners, neither justified by the Law nor by works, should immediately, through faith alone, be advanced to the highest favour. Upon this head, accordingly, Paul has discoursed at length in his Epistle to the Romans, and here again at length. "This is a faithful saying," he says, "and worthy of all acceptation, that Christ Jesus came into the world to save sinners."'

(*b*) The following passage on vain-glory occurs in his *Homily* ii. on the Epistle to Titus :—'There is nothing which is not spoiled by these passions. But as when violent winds, falling on a calm sea, turn it up from its foundation, and mingle the sand with the waves, so these passions assailing the soul turn all upside down, and dim the clearness of the mental sight ; but especially does the mad desire of glory. For a contempt for money any one may easily attain, but to despise the honour that proceeds from the multitude requires a great effort, a philosophic temper, a certain angelic soul that reaches to the very summit of heaven. For there is no passion so tyrannical, so universally prevalent, in a greater or a less degree indeed, but still everywhere. How, then, shall we subdue it, if not wholly, yet in some little part? By looking up to heaven, by setting God before our eyes, by entertaining thoughts superior to earthly things. Imagine, when thou desirest glory, that thou hast already attained it, and mark the end, and thou wilt find it to be nothing. Consider with what loss it is attended, of how many and how great blessings it will deprive thee. For thou wilt undergo the toils and dangers, yet be deprived of the fruits and rewards of them. Consider that the majority are bad, and despise their opinion. In the case of each individual, consider what the man is, and thou wilt see how ridiculous a thing is glory, that is rather to be called shame.'

(c) The following passage is extracted from *Homily* i. on the Epistle to Philemon :—'Considering these things, then, let us also be merciful and forgiving towards those who have trespassed against us. The offences against us here are a hundred pence, but those from us against God are ten thousand talents. But you know that offences are also judged by the quality of the persons : for instance, he who has insulted a private person has done wrong, but not so much as he who has insulted a magistrate ; and he who has offended a greater magistrate, offends in a higher degree ; and he who offends an inferior one, in a lower degree ; but he who insults the king, offends much more. The injury, indeed, is the same, but it becomes greater by the excellence of the person. And if he who insults a king receives intolerable punishment, on account of the superiority of the person, for how many talents will he be answerable who insults God ? So that even if we should commit the same offences against God that we do against men, even so it is not an equal thing : but as great as is the difference between God and men, so great is that between the offences against Him and them.'

CHAPTER VII.

OPPOSITION TO CHRYSOSTOM.

AT this time the influence of Chrysostom was at its zenith. His power was felt in the palace; the clergy were compelled to bend to his will; he exerted no slight authority over the political rulers of Constantinople; and he was held in the highest esteem and affection by the populace. But, nevertheless, the experienced eye could detect, in several quarters, signs of a coming storm. Indications were traceable of disaffection and antagonism both at home and abroad. The sagacious might discover the little cloud of opposition, no bigger than a man's hand, rising in the distant verge of the horizon, which was destined, in no long time, to cover the whole heavens with the blackness of darkness.

The Court appeared, on a superficial view, to be well disposed to him. The emperor, without doubt, trusted and valued him, and paid marked deference to his religious opinions and to his teaching. The empress had, speaking generally, manifested very great favour towards him. She had assisted at his popular services, and had lavished the highest praises upon him. He had regarded her religious principles as genuine, and supposed that her acts of piety had emanated from pure motives and sound religious convictions. When, however, the fervour of her zeal evaporated, and the husk only of piety remained, Chrysostom could not be imposed upon by the mere outward semblance of religion, and did not hesitate to warn and even to censure her—empress though she was—whenever she fell short of the high standard of holiness which he set before her. Nor did he refrain from using strong language to the ladies of her court, when they indulged in anything which, in his estimation, was unworthy of their Christian profession. But the proud empress could not brook such plain speaking even from the Archbishop of Constantinople. Her anger became aroused. The ill-will which she now felt towards him was equal in degree to the favour which she had before manifested. She dreaded, too, his influence over the weak mind of the emperor. It was her great ambition at this time to secure an unlimited sway over her imperial husband. Several of those who had formerly vied with her for the ascendency over his mind had passed away. Eutropius had fallen by the hand of the executioner, and Gainas had perished on the battle-field. Thus the two principal rivals who had thwarted her schemes were removed. Only Chrysostom now remained to dispute with her the pre-eminence over her husband's will. She desired to be the real mistress of the Eastern world. With these ambitious feelings in her mind, she secretly endeavoured to remove Chrysostom out of her path. His influence now appeared to her the sole obstacle that presented itself to the attainment of her ambitious dream of sovereignty. She therefore anxiously looked about her to discover some means by which she might be enabled to weaken his power and influence.

We have already noticed the zeal which Chrysostom displayed in his endeavours not only to correct abuses in the Church, but also to further missionary efforts far and near. The exact boundaries of the different dioceses of the Church were not then so strictly defined as they afterwards were. It had, indeed, been decided by a canon of the Council of Constantinople, in 381 A.D., that the archbishop of that see should hold a rank next to that of the Bishop of Rome ; but though the dignity of the archbishop was thus fixed, the limits of his jurisdiction were not defined with equal certainty. The high political rank which Constantinople held naturally gave an authority and influence to its patriarchs, which the primates and metropolitans of more ancient sees and provinces regarded with ill-concealed annoyance and vexation. The exact jurisdiction of the archbishop was not, in fact, precisely fixed till the year 451 A.D., at the Council of Chalcedon. At the present time, therefore, the Archbishop of Constantinople had no legal jurisdiction in Asia Minor, or, in fact, beyond the limits of Constantinople and his own diocese.

The modern foundation of Constantinople debarred it from being a metropolitan see. It was at first under the ecclesiastical jurisdiction of the Metropolitan of Heraclea, formerly named Perinthus, a large and flourishing town of Thrace, situated on the Propontis, superior even to Byzantium, whose metropolitan was Exarch of Thrace. But subsequently, the claims of Heraclea having become obsolete, the prelates of

Alexandria, by degrees, asserted their rights as metropolitans over Byzantium, on the ground of priority of foundation. But such a subjection to any foreign diocesan was regarded as unsuited to the high status of an imperial capital, and thus, at the Council of Constantinople, in 381 A.D., it was decided that the bishop of the imperial city should hold rank next to the Bishop of Rome, the Bishops of Alexandria and Antioch occupying the third and fourth places. But this priority of rank was not legally established; and though Nectarius had, previously to Chrysostom, exercised jurisdiction in Asia Minor, yet such jurisdiction was not valid in law until the decision of the Council of Chalcedon. When, therefore, at the end of the year 400 A.D., Chrysostom held a visitation at Ephesus, it was by virtue of his being prelate of the imperial city, and also in consequence of his own personal weight of character and great powers of mind.

His visitation at Ephesus originated from the following cause :—Eusebius, Bishop of Valentinopolis, had accused Antoninus, Bishop of Ephesus, at a conference of bishops which had taken place about this time at Constantinople, of appropriating the Church plate for his own private uses, and of simoniacal sales of episcopal ordination. These were two principal articles out of the seven brought against him. Eusebius pressed the charges vehemently against Antoninus, and a meeting was held in Constantinople to ascertain the real state of the case. But they could arrive at no definite certainty as to the truth of the accusations. Delegates were accordingly sent to Ephesus to inquire into these matters. The investigation proceeded slowly and unsatisfactorily; and the commissioners were unable to discover the rights of the case. The defendant, moreover, died before the question was decided. At this juncture Chrysostom received a pressing request from the bishops and clergy of Ephesus and its neighbourhood, to come himself, and rectify, if possible, the abuses that prevailed,—the Arians, they said, infesting them on the one hand, and the covetousness of some of the clergy, like ravenous wolves, disturbing them on the other hand.

It was now mid-winter—January, 401 A.D.—when the request was made; but Chrysostom did not hesitate to respond to the call made to him, though he was in weak health at the time. On his arrival at Ephesus—to which he is said to have walked on foot from Apamea, where he had landed, after a stormy voyage, with Palladius, Paulus, and Cyrinus, whom he had chosen as his associates on the journey,—he deposed, in a synod consisting of seventy bishops, by virtue of his authority as metropolitan, no less than six[1] bishops, who were found guilty of simoniacal practices, and punished with great rigour the clergy who were convicted of mercenary and dissolute conduct. Moreover, on the death of Antoninus, he consecrated, as Bishop of Ephesus, Heraclides, a Cypriot by birth, who had been up to this time a monk at Nitria.

Such severe measures brought down upon Chrysostom the ill-will and animosity of the clergy whom he had punished. They were ready and eager to revenge

---

[1] According to Socrates and Sozomen, he deposed thirteen bishops; but Palladius, as having been present, is probably correct in saying six. He also deposed Gerontius, Bishop of Nicomedia, who was addicted to magic (Sozom. viii. 6), and put Pansophius in his place, against the wish of the people.

themselves upon this stern ecclesiastic, whenever an opportunity should present itself.

During the three or four months of Chrysostom's absence from Constantinople, events occurred which proved extremely injurious to his position there. He had, on leaving the city, delegated his authority as bishop to Severian, Bishop of Gabala, in Cœle-Syria, a famous preacher, and to Serapion, his archdeacon. Severian, we can scarcely doubt, made a dishonourable use of the power which Chrysostom had placed in his hands. He endeavoured, so far as he could, to weaken the character and influence of Chrysostom both with the Court and with those of high rank: He employed all the arts of flattery, with which he was abundantly endued, in his attempts to withdraw from the bishop the favour of the emperor and empress and their suite. A conspiracy was formed against the absent bishop ; and the Empress Eudoxia, and the ladies of her court—against whose personal vanity, luxury, and extravagance Chrysostom had loudly inveighed, together with the rich widows, Marsa, Castricia, and Eugraphia, whom Chrysostom had charged with using for their souls' injury the unjust gains of their husbands—headed the league against him. This conspiracy was strengthened by the appearance at the imperial city of Antiochus, Bishop of Ptolemais, and Acacius, Bishop of Berœa. The latter bishop—previously disgusted at the plain fare of the bishop's table, and at the accommodation provided for him, had been heard to say, in language which savoured of coarseness, 'I will season his soup for him.'

While all this was going on at Constantinople, his archdeacon Serapion had not been silent, but had written to Chrysostom, informing him of Severian's underhand attempts to weaken his influence, and pressing upon him the need there was for his immediate return to the capital.

He returned; but his rash language in preaching soon brought down the storm upon his devoted head. In his very first sermon he inveighed against Severian and Antiochus, whom he described as flattering parasites, whose conduct had become the town-talk of Constantinople. But shortly afterwards he indulged in still more hazardous statements. Taking the history of Elijah as the topic of his address, he cried out, 'Gather together to me those base priests that eat at Jezebel's table, that I may say to them, as Elijah of old, How long halt ye between two opinions?' This allusion to Eudoxia could not be misunderstood. She had been called Jezebel by Chrysostom. Such language the proud empress could not and would not tolerate. Still, she waited her time, and did not yet entirely break with the ecclesiastic to whom she had once been so much attached, even though he had so deeply insulted her.

At this time some words uttered in annoyance by Severian were interpreted by Serapion to imply a denial of the Divinity of Christ, and were reported to Chrysostom as bearing this meaning, Immediately, without further investigation, Chrysostom was said to have pronounced a sentence of excommunication upon Severian, together with banishment from Constantinople.[1] The words were, 'If Serapion die a Christian, then Christ never became man;' which were afterwards brought under the consideration of an

---

[1] There can be no doubt that, at any rate, Chrysostom recommended him to leave Constantinople at once, and attend to his neglected diocese.

assembly of the Church. The people, who still idolised Chrysostom, hearing a rumour that Severian had treated their favourite archbishop with discourtesy, became greatly incensed against him, and might very possibly have had recourse to personal violence had not Severian retired across the Bosphorus to Chalcedon.

The emperor and empress strove eagerly to reconcile Chrysostom to Severian, and Eudoxia even condescended to entreat Chrysostom to be pacified, by placing her infant child, the young Prince Theodosius, who was Chrysostom's godson, on his knee in the Church of the Apostles. Even thus he was with difficulty induced to pardon the offence. The people were only persuaded by Chrysostom himself, and that after much effort, to desist from violence against the insulter of their bishop.

But the conspiracy against Chrysostom was not thus extinguished. The allusion to Jezebel still rankled in the heart of Eudoxia. Severian's treatment at the hand of the archbishop was far from being effaced from his memory. The great body of the ecclesiastics were still eager for the overthrow of Chrysostom, whose high qualities brought out in strong contrast their low standard of life and conduct. And now, in the violent, relentless, unscrupulous, and domineering Theophilus, Bishop of Alexandria, was found one who could organise and command these different forces against Chrysostom. Theophilus had never forgiven him for the part which he had been made unwillingly to play at his consecration. A plea was found for his interference in this sad dispute in the friendly feeling which had been shown by Chrysostom to some Egyptian monks—called, from their lofty stature, 'The Tall Brethren'—who had suffered very severe and cruel treatment at the hands of Theophilus, under the pretence of their holding the views of Origen, but in fact because they were cognizant of the private affairs of Theophilus, which two of them, Eusebius and Euthymius, had been employed by him to investigate and administer. They were, however, so scandalised by what they saw of the means by which Theophilus obtained funds for church-building, that they quitted the bishop.

One of the four brethren was Ammonius, who had cut off his ear when it was proposed to make him a bishop, supposing that such a blemish, as would have been the case under the Levitical law (Levit. xxi. 17, seq.), would have prevented his being made a priest; but finding that it would prove no obstacle in the Christian Church, he declared that he would cut out his tongue also. The other three were Dioscorus, Bishop of Nitria (a mountain with 500 hermits' cells), and Eusebius and Euthymius, who have been already named.

The four brethren, together with about eighty companions—according to Tillemont, three hundred, —had been expelled with the greatest cruelty from their place of abode in the Nitrian desert, their cells having been burnt, their books destroyed, and their lives imperilled by the soldiers of the Governor of Alexandria, whom the bishop influenced against them, charging them with insubordination, and had fled to Scythopolis, in Palestine.

But the cruel hatred of Theophilus had pursued them even there, and they were compelled to leave their retreat, and hasten with about fifty others to Constantinople, in order to supplicate the protection of Arcadius and Chrysostom. They were received with friendly sympathy by Chrysostom, who asked them with tears, 'Who is it that has injured you?' They answered, 'Pope Theophilus; prevail upon him, father, to let us live in Egypt, for we have never done aught against him, or against our Saviour's law.' He allowed them to attend the service in the church called Anastasia,. near which he lodged them, but not to communicate.[1] He entered, moreover, into a correspondence with Theophilus in their favour, before admitting them into communion.

Theophilus replied in indignant language to Chrysostom, whom he charged with bolstering up the cause of heretics, and with interference in the affairs of another diocese. He had, it would seem, been told that the brethren had been actually received into communion by Chrysostom.

He also sent agents to Constantinople to bring forward an accusation against the 'Tall Brethren' before the emperor. Chrysostom had warned them against making any appeal to the civil authorities, and had told them that his interference in their behalf must in that case cease. But the insolent treatment which they had received in the city induced them to have recourse to the emperor's protection. They were favoured in their appeal by Eudoxia.

The Bishop of Alexandria was cited to appear before a council summoned to meet at Constantinople, in order to consider the question of these Nitrian monks, and to hear the proofs of the charges which Theophilus had brought against them. As Theophilus delayed to appear after being summoned, his agents were brought before a prefect for examination, and received punishment for bringing forward false

[1] See Bright's *History of the Church*, p. 240.

accusations, and some of them died during the imprisonment to which they were subjected.

Theophilus, however, craftily contrived that the council should not simply meet to consider the matter of the 'Tall Brethren,' but should rather pronounce a verdict upon the character and conduct of Chrysostom, which might pave the way to his ultimate deposition. Theophilus laid his plans astutely and craftily, urged on by a bitter feeling of personal animosity against Chrysostom. In the first place, he succeeded in bringing to Constantinople the Bishop of Salamis, the aged Epiphanius, whom, no long time before, Theophilus had branded as heretical. Epiphanius brought with him the decisions of a council recently held at Cyprus, in which the Origenistic views of the monks of the Nitriote nome had been formally condemned. These decisions were to be laid before Chrysostom for his signature. Epiphanius, on his first entrance into Constantinople, bluntly refused all offers of hospitality on the part of Chrysostom, until he had entered his protest against the tenets of Origen, and expelled the Nitrian monks from his diocese. But Chrysostom declined thus to prejudicate the case, and left the decision to the council.

Further exasperation was caused by Epiphanius, in violation of the ecclesiastical laws, venturing to ordain a deacon at Constantinople.

We may observe, in passing, that it is scarcely possible that Theophilus, from what is known of his previous history, as well as of his after conduct, was really influenced by any genuine antipathy to the views of Origen. He is said to have been a diligent reader of the works of Origen, and, when charged with being so, to have replied, 'Origen's books are like a meadow beset with all sorts of herbs and flowers : where I find anything that is good and wholesome, I take it to my own use ; where I meet with what is prickly and useless, I pass it by.'[1]

Failing to secure a condemnation at the hands of Chrysostom, Epiphanius endeavoured to procure it from the bishops who were present. But here again he was unsuccessful in his attempt. He then held an interview with the ' Tall Brethren,' who, at Eudoxia's desire, paid him a visit. 'Who are ye ?' he asked. 'Father,' they replied, 'we are the " Tall Brethren." What do you know of our disciples or of our writings?' 'Nothing,' was his answer. 'Why, then,' asked Ammonius, 'have you condemned us as heretics unheard ?' All that the hasty old man could say was, 'You were reported to be so.' They shamed him by replying, 'We treated you far otherwise, when we defended your books against a like imputation.'[2] He was obliged to acknowledge that he had condemned them without having read any of their writings. In consequence of this interview he became aware of the deceit which had been practised upon him by Theophilus, and of the real character of that crafty and revengeful prelate, and he immediately declined to have anything more to do with his plot, and set out for Cyprus at once. When bidding farewell to the bishops who accompanied him to the vessel on which he was to sail, he is reported to have said, 'I leave to you the capital, the Court, and hypocrisy.'[3] He died, at the age of nearly a hundred years, either during the voyage or directly after his return. The unchristian

---

[1] Cf. Socrat. *Hist. Eccles.* v. 17.

[2] Cf. Sozom. viii. 15. See Bright's *History of the Church*, p. 241.

[3] The original words were : 'Αφίημι ὑμῖν τὴν πόλιν, καὶ τὰ βασίλεια, καὶ τὴν ὑπόκρισιν.

wishes said to have been uttered by Chrysostom and Epiphanius on the departure of the latter for Cyprus, to which Socrates refers, but only as a report—'I hope you will not die a bishop,' and ' I hope you will not arrive in your own country,'—are probably wholly destitute of any foundation.

The departure of Epiphanius was closely followed by the arrival of Theophilus at Constantinople, attended by many Egyptian bishops in great state. A strong escort of Alexandrian sailors came with him, who brought with them ample gifts for those whom he wished to win over to his side. He was not publicly received by the bishop and the clergy, but had a noisy welcome from the sailors of the Egyptian corn-vessels in the harbour. He peremptorily declined all Chrysostom's offers of hospitality at the bishop's palace, but lodged in one of the emperor's houses in the suburbs, called ' Placidiana,' which had apparently been prepared for his reception. Conducting himself as though he were Chrysostom's superior in the Church, he appeared not as one who had come to stand a trial, but as one who intended to degrade Chrysostom for faults which he had committed. He ostentatiously affirmed that he was 'going to Court in order to depose John.' During the three weeks which intervened between his entrance into the city and the opening of the council, he endeavoured to gain the favour both of the principal citizens, and also of the clergy who were opposed to their bishop, by costly presents, rich entertainments, flattery, and other means.

Chrysostom was urged by the emperor to hasten on the trial of Theophilus, but he hesitated, on the ground that he did not feel sure of his episcopal jurisdiction. Theophilus, on the other hand, felt no such scruples, but claimed, as Patriarch of Alexandria, the chief place, and asserted his power of citing Chrysostom to attend before him as his subordinate.

Afraid to summon a synod at Constantinople, where the influence of Chrysostom with the people was predominant, Theophilus selected a suburb of Chalcedon, across the Bosphorus, known by the name of 'The Oak,' near which was a spacious church dedicated to St. Peter and St. Paul, and houses for the clergy and the monks, and convened the meeting at the noble palace or monastery built by Rufinus, a man of consular rank. Thirty-six bishops in all assembled there,—some writers say forty-five,—all of whom, with the exception of seven, were Egyptians, and the suffragans of Theophilus. The bishops present from Asia Minor were chiefly those whom Chrysostom had offended during his visitation at Ephesus. Gerontius, Bishop of Nicomedia, whom Chrysostom had deposed, was there, inspired with feelings of bitter hostility. The Bishop of Heraclea-Perinthus, occupied the place of president, as being metropolitan. Before this packed synod, whose members were, as Photius describes them, 'judges, accusers, and witnesses,' in July, 403 A.D., Chrysostom was summoned to reply to the charges brought against him in twenty-nine articles, drawn up by the Archdeacon John, who was Serapion's successor. Many of these charges were utterly trifling, others were greatly exaggerated, and several totally destitute of foundation. Agents had even been despatched to Antioch to discover, if possible, some ground of accusation in his former life ; but all in vain. Some writers assert that these twenty-nine articles had been drawn up by two deacons of indifferent character, who had been ejected from their office by Chrysostom, and who drew them up in order that they might by this service obtain the restoration of their forfeited positions. The charges referred to his mal-administration of the Church funds ; to his imperious treatment of the clergy ; to his having beaten and chained a monk, and struck a man in church so as to draw blood ; to his having slandered the clergy in writing, and having said that they were 'not worth three obols;' to his having accused three deacons of stealing from him his pall ; to the dinners which he gluttonously ate all alone (although his biographer, Palladius, explains satisfactorily the reason of his solitary meals); to irregular ritual practices, as, for example, to his putting on and taking off his robes on the episcopal throne ; to his violation of the rule of fasting-communions ; to his ordination of unsatisfactory candidates ; to his eating wafers on the episcopal throne ; to his having sold the furniture of the church ; to his having excited officers of the Church against Severian, and to having abused Epiphanius, and refused to speak to Acacius; to his use of certain enthusiastic expressions in his sermons, from which were drawn various inferences that savoured of heresy. Amongst the indictments brought against him was the charge of inhospitality, of violence of behaviour, of trespassing on the jurisdiction of other bishops, of comparing the empress to Jezebel—a charge which was regarded as identical with instigating the people to rebellion. Strange to say, no charge was made against Chrysostom for favouring the views of Origen, though that very subject was the ostensible cause for holding the synod.

The synod sat during fourteen days. Four times

R

(it is said by Sozomen and Photius) was Chrysostom summoned to appear before it; but he refused with dignity to present himself before a packed synod composed of those who were opposed to him—Theophilus, himself an accused party, being a member—before which he was summoned by his own disaffected clergy. He demanded to be tried by a legally constituted council; but still, to prevent all public disturbance, he declared himself willing to appear before it, on condition that his four most embittered enemies, Theophilus, Severian, Antiochus, and Acacius, were removed from the number of judges. To this proposal no answer was vouchsafed. Many summonses and counter-summonses took place, which, though made and replied to with noise and violent language, ended in nothing which might be regarded as final.

A fresh list of charges—many of them like those brought against him before—was now preferred against him by a bishop, according to Photius, called Isaac, though Cave regards him as Isaac the Monk.

Three of them were remarkable. One was, that Chrysostom had spoken in a strong and unseemly manner respecting the ' fervour of rapturous devotion ;' another, that he had uttered, in unqualified language, ' assurances of the Divine long-suffering,'—' If you sin again, repent again,'—which was regarded as an inducement to the sinful to continue in sin, and afforded grounds for the title of ' John of Repentance' being given him ;[1] a third, that ' he had eaten before administering baptism, and given the

---

[1] Sisinnius, the Novatian bishop, whom Socrates much admired (vi. 4), wrote a treatise against Chrysostom in regard to his views on this subject.

eucharist to persons who were not fasting;'—which
latter charge he vehemently denied, praying that,
if he had done this, his name might be effaced
from the roll of bishops, and that he might be
anathema. .

Chrysostom now convened another synod, more
fairly constituted, consisting of forty bishops who
were not unfavourable to his cause. This counter-
synod wrote a letter of remonstrance to Theophilus,
but it only met with silent contempt.

The Synod of the Oak, at its twelfth sitting,
received a communication from Arcadius, requesting
a speedy settlement of the case. The members
proceeded accordingly, with all expedition, to examine
into the twenty-nine articles brought against Chrysostom. Of these they pronounced twenty-five to be
frivolous ; but they admitted the truth of the others.
At last they condemned him unanimously as con-
tumacious, and deposed him. The count which
charged him with sedition, and with calling the
empress ' Jezebel,' they left to the emperor, with
the full expectation that the civil power would find
him guilty of high treason. Disappointment was
felt by many members of the synod when the
emperor simply confirmed the judgment of the
synod, and pronounced on him the sentence of
banishment for life. So ended the Synod of the
Oak. 'Chrysostom,' remarks Milner,[1] 'foreseeing the
effect of the storm which was gathering round him,
addressed himself to the bishops who were his
friends, assembled in the great room of his house.
" Brethren," he said, "be earnest in prayer ; and as

---

[1] *Church History*, ii. p. 102. The passage is also quoted by Cave, ii.
p. 484.

you love our Lord Jesus, let none of you for my sake desert his charge. For, as was Paul's case, I am ready to be offered up, and the time of my departure is at hand. I see I must undergo many hardships, and then quit this troublesome life. I know the subtilty of Satan, who cannot bear to be daily tormented with my preaching. By your constancy you will find mercy at the hand of God; only remember me in your prayers." The assembly being afflicted with vehement sorrow, he besought them to moderate their grief; "for to me to live is Christ, and to die is gain." "I always told you this life is a road in which joys and sorrows both pass swiftly away. The visible scene of things before us is like a fair, where we buy and sell, and sometimes recreate ourselves. Are we better than the patriarchs? Do we excel the prophets and apostles, that we should live here for ever?'

When one of the company passionately bewailed the desolations of the Church, the bishop, striking the end of his right fore-finger on the palm of his left hand (which he was accustomed to do when much in earnest), said, 'Brother, it is enough; pursue the subject no further. However, as I requested, desert not your churches. As for the doctrine of Christ, it began not with me, nor shall it die with me. Did not Moses die? and did not Joshua succeed him? Paul was beheaded, and left he not Timothy, Titus, Apollos, and many more behind him?' Eulysius, Bishop of Apamea, answered, 'But if we keep our churches, we shall be compelled to communicate and subscribe.' 'Communicate,' returns he, 'you may, that you make not a schism in the Church; but subscribe not the decrees,—for I am not conscious

of having done anything for which I should desire
to be deposed.'

Chrysostom was a stranger to all personal fear.
'What,' he exclaimed, 'can I fear? Will it be death?
But you know that Christ is my life, and that I shall
gain by death. Will it be exile? But the earth and
all its fulness is the Lord's. Will it be the loss of
wealth? But we have brought nothing into the
world, and can carry nothing out. Thus all the
terrors of the world are contemptible in my eyes ;
and I smile at all its good things. Poverty I do
not fear ; riches I do not sigh for. Death I do not
shrink from ; and life I do not desire, save only for
the progress of your souls.' 'You know,' he once
remarked, 'my friends, the true cause of my fall. It
is that I have not lined my house with rich tapestry.
It is that I have not clothed myself in robes of silk.
It is that I have not flattered the effeminacy and
sensuality of certain men, nor laid silver and gold
at their feet.'

CHAPTER VIII.

CHRYSOSTOM'S FIRST EXILE AND RETURN.

> ' And thus for thee, O glorious man, on whom
> Love well-deserved, and honour waited long,
> In thy last years, in place of timely ease,
> There did remain another loftier doom,
> Pain, travail, exile, peril, scorn, and wrong—
> Glorious before, but glorified through these.'

CHRYSOSTOM was condemned to exile, but the people, who were devoted to his cause, raised a loud and indignant clamour against the sentence which had been pronounced upon their favourite prelate. As the sentence of exile became more and more known, the rage and fury of the populace became greater and greater. A vast crowd assembled around the doors both of his own house and of the church, in order to prevent him from being hurried away by his enemies. For three days and three nights this popular guard protected their beloved archbishop. At this time he possessed unlimited power over the people, and a mere hint from him would have produced rebellion. But never in his sermons during this supreme crisis did he excite the populace to any deeds of violence, but, on the contrary, urged them to acquiesce in the decrees of Providence, and to a spirit of resignation to the will of the Almighty. ' Chrysostom,' remarks Dean Milman,[1] 'shrank, whether

[1] *History of Christianity*, iii. ix. p. 141.

from timidity or Christian peacefulness of disposition, from being the cause, even innocently, of tumult and bloodshed.   He had neither the ambition, the desperate recklessness, nor perhaps the resolution of a demagogue.   He would not be the Christian tribune of the people.'

On the third day, during the time of the mid-day meal, he secretly went out by a side door, and, escaping the notice of his audience, surrendered himself up to the officers of the imperial guard. He uttered no word of complaint.   He simply thanked God and said, 'The Lord gave ; the Lord hath taken away : blessed be the name of the Lord.'

He was cautiously conducted by them, under the favouring shelter of darkness, to the harbour, where he was placed on board a vessel, in which he sailed to Hieron, on the opposite side of the Bosphorus,[1] and was conveyed thence to Prænetum, near Nico-media, in Bithynia.   Thus were the citizens, who crowded every street in order to rescue the bishop, eluded ; and Chrysostom was kept in confinement in a villa on the shore.

The triumph of Chrysostom's enemies, it has been said, now seemed to be complete and final. His relentless opponent Theophilus made his way to Constantinople, and not only so, but proceeded to revenge himself on the followers of Chrysostom. The empress, too, exulted in being able to shake off the ascendency of one who interfered with her own ambitious schemes.   The very people who had been hitherto his staunch supporters seemed at the first moment dazed and stunned with the blow

---

[1] See Soc. vi. 15, and Sozom. viii. 18.

inflicted on their favourite, and maintained a gloomy silence, irresolute how to act in the emergency.

Soon, however, they crowded to the church, and poured forth bitter lamentations. They were violently driven thence by the imperial officers. Indignant and enraged at the grievous loss which they had sustained, they loudly clamoured at the doors of the emperor's palace, and demanded not only the bishop's return, but also that a proper and lawful council should be summoned to try his case. A popular insurrection seemed imminent.

But on the night of the following day 'strange and awful sounds were heard throughout the city,' which was convulsed by an earthquake. The palace was shaken with peculiar violence. The couch of Eudoxia rocked to and fro beneath her. The empress, as superstitious as she was headstrong, shuddered at what she ascribed to the wrath of Heaven, and fell down at the feet of her imperial husband, earnestly beseeching him to recall Chrysostom from exile, and so avert God's anger against them. She herself wrote in haste a letter, in which she disclaimed all feelings of anger against the exiled bishop, and protested that she was innocent of his blood. The following day a clamorous crowd besieged the palace, demanding the bishop's restoration. The voice of the people —so it has been said—and the voice of God seemed to join in the vindication of Chrysostom. Emissaries were sent in different directions to find the exiled bishop, taking with them letters, written in a most humble and even servile spirit. The edict of recall was published. The news diffused the utmost joy amongst his friends. The Bosphorus was alive with boats, eager to convey back the idol of the people.

Torches blazed on every side. Hymns of triumph, composed for the occasion, were sung before him as he advanced on his way. The whole population, as it seemed, went out to meet and to welcome him. His enemies retired into obscurity.

Chrysostom halted at first outside the city, at a village called Marianæ, near Anaplus, about four miles from Constantinople, demanding his acquittal by a general council before his restoration to his see. The populace imagined that another plot was being contrived, and employed strong language against the emperor and the empress. The emperor, fearing an insurrection, wrote to Chrysostom, urging him to enter the city. He obeyed the royal summons. The empress also sent. a congratulatory message to him on his return, expressing her satisfaction that now the head was restored to the body, the shepherd to his flock, the helmsman to the ship.

No sooner had he entered the gates than he was borne on high by his friends, in the midst of torches and the singing of hymns, carried into the church, seated on his archiepiscopal throne, and compelled to deliver an address on the spur of the moment. 'What shall I say?' he exclaims. 'Blessed be God! These were my last words on my departure—these the first on my return. Blessed be God! because He permitted the storm to rage. Blessed be God! because He has allayed it.'[1]

The triumph of Chrysostom was now consummated. His influence with the people was unbounded.

His enemies did not even yet despair. Theo-

---

[1] Doubts are entertained as to the authenticity of Chrysostom's first discourse on this occasion. Baronius thinks that it is lost; but it is found in the *Life of Chrysostom* by George, the Patriarch of Alexandria.

philus still tarried in Constantinople, hoping that some change of feeling might occur. But their cause was thoroughly unpopular, and they could not appear in public without being insulted and attacked. Theophilus, indeed, felt that his person was no longer safe in Constantinople; nor was it, for the people searched for him, with the intention of throwing him into the sea: and he dreaded also the decision of a general council that might be convened to examine into his conduct. Accordingly, putting forward the excuse that his diocese required his presence, he left the city suddenly and unexpectedly, and sailed away, under cover of night, to Alexandria. Before leaving, wishing to be at peace with the monks, he is said to have compelled, by virtue of their monastic obedience, the two surviving 'Tall Brethren' to beg his pardon. Two of them, Dioscorus and Ammonius, were already dead—the former before his death having earnestly prayed to God, either 'that he might see the peace of the Church, or be himself translated into a better land;' the latter having foretold persecution and then peace for the Church, which subsequently came to pass.

Sozomen (viii. 18) relates that Severian was also expelled from Constantinople for daring to preach a sermon against Chrysostom.

The departure of Theophilus was speedily followed by the summoning of another synod, consisting of about sixty bishops, which entirely set aside the decrees of the Synod of the Oak, and pronounced Chrysostom to be the lawful Bishop of Constantinople. Such a decree as this removed all the scruples which Chrysostom entertained as to the legality of his status as bishop; and he forthwith returned to the fulfilment of his customary duties.

He was, moreover, reinstated in the favour of the empress, who seemed to have forgotten all her former animosity against him. Extravagant compliments were again reciprocally expressed between the empress and the archbishop. They appeared unable to praise each other too much or in too strong language. But the reconciliation between them was not destined to be permanent. It was the result more of fear and self-interest, on the part at least of the empress, than of real attachment. When her fears diminished, the long-standing animosity between them began again to show itself. She could not quite lull the suspicions that rankled in her mind, that the eloquent preacher had alluded to her and to her foibles not unfrequently in his sermons. Her ambition, too, did not seem satisfied with the supremacy which she had acquired over the sovereign of the East, but she even aspired to divine honours and worship.

On a lofty column of porphyry was erected a silver statue of the empress, in the lesser forum, near the front entrance of the Church of St. Sophia. It was dedicated in September, 403 A.D., under the superintendence of the prefect of the city (who was a Manichæan), with loud and licentious revelry, accompanied with wild dances, and with almost pagan adoration on the part of the people. The uproar from this unbecoming consecration was heard within the walls of the church, and marred the solemnity of the sacred services. Chrysostom's indignation was aroused at this, and, urged on by feelings of inconsiderate zeal, he delivered a sermon from the pulpit of the church, in which he denounced in the very strongest language all who were concerned in the erection of this statue and in its consecration, from the empress and the prefect down to the lowest of the people. Such intemperate language was naturally reported to Eudoxia, who was greatly exasperated by what Chrysostom had said of her.

When her feelings of indignation were reported to him, he exclaimed, at a festival in commemoration of John the Baptist, 'Herodias is again raging; Herodias is again dancing; once more she demands the head of John in a charger.'[1]

This strong language was conveyed, as a truthful report, to Eudoxia. It is scarcely strange that the empress was violently enraged with the audacious prelate, who had dared, according to the report brought to her, thus to speak of her in public, and that she required from Arcadius full redress for such an insult offered to her. The time for reconciliation seemed past and gone. No compromise appeared to be possible. The haughty prelate must be humbled.

---

[1] Both Montfaucon and Tillemont regard the address which begins in these words as spurious.

CHAPTER IX.

CHRYSOSTOM'S SECOND CONDEMNATION AND EXILE.

> 'O comrade bold of toil and pain !
>   Thy trial how severe,
> When severed first by prisoner's chain
> From thy loved labour-sphere.'

No sooner did Chrysostom incur the odium of the Court and the nobility, than his old enemies started up again into active life from every side. They came trooping into Constantinople from Syria, Egypt, and Asia, all impelled with the one desire of crushing and ruining the prospects of Chrysostom. Again we find Severian and Antiochus and Acacius at Constantinople, carrying on their intrigues together, and endeavouring to weaken the influence of Chrysostom with the recusant clergy and the rich widows in the city. For some time past Chrysostom had been importuning the emperor to convene a general council. They also thought it well that such a council should be assembled ; and they imagined that much might be done to further their plans, if its members were judiciously selected. They proposed that the latest expressions of Chrysostom, which might be regarded as treasonable, should be laid before the council, and its opinion taken upon them. Theophilus was too crafty to appear in person on the scene. He deemed it the wiser and more prudent course to direct the movements of the conspiracy from a distance. He artfully suggested that they should employ against Chrysostom the 12th canon of an Arianising council held at Antioch in 341 A.D., which had been brought to bear against Athanasius. In this canon it was enacted that any bishop should at once be deprived, if, after his condemnation, he appealed to the civil power for restoration to his see.

The council which was to try Chrysostom met at the close of the year 403 A.D. On Christmas-day Arcadius declined to communicate, as he usually did, at the great church, alleging that Chrysostom's position as archbishop was not legally fixed. So decisive a step as this on the part of one ordinarily so irresolute was regarded as indicating a clear bias on his part against Chrysostom. In the council there were forty-two bishops who sided with Chrysostom, and averred that the canon did not apply to his particular case. He himself was calm and undaunted. He never ceased to address his flock from the pulpit, and never addressed them with greater power and persuasiveness than during this time of anxiety and peril.

When the council could come to no practical conclusion on the point at issue, they proposed to request the emperor to decide the question for them. Elpidius, the venerable Bishop of Laodicea, who was himself a confessor, acting in the interest of Chrysostom, suggested that Antiochus and Acacius, who were the chief advocates of the authority of the 12th canon of the Council of Antioch, should sign a statement, in which they affirmed that their theological views were in agreement with the sentiments of those who were the original promoters of the council. It was notorious that these men were for the most part Arians. The emperor saw through the artifice, and entering into it, at once advocated the proposal. The two bishops, when they perceived that they were thus entrapped in the meshes of the net which had been set for them, became livid[1] with anger. They were, however, obliged to conceal their vexation, and agree in words to a compliance.

The council ultimately held that his violation of the Council of Antioch had, in their final judgment, *ipso facto* deposed him. Chrysostom's friends asked, in reply to this decision, 'Will you then commit yourselves to a council which condemned Athanasius, and to a canon repudiated at Sardica?' Easter, however, was now rapidly drawing near. Could the emperor be allowed a second time to be excluded from the reception of the Holy Communion on the highest festival of the Church? They accordingly came to the conclusion that Chrysostom must be deposed even by force, should force be needed ; and that he ought not to be permitted, on a chief festival, to address the congregation in the cathedral, lest the people, who still idolised him, should be led into insurrection.

Induced by such arguments as these, and by the assertion of Antiochus and those who thought with him, that Chrysostom was actually deposed, and no longer Archbishop of Constantinople, the emperor gave orders for his removal, notwithstanding the urgent appeal in his favour of the forty bishops who were keeping Lent with him. To an officer of the

---

[1] Ἐπὶ τὸ πελιδνότερον μεταβαλόντας τὴν μορφήν. Pallad., p. 80. Quoted in Dr. Smith's *Dictionary of Christian Biography.*

emperor, who was sent to order the archbishop to quit the church at once, Chrysostom replied that duty forbade him to desert his post. If the emperor chose to drive him out by force, he would then be able to feel that his conduct, as being involuntary, was excusable. Arcadius, dreading again to incur the wrath of Heaven, hesitated to employ force, and commanded him to remain in close confinement in his palace, and not to enter the church without permission.

But the courage of Chrysostom did not fail. He felt that he could not be absent from the church on Easter-eve, when the great body of catechumens presented themselves for baptism. On this occasion no fewer than 3,000 catechumens would desire to be baptised. The time for the celebration of this great function had now arrived, and Chrysostom, feeling that he must obey God rather than man, walked quietly into the church. The soldiers had received orders not to make use of any forcible method of procedure, and were accordingly unable to act in the emergency. Arcadius, in his difficulty, consulted Antiochus and Acacius as to the course which he ought to follow, upbraiding them for having led him into such a dilemma. They boldly replied that Chrysostom, being deposed, would violate the law in administering the sacraments. They were willing, they said, to bear the brunt of his deposition. Arcadius was delighted to have the onus of the responsibility in regard to the bishop's condemnation laid on the shoulders of others, and gave orders to his officers to remove Chrysostom from the cathedral, inasmuch as he was performing functions which he was not legally qualified to discharge, and to place him in confinement in his own house.

It was the vigil of the Resurrection, and a vast congregation thronged the cathedral to celebrate the occasion. Long rows of catechumens were being led up for the sacrament of baptism, after the deacons and deaconesses had respectively prepared the candidates for the solemn rite by the removal of their outer garments. It was at this solemn moment that the hoarse clamours of the rude soldiery filled the sacred building. These rough barbarians burst into the church, and rushed to the places where baptism was taking place, advancing to the pulpit, and even to the altar. They drove with their swords the catechumens from the font, which was actually defiled by blood. They also proceeded to the baptisteries where the female candidates were preparing for the rite, and drove them, with brutal violence, half-clothed into the streets. It was rumoured that some of these idolatrous troops had even broken open the sanctuary, and touched with profane hands the sacred elements that were there. No one was safe from their rude assaults. The clergy, in their vestments, together with a vast crowd of men, women, and children were expelled from the church at the point of the sword, and pursued along the dark and gloomy streets. With a holy courage, the catechumens reassembled at the Baths of Constantine, together with the officiating clergy. Just as they were about to recommence the ceremony, 400 fierce and brutal Thracians, commanded by Lucius, attacked them with revolting violence : wounded in the head the chief of the staff of the clergy ; injured the arm of one of the deacons ; stripped the altar, which had been hastily arranged, of its valuable vessels ; and carried off the vestments of the clergy and the ornaments and dresses of the women. Many of those who were driven out by the soldiers were wounded, and some were taken off to prison, where they sang hymns and celebrated the Holy Communion. The unutterable terrors of that fearful night were stamped deeply and ineffaceably on the memories of those who endured or witnessed the awful scenes.

During the whole of the Easter week, Constantinople continued like a besieged city. Private houses were broken into and ransacked in order to search for any secret meetings. The Joannites, the followers of John Chrysostom, were ill-treated, scourged, tortured, cast into prison, on the very slightest suspicion of guilt or complicity. It was said that the sound of the scourge and the blasphemies of the soldiers could be heard even in the church itself. For two long and anxious months Chrysostom remained in his palace, unceasingly guarded by relays of his own followers. Twice was his life in jeopardy from the hands of assassins—in one instance by a man pretending to be insane; in another by a servant of Elpidius, a presbyter, a violent opponent of Chrysostom, who murdered several persons before he was captured. Chrysostom sent an account of these terrible events to the bishops of Rome, Aquileia, and Milan. But not yet could Arcadius make up his mind to attach his signature to the rescript for his exile. Finally, however, on June 5th, 404 A.D., he was induced to sign the decree, which was sent by Patricius, secretary to the emperor, in the following form to Chrysostom :—' Acacius, Antiochus, Severianus, Cyrinus, and their party, have taken your condemnation upon themselves ; as soon, therefore,

as you have disposed and commended your affairs
to God, depart from the church.'

With perfect calmness was the order received by
the archbishop. He offered up one last prayer in
his beloved cathedral, with some bishops who still
remained faithful to his cause, and then prepared to
obey the decree. To avoid all fear of insurrection
by the people on his behalf, he ordered his horse
to be led round, saddled, to the principal entrance
on the west side of the palace ; but in the meantime,
after a tender parting with his dear friend Olympias
and the attendant deaconesses, Silvina—the widow of
Nebridius—Procla, and Pentadia, who could with
difficulty be removed, and whom he urged to yield
to the authority of his successor, he passed quietly
out at a side door of the palace. His language to
the deaconesses was,—' Come hither, daughters, and
hearken to what I say. The things that concern me
have, I perceive, an end. I have finished my course,
and perhaps ye shall see my face no more. This
is that which I earnestly beg of you, that none of
you would lay aside your accustomed care and
diligence towards the Church. If any one that is
unwilling shall be ordained to this place, and shall be
chosen by common consent, and not ambitiously
seek it, submit to him as if it were myself ; for the
Church cannot be without a bishop. So shall you
obtain mercy from God. Be mindful of me in your
prayers.' He then resigned himself into the hands
of the officers of the imperial guard, calling to mind,
in regard to his exile, that 'the earth was the Lord's,
and the fulness thereof,' and repeating the words of
Job, ' Naked came I out of my mother's womb, and
naked shall I return thither.' Accompanied by two

bishops, Cyrinus and Eulysius, who refused to leave him, he was placed, in the darkness of the night, on board a vessel, and conveyed to the coast of Asia.

Scarcely had Chrysostom quitted the city, when a fire, which was said to have originated in the bishop's throne, caught the roof of the cathedral, and quickly spread to every part of the buildings except the sacristy. It extended, moreover, to the senate-house —an equally magnificent building, and rich in specimens of ancient art—as well as to some other public edifices. The real origin of the fire was never discovered. By some it was ascribed to incendiaries; by others it was regarded as an evidence of the just anger of Heaven; but, as was natural, suspicion fell on the Joannites, or partisans of Chrysostom, who were said to have caused the fire in order that no one should minister in the church which was so deeply associated with the preaching of Chrysostom. His adherents were, on this suspicion, which was no doubt baseless, subjected to a most severe persecution. They were put to the torture by Optatus, the prefect of the city, that they might be induced to denounce the guilty parties, but with no effect. In some cases, as in that of the presbyter Tigrius, and of Eutropius, his youthful reader, the torture was carried to such an extent that the victims expired under it; while others were mutilated for life by their relentless persecutors. The accounts of the sufferings of his adherents, and especially of the noble-hearted Olympias, greatly affected Chrysostom. When Olympias was interrogated as having been concerned in the fire, she nobly replied, ' My life up to this time is an answer to such a charge. A person who has expended so much on church-building is not likely to destroy churches.'

Chrysostom's followers, moreover, were charged with contumaciously refusing to communicate with his successors in the bishopric: namely, Arsacius, who was eighty years old, the brother of Nectarius, the predecessor of Chrysostom, who died a year after his appointment, on November 11th, 405 A.D.; and Atticus, who succeeded Arsacius in 406 A.D. Atticus had been one of the chief accusers of Chrysostom at the Synod of the Oak, and is called by Palladius πάσης μηχανῆς τεχνίτης, the man who had devised the whole plot against him. He was born at Sebastea, in Armenia, and educated among the monks. He was, according to Cave, 'a man rather subtle than learned, and fitter to lay a crafty plot than to dispute for and defend the faith.' He was endued with no eloquence, but 'in his conversation smooth and plausible, and knew how to adapt himself to the persons that he had to deal with.' He proved a stern persecutor of the Joannites. The refusal to communicate constituted an offence to which the most severe penalties were attached.

The faithful deaconesses remained true to the cause of Chrysostom after his expulsion from the city, and were exposed to many cruel sufferings in consequence. Olympias—who was attached to Chrysostom by spiritual ties of the closest character—was nobly born and of great beauty, the daughter of Count Seleucus, the granddaughter of Ablavius, one of Constantine's prætorian prefects, and the widow of Nebridius, a prefect, to whom she was married less than two years. The Emperor Theodosius desired her as a wife for his kinsman Elpidius, but in vain. Rich, devout, and well known, she was not only accused of having set fire to Chrysostom's church, but also fined, and afterwards banished to Nicomedia, in Bithynia. From Chrysostom's letters—no less than seventeen in number—addressed to her in her exile, we see that she bore her sufferings with the greatest fortitude and resignation. Another deaconess, whose name has been already mentioned, Pentadia, who was also of high rank, the widow of the consul Timasius, suffered with patient endurance the afflictions which befel her in the city after Chrysostom's departure, and became an example of holiness of life to those among whom she dwelt. The faithful clergy, too, were expelled from their sacred offices and driven into banishment; while those six bishops whom Chrysostom had deposed were restored to their sees. So savage was the treatment to which the persecuted were exposed, that many died before they reached their places of exile. No efforts, however cruel, were spared to crush the adherents of the exiled prelate. Their religious meetings were forbidden, and masters were ordered to prevent their servants going to them. If they permitted it they were heavily fined. Soldiers broke up their meetings with brutal violence. The bishops, also, who were favourable to Chrysostom endured the most terrible sufferings during the persecution. These efforts of repression were not confined to Constantinople, but extended also to Syria and Asia Minor. As is usually the case, however, such acts of cruelty only tended to enhance the love of his followers for their banished bishop, and to render their determination to resist all the stronger.

At last, when the persecution to which they were exposed did not diminish, they resolved to make an appeal to the bishops of the Western Church. Chrysostom himself, the forty bishops who were his friends, and the clergy of Constantinople, despatched letters to Innocent, Bishop of Rome, Venerius of Milan, and Chromatius of Aquileia. Theophilus and his party made also a representation of their own views, in opposition to that which Chrysostom and his friends had made. Innocent at once perceived which side was in the right. He declared that Chrysostom had been unfairly deposed, and set aside his deposition, because it had been pronounced when Chrysostom was absent. He also wrote to the principal persons concerned in the matter. His letter to Theophilus was one of decided rebuke. 'Brother Theophilus,' he wrote, 'we hold communion both with yourself and our brother Chrysostom, as we gave you to understand in our former letters, and do still continue in the same opinion and resolution, now again plainly declaring to you (and so we shall as oft as you send) that unless a more just and equal determination be made about these things that have been so childishly and ridiculously managed, we cannot with any reason or justice withdraw ourselves from Chrysostom's communion. If, therefore, you dare abide by the judgment you have made, make your appearance before a synod to be assembled according to the laws of Christ, and there unfold your accusations, and prosecute the charge according to the canons of the Nicene Council (for no other rule does the Church of Rome allow of), and then you will gain unquestionable strength and security to your cause.'

To the clergy of Constantinople, Innocent wrote in cordial sympathy; and to Chrysostom himself his letter was full of affectionate and cheering condolence. 'A good man,' he wrote, 'can be exercised, but he cannot be overcome while the Divine Scriptures strengthen his mind. Venerable brother, let your conscience comfort you.'

He also induced the Emperor Honorius to write to his brother Arcadius, pressing earnestly upon him the duty of summoning a general council at Thessalonica. A deputation of Western bishops conveyed the letter to Constantinople. But they were never permitted to see Arcadius. The letter was rudely taken from them, and in the struggle the thumb of Marianus, one of the bishops, was broken. They were treated with the greatest rudeness and violence, robbed, subjected to most shameful insults, and compelled to return home. It would appear that Chrysostom wrote three letters to them, thanking them for their kindness and courage in thus befriending his cause. After encountering many perils, and having narrowly escaped foundering at sea from the wretched state of the vessel on board which they were put, they at length landed on the coast of Calabria, and made their way to Rome, after an ineffectual journey, which had occupied four months.

CHAPTER X.

CHRYSOSTOM'S EXILE AT CUCUSUS, AND DEATH.

' In a series of trials which conducted him towards a glorious end,
Chrysostom had every opportunity of manifesting the greatness, power,
and tranquillity of a soul wholly penetrated by the faith of the Gospel.
—Neander.

> ' I would not miss one sigh or tear,
> Heart-pang, or throbbing brow ;
> Sweet was the chastisement severe,
> And sweet its memory now.'

THE spot chosen by Eudoxia for the exile of
Chrysostom was cruelly selected. It was, perhaps,
chosen as having been the place where his predecessor Paulus, in the reign of Constantine, had
been banished, and where he had died under the
hands of Philip, the governor. Cucusus—such was
its name—was a secluded and solitary village of
Cataonia, situated in a deep valley of the range
of Taurus, in Lesser Armenia, and on the border-
land of Cilicia. Not only was the climate of this
mountain-village most rigorous, but it was also subject to the fierce attacks of marauding Isaurians.
Chrysostom was not informed of his place of exile
until he reached Nicæa. Scythia had first been
named ; and afterwards Sebaste, in Pontus. However great his regret might have been when he
was told of the place of his exile, he felt that all

objection on his part would be utterly futile. The healthful breezes that blew from the lake Ascanius, on the eastern end of which the Bithynian Nicæa— sacred as the spot where the great council had been held about eighty years before—was situated, refreshed and strengthened the worn and weary frame of Chrysostom, and prepared him in some degree for the long journey of seventy days to Cucusus. 'The lake of Ascanius,' observes Leake, in his *Asia Minor*, 'is about ten miles long and four wide, surrounded on three sides by steep woody slopes, behind which rise the snowy summits of the Olympus range.'

While at Nicæa, Chrysostom wrote several letters to his friends, and one or two to Olympias. In one addressed to her, he says:—' My consolation increases with my trial. I am sanguine about the future. Everything is going on prosperously, and I am sailing with a fair wind. There are, indeed, hidden rocks, there are tempests, the night is moonless, the darkness thick, and crags and cliffs are before me ; yet, though I am navigating a sea like this, still I am not at all in worse case than many a man who is tossing about in harbour. Reflect on this, my religious lady, and rise above these alarms and troubles ; and please to tell me about your own health : for myself, I am in health and in spirits. I find myself stronger than I was ; I breathe a pure air ; the soldiers of the prefecture, who are to accompany me, are so atten- tive as to leave me no need even of domestics, for they take on themselves domestic duties. They actually volunteered this charge of me for love of me ; and wherever I go I have a bodyguard, each of them thinking himself happy in such a ministry. I have one drawback—my anxiety for your health. Inform me on this point.'—(*Ep.* xi.). A few days after he again writes to her: ' Have no fear,' he says, 'about this either—I mean my journey ; as I have already written you word, I am improved in health and strength. The climate has agreed with me ; and my conductors have shown every wish, and done all in their power—more, indeed, than I desired myself—to make me comfortable. I have written this when on the point of starting from Nicæa, the 3rd July. Give me some account from time to time of your own health ; and also tell me that the cloud of despondency has passed away from you.'[1]

It is not impossible that, in writing to Olympias, he may have spoken in the most hopeful manner, in order to mitigate her grief. We have another letter, written about this same time, addressed to Constantius, a friend, and a presbyter of Antioch, in which he enters into more particulars respecting himself and his feelings. ' I am to set off,' he writes, ' on July 4th from Nicæa. I send you this letter to urge you, as I never cease to urge, though the storm increase in fury and the waves mount higher, not to fail to do your part in the matter which you originally undertook—I mean the destruction of the Greek worship, the erection of churches, and the care of souls,—and not to let the difficulties of things throw you upon your back. For myself, if I do not take my share of the work, but am remiss, I shall not be able to excuse myself by my present trouble. Remembering this, do not give over your duties towards Phœnicia, Arabia, and the churches of the East, knowing that your reward will only be the

---

[1] See Dr. Newman's *Historical Sketches*, vol. iii. p. 241, seq.

greater if, amid so many hindrances, you contribute
towards the work.   And do not be backward in
writing to me from time to time, nay, very frequently ;
for I now know that I am sent, not to Sebaste, but
to Cucusus, whither it will be easier for you to get
letters to me.   Write me word how many churches
are built every year, and what holy men have passed
into Phœnicia, and what progress they have made.
As to Salamis, in Cyprus, which is beset by the
Marcionite heretics, I should have treated with the
proper persons, and set everything right, but for
my banishment.   Urge those especially who have
familiar speech with God, to use much prayer with
much perseverance for the stilling of the tempest,
which is at present wrecking the whole world.'

The journey to Cucusus was painfully fatiguing.
The sultry heat of the summer was sufficiently
oppressive ; but it was rendered all the more trying,
because his escort had received orders from headquarters to press forward as fast as they could,
without any regard to the archbishop's infirmities.
The two officers to whom he was intrusted, Ana-
tolius and Theodorus, did all they could by kindness and personal services to lessen his sufferings.
But the summer sun was shining down with all its
fiery force upon the wide and torrid plains of Galatia
and Cappadocia.   Instructions had been given to
avoid all the cities and towns, and to put up for the
night at wretched villages, where but little suitable
food could be procured.   Black bread was all that
they could generally obtain, and this was so dry
and hard that Chrysostom could not eat it until
it had been soaked in water.   The drinking-water,
too, was impregnated with bitumen, and unwholesome,

and was little suited to quench the insatiable thirst which the heat and dust created. The bishop was attacked by ague and fever combined, and could scarcely travel. Still the orders to press on with all speed must be obeyed. No delay was tolerated, though he felt cheered by the sympathy of the crowds who condoled with him on the way (*Ep.* ix.); and in a state of utter exhaustion he reached the city of Cæsarea.

He might have expected to find a warm welcome and kindly consideration from a successor of the saintly Basil ; but Pharetrius, who now filled the episcopal chair, was decidedly inimical to Chrysostom, though he was afraid to display openly his ill-feelings towards him, on account of his people, who favoured the cause of the archbishop. He had, indeed, sent clandestinely his agreement to whatever decrees the council might think proper to make against him. Chrysostom's stoppage at Cæsarea was consequently very displeasing to Pharetrius. If he treated Chrysostom with indifference, or neglect, or harshness, his clergy would all rise up in indignation against such treatment, for they were almost all Joannites. On the other hand, by treating him with kindness and consideration, he would fall under the displeasure of the angry empress. Distracted by these conflicting opinions, he avoided, on different excuses, any intercourse with Chrysostom, and contented himself with sending messages which were apparently of a friendly character. He secretly longed for the time when the archbishop would have quitted his city. But a still more severe attack of ague and fever rendered it impossible for Chrysostom to leave Cæsarea at the present moment. Medical assistance had to be called in. The love and affection which the whole population of the city manifested towards him was far from agreeable to Pharetrius.

From Cæsarea he wrote as cheerfully as he could to Olympias :—'Now that I have got rid of the ailment which I suffered on my journey, the remains of which I carried with me into Cæsarea, and am already restored to perfect health, I write to you from that place. I have had the advantage here of much careful treatment at the hands of the first and most celebrated physicians, who nevertheless did even more for me by their sympathy and soothing kindness than by their skill. One of them went so far as to promise to accompany me on my journey ; so, indeed, did also many other persons of consideration. Now, I am often writing to you of my own matters, and you, as I have already complained, are very remiss in that respect yourself. I can prove to you that it is your own neglect, and not the want of letter-carriers. . . . . . . For yourself, write me word frequently how you are, and about my friends ; but as for me, have no anxiety about me, for I am in health and in good spirits, and in the enjoyment of much repose up to this day.' His style, however, sadly changes when writing to Theodora, when at his worst at Cæsarea : —'I am done for ; I am simply spent ; I have died a thousand deaths. On this point the bearers of this will be the best informants, though they were with me only for a very short time. In truth, I was not in a state to converse with them ever so little, being prostrated by continual fever. In this condition I was forced to travel on night and day, stifled by the heat, worn out with sleeplessness, at death's door for want both of necessaries and of persons to attend to me. Hardly and at length I arrived at Cæsarea ; and

I find the place like a calm, like a port after a storm: not that it set me up all at once, after the severe handling that preceded it ; but still, now that I am at Cæsarea, I have recovered a little, since I drink clean water, bread that can be chewed and is not offensive to the senses.   Moreover, I no longer wash myself in broken crockery, but I have contrived some sort of bath ; also I have got a bed to which I can confine myself.'

Another cause also combined to render Chrysostom's stay at Cæsarea somewhat longer. The Isaurian marauders made an attack, which tended to delay his departure. The Isaurians were a bold and hardy race, who lived in the immediate neighbourhood of Mount Taurus, between the countries of Cilicia and Lycaonia. They lived on plunder, and Strabo calls their villages nests of robbers. Their country had, indeed, been overrun by P. Servilius, who derived from the exploit the title of ' Isauricus,' but he had not effectually crushed them.

The impatience of Pharetrius was severely tried by this protracted stay. It would seem probable that he instigated some fanatical monks to attack the house at which Chrysostom was residing, and to threaten to burn it to the ground if he did not instantly leave it. Thus expelled by their fury from the town, the archbishop was unable to proceed on his journey owing to a fresh accession of fever, and was compelled to find a resting-place in the house of a .rich lady, whose residence was outside the city, and whose name was Seleucia, the wife of Ruffinus. But so violent were the threats of Pharetrius, that Seleucia was induced through fear to infringe the duties of hospitality, and to force Chrysostom to quit the house

in the middle of the night, on the plea of an attack
of the Isaurians being imminent, and that his only
chance of security lay in flight.   He had to undergo a
sad and terrible night.   The journey was performed in
utter darkness.   Their torches were extinguished, lest
they should afford a mark to the Isaurians.   His mule,
also, fell down under the burden of his litter, and
Chrysostom was at first picked up as dead.   He was
subsequently carried along mountain paths which
were steep and rugged.   He describes in graphic language, in a letter written to Olympias, the dangers
and sufferings of that midnight march.   The latter
portion of his route during those terrible seventy days
was a little relieved by the presence and kind services
of a physician from Cæsarea, who travelled with him.
He would seem also to have met with much friendly
sympathy from some monks and nuns, who loudly
expressed their sorrow that the voice of the archbishop should be silenced.   He was deeply affected
by their kind solicitude on his behalf.

At length, after the greatest fatigue and peril, he
reached Cucusus in the autumn of 404 A.D.   His reception at his place of exile was far more friendly and
cordial than he could possibly have expected.   It
afforded some compensation for all the sufferings he
had undergone, and the fatigues which he had endured.
Not one, but many residences were immediately placed
at his disposal.   He chose the house of Dioscorus,
who at once, regardless of expense, proceeded to
render it suitable for the residence of one thus
broken down by labours, fatigue, and exposure.   Nor
did he receive less kindness from Adelphius, the
Bishop of Cucusus, who emulated the friendly spirit
evinced by Dioscorus, and even desired to resign

his bishopric into his hands.   Though Cucusus lay so far away from Constantinople, yet many of Chrysostom's friends and adherents at the latter place owned estates in this remote spot.   They wrote accordingly to the managers of their farms, instructing them to supply Chrysostom with all that their estates furnished. Some of those still more attached to him followed him even from Constantinople, and shared his exile with him.   Nor was he without the sympathy of his old friends in Antioch, to whom Cucusus (only about 120 miles distant) was more accessible than Constantinople.   Many of these friends now rallied round him, and comforted him in his exile.

In such intercourse with sympathetic friends he could not fail to have passed many agreeable hours.   He moreover engaged in an extensive correspondence with friends in all quarters, and received many letters from friends in return.   Such employment must have greatly relieved the tedium of his banishment.   He comforted himself by writing to his faithful friend Olympias two treatises—one on the topic that 'No one can be hurt by any one but himself,' and the other addressed 'To those who are scandalised by persecution.'   In one of his letters to her he writes :—'Hardly at length do I breathe again, now that I have reached Cucusus, from which place I write to you ; hardly at length am I in the use of my eyes after the phantoms and the various clouds of ill which beset me during my journey. Now then, since the pain is passed, I will give you an account of it ; for while I was under it I was loth to do so, lest I should distress you too much' (*Ep.* xiii.).   Subsequently, in another letter to her, he says :—' All these evils have vanished.   On arriving

T

at Cucusus, I got rid of all remains of my malady. I am released from my fear of the Isaurians, for there is a strong force of soldiers here. And now I have told you all about me, lest any friend should be precipitate in getting me removed elsewhere.' Again he writes to her :—' Why do you bewail me ? Why are you grieved because you have failed in effecting my removal from Cucusus? What can be more pleasant than my sojourn here ? I have quiet, calm, much leisure, excellent health.'

Writing subsequently to thank Innocent for his sympathy, Chrysostom says that ' in this third year of exile, amidst famine, pestilence, war, sieges, indescribable solitude, and daily peril from Isaurian swords, he was greatly comforted and gratified by the true, constant, and abounding love of Innocent to him.'

But his influence at this time was immense. Never, even as Archbishop of Constantinople, did he wield a greater power and authority than in his lonely retreat at Cucusus. The religious destinies of the East might truly be said to be regulated from a mountain village of distant Armenia, and from Chrysostom's solitary cell there. He received letters, asking for his judgment and advice, from every side. No ecclesiastical movements seemed to be attempted except after consultation with him. Gibbon himself (ch. xxxii.) has said that ' the three years which Chrysostom spent at Cucusus, and the neighbouring town of Arabissus, were the last and most glorious of his life. His character was consecrated by absence and persecution ; the faults of his administration were no longer remembered ; but every tongue repeated the praises of his genius and virtue ; and the respectful attention

of the Christian world was fixed on a desert spot
among the mountains of Taurus. From that solitude
the archbishop, whose active mind was invigorated by
misfortunes, maintained a regular and frequent correspondence with the most distant provinces ; exhorted
the separate congregations of his faithful adherents to
persevere in their allegiance ; urged the destruction
of the temples of Phœnicia, and the extirpation of
heresy in the isle of Cyprus ; extended his pastoral
care to the missions of Persia and Scythia; negoti-
ated, by his ambassadors, with the Roman Pontiff and
the Emperor Honorius ; and boldly appealed, from a
partial synod, to the supreme tribunal of a free and
general council. The mind of the illustrious exile was
still independent ; but his captive body was exposed
to the revenge of the oppressors, who continued to
abuse the name and authority of Arcadius.'

His influence at Constantinople was never greater
than now. He might be deposed from his see, but
no successor to his office could exert a hundredth
part of the influence that he did. He ruled in the
hearts of men with an almost miraculous power. His
numerous letters bear testimony to the interest which
he felt in his old diocese, and show how intimate was
the connection between himself and his friends there.
His letters abound with encouragement, with warning, with exhortation to his followers in that city.
Acutely feeling for the sufferings which their affection
for him and his cause had brought upon so many
bishops, clergy, and laymen at Constantinople, he wrote
to them in terms of the warmest and most tender
sympathy, and endeavoured in all practical ways to
relieve them from the sufferings they endured for his
sake.

His affections also went forth to the poor and the afflicted in and around Cucusus. Much of the money which was sent to him by kind and sympathising friends to supply his own pressing wants, he liberally gave towards the relief of those who were suffering in his own immediate neighbourhood. A famine had pressed severely upon many of the poor in that district. He was ready to supply their wants; and also to redeem the prisoners whom the Isaurian marauders had carried off.

His exile at Cucusus was not without its blessings and its compensations. The intercourse of the bishop Adelphius was sweet and pleasant to him. He could derive much comfort from the greater leisure which he now enjoyed for spiritual meditation and prayer, and for the devout reading of the Word of God. His letters to his friends afforded a pleasing and delightful exercise both to his heart and mind. His consolations to his beloved Olympias assumed the form and size of treatises rather than of letters. In one of his epistles to her he remarks—'There is but one thing to be dreaded, O Olympias, in this world, and that is sin. Nothing besides is alarming. Nothing else can affect the only true life—life eternal.' His life at Cucusus thus became not only tolerable, but agreeable and happy. In a letter to Carterius, the President of Cappadocia, he says,—'Cucusus is a place desolate in the extreme; however, it does not annoy me so much by its desolateness as it relieves me by its quiet and its leisure. Accordingly, I have found a sort of harbour in this desolateness, and have sat me down to recover breath after the miseries of the journey, and have availed myself of the quiet to dispose of what remained both of my illness and of the other troubles which I have undergone. I say this to your illustriousness, knowing well the joy you feel in this rest of mine.'

He wrote also to several other friends at Cæsarea, thanking them for different acts of kindness shown towards him : among them may be mentioned Leontius, in love and recollection of whom he says that he revelled ; Hymnetius, who proved the best of friends and physicians ; and Firminus, who took him captive at first sight, and bound him to himself. But he never, or scarcely ever, calls to mind the harshness and the cruelty which he had received from enemies on his journey. Of such treatment—so far as his letters are concerned—he seems to retain no recollection. He tells Diogenes that in his 'affection he possesses a great treasure and untold wealth,' even though he returns, because he does not need, the presents he had sent him. He thanks Carteria, adding, 'That warm and true charity of yours, so vigorous, so constant, suffices to make me very happy. Such pledges of your warm and true charity have you stored up for me, which length of time can never obliterate.' He felt that he could still do good to others, and share in their sympathies, their labours, and their prayers.

Chrysostom was thus enabled to make manifest the truth and the reality of the Christian religion. He could show in his own life and character the living power which the Gospel could exert over the hearts and wills and affections of men. He could give 'practical evidence of the truth of Christianity, as contrasted with the philosophy and literature of paganism, which had vented themselves in such querulous elegiac dirges as were composed by the

Roman poet Ovid, banished to the same country ; and in such piteous wailings as those of the Stoic Seneca, in his solitary exile in Corsica.'

His practical piety also led him to think of others more than of himself. He often, as we learn from Palladius, preached to the people. His charity, as we have seen, was unstinted towards the poor around him, the captives, and all in distress. His religious spirit led him to foster missionary enterprise in Phœnicia, Cilicia, Persia, and among the Goths. He .was willing even to take the initiative in a reconciliation with Maruthas, Bishop of Mesopotamia, who had been one of those who endeavoured to effect his condemnation, if by that means his missionary projects might be more readily carried out. In one of his letters to Olympias he refers to the death of the great Bishop Unilas, whom he had consecrated, and mentions the fact that the king of the Goths had written to request him to send another bishop like him. He even found time to rebuke two presbyters at Constantinople, who either had not preached at all, or only a very few times, since his departure. 'It has,' so he writes to one of them, 'given me no common pain, that both you and the presbyter Theophilus should have relaxed in your duties. I have received information that one of you has only preached five sermons up to October, and the other none at all. This information has tried me more than my state of desolation here.' With regard to the mission to Phœnicia, he says that he will do all that he can to furnish a missionary for them, even if he has to write to Constantinople a. thousand times about it.

The sufferings of Chrysostom at this time were perhaps physical rather than mental. The changeful nature of the climate at Cucusus, and the long and severe winter, tried him greatly. His worn and exhausted frame could not stand the rapid changes from heat to cold, and from cold to heat. Even with a fire constantly burning, and with abundance of warm coverlets, his ague-stricken body was unable to endure the severity of the weather. He was very frequently compelled to keep his bed for weeks at a time, in consequence of the intense headaches from which he suffered; and on more than one occasion his life was despaired of. Added to this was the constant dread of attacks from the Isaurian banditti. In the winter of 405 A.D., tidings reached Cucusus that the Isaurians meditated a sudden attack upon the place. The great bulk of the inhabitants fled from the town. Chrysostom joined them in their flight. In weakness and feebleness he wandered on from one place to another, accompanied by Evethius, a faithful presbyter, and Sabiniana, an aged deaconess of Constantinople, and other trusty friends, compelled, not unfrequently, to spend the night in rocky ravines and in forests, with the fear of the Isaurians ever haunting them, until at length they arrived at the mountain castle of Arabissus, resembling more nearly a prison than a home, situated about sixty miles from Cucusus.

Here he passed a wretched winter of suffering and anxiety. The fear of famine and pestilence pressed heavily upon him. Invalided though he was, he could procure no medicine to relieve his sufferings. No letters reached him from his friends, and no friends save Theodotus the deacon and Theodotus the reader came to him, since the roads were impassable from snow, and closely beset by the Isaurians, who laid the whole country waste with fire and sword. All these miseries he recounts in different letters, and he also tells us of an attack by night upon the place, in which he was nearly made a prisoner. When winter had passed away, he was able—the Isaurians having, according to their custom, departed also—to go back to Cucusus at the commencement of the year 406 A.D. Cucusus appeared to him almost a paradise after the loneliness and isolation of Arabissus. He was once more brought within the circle of his friends, and he could receive with far greater regularity letters from those who were at a distance from him.

'The spirit of the man,' it has been said, 'and some idea of his style, may be learned from the following literal translation of a paragraph in one of his private letters to a friend, written during his exile, in reference to his banishment :—" When driven from the city, I cared nothing for it. But I said to myself, If the empress wishes to banish me, let her banish me : the earth is the Lord's, and the fulness thereof. If she would saw me in sunder, let her saw me in sunder: I have Isaiah for a pattern. If she would plunge me in the sea, I remember Jonah. If she would thrust me into the fiery furnace, I see the three children enduring that. If she would cast me to wild beasts, I call to mind Daniel in the den of lions. If she would stone me, let her stone me : I have before me Stephen the Protomartyr. If she would take my head from me, let her take it : I have John the Baptist. If she would deprive me of my worldly goods, let her do it : naked came I from my mother's womb, and naked shall I return. An apostle has told me, 'God respecteth no man's person,' and 'if I yet pleased men, I should not be the servant of Christ.' And David clothes me with armour, saying, ' I will speak of Thy testimonies before kings, and will not be ashamed.' " [1]

And now a third winter of exile had arrived. Use had rendered him more capable of enduring the cold and the privations which it brought with it. He tells us in his letters that he had no return of his malady during this winter. ' I have at length learnt,' he writes to Elpidius, ' how to endure an Armenian winter, with some suffering, indeed, such as might be anticipated in the case of so weak a constitution of body, but nevertheless with real success.' He anticipated at this time a return to his work in his old diocese, so mercifully had he been rescued from dangers, and so wonderfully had his health not only been preserved, but even strengthened, in the midst of all his sufferings and privations. ' I do not despair,' he writes to Olympias, ' of happier times, considering that He is at the helm of the universe who overcomes the storm, not by human skill, but by His fiat.' He bids her cherish a full conviction that she would see him once again : ' I speak not simply for the sake of comforting you, but I am sure that thus it shall be. For, had not this been the case, I should have died long since—such are the trials that have befallen me.' These hopes, however, were not destined to be fulfilled.

On September 30th, 404 A.D., a dreadful hail-storm burst over Constantinople. Within the following week Eudoxia died, after prematurely giving birth to a still-born child. She thus preceded Chrysostom to the grave. Cyrinus, Bishop of Chalcedon, one of Chrysostom's avowed enemies, also died. Various calamities took place, which, as we learn from

---

[1] See Mosheim's *Ecclesiastical History*, vol. i. p. 325.

Palladius and Sozomen, were accounted as evidences of the wrath of Heaven against his opponents. But not a few relentless foes still remained. Disappointed that the severity of the climate of Cucusus had not, as they desired, cut off the victim of their hatred, and vexed that his influence, even from his distant place of exile, did not diminish, they succeeded in getting a rescript from Arcadius, in which his place of banishment was changed from Cucusus, first to Arabissus, and then, at a still greater distance from Constantinople, to the little town of Pityus, which lay on the cold, bleak north-eastern shore of 'the Euxine, that strange mysterious sea, which typifies the abyss of outer darkness, the scene of wild unnatural portents, with legends of Prometheus on the savage Caucasus, of Medea gathering witch-herbs in the moist meadows of the Phasis, and of Iphigenia sacrificing the shipwrecked stranger in Taurica.'

Pityus was selected as being the most wind-swept and inhospitable place in the limits of the Roman empire, at the base of Mount Caucasus, and, therefore, as the most likely to bring his existence to a close, even on the supposition that the long and fatiguing three months' journey did not, before his arrival, extinguish his frail life.[1]

Such was the murderous design that received the emperor's approval. Two prætorian guards of notorious ferocity were picked out to execute this deadly commission. No pity was to be shown to their feeble prisoner. They were ordered to accomplish the

---

[1] ' While thus thy deeds declare
Christ's presence, wonder not if fiends conspire
Against thee, forced near the rude Caspian main,
To drink thy Master's cup, in exile, want, and pain.

journey with remorseless expedition. No consideration for the health or comfort of their victim was for a moment to be entertained. Promotion, it was hinted, might be expected if their cruel treatment brought about his death on the journey. He was not to be allowed any conveyance; the journey must be performed on foot. The solace of a hot bath was not to be permitted to the sufferer. No towns, at which comforts could be procured, were to be selected as places for a halt; poor and miserable villages were to be chosen in preference, or they were to spend the night at unsheltered places in the open country. He was to receive no letters; and all communication with strangers or passers-by was to be sternly prevented.

One of the guards was disposed to relent a little in his conduct towards him; but the time of that sad and dreadful journey must have been terrible indeed to the toil-worn and ague-stricken sufferer. His body was scorched by the heat of the glaring sun, so that, as Palladius has remarked, it resembled a ripe apple ready to fall from the tree.

He reached Comana,[1] in Pontus, but it was evident that he could advance with safety no farther on the road. His unrelenting escort, however, hurried him through the town without any halt, till, at about five or six miles beyond Comana, they reached a chapel, with some residences attached to it, which had been erected over the tomb of Basilicus, a martyred bishop of Comana, who had died for the faith of Christ in the reign of Maximin. Here a halt for the night was made. We are told that, during sleep, Chrysostom beheld the martyred bishop

---

[1] Comana Pontica, not Comana in Armenia, as Sozomen asserts.

standing near him, and telling him to 'be of good cheer, for to-morrow they should be together.' A similar vision, it is reported, was previously seen by the priest of the chapel, who was bidden to 'prepare a place for our brother John.' In the morning, Chrysostom earnestly pleaded for a short rest. His entreaty, however, was fruitless. He was urged forward once more on his sad journey; but they had not advanced more than four miles on their way, when a very violent access of fever came upon him, and they were reluctantly forced to go back to Comana. When Chrysostom reached the chapel, he was supported to the communion table, and having been attired, according to his request, with the white robe of baptism, he gave away the clothes which he had worn to those who were standing near him. He then received the Holy Communion, uttered a last prayer, which he concluded with his usual doxology, 'Glory to God for all things. Amen '—and peacefully fell asleep in Jesus, on September 14th, 407 A.D., in the sixtieth year of his age, or, according to others, the eighth month of his fifty-second year.[1] It was the third year and third month of his exile, and the tenth year of his archbishopric.

It has been remarked that 'no comment on his glorious life could be so expressive as the doxology with which it closed, and which, gathering into one view all its contrasts, recognised not only in success and honour, but in cruel outrage and hopeless desolation, the gracious presence of a never-changing Love.'[2]

---

[1] *e.g.*, Mosheim, Cave, Perry, Wordsworth, and Milner are in favour of the fifty-second or fifty-third year.

[2] Bright's *Church History*, p. 255.

His feelings had ever been embodied, in these
words :—

> 'Lead Thou me, Spirit, willing and content
> To be, as Thou would'st have me, wholly spent ;
> I am Thine own, I neither strive nor cry :
> Stretch forth Thy hand—I follow, silently.'

'Two Christian sufferers, in widely different
ages of the Church, occur to the memory as we
look on the map of Galatia. We could hardly
mention any two men more thoroughly imbued
with the spirit of St. Paul than John Chrysostom and Henry Martyn. And when we read how
these two saints suffered in their last hours
from fatigue, pain, rudeness, and cruelty, among the
mountains of. Asia Minor, which surround the place
where they rest, we can well enter into the meaning
of St. Paul's expressions of gratitude to those who
received him kindly in the hour of his weakness. . . .
There was a great similarity in the last sufferings of
those apostolic men : the same intolerable pain in
the head, the same inclement weather, and the same
cruelty on the part of those who urged the journey.
It is remarkable that Chrysostom and Martyn were
buried in the same place. They both died on a
journey, at Tocat or Comana in Pontus.'[1]

Chrysostom was buried in the Martyr Chapel by the
side of Basilicus, in the presence, so Palladius affirms,
of a large number of monks and nuns, who came
from the neighbouring provinces—from Cilicia, Syria,
Armenia, and Pontus—to celebrate his burial. He
was always regarded with deep respect by the Western
Church, but his name was not restored to any of the
'diptychs'—the folded tablets, consisting of plates of
wood, silver, gold, or ivory, on which were recorded

1 Conybeare and Howson's *Life of St. Paul*, vol. i. p. 295.

those who were mentioned at the communion—of the Eastern Church, until 415 A.D. This restoration was due to Alexander, the Bishop of Antioch, who, after composing the differences which existed in his own diocese, subsequently by this act benefited Constantinople also. On January 27th, 438 A.D., thirty-one years after his death, in the reign of Theodosius II., the son of Arcadius, when Proclus, formerly a disciple of Chrysostom, was Bishop of Constantinople, the emperor was induced by that prelate to give orders that the mortal remains of Chrysostom should be removed from their grave at the Martyr Chapel of Basilicus, and be conveyed with pomp—with even greater pomp than that which attended his first return from exile—to his own episcopal city, and be placed near the altar in the Church of the Holy Apostles, the burial-place of the imperial family and of the bishops of Constantinople. The youthful emperor with his sister Pulcheria assisted at the solemn ceremony, and humbly prayed for pardon for the wrong inflicted by their parents on the holy bishop. This action on the part of Proclus is said to have been the means of appeasing the Joannites, and of inducing them once again to unite themselves to the Church.

On this sad story of injustice, cruelty, and persecution, we cannot refrain from quoting Dean Milman's philosophical commentary :—' The remarkable part in the whole of this persecution of Chrysostom is that it arose not out of difference of doctrine or polemic hostility. No charge of heresy darkened the pure fame of the great Christian orator. His persecution had not the dignity of conscientious bigotry ; it was a struggle for power between the temporal and ecclesiastical supremacy ; but the passions and the personal animosities of ecclesiastics, the ambition, and perhaps the jealousy of the Alexandrian Patriarch as to jurisdiction, lent themselves to the degradation of the episcopal authority in Constantinople, from which it never rose. No doubt the choleric temper, the over-strained severity, the monastic habits, the ambition to extend his authority, perhaps beyond its legitimate bounds, and the indiscreet zeal of Chrysostom, laid him open to his adversaries ; but in any other station, in the episcopate of any other city, these infirmities would have been lost in the splendour of his talents and his virtues. Though he might not have weaned the mass of the people from their vices or their amusements, which he proscribed with equal severity, yet he would have commanded general respect ; and nothing less than a schism arising out of religious difference would have shaken or impaired his authority. At all events, the fall of Chrysostom was an inauspicious omen, and a warning which might repress the energy of future prelates ; and, doubtless, the issue of this conflict materially tended to degrade the chief bishop in the Eastern empire. After this time the Bishop of Constantinople almost sank into a high officer of state. Except on some rare occasions, he bowed with the rest of the empire before the capricious will of the sovereign or the ruling favourite ; he was content if the emperor respected the outward ceremonial of the Church, and did not openly espouse any heretical doctrine.'[1]

[1] *History of Christianity*, vol. iii. pp. 148, 149.

BOOK IV.

* * *

*THE CHARACTERISTICS, INFLUENCE,
THEOLOGY, AND ASPECT OF THE TIMES OF
CHRYSOSTOM.*

CHAPTER I.

THE CHARACTERISTICS OF CHRYSOSTOM.

No one who has studied his life, can doubt that Chrysostom was a man of high and even transcendent intellectual powers. His mind had been diligently trained and educated from his earliest days. He had read carefully and almost exhaustively all the literature of Greece—its poets, historians, and philosophers. He was brought up in the school of one of the most noted and conspicuous Sophists of the day, who taught him the art of rhetoric and dialectics, and forensic and epideictic oratory. So apt a scholar did he prove, that his master, the famous Libanius, was in the habit of saying that John was the most qualified of all his pupils to succeed him in his school of rhetoric. 'Nature,' says an old biographer of his, 'had enriched him with very exquisite abilities and endowments, a clear apprehension, prompt wit, acute reasoning, pregnant invention, and all these attended with a nimble and ready utterance, and an apt way of expressing his conceptions. Notions flowed quick into his imagination, and found words ready to clothe and dress them up in their proper shapes.' Together with an intellect capable of grasping all subjects placed before it, he possessed a refinement of thought, a delicacy and nicety of expression, and a richness of illustration, that fall to the lot of few indeed.

His study of Holy Scripture was exceptionally deep and extensive. He appeared to be perfectly familiar with the Old and New Testament alike. He is reported to have known the whole Bible by heart. Nor did he ever seem to be at a loss for some scriptural quotation with which to illustrate his remarks. These are all acknowledged facts, which no intelligent reader of his life could for a moment venture to dispute.

His moral and theological character, as contrasted with his intellectual, stood also on a high and exalted pinnacle ; but a greater difference of opinion, on certain points, may be admitted here, than could be admitted in regard to his mental endowments.

Though fearless and undaunted in speech, and somewhat inflammable in temper, so that his opponents at least called him proud and choleric, he was nevertheless, in many respects, modest, humble, and a sincere friend of the people. He never scrupled in his writings and sermons to lament his own short-comings, to bewail his sinfulness, and to express his sad conviction of the many spiritual blots in his character. The fault and corruption of his nature lay often upon him, like a heavy burden, that could hardly be borne. He was faithful in the highest degree to his duties as a bishop and pastor of his flock. Whenever he chanced to be kept away from his church by illness, he was 'wont to account this forced silence and absence from his people worse than the disease itself.'

And it is said that, ' no sooner was he restored to any
measure of strength, but he returned to the pulpit
with a kind of triumph and rejoicing, declaring that
he looked upon this opportunity of conversing with
his beloved auditory as the sweetest accent of his
health, and was as much affected and delighted with
it, as men are wont to be, that after a tedious absence
and a long journey are come home safe.'   He pleaded
so earnestly and so successfully in behalf of his
poorer brethren, that he was named, not unfrequently,
' John the Almoner.'   From the fact of his constantly
scrutinising his own heart and feelings, he had
acquired the ability to scrutinise the hearts and feelings
of other men.   He has been described as 'a mirror
which displayed men to themselves, and thus enabled
them to correct the defects of which they would
otherwise have remained unconscious.'

Though a Church historian[1] has even gone so far as
to say, ' It would have been easy to produce abundance of instances of his oratorical abilities ; I wish
it were in my power to record as many of his evangelical excellences ' ; and again, ' Had he known
Divine truth more exactly, and entered more experi-
mentally into the spirit of the Gospel, he would have
known better how to govern his own temper ;'—yet he
is obliged to confess ' that the connection between the
doctrine of the Gospel and holy practice is sufficiently
plain in the history of Chrysostom,' and that ' this great
man, though dead, yet speaks by his works.'   He
further states, ' He laboured much in expounding the
Scriptures, and though not copious in the exhibition
of evangelical truth, still he everywhere shows that he
loved it ' ; adding that in his interpretation of the

[1] Milner, *Church History*, vol. ii. ch. I.

passage, 'That we might be made the righteousness of God in Him,' when he says, 'What a saying ! What mind can comprehend it ?   It is of God, since not of works (which would require spotless perfection), but by grace we are justified, where all sin is blotted out,' Chrysostom bears 'a plain testimony to the Christian doctrine of justification, and under this shelter this holy man no doubt found rest for his own soul.'

Finally, he is led to use such language as this when describing Chrysostom : 'Behold a bishop of the first see, learned, eloquent beyond measure, of talents the most popular, of a genius the most exuberant, and of a solid understanding by nature ; magnanimous and generous,—liberal, I had almost said, to excess; sympathising with distress of every kind, and severe only to himself; a man of that open, frank, ingenuous temper which is so proper to conciliate friendship ; a determined enemy of vice, and of acknowledged piety in all his intentions !   Yet we have seen him exposed to the keenest shafts of calumny, expelled with unrelenting rage by the united efforts of the court, the nobility, the clergy of his own diocese, and the bishops of other dioceses . . . Such seems the just conclusion from the case: real godliness, under Christian as well as heathen governments, is hated, dreaded, and persecuted.'

Such a testimony in Chrysostom's favour from one who was not disposed to acquiesce in all· his views, and who was ready to indicate the points in which he differed from him, is very valuable.

It is quite possible that some of the errors and infirmities which Chrysostom manifested at Constantinople may be accounted for by the marvellous powers which he had exercised as a preacher at

Antioch. A brilliant and distinguished preacher does not necessarily, or even frequently, become a great, wise, and judicious bishop. The characteristics required for success in each condition are different. The unlimited sovereignty which Chrysostom exercised over men's minds at Antioch—the absolute sway which he there enjoyed—may have unfitted him, in some respects, for performing all the delicate functions which he had to discharge at Constantinople, and may have led him to lay down the law in too unqualified a manner, to brook no opposition to his will, and not to cultivate those more persuasive and gentle methods, by which successes are more often achieved in the intercourse of man with man. The administrative qualities which are essential to the judicious and successful bishop are not needed in the great orator and preacher. The difficulties which surround a bishop often require to be met by a conciliatory spirit, and to be escaped from by the exercise of prudence and judgment. Such qualities may seem poor and even mean to him who is accustomed to sway thousands by his eloquence. They may appear to savour of worldly policy and temporising expediency. But, nevertheless, such caution, prudence, and judicious knowledge of men, and even such concession to their feelings and weaknesses, are needful for one placed in an imperial city, amidst a crowd of educated nobles and wealthy citizens, as Chrysostom was in the eastern metropolis of the Roman empire.

' A bright, cheerful, gentle soul '—such is the testimony borne to him by a well-known writer, in his *Historical Sketches*—' a sensitive heart, a temperament open to emotion and impulse, and all this elevated, refined, transformed by the touch of heaven ; winning followers, riveting affections by his sweetness, frankness, and neglect of self. In his labours, in his preaching, he thought of others only.' 'I am always in admiration of that thrice-blessed man,' says an able critic (*Photius*, p. 387), 'because he ever, in all his writings, puts before him as his object, to be useful to his hearers ; and as to all other matters, he either simply put them aside, or took the least possible notice of them.' He was, indeed, a man to make both friends and enemies—to inspire affection, and to kindle resentment ; but his friends loved him with a love stronger than death ; and it was well to be so hated, if he was so beloved.'

Moreover, there was another characteristic in Chrysostom, which perhaps gained for him 'this great blessing of warm, eager, sympathetic, agonised friends. He had, as it would seem, a vigour, elasticity, and what may be called seriousness of mind, all his own. He was ever sanguine, seldom sad. He had that noble spirit which complains as little as possible, which makes the best of things, which soon recovers its equanimity, and hopes on in circumstances when others sink down in despair ; a spirit which forgets an enemy, but ever beats true to the claims of friendship. No one could live in his friends more closely and intimately than Chrysostom did. He had not a monk's spirit of detachment in such severity as to be indifferent to the presence, the handwriting, the doings, the welfare, soul and body, of those who were children of the same grace with him, and heirs of the same promise' (cf. *Ep.* 2).

CHAPTER II.

THE INFLUENCE OF CHRYSOSTOM.

WHAT was the impress stamped by Chrysostom upon
his day and generation ? Did he, by his holy character and his vast powers as a preacher, change the
whole state of society at Antioch and Constantinople,
and effect a 'revival,' so to speak, in those two
luxurious and dissipated cities? Or are we to
suppose that, after all, his influence was only slight
and transitory? It is probable that the truth lies
between the two extremes that we have indicated.
To conceive that any single individual—however
great, or good, or eloquent—could have permanently
reformed the tone of society, the state of feeling, and
the lives and conduct of men in two such capitals as
Antioch and Constantinople, is an almost impossible
supposition. The servant could not be thought
capable of effecting what his Divine Master Himself
did not in His own sphere accomplish. But still we
believe that among the leading fathers of the early
Church, no one has exerted a greater influence among
men of his day (with the exception, perhaps, of

Augustine in a narrower sphere), or has been more valued, appreciated, and venerated in after ages than Chrysostom. He destroyed no ecclesiastical polity, he founded no sect ; but he built up the edifice of the Christian Church on a solid basis, he placed before the eyes of men a pattern of a pure and godly life, and he stimulated all around him to admire virtue, to love justice, to reverence piety, and to practise holiness.

Moreover, a marked and decided contrast existed, in regard to ecclesiastical influence and authority, between the bishops of Rome and Constantinople. We find Anastatius, who was elected to the see of Rome about the same time as Chrysostom, able to publish his edicts over the West with but little opposition or contradiction. The Bishop of Constantinople, on the other hand, as presiding over a comparatively new see, possessed far less influence. At Rome, the bishop was, in fact, a sovereign pontiff, while at Constantinople the Emperors of the East lorded it over the prelate of that church. The vigour and the eloquence of such a man as Chrysostom tended, no doubt, to draw forth the latent energies of the Christian Church, in opposition to the power and authority of the State. But, nevertheless, such a manifestation of spiritual influence could, in the nature of things, only be temporary, and dependent on the extraordinary abilities of the bishop for the time being.

As bearing on the question of Chrysostom's influence, it is interesting to inquire what congregations were attracted by so great a preacher as he undoubtedly was, and what success attended his preaching.

No doubt both at Antioch and at Constantinople

his eloquence generally drew together overwhelming congregations, who listened to the gifted preacher with rapt attention. So vast was the number of his hearers, that at Constantinople, in order to be heard, he not unfrequently preached from the desk of the reader, called the ambo, which was placed in the centre of the large church.

Men of every rank, of every profession, from the highest to the lowest, even workmen and artisans, left their various occupations and crafts, and thronged to listen to the golden-mouthed preacher. It was not once only that they came ; but, on every occasion that presented itself, they eagerly drank in his burning words, never appearing to have heard too much, or to have listened too long. Such large attendances would seem to have been the rule rather than the exception.

But, we must add, the gifted preacher had clearly at times to complain of a much smaller number of hearers. He speaks now and then of the church as being empty and neglected, while the theatre and the race-course, and other places of public resort, were crowded with spectators. He not unfrequently in his sermons bewails such a desertion of the house of God, and sadly and mournfully expostulates with his hearers, expressing his conviction that all his labour on their behalf had been in vain. But this could not possibly have been the case. Such teaching as his must have produced results of the most important kind, though he, in his moments of despondency, could not perceive them. He strove, moreover, so far as it was possible, to affect individuals. He did not rest satisfied with his earnest appeals to the 'great congregation.' At such a time as that of the sedition at Antioch, we know, from the best authority, that the most marked and lasting effects followed his impassioned addresses, calamity, fear, and sorrow having affected the hearts of the people, and pre-disposed them to hear and to derive consolation from his words.

The impressions which at times were made on his hearers were no doubt temporary, passing away when the immediate cause of their sorrow or depression had vanished. But, in many instances, the seed sown germinated, and brought forth fruit to perfection.

As we have already seen, he never failed to impress upon his hearers the deep importance of a careful and diligent study of Holy Scripture. He knew how inestimably advantageous such a study had proved in his own case, and he desired that others also should derive similar benefits in their own religious experi-ence. Anxious to confer the greatest amount of good on others, he addressed in his sermons all characters, and men and women of every rank and condition. He warned the thoughtless and negligent professors of Christianity that their ill-conduct and careless habits bolstered up the cause of heathenism. He pointed to the life of the soldiers (many of which class were among his hearers), and drew a moral from it, that both they and others should strive with earnestness to 'fight the good fight of faith.'

Faultless, indeed, Chrysostom was not. He had, without doubt, his weaknesses, his besetting sins, his errors of judgment, and his impetuous temper to contend with. But he was a noble specimen of regenerated humanity—one whom we cannot help loving, admiring, reverencing, and sometimes fearing ; one who, like St. Paul, stamped the whole age in which he lived with the broad seal of his genius, piety, eloquence, and moral grandeur ; one who seems to fill up the entire field of vision during the period in which he flourished, and to cast all other characters into the dark background of shade; one who has shaped and moulded the hearts and minds of successive generations of men, who has spoken to mankind through the long space of nearly fifteen hundred years, and who will continue to speak by his writings, his example, and his influence to generations yet unborn, until the time of the restitution of all things.

A living writer has asked the question, 'Whence arises his devotion to Chrysostom, which makes him kindle at his name, and dwell upon the thought of him ?   Many holy men,' he says, 'have died in exile, many holy men have been successful preachers ; and what more can we write upon St. Chrysostom's monument than this, that he was eloquent, and that he suffered persecution?   He is not an Athanasius, expounding a sacred dogma with a luminousness which is almost an inspiration ; nor is he Athanasius, again, in his romantic, life-long adventures, in his sublime solitariness, in his ascendency over all classes of men, in his series of triumphs over material force and civil tyranny ; nor, except by the contrast, does he remind us of that Ambrose, who kept his ground so obstinately in an imperial city, and fortified himself against the heresy of a Court by the living rampart of a devoted population.   Nor is he Gregory or Basil, rich in the literature and philosophy of Greece, and embellishing the Church with the spoils of heathenism. Again, he is not an Augustine, devoting long years to one masterpiece of thought, and laying, in successive controversies, the foundations of theology. He has not trampled upon heresy, nor smitten emperors, nor beautified the house or the service of God, nor knit together the portions of Christendom, nor founded a religious order, nor built up the framework of doctrine, nor expounded the science of the saints.

'Whence, then,' he asks, ' has he this influence, so mysterious, yet so strong?'   He considers that charm to lie in his infinite sympathy and compassionateness for the whole world, not only in its strength, but in its weakness ; in his habit and his power of throwing himself into the minds of others, of imagining with exactness and with sympathy circumstances or scenes which were not before him, and of bringing out what he has apprehended in words as direct and vivid as the apprehension.   He writes as one who was ever looking out with sharp but kind eyes upon the world of men and their history ; and hence he has always something to produce about them, new or old, to the purpose of his argument, whether from books or from the experience of life.   Head and heart were full to overflowing with a stream of mingled 'wine and milk,' of rich, vigorous thought, and affectionate feeling.   This is why his manner of writing is so rare and special ; and why, when once a student enters into it, he will ever recognise him, wherever he meets with extracts from him.'[1]

The opposition to Chrysostom was not confined to one sect, or party, or class. A character such as his, with all his unshrinking repugnance to every form of evil, could not fail to excite a storm of ill-will from every quarter. If the Novatians assailed him for admitting to the Holy Communion, after repentance,

_____

[1] *Historical Sketches.*

those who had fallen into sin ; those, on the other hand, whose lives and conduct were lax and licentious, upbraided him for what they considered the sternness and severity of his moral code. There was an uncompromising character about his religious life and teaching that naturally tended to provoke opposition, not only in the case of the irreligious, but also in the case of the formalist. Chrysostom did not possess the bland courtesy, the worldly compliance, the studied moderation, the faculty of pleasing all men, the power of making himself agreeable to those in authority, which the polished Sisinnius, the Novatian Bishop of Constantinople (as described by Socrates the Historian, iv., 21), or the urbane Atticus possessed. He might have escaped all persecution, as they did, had he exhibited such qualities. Calumny would not, under such circumstances, have directed its envenomed shafts against him. But when his piety was of so exalted a character, when his candour was so conspicuous, when he never shrank from branding impiety and vice wherever they appeared, we cannot wonder at the odium which was excited against him. Chrysostom possessed, in a great degree, the different qualities usually found in a reformer,—the same ardour, the same zeal, the same excitable temper.

It has been remarked by Waddington,[1] that 'in the tedious and delicate office of ecclesiastical reformer, that zeal which is not tempered with moderation, and qualified by due regard for existing circumstances, will commonly ruin the advocate, without benefiting the cause.' In his estimation, 'the disposition of Chrysostom was naturally choleric and impatient, and

---

[1] See his *Church History*, ix. 139.

his noblest intentions were frustrated by his passionate imprudence.'   It is not, indeed, improbable, that had his fiery zeal been toned down by greater moderation of temper, he might not have aroused the angry passions of the court, the clergy, and the higher ranks, and so have been enabled to carry out his reforms more successfully, and to have established them on a more durable basis.

In the same spirit, another Church historian[1] has remarked, that the stern and uncompromising inflexibility, the rigid asceticism, the heroic courage, ardent enthusiasm, and vehement impetuosity of Chrysostom, disqualified him, in a certain sense, for the task which was before him.   Chrysostom was a martyr to the cause of Church discipline.

His character, perhaps, was too unworldly, too much impregnated with the monasticism of his earlier years, his temperament too enthusiastic, and his mind somewhat too deficient in that practical wisdom which would have led him safely, as Ambrose was led, through the thorny paths of reformation of life and morals.

[1] Bishop Wordsworth's *Church History*, iv. 149.

CHAPTER III.

THE THEOLOGY OF CHRYSOSTOM.

' St. Chrysostom is brought on both sides, and his rhetoric hath cast
him on the Roman side [respecting the sacrament of the Lord's Supper],
but it also bears him beyond it ; and his divinity and sober opinions
have fixed him on ours. How to answer the expressions hyperbolical,
which he often uses, is easy, by the use of rhetoric and the customs of
the words.'—JEREMY TAYLOR, x., 84.

IN inquiring into Chrysostom's theology, it will be
necessary to refer to different doctrinal topics, and to
see what were the opinions which he held respecting
them. Without such a subdivision of the matter,
our review would be confused and unsystematic, and
would fail to give an accurate account of his religious
sentiments. The points in question will be discussed
as briefly as possible—indicated often, rather than
fully dwelt upon.

1. It is obvious to all who have read his writings
with any attention, that Chrysostom cherished with
great care and consideration the *relics of martyrs
and saints.* He attributed to them no slight efficacy.
He always speaks of them with much respect and
veneration. He even alludes to miracles as wrought
at the tombs of the martyrs : and yet, in other places
in his works, he distinctly speaks of the cessation of
miracles.[1]

[1] See *Hom. in Cor.* vi. xi. Cf. also Milman's *History of Christianity*, iii. 160.

Such respect seemed to him—who looked at things through a practical medium—as likely to induce men to put before them the lives, and the virtues, and the excellences of those who had departed, as patterns which they might follow in their own practice. We know that from the very early ages of Christianity, it was the custom to assemble together at the tombs of the martyrs, and to celebrate the anniversary of their martyrdom, or, as it was called, their birthday. Thus what arose at first from feelings of respect, degenerated subsequently into superstition.

When, indeed, Chrysostom thought strongly on any matter, he expressed himself ordinarily in somewhat vehement and unrestrained language, and hence his views have often been greatly misinterpreted on these points, and opinions have been ascribed to him which he did not really hold. It is clear to any one who has studied the writings of Chrysostom, that he never contemplated the idea of such relics being worshipped. In this view Jerome strongly sympathised. 'Not only,' he says, 'do we not worship relics, but not the sun, the moon, angels nor archangels, cherubim nor seraphim, nor any name that is named in this world or in the world to come; lest we should serve the creature rather than the Creator, who is blessed for ever. We honour the relics of the martyrs, that we may worship Him whose martyrs they are. We honour the servants, that their honour may redound to their Lord's.'

'It has been proved,' says Bishop Browne, 'that, in the early ages, the Church never permitted anything like religious worship to be offered to the relics of the saints. The respect paid to them sprang from the natural instinct of humanity, which prompts us to cherish the mortal remains, and all else that is left to us, of those we have loved and honoured whilst in life ; and the belief of the sacredness and future resurrection of the bodies of Christians, joined with the wish to protect them from the insults of their heathen persecutors, added intensity to this feeling. With the progress of image-worship and of the invocation of saints, grew (and perhaps still more rapidly) the undue esteem of relics, to which sanctity seemed to belong, until at length the relics of saints were formally installed amongst the objects of worship, and set up with images for the veneration of the faithful.'

It would seem evident that no religious worship was allowed to be given to the relics of saints and martyrs, till after the time of St. Augustine.[1]

Invocation of saints was, we cannot doubt, a practice in the time of Chrysostom, who thought that a mutual relation subsisted between martyrs and saints who had gone to their rest with the members of the Church of Christ struggling in their conflict in this world.

But this view never led him to the worship of saints and angels, which he always strongly repudiated and deprecated. He says, in his homily on Colossians v. § 1, 'that not stones, not animals, not plants, not elements, not things above nor things below, not man, not demons, not angels, not archangels, not any other of those powers above, ought to be worshipped by the nature of man.' In another place (homily on Colossians, ix.), he protests most strongly against

---

[1] This is the judgment of Bingham in his *Antiquities of the Christian Church*, vii. 457.

angel-worship, and ascribes its origin to the invention of Satan.

There can be no doubt that 'the affectionate interest which the first Christians felt in the repose of the souls who had gone before them to paradise, their belief that they still prayed with them and for them, in course of time engendered an inclination to ask the departed to offer prayers for them, and so by degrees led to the Mariolatry and saint worship of the Church of Rome.'

No early testimony in favour of the invocation of saints can be advanced. Justin Martyr, Tertullian, Origen, Lactantius, and Athanasius, all speak strongly against it.

It has been well and forcibly remarked, that the temptation to turn the mind from God to His creatures is nowhere more likely to assail us than in our devotions. The multitude, converted from heathenism, who had all along worshipped deified mortals, readily lapsed into the worship of martyrs. The noxious plant early took root, and though for a time the wise and pious pastors of the Church kept down its growth, still it gained strength and sprang up afresh, until in ages of darkness and ignorance it reached a height so great, that, at least among the rude and untaught masses, it overshadowed with its dark branches the green pastures of the Church of Christ.

Prayers for the dead seem to have been advocated by Chrysostom at the Holy Communion, and also at the anniversaries of the deaths of dear relatives and friends. There is, however, in these prayers no reference to purgatory. The custom of prayers for the dead existed at a very early period of the Christian Church. Tertullian speaks of it as a common practice to offer prayers for the dead on the anniversary of their death. The same thing is referred to as of common occurrence by the other early fathers of the Church up to the time of Chrysostom; and prayers and thanksgivings for the dead are said to occur in all the ancient liturgies, as, *e.g.*, that of St. James, St. Mark, St. Basil, and St. Chrysostom.

2. *Confession.*—Chrysostom, without denying the advisability at times and in certain cases of confession to man, never for a moment regards it as binding upon any one. He would have us confess our sins to God, without reserve, and often. Such was his constant advice to penitents. In reference indeed to penitence—in spite of some apparent divergences of opinion upon which Roman Catholic writers have fastened—it is evident that in his writings he always dwells upon the duty of confession in our prayers to God, and never inculcates the necessity of any intervention on the part of God's ministers, except, perhaps, in particular and exceptional cases. Previous to the time of Nectarius, the office of 'penitentiary presbyter' used to exist, but it was abrogated by him. To God then, according to Chrysostom, were men to confess their sins, and not to man. To Him were all our secret sins to be laid bare, and our hearts to be unburdened. For public offences public penance was to be employed.

'If therefore,' to employ the words of a well-known writer, 'private confession and private absolution were, as some say, necessary to the spiritual health of the soul, it must be acknowledged that the Church of God was in a state of spiritual sickness from the time of the apostles for 1200 years ; it was not till A.D. 1215 that private confession was made obligatory by the Church of Rome, at the fourth Lateran Council, and then only once a year.'

The language of Hooker [1] is equally clear :—' I dare boldly affirm that for many hundred years after Christ the fathers held no such opinion ; they did not gather by our Saviour's words any such necessity of seeking the priest's absolution from sin, by secret and (as they now term it) sacramental confession ; public confession they thought necessary by way of discipline, not private confession, as in the nature of a sacrament, necessary.'

3. On the doctrines of *free-will, grace,* and *original sin,* there can be but little doubt that Chrysostom expressed himself somewhat carelessly, especially concerning the relation of grace and man's free-will. But we must recollect that, in his day, no controversy existed on these subjects which would have caused him to study accuracy and nicety in his statements. Hence his opinions, as expressed at different times, would seem to be in collision with each other, and even appear to be in opposition. In consequence of this unstudied language, Anianus and Julian, themselves Pelagians, claimed Chrysostom as adopting their views.

Perhaps also, it has been remarked, though he was a zealous champion of Divine grace, and boldly asserted the absolute need of the regenerating and sanctifying gifts of the Holy Spirit, he may, in his character of a great ethical teacher, and as an eloquent advocate of religious practice, have seemed sometimes to approach the verge of Pelagian exaggerations of

---

[1] Book vi., ch. iv.

the power of the human will. 'We are virtuous or wicked (he says), not by nature, but by our own purpose. If we will, we can shake off our sin. Satan cannot force us to do evil ; nor will God force us to do good. He will not be served by slaves, but freely ; our salvation or our destruction depends on ourselves.' At the same time, he no less distinctly affirms, that 'we cannot resist the slightest temptation without Divine help ; and that we cannot do the least good without God's grace. God wills all men to be saved, and gives grace freely to all ;' and in one of his last letters he expressed his antipathy to Pelagianism.[1]

Milner[2] observes that Chrysostom, in occasionally speaking of that passage of St. Paul to the Romans, 'It is not of him that willeth, nor of him that runneth,' introduces the doctrine of free-will in the same manner as most of the fathers did, who spoke of it at all, from the days of Justin, and observes that the whole is said to be of God, because the greatest part is, so hard pressed is he with the plain words of the apostle, which are directly opposite to the system he had imbibed. But Platonic philosophy (he adds) had done this mischief to the Church, to the great hurt of Christian faith and humanity.

Those who are named the apostolical fathers have not expressed with any definite clearness their opinions on the subject of free-will. They wrote in a practical rather than a controversial spirit. Nevertheless, they manifestly hold the need of Divine grace, as well as the weakness of man. The same

---

[1] Cf. Jeremy Taylor, ix. 101, for passages from Chrysostom on original sin.

[2] *Church History*, ii. 109, *et seq.*

remark holds true with regard to original or birth-sin. All who are in the least degree familiar with the writings of St. Augustine are aware that the origin of evil was a subject which exercised a great influence on his mind, and formed a constant subject of speculation. We can scarcely doubt that the early fathers of the Christian Church maintained the doctrine of the universality of man's corruption. ' Besides the evil (says Tertullian) which the soul contracts from the intervention of the wicked spirit, there is an antecedent, and, in a certain sense, natural evil arising from its corrupt origin.'

If, then, it is certain that man is not in possession of free-will, inasmuch as his nature is corrupted by the fall ; or, in other words, that man's will, though not restrained by God, is subjected to the influence of evil from without and evil inclinations from within : it is clear that the grace of God is necessary to act upon the will, and release it from its natural bondage.

' God,' it has been said, ' must give the will, must set the will free from its natural slavery, before it can turn to good ; but then it moves in the freedom which He has bestowed upon it, and never so truly uses that freedom as when it follows the motions of the Spirit.'

The rationale of Chrysostom's views on the subject has thus been presented to us by Neander[1] :—' It appeared to the moral zeal of Chrysostom an object of the highest importance to deprive man of every ground of excuse for failing to put forth moral efforts. His fields of practical labour at Antioch and Constantinople encouraged and promoted in him this bent of mind ; for in these great cities he found many, who, in the weakness of human nature, in the power of

Church History, iv. 429, *et seq.*

Satan, or of fate, sought grounds of excuse for their deficiencies in practical Christianity. These motives, from within and from without, had no small influence in giving direction to the development of Chrysostom's habit of thought, especially on these subjects ; and with his peculiar style of homiletic composition, calculated upon, and adapted to, immediate practical needs, his mode of exhibiting his thoughts and views depended very much on the predominant interest which he was pursuing at the moment. He was deeply penetrated with the feeling of the need of redemption, of the need of a fellowship of life with Christ. With great emphasis he announced the truth, which he found in the epistles of St. Paul, as well as in his own heart, that justification, by which he understood not merely forgiveness of sin, but also the communication of that more exalted dignity and worth which far transcended the powers of the limited finite nature, by means of the fellowship of life with Christ, was acquired, not by any merit or doing on the part of man, but by faith alone. In the eighth homily on the First Epistle to the Corinthians, sect. 4, he says, 'Christ is the Head, we are the body. Can there be anything intervening between the Head and the body ? All this points to union, and leaves no room for the least intervening space.' But he felt it to be important also, to set everywhere distinctly forth, that to believe or not to believe depends on man's self-determination ; that there was no such thing as a constraining grace, not conditioned in its operations on the peculiar bent of man's own will ; but that all grace is imparted according to the proportion of the will's determination. Here, too, he attached the most importance to the practical element to counteract as well a proud self-confidence, as moral inactivity and self-neglect. God draws us to Himself, not by force, but with our free-will, says he in the fifth homily on John, sect. 4, 'Only shut not the door against the heavenly light, and thou shalt enjoy it abundantly.' 'God comes not with His gifts before our will ; but, if we only begin, if we only will, He gives us many means of salvation' (see *Hom.* vii., viii., *ad Roman*).

On this point the philosophically-expressed views of Dr. Shedd, in his *History of Christian Doctrine*, may fairly be quoted. 'The Antiochian school, represented by Theodore of Mopsuestia, Chrysostom, and Theodoret, adopted substantially the same anthropology with the later Alexandrines. They held the doctrine of the Adamic connection only so far as the physical nature is concerned, and taught that there is an inherited evil, or corruption, but not an inherited sin. The best representative of this school, and perhaps of the Greek anthropology generally, is Chrysostom. He concedes that the mortal Adam could beget mortal descendants, but not that the sinful Adam could beget sinful descendants. The doctrine of propagation, according to him, applies to the physical nature of man, but not to his spiritual and voluntary. The first progenitors of the human race brought corruption, *i.e.*, a vitiated sensuousness, but not a sinful will into the series of human beings, and these latter universally adopt it, and strengthen it, by the strictly individual choice of their will. In his commentary upon Rom. v., Chrysostom thus expresses his views :—' It is not unbefitting (οὐδὲν ἀπεικός) that from that man who sinned, and thereby became mortal, there should be generated those who should also sin, and thereby become mortal ; but that by that single act of disobedience another being is made a sinner, what reason is there in this ? No one owes anything to justice, until he first becomes a sinner for himself (οἴκοθεν). What, then, is the meaning of the word ἁμαρτωλοὶ, in the phrase 'were made sinners'? It seems to be, to denote liability to suffering and death.

Here, plainly, Chrysostom limits the connection of Adam with his posterity to that part of man which is other than the strictly voluntary part. The union of Adam and his posterity accounts for the origin of strong animal passions, of inordinate sensual appetites, but not for the origin of voluntary wickedness. This, as it is the act of the will, and not the mere working of sensuous appetite, has a purely individual origin. Chrysostom's theory of regeneration was firmly synergistic. If man, upon his side, works towards holiness, God's grace will come in to succour and strengthen him. In his sixteenth homily on the Romans, his exegesis is as follows :—'The phrase, "it is not of him that willeth, nor of him that runneth," does not denude man of power altogether, but indicates that the *whole* power is not of man. Assisting grace is needed from above. For it is necessary that the man himself should both will and run ; but he is to be courageous (θαῤῥεῖν) and constant (in well doing), not by his own efforts, but through God's loving-kindness.' Again, Chrysostom remarks, that 'it is necessary for us first to choose goodness, and when we have chosen it, then God introduces (ἐισάγει) goodness from Himself. . . . . It· is our function to choose beforehand, and to will, but it is God's function to finish and bring to completion' (*Hom. ad Heb.*, xii.).

4. Chrysostom's views on the *sacraments.*

With regard to the sacrament of *baptism*, Chrysostom would seem to be in agreement with the opinions of the primitive Church of Christ. He speaks of the blessings and benefits derivable from it in very strong language. He says that it is named in Holy Scripture the 'laver of regeneration,'[1] and as a burial. It was regarded by the early fathers as a 'complete illustration of the soul.' The neophyte was said to 'emerge from the waters of baptism in a state of innocence.' We read that ' the heart was purified ; the understanding illuminated ; the spirit clothed with immortality.' But we must not forget that, though Chrysostom strongly advocated the practice of infant baptism, the great majority, probably, of those whom he baptised were of ripe years, capable themselves of repentance and faith.

In two places Chrysostom gives the Eastern profession of Christian faith, which was of a very simple nature :—'I renounce Satan, his pomp and worship, and am united to Christ. I believe in the resurrection of the dead.'

In the same manner Chrysostom's language respecting the *Holy Communion* is, in some of his writings, far stronger than we should employ,—so strong, indeed, in some instances, that many writers have affirmed that his views approach not only to 'consubstantiation,' but even to 'transubstantiation.' At other times he speaks in a far more qualified manner, saying that the nature of the bread and wine remains, and that it is only *mystically* the body and blood of Christ.

There is, in short, a vagueness and uncertainty in

<hr>

[1] λουτρὸν παλιγγενεσίας, Tit. iii. 5.

his statements, which render a specific definition of them very difficult.

A standard author, Bishop Browne, when treating of the XXVIII. Article of the Church of England, has observed :—'St. Chrysostom writes, "when you behold the Lord sacrificed and lying, and the priest standing by the sacrifice and praying, and the congregation sprinkled with that precious blood, are you not immediately transported to heaven, and dismissing from your soul every fleshly thought, do you not, with naked spirit and pure mind, see the things which are in heaven?   Oh, wonderful! oh! the love of God! who, seated with the Father above, is held at that moment by the hands of all ; and who gives Himself to those who desire to receive Him.   And all see this by the eyes of faith" (*De Sacerdot.*, iii., sect. 4).   Again, "Behold, thou seest Him, thou touchest Him, thou eatest Him.   He gives Himself to thee, not only to see, but to touch, to eat, and to receive within. . . . .   How pure should he be who partakes of that sacrifice! the hand that divides His flesh, the mouth filled with spiritual fire, the tongue empurpled with His awful blood!" (*Hom.* lxxxiii. *in Matt.*, cap. 26).   Now these expressions (adds the same writer) are so strong, that even believers in transubstantiation could hardly use them without a figure.   The Roman Catholics allow that the *accidents* of the bread and wine remain unchanged ; and would hardly, therefore, in literal language speak of the tongue as assuming the purple colour of Christ's blood.   But hyperbolic expressions are common with St. Chrysostom and his contemporaries ; and they use such language, that they may exalt the dignity of the blessed Sacrament ; that they may induce communicants to approach it with devotion and reverence ; that they may turn their minds from the visible objects before them to those invisible objects which they represent, and which, as Chrysostom says, they may " see by the eye of faith." '

Collier, in his *Ecclesiastical History of Great Britain*,[1] confirms the opinion which has just been stated. His language is: 'It must be confessed Chrysostom's words sound high, at least towards consubstantiation ; but these expressions being either in his homilies or his book of the priesthood, are not to be strained up to the letter. The design of the father in these discourses being only to give a solemn idea of the dignity of the sacrament, to awaken the reverence and heighten the devotion of the receivers. To this purpose he made use of strong affecting metaphors. That his phrase is sometimes figurative must be owned, even by those who maintain transubstantiation. For instance, in one place, he speaks thus :—"The mouths of those who receive are tinged and empurpled with the blood of our Saviour." Thus he makes the corporeal presence an object of sense, which is neither true nor maintained by those of the Roman communion. It is evident, therefore, these strong passages of St. Chrysostom are to be construed with allowance, and pass for no more than figures of rhetoric. To make a right judgment of this father's opinion, we must consult him in those discourses where strict logic is his business, and where he pretends more to argue than flourish. And of this kind we may reckon his epistle to Cæsarius. In this tract he attempts close reasoning, and discovers his opinion without

[1] Vol. vi. p. 76.

heightenings and swelled expressions: and therefore, by all reasonable construction, the passages in his rhetorical discourses ought to be interpreted by what he delivers here.'[1]

The passage in his epistle to Cæsarius especially bearing upon the subject is this: 'For, as before the bread is sanctified, we name it bread, but the Divine grace sanctifying it, by means of the presbyter, it is freed from the name of bread, but it is esteemed worthy to be called the Lord's body, although the nature of bread remains in it.'

We must not, however, forget that while in our day such doctrines as these have been formulated with strict and rigid accuracy in our creeds and confessions and articles of faith, in the age of Chrysostom no definition of transubstantiation was known, and no fears of the dogma entertained; so that he and the early fathers indulge in an indefinite and enthusiastic mode of thought and language, into which at a later age they would probably never have been hurried by their strong feelings and intense devotion, which could scarcely then find an adequate expression in any language, however exaggerated.

Thus 'the poetry of devotional language kindled into the most vivid and realising expressions of awe and adoration. No images could be too bold, no words too glowing, to impress the soul more pro-

---

[1] It is stated by Robertson (i. 360, note) that one of Chrysostom's letters from Cucusus, addressed to Cæsarius—which is preserved only in a Latin translation—is important, as containing a distinct contradiction of the doctrine of transubstantiation. Some members of the Romish Church have questioned its genuineness; but Tillemont (xi. 475-9) honestly avows his opinion in favour of it. Cf. Jeremy Taylor, x. 84, *et seq.*

foundly with the sufferings, the divinity, the intimate union of the Redeemer with His disciples.'

Chrysostom never speaks of more than two sacraments, in. the strict sense of the word. In his church the Holy Communion was administered every day. He wished all to partake of it as often. He did not require from the people a lengthened preparation for it. What he required was a determined renunciation of sin, and a resolution to abstain from it, if possible, for the future.

5. Of Chrysostom's opinions respecting *monasticism* and *celibacy* we have already said much.

It is evident from his language that he entertained a strong partiality for monastic institutions and for the state of celibacy. He writes in the most glowing language of the blessings and the privileges of both these conditions. The monastic life appeared to him as one of unsullied happiness. But still his enthusiasm in their favour was neither blind nor indiscriminate. He could detect the sins and evils and defects that had crept into the cloister, and he not unfrequently recommended marriage, as well as a continuance in the world, to those whose influence he thought likely to prove beneficial to their fellow-men. It is certain that, in his younger days, when he lived an ascetic life himself, he advocated monasticism and celibacy more strongly than in his later days, when, from an enlarged acquaintance with men, he saw the importance of retaining in the midst of the active life of the world, as examples and guides to others, the great and the good. Neander remarks that although Chrysostom was largely indebted to monachism for the character of his inner life ; although everywhere inclined to place a very high value on the victorious power of the will over the sensuous nature, where it was enlivened by the spirit of love; although enthusiastically alive to the ideal of holy temper and holy living in monachism; yet he was too deeply penetrated by the essence of the Gospel not to be aware that the latter should pervade *all* the relations of life. His large experience gained at Antioch and at Constantinople had led him to see how mischievous the delusive notion that men could not strive after the ideal of the Christian life amid ordinary earthly relations must be, and had actually been, to practical Christianity. This delusion, therefore, he sought in every way to counteract. He attacked the exaggerated opinion of monachism, by assuming for his position the consciousness of the universal Christian calling, the sense of the principle of holy living, which he recognised as belonging in common to all true believers; but he was still too much influenced by the prevailing views of his time to be able always to carry out and apply that position with logical consistency. It is apparent here, as it often is in his case, that on one side he was confined by the prevailing spirit of his age; while, on the other, by his profound insight into the essence of the Gospel, he rose above it, and was thus betrayed into self-contradiction.

Thus, in that age, marriage was regarded as 'a necessary evil,' and as 'an inevitable infirmity of the weaker brethren'; while virginity was viewed as the 'transcendent virtue,' and as the 'pre-assumption of the angelic state, the approximation to the beatified existence.' It has been noticed that Basil, with the Gregories, Ambrose, Augustine, and Chrysostom, wrote a treatise or treatises upon virginity, on which subject each expatiates with all the glowing language which he can command. And Jerome's language on the subject is still stronger than that of the fathers already quoted : *Nuptiæ terram replent, virginitas paradisum.* Celibacy, however, produced that 'false antithesis between the spiritual and the secular,' which was so prejudicial to the whole Christian life ; and it fostered the erroneous idea that the clergy, from their spiritual character, ought to free themselves from everything earthly, and that marriage marred their dignity as priests.

6. No reader of Chrysostom's work on the priesthood, or, as it might perhaps be better named, on the episcopate, can fail to notice the very high standard which the archbishop has laid down for the conduct and character of a *bishop* of the Church. In his estimate a bishop must be raised far above mere earthly feelings and mere human interests into a region that almost borders on heaven itself. He must shun all imperfections of temper, disposition, and conduct, inasmuch as any failings on his part are infinitely more injurious to the brethren than those of other men, and cause a greater disgrace and scandal to true religion. He must be conspicuous for self-denial, moderation, capability of enduring injuries, and freedom from all arrogance and pride. He must possess learning, the power of speech, and the gift of persuasion, as well as energy, activity, and zeal.

Such being some of the exalted qualities which Chrysostom felt should be found in the bishops of the Christian Church, we cannot wonder that, when he endeavoured to bring bishops, who had been living in easy luxury and idleness, up to his high and pure standard of the episcopal office, he found the task one which exceeded his powers, and he quickly aroused their ill-feelings against him, and placed them in the ranks of his most embittered enemies.

We have, indeed, already seen that there were many really apostolic bishops existing in the Church during the time of Chrysostom or just before his day. Who could name except with praise Gregory of Nazianzum, that devout and spiritually-minded prelate, who preceded Chrysostom at Constantinople? We have seen how gentle, loving, and affectionate was Meletius, who was adored by the people of Antioch. Nor was the character of Flavian less self-sacrificing, tender, and disinterested. But without doubt the *election* to the episcopal office had lost the simplicity which had characterised it in the earlier and purer days of the Church. Many evils had now crept in. The position was at this time a coveted honour. Intrigues, dissensions, feuds, tumults, and even bloodshed now marked the election, especially in the larger and more important cities. After his election, the bishop's conduct was subjected to the most searching scrutiny. Every act of his life, every visit he paid, even the mode in which he greeted his friends and acquaintances, was exposed to severe criticism and often to obloquy.

7. No doubt among the ardent and susceptible temperaments of those Eastern communities, there existed a strong element of superstition, which the reformed Churches have discountenanced. But we cannot hesitate for a moment to award to Chrysostom the highest meed of praise for the noble and exalted supremacy which he assigned to *Holy Scripture*, and for his constant and unwavering assertion, that all

doctrine and theological truth must be based upon it and derived from it. It is the peculiarity of his teaching, that he did not ground his arguments upon the formularies of his Church, or upon the writings and traditions of men, but goes up direct to the well-head of Holy Scripture. He insists upon the literal and grammatical interpretation of the Bible and is not led aside into mystical or allegorical explanations—'a happy talent,' remarks Cave, ii. 529, ' almost peculiar to him, the main humour of those ages being to wire-draw Scripture into allegories, and to make witty allusions, and pick out mystical and far-fetched expositions, which were never intended, and when found out, served to little or no use or purpose. And, indeed, so happy a talent had he in expounding Scripture, that an ancient writer assures us that his judgment herein was accounted the common standard of the Church, insomuch that although all the rest of the fathers unanimously concurred in the exposition of any one place, yet if his sense differed from it, his exposition was immediately chosen, and preferred before, yea, against all the rest.' Thus it has been said, that ' Chrysostom was to the East what Augustine was to the West—the fountain of scriptural exposition.'

' It adds not a little (continues Cave) to the reputation of his learning, that he bred such a race of excellent men, who were his scholars, men famous both for the contemplative and practical philosophy of Christianity: such were Palladius, Bishop of Helle-nople, Isidore the Pelusiote, Nilus, Marke, and Theodorit, Bishop of Cyrus, and many more, who accounted it their honour, as it was their interest, to have been brought up under such a tutor.'

One passage will enable us to form an estimate of the lofty pedestal upon which he placed the Holy Scriptures. 'Tarry not' (he says) 'for another to teach thee, for thou hast the oracles of God. No man teacheth thee as they; for he indeed oft concealeth much for vainglory's sake and envy. Hearken, I entreat you, all ye that are careful for this life, and procure books that will be medicines for the soul. If ye will not any other, yet get you at least the New Testament, the Acts of the Apostles, the Gospels, for your constant teachers. If grief befall thee, dive into them as into a chest of medicines; take thence comfort of thy trouble, be it loss, or death, or bereavement of relations; or rather, dive not into them merely, but take them wholly to thee; keep them in thy mind. This is the cause of all evils, the not knowing the Scriptures. We go into battle without arms, and how shall we come off safe? Well contented should we be if we can be safe with them, let alone without them' (*Coloss.*, *Hom.* ix. *init.*).

Moreover, he insists upon the duty of the laity, as well as the clergy, to read for themselves the Holy Scriptures. They should go themselves to this great source of spiritual enlightenment. He allows of no excuses on this point. 'I am a man of business,' pleads some one, 'I am no monk; I have a wife and children to provide for.' Such an excuse he regards as worthless and futile, and affirms that such a man, tossed to and fro by the storms of the world and temptation, requires to consult the Scriptures even more than the monk who was buried in the retirement of the cloister, and hence relieved from many temptations which tried that man who was immersed in worldly affairs. Accordingly, he was in the habit of giving his hearers certain passages of Scripture to look over and examine before he spoke upon them. He attributed the spread of error in doctrine and practice among them to their non-acquaintance with the sacred volume.

No doubt, at that time, copies or MSS. of the Scriptures were costly ; but he argues that even the poor man could, if he had the will, procure a Bible for himself.

Moreover, he held remarkably clear views on the subject of inspiration at a time when men's opinions of such and similar doctrines had not been formed with the stricter accuracy and the greater minuteness of a more recent age. He perceived in Scripture the presence both of the Divine and the human element. He could trace God as inspiring the writers of the different books, and yet could mark that human element which God, in His mercy, permits us to discover in His sacred volume ; by which He makes use of, without crushing or annihilating, human feeling and thought, as well as the peculiarities and distinguishing characteristics of different men.

8. The different churches under the Patriarch of Constantinople long used a liturgy, varying from that of St. Basil, though probably based upon it, which was sometimes named the *Liturgy of St. Chrysostom.* There are not many allusions made by writers to a work of this title. A tract ascribed to Proclus, a bishop of Constantinople, in the early part of the fifth century, which by many is regarded as spurious, speaks of the Liturgy of Chrysostom. No doubt there are many references in the writings of Chrysostom to the rites and services of the Church, which have been collected by Montfaucon in his *Life*

of Chrysostom; but these passages are found in writings composed before he came to Constantinople. The liturgy of Constantinople would appear to have been older than the time of Chrysostom, though naturally named after so famous an archbishop of the Church in after days.[1]   This liturgy is at the present time commonly in use in the Eastern churches.[2]

It would seem probable that Chrysostom, at different times and places, employed different liturgies.   When at Antioch, he used the liturgy styled that of St. James, just as at Constantinople that of St. Basil.   There would seem to have been a systematic order of lessons for the year.

The prayer which precedes the benediction in the morning and evening services of the Church of England is styled 'A Prayer of St. Chrysostom.' This prayer (remarks Palmer, *Orig. Liturg.* i. 249) occurs in the liturgy of the Church of Constantinople, which bears the name of Chrysostom.   It must be confessed, however, that it is not found in the most ancient manuscripts of that liturgy, but in those of the liturgy of Basil.   Whether this prayer be as old as the time of either Basil or Chrysostom, is very doubtful ; but it certainly has been anciently used in the exarchate of Cæsarea and the patriarchate of Constantinople.

9. Chrysostom, in the construction of his immortal *sermons,* was not bound by any strict and iron rule. They were not conformed to one particular or stereotyped model.   Sometimes they were more expository, sometimes more hortatory.   At one time they were elaborate, at another simple and unpre-

---

[1] Cf. Palmer's *Origines Liturgicæ,* i. sec. 3.
[2] Hammond's *Liturgies,* Pref. 47, *et seq.*

meditated. Sometimes the exordium was long and carefully prepared, at other times the peroration claimed the greater care and attention, and was more systematically worked out. But however much in form and substance his sermons might differ from each other, they all, with very rare exceptions, pressed home the truths which the passage of Scripture involved with zeal and earnestness to the hearts and consciences of his hearers. It was his intense desire to promote not a 'formal orthodoxy, but vital Christianity,' and to sweep away all confidence in mere outward piety. No preacher was ever more perfect and polished in his style—richer in highly-wrought metaphors and similes—more argumentative in his reasoning—more stern and terrible at times, and yet more gentle and persuasive on other occasions—more copious in matter—more clear in exposition—more subtle and ingenious in thought—more capable of gaining the ear, appealing to the feelings, and influencing the judgment of his hearers. A heart (says Neander, iv. 478) full of the love which flows from faith, gave to his native eloquence, cultivated by the study of the ancients, its animating charm.

'He managed preaching with such clearness and perspicuity, such force and evidence, such freedom and smartness, and yet with such temper and sweetness, that, in the whole train of ancient fathers, none (says a biographer) went beyond him, and few came near him' (Cave, ii. 528).

Though he indulged sometimes in the most homely remarks, and referred to the common every-day occurrences of life, yet no preacher, either of ancient or modern times, could have reached a loftier height of sublimity, employed grander language on the grandest themes, proclaimed the highest truths with a greater boldness and authority, and appealed to the heart of man with more power and pathos, than John Chrysostom.

His masterly acquaintance with the Word of God was probably the chief cause of his success as a preacher. It enabled him, in the midst of much surrounding error, superstition, and false doctrine, strictly to maintain the analogy of the faith, and prevented him from being led away by one-sided views, and specious, though false, inferences from Scripture. It no doubt gave him that wonderful hold upon the minds, hearts, and feelings of the great middle classes, to whom there would have been a living power in such a handling of religious truth, which no mere dogmatic statements, no philosophical or mystical interpretations, could have ever exerted over them.

As he stood before the thronging multitude at Antioch or Constantinople, anxious lest they might lose a single word that he uttered; as their voices rose into loud acclamations at his brilliant oratory; as their eyes filled with tears at his touching appeals and his home-thrusts at their besetting sins; as they felt consoled in the midst of their troubles by his words of comfort, or became alarmed by his denunciations of future woe if they persisted in their sinful courses; as they thus drank in his words of practical and heavenly wisdom; you cannot fail to recognise one of those grand and master minds, one of that comparatively small array of splendid preachers, who have been raised up at sundry times by Providence to declare to man the mind of the unseen God, to reveal the deep and hidden mysteries of the human heart, and to lead many into the path of truth and righteousness.

On this point we would quote, in confirmation of what has been advanced, the opinion of well-known writers on the subject.

For overpowering popular eloquence (remarks Mosheim, *Eccles. History*, i. 325, note) Chrysostom had no equal among the fathers. His discourses show an inexhaustible richness of thought and illustration, of vivid conception and striking imagery. His style is elevated, yet natural and clear. He transfuses his own glowing thoughts and emotions into all his hearers, seemingly without effort, and without the power of resistance. Yet he is sometimes too florid: he uses some false ornaments, he accumulates metaphors and illustrations, and carries both his views and his figures too far.

His style (says Cave, ii. 529) is clear, chaste, easy, and elegant ; his conceptions flow in the most apt, familiar, and intelligible expressions, though whenever his argument required it, or his leisure permitted it, he could clothe his mind with a more accurate eloquence; witness his elaborate compositions while he was at Antioch, where he enjoyed ease, and more calm and retired thoughts than he did afterwards.

Suidas has quaintly remarked that no man in any age was master of such a copiousness and plenty of words, which ran from him with a fluency beyond the cataracts of the Nile. Another writer has said: There was a strange impetus and nervous efficacy in his reasonings, in comparison to which the most celebrated orators of Greece were but children to him.

His sermons and homilies are extremely numerous. Their style (so it has been remarked by Waddington, in his *Church History*, 140) is not recommended by that emulation of Attic purity which adorns the writings of Basil, or Gregory Nazianzen ; but it is elevated and unconstrained, pregnant with natural thoughts and easy expressions, enriched with metaphors and analogies, and dignified by boldness and grandeur. And, what is more important, the matter of his discourses, while it declines the affectation of subtlety, and avoids the barren fields of theological speculation, is directly addressed to the common feelings and principles and duties of mankind. The heart is penetrated, the latent vice is discovered, and exposed in the most frightful colours to the detection . of Christians. Such was the character of that eloquence which, by captivating the people and scandalising the great, occasioned such tumultuous disorder in the metropolis of the East. Yet the historian finds more to admire in the bold and impetuous enthusiasm of the orator, than to censure in his indiscretion. One object alone filled his mind and animated his efforts— and that the noblest object to which the genius of man can be directed—to stimulate the religion, to purify the morals, and to advance the virtue and happiness of those whom he influenced.

10. Chrysostom was no advocate of *persecution*, fervent and earnest though he was. He denounced in the strongest language error and false doctrine, but he never wished to see those who held them persecuted for their opinions. He commended those emperors who abstained from it. He looked to persuasion and argument to bring error home to those under its influence.

He inveighed against the *theatres and the stage* in language too strong to be palatable to modern ears. He denounced the stage as an 'academy of incontinence.' He was, of course, familiar with the effects which it produced, both socially and morally, inasmuch as he lived in two great capital and distinguished cities, where plays were constantly performed and theatrical shows abounded. His religious opinions were of too practical a character, and his piety too exalted, to suffer him to abstain from protesting against the licentiousness of the stage.

The tendency to *astrology* at Antioch has already been noticed. Other heathen predilections and practices were rife at Constantinople. To all such superstitions Chrysostom was strongly opposed. He unsparingly ridiculed their fondness for omens and auguries and similar follies. His piety was of a practical character. 'If any (observes Waddington), engaged in a pilgrimage to the holy places, he assured them that their principal motive should be the relief of the poor; if any were bent upon offering up prayers for the dead, he exhorted them to give alms for the dead also.'

He inculcated in his sermons the value of a liberal spirit of *almsgiving;* the duty of abstaining from worldly pleasures and pursuits; moderation and temperance in the use of wine; and more especially the obligation laid upon the Christian to offer earnest, persevering, continual *prayer*, which may be offered not only in church, but anywhere; since, as he remarks, neither place nor time are any obstacle to it. Every house, in this respect, should be a church. We may everywhere, he says, lift up holy hands. The man in the court of justice, the woman as she plies her spindle, can call on the name of the Lord. He even instituted nightly prayers in the churches, to the great annoyance of the more idle clergy, in addition to the prayers in church which were offered three times a day. On all these duties he dwelt very zealously in his addresses to the people.

He complained not unfrequently of the noise and laughter and disturbance which took place in church, and pointedly told them that, instead of finding sheep there, he found only a stable for oxen. The singing in church was congregational, and much cultivated. Instrumental music does not appear to have been in use in that day. He gave permission to the weak, if tired, to leave the church before the conclusion of the sermon, if a long one.

He urged them in his sermons not to trust to escape future punishment on the strength of the mercy and long-suffering of God. Chrysostom, says Dr. Shedd, in his history of *Eschatology*, employs his powerful eloquence in depicting the everlasting torments of the lost; but remarks that it is of more consequence to know how to escape hell, than to know its locality or its nature. Chrysostom, moreover, asserted the identity of the two bodies (*i.e.*, the resurrection body and that laid in the grave), but directs particular attention to the Pauline distinction of a 'natural body' and a 'spiritual body.'

It almost appears strange that many of the Jews were well inclined towards Chrysostom. We read that many half-hearted Christians attended some of the Jewish feasts, and regarded an oath administered by them as superior in binding force to that administered by Christians. To such views and practices Chrysostom offered a strong opposition.

The strong *missionary* spirit of Chrysostom was exemplified throughout his life. No man was ever more truly devoted to the encouragement of missionary work. When arguing with the heathen it was his method to start from some generally-admitted truth on both sides, as, for example, the planting of Christianity by Christ and the consequent spread of the Gospel.

Chrysostom was naturally trammelled by the peculiar *physical* theories which prevailed amongst the philosophers of Greece from whom he had derived his knowledge. He held to the view common to the physical philosophers of that age, that the firmament was a solid body, which divided the waters above from those which were below ; and he would seem to have conceived that the earth rested on the ocean (*Hom. ad Pop. Antioch*, ix. sect. 3, 4). But, nevertheless, he entertained views on *natural theology* which corresponded with the beautiful theories of Xenophon's Socrates as described in his *Memorabilia*, and which would be worthy of a place in the writings of Paley on this subject. He delighted to dwell upon the wonderful construction of the human body, the various processes of nature, the different properties of the animal creation, and the instinct that guides their conduct.

The *sign of the cross*, says Neander, iii. 385—as the sign of the victory of Christ over the kingdom of evil, as the token of redemption—passed over from the actions of daily life, in which it was customarily employed at an early period, to the Christian Church. A true and genuine Christian feeling lay at the basis of the practice,—the feeling that the Christian's whole life, in sorrow and in joy, should be passed with one constant reference to the redemption, and sanctified thereby. But with most (he adds) this resort to the sign of the cross had become a mere mechanical act, in performing which they either were not conscious themselves of the ideas thus symbolised, or else transferred to the outward sign what should have been ascribed to faith and to the temper of the heart alone. The universal use of this symbol is thus described by Chrysostom :—'The sign of universal execration, the sign of extremest punishment, has now become the object of universal longing and love. We see it everywhere triumphant; we find it in houses, on the roofs and the walls; in cities and villages; on the market-place, the great roads, and in deserts; on mountains and in valleys; on the sea, on ships; on books and on weapons; on wearing apparel, in the marriage-chamber, at banquets, on vessels of gold and silver, in pearls, in pictures on the walls, on beds.'

Chrysostom agrees with Eusebius in disclaiming all knowledge of a sensuous image of Christ, but ever speaks of Christ's moral image alone in the copying of His holy walk.

Many of the doctrines and practices prevalent in the time of Chrysostom we do not hold or maintain in the present day in the reformed Churches of Christ. Some of them were germs of usages which, in after ages, developed into large proportions, and have been commonly denounced by such Churches. They were, no doubt, the result in Chrysostom's age of a deep and enthusiastic love; as, for example, the affection, nay, the adoration, shown towards the relics of saints and martyrs, and the invocation of saints, which the Anglican Church in her Articles has pronounced to be ' a fond thing, vainly invented and grounded upon no warranty of Scripture, but rather repugnant to the Word of God.'

We naturally meet in his writings with many references to the different forms of *heresy* and false doctrine prevailing in and about his age. He speaks of the errors of Valentinus, and Marcian, and Macedonius, of Sabellianism, and Arianism, and Manichæism. But he was not, as we have before seen, mixed up with controversy like St. Augustine was ; and hence the practical nature of his teaching. Chrysostom, however, was no latitudinarian in his views. He firmly maintained doctrinal accuracy of statement.[1]

[1] We need not enter into any account of his opinions respecting the festivals and fasts of the Church, or respecting the Christmas feasts which, he says, had first become known at Antioch less than ten years before. (Cf. Neander's *Church History*, iii. 398, 409, 416.)

CHAPTER IV.

ASPECT OF CHRYSOSTOM'S TIMES.

Eheu! eheu! mundi vita,
Quare me delectas ita?
Cùm non possis mecum stare,
Quid me cogis te amare?

Vita mundi, res morbosa,
Magis fragilis quàm rosa,
Cùm sis tota lacrymosa,
Cur es mihi gratiosa?

THE Life of Chrysostom would be obviously imperfect without, at least, a passing glance at the moral and social condition of the times in which he lived.

1. In regard to the *moral* condition of the times, Chrysostom himself acknowledges that a sad degeneracy had taken place in the Church since the age of the apostles. He speaks of the Church of his day in one of his homilies (*Hom. in Cor.* xxvi. sect. 5) as resembling a woman who had sunk down from her former prosperity, and who preserved only the signs of what she once was; who can show, indeed, the cases in which her former gold and jewels were kept, but whose riches had all vanished. With such a decay existing, it is scarcely to be wondered at, if Chrysostom himself is not in all particulars quite perfect according to our standard of religious excellence.

Very little difference can be traced between the

Z

moral and social condition of the inhabitants of Antioch and Constantinople. The moral state of each was rotten to the core, and their social habits and practices were almost in as low a state. The royal palace at Constantinople was stained with blood. Its occupants murdered, almost without hesitation, both relatives, friends, and dependants, who seemed either to stand in the path of their ambition, or to be the object of their dread. The great Constantine himself shed the blood of his son Crispus at the instigation of the jealous Fausta. And if life in the palace was thus insecure, we cannot doubt that it was held on an equally insecure tenure among the citizens themselves. When war, or tumult, or earthquake, had driven out in panic haste the inhabitants from the city, they returned to find their houses pillaged and their property destroyed. But when peace smiled on them, they at once yielded to all the temptations which luxury and vice supplied, and indulged in idleness, dissipation, and sensual pleasures. The bare idea of virtue was repulsive to such men, who merely saw in it a censure of the conduct in which they indulged. They did not believe in it, and laughed with scorn at the very idea of its existence. The moral code was completely inverted in their practice. What Christianity held sacred they despised; what Christianity reprobated they pursued. Mammon was the god they worshipped. Humility and forgiveness of injuries they ridiculed. They called vices and virtues alike by false and unfair names. They confused the very nature of right and wrong.

Such was the character of the people whom Chrysostom was called upon to address, and amongst whom he lived. There were, of course, amongst his hearers men and women imbued with a deep love of piety and holiness, who were striving to do what they could to ameliorate the moral condition of their fellow-citizens, and to raise the tone of society. But neither the bishop nor the Christian population could look for support in such a cause from the palace and from those in authority. It was no interest of theirs to curtail the expense and the luxury in which the richer citizens indulged. If such a disposition of their wealth, if such an employment of their time, were taken away from them, who could tell whether their wealth and their time might not be directed to ends which would be disadvantageous, if not dangerous, to the state? And so the Court took the lead in grandeur and display. The emperor, when he appeared in state, or when he administered justice, was invested with all the insignia of magnificence. Guards with gilded shields accompanied him. He was borne on a chariot of gold, robed in purple. His palace was filled with crowds of officers of the highest rank, who regulated the household. Everything was done to please the eye, excite the desire for wealth, and promote the cause of luxury and display. Law and justice were respected in form, but not in reality. The semblance was there, the spirit had departed. Bribery, coercion, and intimidation, affected the decisions of the judges, and cruelty was practised by means of torture on the prisoners. The prisons to which the accused were consigned were a disgrace to civilisation. Thus, from a government notoriously corrupt, and in which admission to its highest posts was the result of purchase, no Christian preacher could hope for much moral support in his advocacy of virtue and censure of vice. He must rest upon his own powers and his own resources, in dependence upon higher and spiritual aid.

2. The Christian preachers have been aptly styled 'the great painters of Roman manners.' The sketches with which Chrysostom's sermons abound of the wealth, the luxury, as well as of the costly mansions and furniture of the higher classes of his auditors, are singularly striking and graphic. Nor have we any reason to believe that, in the main, his descriptions were overdrawn or exaggerated. He may sometimes have been carried away by his impassioned eloquence into bold and strong language when painting the luxury and the vice of the richer citizens of Antioch or Constantinople, but we have no reason to doubt the general and substantial accuracy of his statements. His mind was too clear, his love of truth too strong, and his knowledge of human nature too accurate, to have allowed him to describe things as they were not. Apart from all other higher considerations, such an untruthfulness recoils on the speaker himself.

We learn from what he has said, that the mansions of the nobles were adorned with mosaics, inlaid pavements, marble columns, precious pictures and vases, richly-embroidered hangings, and were sometimes even roofed with golden tiles. Their couches were inlaid with the precious metals and with ivory; their tables often made of solid silver; all the vessels which they used were formed of silver or gold. Outside their houses were gardens through which cool streams flowed, and trees of varied kinds afforded a pleasing shade from the heat of the sun. Such was the lavish excess—the 'luxury without refinement, the pomp and prodigality of a high state of civilisation with none of its ennobling or humanising effects—which characterised the dwellings of the wealthy, and which called forth the caustic language of Chrysostom, leading him to point out to them higher riches, more enduring goods, and heavenly habitations.'

Nor is it probable that men and women so devoted to luxurious living would be free from the temptation to deck out their own persons with costly dress, and to employ upon them all arts for enhancing their beauty and personal charms. This vanity again furnished a fair and legitimate butt for the ridicule of Chrysostom. He held up to contemptuous notice their dresses of silk, the boots on which they prided themselves, their waste of existence, their absolute buffoonery, though he could (as he says) shed tears while he thus spoke. He mercilessly assailed the topics on which they conversed, which were often frivolous, often indelicate, frequently of a very questionable character, interlarded with oaths, against the use of which, as we have already remarked, he waged an unceasing warfare. He assailed, too, the luxurious extravagance and excess in which they indulged in their meals and in their entertainments. No expense was spared in procuring the most costly viands that could be obtained. The more rare these luxuries were, the more they were prized. They procured the handsomest slaves that their wealth could purchase to wait at their tables. The wines —sought from every land—were presented to them in golden goblets. Music added its attractions to the feast, which did not close till late at night, many of the revellers being then stupefied by intoxication.

Such were some of the besetting failings and sins which Chrysostom endeavoured to root out from among his people ; and, in order to carry out his purpose, he did not scruple to employ the weapon of ridicule with unsparing force and energy.

The follies of the emperor were reproduced amongst his subjects. His was an *exemplar vitiis imitabile.* Just as the emperor was surrounded when in the streets by a gorgeous retinue, so these wealthy nobles, of whom we are speaking, imitated their royal master in the splendour of their chariots, the crowd of their retainers, the gilded trappings of their horses, their pomp and state. Thus they went to the effeminate luxury of the public baths, or to the dissolute performances of the theatres, which last source of pleasure Chrysostom never ceased to brand with unqualified reprehension. The amphitheatre, too, with all its varied attractions, its athletic exhibitions, its wrestling, foot-races, and boxing, and especially its chariot-races, claimed the attention of the wealthy and the noble. The factions which were formed respecting these chariot races nearly led at one time to the ruin of the city of Constantinople.

Nor were the poorer classes without their peculiar pleasures and amusements. They were delighted with acrobatic performances in the streets, with the excitement of the circus, with music, dice, and games of chance. The same kind of pleasures held each class enthralled. Here, again, was Chrysostom furnished with materials for scornful invective or for earnest exhortation.

Nor did Chrysostom fail to attack the special frivolities, vanities, and even indelicacies, of the *female* portion of his hearers. He rebuked them for the costly jewels that they wore, which were sufficiently valuable to have kept from hunger and starvation thousands of the poor. He urged them to cultivate beauty of soul, rather than endeavour to improve their personal charms by pigments and cosmetics,[1] and artificial adornments. He lashed them for their cruel treatment of their female slaves, whom they not unfrequently, in their caprice and ill-humour, inhumanly flogged, and bade them become more merciful and forbearing. He was also severe upon them for indulging in the dances then popular, and was very sarcastic upon the exhibition which they often made of themselves when dancing.

The ridicule which Chrysostom, in his endeavours to lead them to higher aims and nobler pursuits, poured upon the rich ladies of Constantinople, alienated them from him to such an extent that they became in the end some of his most embittered and implacable foes. Their injured vanity, and the open exposure of all the means which they employed in their efforts to set off their personal attractions, rendered them relentlessly hostile to the archbishop, from the offended empress downwards. They united at length with his most persevering enemies, and pursued him with an unpitying persecution.

Such, then, is a brief and outline sketch of the moral and social condition of the different classes of persons whom the great reformer strove by every means to benefit, and to lead to higher thoughts and

---

[1] 'What business (Jerome indignantly exclaims, ep. 54) have rouge and paint on a Christian cheek ? Who can weep for her sins when her tears wash her face bare and mark furrows on her skin ? With what trust can faces be lifted up towards heaven, which the Maker cannot recognise as His own workmanship ?'

more ennobling objects of pursuit. We have already expressed our conviction that such continuous and unselfish efforts as he displayed could not have failed to achieve success, whether great or small. To this grand end of ameliorating the moral condition of those who were spiritually intrusted to his care, and leading them to become Christians indeed, he may fairly be said to have disinterestedly sacrificed his health, his peace of mind, his comfort, and his life. In this noble effort to Christianise his flock, he never for an instant flagged. No fear of injurious consequences to himself deterred him from his self-denying exertions. He went on unmoved amid dangers, discomfort, obloquy, opposition, and persecution, from which the great majority of men would have recoiled. He has his reward. His works will doubtless follow him. His mistakes and errors of judgment, whatever they were, will be forgotten or pardoned before a tribunal higher than that of earth.

> ‘ Rest comes at length ; though life be long and dreary,
>   The day must dawn, and darksome night be passed ;
> Faith's journey ends in welcome to the weary,
>   And heaven, the heart's true home, will come at last.’

Pardon & Sons, Printers, Wine Office Court, Fleet Street, London, E.C.